In the Twilight, In the Evening

BOOKS BY GILBERT MORRIS

THE HOUSE OF WINSLOW SERIES

1. *The Honorable Imposter*
2. *The Captive Bride*
3. *The Indentured Heart*
4. *The Gentle Rebel*
5. *The Saintly Buccaneer*
6. *The Holy Warrior*
7. *The Reluctant Bridegroom*
8. *The Last Confederate*
9. *The Dixie Widow*
10. *The Wounded Yankee*
11. *The Union Belle*
12. *The Final Adversary*
13. *The Crossed Sabres*
14. *The Valiant Gunman*
15. *The Gallant Outlaw*
16. *The Jeweled Spur*
17. *The Yukon Queen*
18. *The Rough Rider*
19. *The Iron Lady*
20. *The Silver Star*

THE LIBERTY BELL

1. *Sound the Trumpet*
2. *Song in a Strange Land*
3. *Tread Upon the Lion*
4. *Arrow of the Almighty*

CHENEY DUVALL, M.D.

(with Lynn Morris)

1. *The Stars for a Light*
2. *Shadow of the Mountains*
3. *A City Not Forsaken*
4. *Toward the Sunrising*
5. *Secret Place of Thunder*
6. *In the Twilight, in the Evening*

THE SPIRIT OF APPALACHIA

(with Aaron McCarver)

1. *Over the Misty Mountains*
2. *Beyond the Quiet Hills*

TIME NAVIGATORS

(For Young Teens)

1. *Dangerous Voyage*
2. *Vanishing Clues*
3. *Race Against Time*

9709

CHENEY DUVALL, M.D.

6

LYNN MORRIS & GILBERT MORRIS

IN THE TWILIGHT, IN THE EVENING

BETHANY HOUSE PUBLISHERS
MINNEAPOLIS, MINNESOTA 55438

In the Twilight, in the Evening
Copyright © 1997
Gilbert Morris and Lynn Morris

Cover by Dan Thornberg,
Bethany House Publishers staff artist.

All rights reserved. No part of this publication may be reproduced, stored in a retrieval system, or transmitted in any form or by any means electronic, mechanical, photocopying, recording, or otherwise without the prior written permission of the publisher and copyright owners.

Published by Bethany House Publishers
A Ministry of Bethany Fellowship, Inc.
11300 Hampshire Avenue South
Minneapolis, Minnesota 55438

Printed in the United States of America.

Library of Congress Cataloging-in-Publication Data

Morris, Lynn.
In the twilight, in the evening / by Lynn Morris and Gilbert Morris.
p. cm. — (Cheney Duvall, M.D. ; 6)
ISBN 1–55661–427–6 (pbk.)
I. Morris, Gilbert. II. Title. III. Series: Morris, Lynn. Cheney Duvall, M.D. ; 6.
PS3563.O874439I6 1997
813'.54—dc21 97–33844
CIP

For Alan, my brother of Norse mythology,

And my pretty sister Stacy, she of Norwegianed poesy,

From the short one with the good personality.

All my love.

GILBERT MORRIS & LYNN MORRIS are a father/daughter writing team who combine Gilbert's strength of great story plots and adventure with Lynn's research skills and character development. Together they form a powerful duo!

Lynn has also written a solo novel, *The Balcony*, in the PORTRAITS contemporary romance series with Bethany House. She and her daughter live near her parents in Texas.

For at the window of my house
I looked through my casement,

And beheld among the simple ones,
I discerned among the youths,
A young man void of understanding,

Passing through the street
Near her corner;
And he went the way to her house,

In the twilight, in the evening,

In the black and dark night . . .

PROVERBS 7:6–9

CONTENTS

PART ONE ▪ MINGLED WINE

PART TWO ▪ BETTER THAN RUBIES

PART THREE ▪ KNOWLEDGE OF WITTY INVENTIONS

PART FOUR ▪ BETTER THAN THE MIGHTY

PART FIVE ▪ STOLEN WATERS

Mingled

Part One

Wine

Wisdom hath builded her house…
Whoso is simple,
Let him turn in hither:
As for him
That wanteth understanding,
She saith to him,
"Come, eat of my bread,
And drink of the wine
Which I have mingled.
Forsake the foolish,
And live…."

Proverbs 9:1, 4–6

1

Tiger in the Garden

"Just look at this diagram of the brain!" Cheney exclaimed.

"Cheney, be still," her friend Victoria ordered crossly.

"It's by Andreas Vesalius! Sixteenth century! Can you believe it?" Cheney waved the enormous book in the air. At such times it was obvious how much Cheney Duvall, M.D. loved her chosen profession. Her maid, Nia, hurried to stand behind her chair so she could look over Cheney's shoulder. "Look, Nia, how intricate the detailing, how finely delineated the separate lobular structures—"

"The what?" Nia asked, bewildered.

"Cheney, I said for you to be still," Victoria repeated. She was sitting across from Cheney with a sketch pad on her lap and a charcoal pencil in her hand. "Stop waving that horrid book around and put it back in your lap."

"Hmm?" Cheney stared at Victoria in surprise. "What did you say?"

As Cheney spoke, she laid the book back on her lap and rested her right hand on top of the open pages. Without bothering to answer, Victoria ducked her head and resumed sketching. Every so often she looked up with the narrow, intense look of the artist at work.

"She's drawin' you," Nia offered helpfully from over Cheney's shoulder.

"So I see," Cheney said with amusement.

"Your hands," Nia added.

"Really?" Cheney couldn't see Victoria's sketch pad, as she was holding it at a slight angle. "Interesting. Anyway, look at this, Nia. It's a perfect illustration of the human brain, drawn in 1543 by a man named Andreas Vesalius. This *De humani corporis fabrica* is still one of the best anatomical treatises available."

"It's in Latin," Nia said mournfully.

"Yes . . . well . . ." Cheney hesitated, trying to think of how to encourage her servant, who wanted to become a doctor. Little Nia, eighteen years old, with her little-girl voice and big doe eyes and tiny hands. Nia, the daughter of slaves, who hadn't a hope of being able to attend a university. Nia, the young black woman whose odds of ever being accepted to one of the three medical colleges that occasionally accepted women were nonexistent. Nia, her maidservant and—Cheney had finally decided—her apprentice.

"You can look at the pictures," she finally told Nia. "Later—when I can use my hands again—we'll go through and I'll dictate the captions. You can write them in the book, in English. It'll help you remember. You can do it, Nia."

"I can do it," Nia repeated softly, then leaned farther over Cheney's shoulder to search the drawing more closely.

"I'm going to see if there is any possibility of getting you some formal medical training here," Cheney said softly, being careful to keep her hands still while Victoria was so avidly drawing them. "Perhaps the hospital will offer some lectures, or at least allow you to observe some dissections. . . . That is, I'll do all this for you *if* I am accepted there," she finished wryly.

"You will be," Nia said confidently. "You're a great doctor, Miss Cheney."

"Let's hope Dr. J. E. Baird thinks so, Nia. It sounds like St. Francis de Yerba Buena Hospital is exactly what I want. I really wanted to go to apply for a position today, but Victoria wouldn't let me."

"After a month on that ship from New Orleans? And you can't even take off your bonnet before you're sashayin' off down to that hospital?" Nia sniffed in outrage. "Good for Mrs. de Lancie. You need to rest."

"Yes, so I thought, but now I'm beginning to think that Victoria just wanted me to stay around the house so she could draw my hands. I hope she finishes in a day or two so I can move." Cheney spoke with exasperated affection. Victoria gave no sign that she'd heard.

Victoria de Lancie had, in effect, made this opportunity possible for Cheney. Victoria's father, Henry Andrew Steen, was a wealthy New Yorker whose riches had originated in the diamond mines of Africa. But he had investments and financial interests all over America, and he was also a dedicated philanthropist. He was one of the founders of St. Francis de Yerba Buena, an experimental private hospital in San Francisco. Victoria was certain that Cheney would be granted a position as a staff physician; in sprawling, ebullient, gold-and-silver-fed San Francisco, even a woman doctor was a valuable addition to a tragically understaffed field. San Francisco's work force consisted mainly of gold miners, ex-gold miners, silver miners, and ex-silver miners.

Cheney looked out over the gardens sprawling below the back veranda of Steen House. Although they had only arrived in San Francisco the previous day, Cheney had already come to appreciate the city's distinct beauty. Gentle veils of mist floated in the rather untamed gardens and grew more tangible as the western sun lit them. The combination of gossamer fog and golden light made the gardens and the glimpses of the city laid out below Russian Hill look as if they glowed from within.

"I don't understand why you don't paint this landscape, Victoria," Cheney declared. "The quality of the light is like nothing I've ever seen."

Victoria grandly ignored her. Actually, she was not consciously disregarding her friend; she was just so engrossed in her sketching that she was oblivious to her surroundings.

"Victoria, dear," Cheney prodded, watching her curiously.

Still Victoria looked at Cheney's hands, then back at her paper, her charcoal moving quickly.

Cheney watched her affectionately for a long time.

Victoria Elizabeth Steen de Lancie was a study for an artist herself. Delicately framed but curvy, silvery-blond, with sparkling blue eyes and an elegant *hauteur* in every movement, Victoria was, by Cheney's estimation, the epitome of fashionable beauty.

Cheney also reflected ruefully that her friend sometimes made her feel mannishly tall and gangly and clumsy. Victoria's tiny feet made Cheney feel as if she herself had frog flippers.

It wasn't true, of course. Cheney was tall, five feet ten inches. Though she'd been coltish when she was younger, now, at nearly twenty-six, her own unique beauty was fully formed. She was animated, energetic, her features were rich. Her green eyes sparkled. Her face was squarish, with a wide mouth, a firm chin, and straight dark brows. From her mother she'd inherited a beauty mark high on her left cheekbone. Her luscious, thick, auburn hair crowned her rather dramatic looks.

Deep down Cheney harbored no serious insecurities about her looks or her demeanor. She knew she wasn't clumsy. She was quick and agile, decisive in her walk and her movements, confident and comfortable with her capable femininity. In 1867 some might have considered these traits contradictory, but Cheney had found mild satisfaction in being a striking woman and great joy in being a successful physician.

These thoughts flitted through her busy mind as Nia continued to squint over her shoulder, and Cheney's eyes narrowed as she considered Victoria's utter absorption in her sketching.

"You know, Nia," she murmured thoughtfully, "stroke victims are fascinating."

Nia sighed. Victoria, of course, had never had a stroke. But by now Nia had grown accustomed to Cheney's teaching her something by approaching it in a somewhat sideways manner. "Yes, Miss Cheney? How's that?"

"If the stroke affects the right side of the body," Cheney said almost inaudibly, as if reciting to herself, "that affects the left side of the brain. This results in a loss of speech capability . . . the victim can't talk. He can't remember simple words."

"Yes, ma'am?"

"But that study . . . what was it? I'll have to look it up. The musician," Cheney muttered to herself. "He had a stroke that paralyzed his left side, and therefore affected the right side of his brain . . . and he could still articulate perfectly, but he couldn't write music, or even understand or . . . or . . . comprehend music anymore."

Nia mulled this over, her brow wrinkling.

Cheney sat up straighter. "Victoria," she said clearly. "Victoria, can you hear me?"

Victoria kept drawing busily, her face absorbed, and never gave a sign that she'd heard Cheney. After long moments she finally murmured vaguely, "Hmm. . . ?"

"Victoria Elizabeth Steen de Lancie," Cheney said loudly, watching Victoria with ardent curiosity.

Victoria kept sketching. This time she didn't respond in any way.

Cheney flashed a smile up at Nia. "I think we might have a study of the brain here, Nia," she told her gleefully. "I theorize that our subject—Victoria—cannot talk and sketch at the same time. I further theorize that since speech capability appears to be centered in the left side of the brain, perhaps the more complex perceptual functions, such as writing music and doing a painting, are functions of the right side of the brain. She literally can't understand speech or figure out how to talk while she's drawing."

"But, Miss Cheney—'course Mrs. de Lancie can understand you and can talk. She's just busy, is all," Nia said tentatively.

Cheney turned back to face Victoria. "Listen, Victoria."

She waited, but the artist was still lost in her art.

"Victoria," Cheney said loudly, "there is a tiger in the garden."

After long moments Victoria hummed, "Hmm. . . ?"

"A tiger," Cheney repeated precisely. "With polka dots instead of stripes. And a big red cravat. He's given you permission to draw him instead of my astounding beauty."

"Hmm. . . ?"

"The tiger," Cheney insisted.

"Um . . . hmm . . ." Victoria responded, still drawing furiously.

"Now watch this," Cheney whispered mischievously. In a quick movement, she swept her hands behind her back.

Victoria visibly started, her otherworldly gaze focused on the denuded book on Cheney's lap, and she frowned darkly. "Cheney," she bit off impatiently, "I told you, do be still!"

"When did you tell me that?" Cheney asked innocently.

"You know I just told you, or tried to!" Victoria retorted. "Now, put your hands back on—good gracious, it's almost night!" She said this accusingly to the air, as if it had suddenly ambushed her with darkness.

Cheney and Nia looked at each other and smiled knowingly.

"And what is so amusing?" Victoria haughtily demanded. "You know, Cheney dear, it's rude to indulge in private jokes when others are present."

"I can't tell that anyone else has actually been present for the last half hour or so," Cheney replied. Nia giggled.

Victoria sniffed. "Just because I don't want to look at your horrible old brain pictures doesn't mean I wasn't paying attention. I heard everything you were saying."

"Did you, Victoria dear?" Cheney asked mildly. "What was I talking about?"

"Andreas Vesalius, sixteenth century," Victoria replied superciliously. "*De humani corporis fabrica*."

Cheney looked triumphantly up at Nia. "See? That's when she started drawing again. Fascinating—I wonder how we could do an organized study of it." Excitedly she turned back to Victoria, who looked both puzzled and outraged. "Victoria, start drawing again," Cheney ordered.

"Dr. Duvall, I am not your trained tiger," Victoria said with stiff politeness, then looked bewildered. "Did I say tiger? I meant to say monkey. How very odd. . . ."

Cheney and Nia laughed, and Victoria began to look belligerent, which on her meant a tightening of her shapely mouth and a scornful lift of her left eyebrow. She started to say something, but at that moment a jarring, screeching crash rent the quietness of the gardens. Horses neighed and screamed in panic, accompanied by a skin-crawling screech of wood splintering.

The three women jumped and stared at one another wide-eyed. Cheney was the first to recover. "Down the street, over that way! It must be a carriage accident! Hurry, Nia, go get a lamp and wait for me in the vestibule!"

Cheney was already hurrying through the Steen house, darting up the stairs to her bedroom to get her medical bag. She grabbed two clean sheets out of the linen press and ran back down to meet Nia in the vestibule. Together they ran out the front door.

The Steen house was on the very summit of Russian Hill, with three roads leading up to the drive. To their right they could hear the unmistakable sounds of men shouting hoarsely, one man crying out in pain, and panicked horses. This road, to the southeast, was narrow, ill-lit, and crooked.

By the time Nia and Cheney rounded the third curve and saw the accident, they were running at top speed from the steepness of the decline. Cheney skidded to a stop and took two deep breaths while she made a fast assessment of the situation. Beside her, Nia held the lamp high and steady.

A wooden cart had been coming down the hill, and a fine carriage coming up. They'd collided as they rounded one of the tight curves. The cart was almost completely demolished, a pile of shards and pikes in the middle of the road. The carriage was intact but was lying on its side half-buried in a ditch. Evidently both vehicles had been moving at a fast clip, because the three horses were still entangled in one another's traces and harnesses, and were screaming and rearing and fighting, adding a nightmarish backdrop to the grisly scene.

"Multiple injured," Cheney breathed, half to herself and half to Nia.

Three injured men lay in the road. The one nearest to Cheney and Nia was an older man, perhaps sixty, dressed in rough clothing. Cheney thought he might be the cart driver. He lay on his left side, his chalk face turned expressionlessly toward them. Kneeling by him was a young man, finely dressed, obviously uninjured.

To their right a young man of about twenty groaned loudly, his face strained, his eyes wide and panicked. He struggled to sit up. Blood streamed from his forehead, and a wicked-looking spike of wood protruded from the fleshy outer part of his right thigh.

Farther along, dangerously close to the storm of horses, another man was lying motionless on his back. Cheney could see he was dressed in pegged pants and a three-tiered coat—a carriage driver's livery. A gentlemanly older man, evidently uninjured, knelt by him, his ear against his chest.

All this took only a few seconds to register on Cheney's mind and in her brain. She stepped forward and called loudly, "You two men! Don't touch them, don't move them! I'm a doctor, and I'll see to them!"

The two uninjured men looked up at her in amazement.

Cheney spoke first to the well-dressed young man. "You! Go back there and attend to those horses, or we'll all end up lying here in the street senseless!" The horses were fighting and stamping, and the traces were still attached to the wreckage of the cart and the overturned carriage. All of them were in danger of being run over by the horses, should they get loose, or of being hit by what was left of the cart and the carriage if the horses bolted.

Then she knelt down swiftly for a closer look at the cart driver. Nia hovered close behind her, trying to hold the lamp to Cheney's best advantage. But the young man stayed where he was and stared at her with surprise and disbelief.

"Sir, are you injured?" she asked him brusquely.

"What? No, no, of course not," he said with some confusion. "I was just—"

"I told you, I'm a doctor," Cheney repeated impatiently. "I'll take care of these men. Now, go get those horses calmed down, please, before they break loose and bolt."

He stood up and looked uncertainly down at her, then behind his shoulder at the other uninjured man. Both of the men were finely dressed, and Cheney thought they must have been the occupants of the carriage. Gruffly the older man jerked his thumb toward the horses, though he was watching Cheney with narrowed eyes. The young man hurried to the horses and tangle of harness.

Sighing, Cheney laid her fingers gently under the man's ear and felt a faint pulse. As she did, she got down very close to the man; he was breathing. "Sir? Can you hear me?" Cheney couldn't tell if he was unconscious; his eyes were open but blank.

He murmured a little and seemed to focus on Cheney's face.

"Don't move, I'll be right back," she told him, then hurried to the man with the bloody scalp wound and the splinter. Nia followed close behind.

"Sir? Calm down, sir. I'm a doctor, and I can help you." The man's face was contorted with fear, and he was gasping.

"Huh?" he grunted, trying to touch his head with shaking hands. "Help me . . . bleeding . . . hurts!"

"I know, sir," Cheney said calmly, feeling of his pulse for only a few seconds. "Fast but strong," she told Nia quietly, "and he's breathing all right." Rising to her feet she told the man, "Be still, try to be calm. I'll be back in just a minute."

"No! No, don't leave me!" he begged.

Cheney turned her back to hurry to the last man. Nia looked back at the bleeding, gory man and whispered uncertainly, "Miss Cheney?"

"Nia, we have to see if any of them have life-threatening injuries," Cheney told her. She cast a glance back over her shoulder at the man who was still groaning and crying out for them to come back. "He looks the worst, but he's not hurt the worst."

Cheney went swiftly to the last man, the carriage driver. The older man kneeling by him hadn't moved, though dangerously close behind him the three horses still stamped and fought. The young man was having a hard time of it trying to separate the tangled harness and calm down fifteen hundred pounds of furious horseflesh.

"His name is Mr. Watts," the older gentleman said calmly. "He's my driver. He has facial contusions and abrasions, abrasions on his right knee and shin, not serious, and I believe his left shoulder is separated." He watched Cheney curiously.

"Mr. Watts? Can you hear me?" she asked the pale man.

"Yes, ma'am, sure can," he answered gamely, if a little weakly.

"Your shoulder hurts?" Cheney asked, probing it gently.

He grimaced with pain. "Sure does, miss. Miss—doctor. But I got it out of whack twice before like this—ball came out of the socket, you know—and it feels just like it did the other two times."

"Bad habit to get into, Mr. Watts," Cheney said with a tight smile, standing up again. "But you'll be all right. That other man"—she pointed behind her—"is very seriously injured, and I need to attend to him first. I know you're in pain, but I have something that will help you, and I'll get my nurse to bring it to you in just a moment. All right?"

"S'fine, miss, you go ahead for sure," he replied quietly.

He exchanged an odd look, heavy with some meaning that Cheney couldn't understand, with the older well-dressed man close by him. Cheney was too busy to spend much time wondering about it. She did see with some satisfaction that the older man stood and was helping calm the horses and get them in order.

"Come with me, Nia," she ordered, hurrying back close to the first man but staying out of earshot. Cheney was satisfied to see that Nia was alert and ready to help, and although she was somewhat nervous, she was in complete control of herself. "First, give both Mr. Watts and the bleeding man some laudanum."

"Yes, ma'am. I know what it is and how much to give them."

"Good. Medicate Mr. Watts first, and then you can leave him; he's fine. Go to the bleeding man. Be very, very calm, Nia. If you are calm, it will help him to be. Speak quietly to him while you're working on him. Do you know what to do?"

"I think so," she answered tentatively. "The scalp wound? Stop the bleeding?"

"Yes, it's scary how much they bleed," Cheney stated, "but unless you can feel an indentation around it, it's usually just a laceration of the skin and not a skull fracture. Even if it does feel funny, Nia, just gently press a dressing to it, and it should stop bleeding in a few minutes. Now, for that splinter—"

"I know," Nia said hurriedly. "I already know. Pour some carbolic acid around it, then pack around it with bulky dressings and bandage them to keep it still. I know not to pull it out."

"Excellent!" Cheney declared. "But be sure and give Mr. Watts a good solid dose of laudanum. He's the least seriously injured, but a separated shoulder is very painful. And then be sure and get the bleeding man calmed down. And don't let him touch that splinter!"

Cheney hurried back to the first man, the cart driver. He still lay on his side, motionless, staring straight ahead.

Cheney lay down almost prone in the road to look at the man's eyes. "Sir? Sir? Can you hear me?" she asked loudly.

"Yes," he said faintly, almost unconcernedly.

Cheney picked up his wrist and with one compartment of her brain registered an even but somewhat slowed pulse rate. "Sir? What is your name?"

It took him a few seconds but finally he said, "E-Ethan . . . Sanford."

"My name is Dr. Duvall. I'm going to help you, but I need some information," Cheney said in a calm but commanding voice. "Mr. Sanford, did you get thrown out of the cart and hit your head?"

"Don't know . . . don't know . . ." he whispered.

"No, don't move yet, Mr. Sanford! Just be still for a few minutes, and I'm going to examine your eyes and head. But I really need to know about the accident. Think back and tell me exactly what happened," Cheney urged him.

As she talked to him and made him respond, she conducted a quick but thorough physical examination. She checked his pupils and noted that the left was slightly more dilated than the right. She could see a small pool of blood beneath his left ear, but she couldn't yet tell if there was a laceration or if it was coming from inside his ear. But she wasn't ready to move him yet, as she hadn't been able to determine if he'd sustained a spinal cord injury. At least his pulse was steady, but it seemed to be slowing. His respiration was slow. His heart rate was slow but sounded solid and regular. Running her hands down his chest and thorax, she pressed lightly here, there, but felt no abdominal stiffening or broken ribs.

He had stopped talking, and his eyes were growing glazed and dull. "Mr. Sanford! Don't go to sleep!" she ordered sharply. "Keep talking to me!"

Again she bent down to see his pupils, but it was getting too dark to see details. Nia had the lamp, and Cheney started to scramble up to see if she could find one of the carriage lamps. At that moment the younger carriage gentleman loomed over the two of them with one already lit. "Here, you need this, Dr. Duvall," he said.

"Thank you." Grabbing it, she put it as close to the man's face as she could. With a measure of satisfaction she saw that his eyes tracked the bright circle of yellow, then squinted a little. "Mr. Sanford? Tell me, do you feel any pain? Anywhere?"

"N-no . . . n-no . . .'cept a headache. . . ."

"Any tingling? Numbness anywhere?" Lightly Cheney ran her hands down his arms and legs, then carefully began to touch the back of his neck with her fingertips, then trace the spinal cord all the way down.

"D-don't . . . think so . . . I don't feel anything, much . . . 'cept uncomfortable . . . and scared," he whispered.

"I know," she said quietly, then took his hand between both of hers. "I'm going to help you, Mr. Sanford. In just a minute I'll move you to a more comfortable position. I want you to stay still until then."

She looked at the young gentleman, who had knelt behind Mr. Sanford's back and was watching Cheney gravely. She signaled him to step away from the injured man. "I need your help," she said simply.

"What do you want me to do?"

"This man needs to be transported to the nearest hospital by ambulance. He has a basal skull fracture and intracranial hemorrhage. That means—"

"I know what it means, Dr. Duvall," the young man said evenly. "I can ride one of the carriage horses to St. Francis. I should be back with the ambulance in about half an hour."

Without another word he turned and jumped onto one of the carriage horses. Evidently the two uninjured men had anticipated this. They'd cut the horse loose from the carriage harness but had left a length of trace attached to the bridle so the horse could be ridden, although it was, of course, unsaddled.

Cheney hoped that the young man was a good and fast rider.

If he wasn't, Ethan Sanford would die.

2

The Mission

Cheney hurried to check on Nia and the man with the spike in his leg. With satisfaction she saw that the man was calmer now, though his eyes were still wild and scared. He was pressing a clean dressing to his head while Nia attended to his leg. Nia had positioned herself effectively to block the man's view of the terrible splinter protruding from his leg as she packed it to prevent further damage. This was good; if the patient couldn't see such a frightening injury, it was easier to calm him. Cheney had never told Nia this, for they'd never been in a trauma situation together. The girl must have just known it instinctively.

When Cheney knelt beside them, Nia said quietly, "Dr. Duvall, this is Mr. Ike Trimble. Mr. Trimble, this is Dr. Cheney Duvall, and you don't know how lucky you are that she's here to take care of you."

"And how fortunate you are that Nia is such a good assistant," Cheney added. The man's panicky gaze went from Nia to Cheney, then back to Nia, but he did seem to relax just a bit. Cheney picked up his hand, pressed it reassuringly for a moment, then took his pulse. It was stable, though elevated. Then she gently moved the dressing aside and touched all around the laceration on his forehead.

"This is going to take some stitches, Mr. Trimble, but it's not at all serious. The bleeding's already slowing. That's right, just hold this dressing against it for a few more minutes. Now, I know you're in pain and you're scared. But an ambulance is on the way, and we're going to take you to St. Francis de Yerba Buena Hospital. Your leg will be taken care of there, and I promise you, Mr. Trimble, that you're going to be all right. Now, do you remember the accident?"

"Y-yes'm. We . . . we just crashed into that carriage."

"I need to know what happened to Mr. Sanford," she said intently. "Do you remember? Did you see?"

"He—I think he got thrown over the front of the cart. He was driving. Yes, he went right over the front of the cart, and I guess he got . . . tangled up with the horses. . . ." Trimble began to look panicky again. "He gonna be all right? He . . . he's . . . my friend . . . he helps me. . . ."

Again Cheney took Trimble's free hand and stroked it. "Don't worry, Mr. Trimble. I can help him. He is seriously injured, but I know what to do. Now, Nia, here, is taking very good care of you, and she's an excellent nurse. I need to get back to Mr. Sanford. You just stay calm, all right?"

After a few moments he took a deep, gulping breath and nodded. "Miss Nia's doin' fine," he said tremulously. "She's real nice. You go see about Ethan, Dr. Duvall."

Though every nerve in Cheney strained to hurry back to Ethan Sanford, she knew she needed to at least say a word to Mr. Watts. She rose and turned back toward where he lay, but she was amazed to see that the older carriage gentleman was helping him to walk to the carriage, and then helping him to sit down with his back to it so he could be in a semiprone position. Cheney ran to them, calling, "Wait! Wait, sir! I don't want to move him yet!"

As she neared them, however, she could see that Mr. Watts's arm was in a sling. An expert sling. His left hand was folded across his chest, and a bandage—the carriage gentleman's cravat, she noted—was wrapped in a tight diagonal to keep it immobile in the most comfortable position possible.

The older gentleman rose and regarded Cheney gravely.

Cheney stopped and searched his face. He was about fifty-five, with thick, coarse gray hair combed straight back from a high forehead, a thick gray mustache, and no-nonsense dark eyes. "Who are you?" she demanded.

He put out his hand. "I am Dr. J. E. Baird, Dr. Duvall. It's a pleasure to meet you, although it is under such unfortunate circumstances."

"Oh, dear," Cheney sighed. Dr. J. E. Baird was a highly respected San Francisco physician, a forty-niner who'd struck it rich in 1850 and then had the courage to go to medical school at thirty-five years of age. He was the senior physician and administrator of St. Francis de Yerba Buena Hospital, and Cheney had an interview scheduled with him the next day to ask him for a job. "Wonderful," she breathed wryly, "Dr. Baird, I—"

"Never mind all that now," he interrupted and hurried toward the wreckage of the cart. Cheney kept pace alongside him. "Looks like we—you—have these two patients settled. What about that one?" He jabbed a thick forefinger toward Ethan Sanford, who still lay forlornly in the middle of the dusty road.

"Skull fracture, intracranial hemorrhage," Cheney answered. "I don't believe he has a spinal injury, but he's lethargic and vague. I haven't had time to conduct a thorough enough examination to feel confident about moving him yet."

"Go see to him," Baird ordered. "I'll try to find a board in this wretched pile of sticks good enough to hold him steady. The ambulance will be here soon, and we can at least get him ready for transport."

Cheney hurried back to Ethan Sanford and without hesitation threw herself on the ground beside him. "Mr. Sanford? Mr. Sanford, it's Dr. Duvall! Can you hear me?" His eyes were half-closed. The eyelids fluttered, then opened very slowly. He seemed unable to respond, however, and his gaze was empty.

"Listen to me, Mr. Sanford!" Cheney almost shouted, then roughly pinched the skin on his left hand. "Can you feel this?"

"Hmm . . . yes, yes, my hand . . ." he muttered almost inaudibly.

"This?" She pinched his right arm.

Cheney pinched and poked his arms and legs and feet, and he did have pain sensation throughout his body. She could tell, however, that he was noticeably weaker on his right side than on his left—which was another sign that he had bleeding, probably on the left side of his brain.

Dr. Baird hurried up with a piece of a sturdy two-by-twelve about three feet long. "This will have to do. You check his vital signs, Dr. Duvall, and I'll tear these sheets into strips. Talk to me, tell me about him."

As Cheney checked his pulse, respiration, and heart, she gave Dr. Baird a synopsis of his condition. "I think he was kicked in the head by a horse. Leakage from left ear, blood and maybe cerebrospinal fluid. When I first arrived on the scene his respiration was slow, but now he's beginning to go into tachypnea. His pulse is growing progressively slower. His heart rate is stable but slow. I think his temperature is rising." She bent closely over his head. "Ecchymoses behind the ears."

"Huh?" Dr. Baird said gruffly as he busily tore one of the Steens' fine linen sheets into strips.

"Um . . . ecchymoses, Dr. Baird," Cheney repeated hesitantly. "Battle's sign."

"What's that?" he demanded unselfconsciously.

"Dark purple bruising," Cheney explained. "Blood pooling in the sinus cavities." She bent over Sanford, who seemed either uncaring about the conversation or unable to hear. "Mr. Sanford? Listen to me! Can you hear me?" She looked up at Dr. Baird. "He's unconscious. CSF trickling from left nostril."

"All right, let's get him trussed up."

Cheney said quietly, "You know we need to prop him up on his left side, with his head slightly elevated, sir."

"No, sure didn't," Dr. Baird rasped. "But I'll take your word for it, Dr. Duvall. Let's get him strapped up, then I'll go find something to wedge behind and under him. At least I'm good for that!"

"I think you might want to lay these binding strips down behind him, sir, so we can lay him and the board on top of them, don't you think, Dr. Baird?" Cheney suggested gently.

"Woman," he grunted, "all this polite tea-talk is nice, but you and I both know I haven't got a notion of what to do. You might as well just keep on ordering me around like you've been doing. Save us and Mr. Sanford a lot of time."

Amused and resigned, Cheney instructed Dr. Baird how to lay out the strips and the board. Then, while he held it securely against Sanford's back and neck, Cheney gently pushed the injured man over on his back while Baird eased him down. Then she crossed Sanford's arms securely on his chest. "No, don't tie these strips directly across him," she told Baird. "Pad it with dressings—no, I guess we don't have enough of those—go tear up the sheet so we can make pads two or three inches thick."

"Yes, ma'am," he agreed wryly, but Cheney could see a ghost of a smile on his craggy features.

Sanford had a definite blunt trauma to the left side of his head, and Cheney knew all she could do right now was to gently dab at the fluid leaking from his ear. Every few minutes she checked Sanford's pulse, respiration, and heartbeat. He was worsening fast.

They finally got him securely bound to the backboard, and Dr. Baird scrounged some chunks of wood to position him in an upright position as Cheney had instructed. Then came the hard part; they sat by the injured man and waited.

Dr. Baird asked without preamble, "Obviously you know how to handle this kind of trauma in an emergency situation. But what's your plan of management, Dr. Duvall?"

"He needs surgery," she said firmly. "Immediately."

Dr. Baird's eyes narrowed to slits. "Surgery," he repeated in disbelief. "Brain surgery?"

"No. His brain hasn't been traumatized." Cheney felt gently around the left side of Sanford's head. "I can feel a definite indentation but no skull shards. But this hemorrhage must be drained."

The older man considered her dispassionately for a long time. "I'm not familiar with this surgical procedure, Dr. Duvall," he finally said evenly but not rudely. "Are you?"

"I've never done it," Cheney admitted. "But I know it must be done. The logic is inescapable. This man's going to die if the pressure on his brain isn't relieved. Exploratory surgery is the only way to do that."

Again Dr. Baird was silent for long moments. "Can you do it?" he asked her with an expression that was both withering scrutiny and curiosity. "Will you do it?"

Cheney considered her answer carefully. At length she said, "It's a fairly simple procedure; that is, there are fewer steps than, for example, gall bladder removal. So, yes, I am physically and intellectually capable of doing it." She hesitated, and Dr. Baird waited, watching her. "I would do it, yes, if you or another more experienced doctor won't. I would prefer—it would be much better for me, and for Mr. Sanford, if my nurse could assist me."

Dr. Baird's eyes cut to Nia, who was still holding Ike Trimble's hand and talking softly to him. "Her?" he asked in disbelief.

"No, she's . . . I'll . . . explain about Nia later," Cheney said hastily. "No, I meant my medical assistant. He's here in San Francisco. He escorted me and Mrs. de Lancie here. He's been my medical assistant for two years now, and he's quite . . . expert. He was a medic in the war, and he has a great deal of experience with trauma victims. In fact, he is the one who brought an article in *The Lancet* to my attention a month or so ago on this exact procedure."

"Hmm," Dr. Baird growled. "And who is this wonderful nurse?"

"His name is Shiloh Irons," Cheney replied.

Dr. Baird's bushy gray eyebrows shot up. "Shiloh Irons? The Iron Man? He's your nurse?"

Cheney's eyes widened. "You know him? No, wait—The Iron Man! Don't tell me he's fighting again!"

"Hmm, I see that's not a topic," Baird rumbled with spare amusement. "No, he's not fighting . . . yet. But if my son has his way, he will be soon."

"Your son?"

Dr. Baird's severe countenance softened almost imperceptibly. "My son, Walker. Dr. Matthew Walker Baird. That was Walker that you were ordering around like a stable boy. He should be back with the ambulance soon."

At that moment they heard the insistent jangling bell of an emergency vehicle far down at the base of Russian Hill and coming closer.

★ ★ ★ ★

A few minutes later the ambulance came careening around the curve, with Dr. Walker Baird still riding the carriage horse and, Cheney was profoundly grateful to see, Shiloh Irons riding beside him. Cheney ran to Shiloh as he slid off the horse.

"How did you—where—"

"Hi, Doc," he said casually, as if they'd just met on the Ladies' Mile in Manhattan. "You glad to see me?"

"Yes," Cheney breathed gratefully. "I really need you, Shiloh."

"Yeah, I know. I always know," he said lightly as he took her arm and made a beeline to Mr. Sanford. "This guy's pretty done in, huh?"

"Yes, he's—"

"Skull fracture?" Shiloh knelt beside the injured man, pulled up his eyelids, peered behind his ears, felt his wrist, put his head down on his chest.

"Yes. And he—"

"Cerebral hemorrhage?"

"Yes. I—"

"Don't know about the spine?"

"No," Cheney answered, rolling her eyes.

"Okay, let's get them loaded up." Shiloh stood, and Dr. Baird, still seated by Ethan Sanford, took a long, long look up at him.

Shiloh was six five and weighed about two hundred pounds. He was an intimidating size but not a frightening man. Not usually, anyway. His movements were calm, easy, almost indolent but purposeful.

He was golden-boy handsome, with light blond hair and mild blue eyes and clear, clean features.

Shiloh put his hand down to Dr. Baird, both as a greeting and to help him up. "Shiloh Irons."

Dr. Baird rose. "Dr. J. E. Baird. I've heard about you from my son, Mr. Irons. It's a pleasure to meet you."

"My pleasure, sir," Shiloh said briskly, then turned away to instruct the two burly ambulance attendants who had hurried up to hover uncertainly over Ethan Sanford. "Here, you! Go get that man—" Shiloh pointed toward Ike Trimble—"a stretcher and a pillow, so we can prop him up into a sitting position. Get him onto the stretcher and I'll come help you get him." He addressed the second attendant. "You go back into the ambulance and make sure one of the hammocks is cleared. Then come back and help me load this man. We're going to put him, backboard and all, on a hammock, and we'll need two pillows to prop him up just like this."

Walker Baird was helping Mr. Watts into the ambulance already, and Shiloh shouted, "Walker! Put him in a top hammock, okay?"

Walker turned and made a jaunty thumbs-up sign to Shiloh.

Shiloh turned back and frowned darkly at the ambulance attendants, who were still standing mute, staring at Dr. Baird.

Dr. Baird crossed his arms. "You two men do what Mr. Irons says." They both turned and sprinted back toward the ambulance wagon. Baird turned back to Shiloh. "All of you people sound like you know what you're talking about. Hope you really do, because I've been 'yes ma'aming' ever since I climbed out of that carriage."

Shiloh nodded sagely. "The Doc been bossin' you around, sir?"

"Yep." The older man shrugged. "Might as well. You and she seem to be the only people around here who know what they're doing. You two and the little colored girl. She hasn't given me any orders yet, but I guess if she did I'd hop to it."

"Easier that way," Shiloh stated. "Believe me, I know."

"Two years, I hear," Baird said sympathetically.

"Yes, sir. I gotta tell you, I only thought the war was exciting and dangerous. That was before I started working for Dr. Cheney Duvall."

The attendant returned from the ambulance wagon and was solicitously checking the strapping on Ethan Sanford. Shiloh moved toward them, but Dr. Baird stopped him by gripping his arm. "Mr. Irons, Dr. Duvall wants to do an exploratory skull surgery on that man."

Shiloh nodded. "Only thing to do for him."

Baird considered him with shrewd dark eyes. "She was reluctant to do it unless you could assist her. How do you feel about it?"

Shiloh had a certain intuition about people. Sometimes he just knew things, understood things about people, sometimes even with people he'd only just met.

Right now he knew that Dr. J. E. Baird wasn't asking him about his own ability to assist at such a delicate operation. And the doctor wasn't asking him how he felt about such an unproved surgery. Dr. Baird was asking him about Dr. Cheney Duvall.

Shiloh returned his questioning gaze with an iron-steady stare of his own. "She's about the best doctor I've ever worked with. She's smart and she's strong. She never wavers, never weakens, and never gives up."

Long moments passed; J. E. Baird searched Shiloh's open face, his clear direct gaze, and then nodded firmly. "So," he muttered, "I guess we'd better pack up this whole circus and head to St. Francis."

★ ★ ★ ★

Mission St. Francis de Yerba Buena was built in 1799 by the Spanish monks and their converts, the Ohlone Indians. The original mission had actually been a small community, centered around the church. The cluster of buildings had consisted of cloisters for the monks, living quarters for the Indians, workrooms, shops, and warehouses. The land had encompassed farm fields and a cemetery.

In 1821 Mexico took advantage of the crumbling Spanish regime and declared its sovereignty. Naturally, the new empire considered Alta California part of its property. Twelve years after declaring its independence, the Mexican government passed a Secularization Act stripping the Spanish missions of all their landholdings, which were indeed vast. So in 1833 almost all of the missions had been abandoned and left to ruin.

Henry Andrew Steen, Victoria de Lancie's father, had bought large parcels of San Francisco real estate during the Gold Rush, and one of these parcels included the mission of St. Francis de Yerba Buena. Although he had not upgraded or maintained the deserted mission, neither had he sold the four acres that included the church, the cloister, and the outbuildings. In 1860, when he had invested heavily in the Comstock, his miners approached him to make some provision for their medical care. He established an emergency care clinic in Virginia City, then decided to convert St. Francis into a private convalescent hospital. And so St. Francis de Yerba Buena became a house of healing.

Cheney Duvall, her hair tightly bound up in a French twist, her hands yellow from scrubbing with carbolic acid, her blood-and-dirt-stained tea gown completely covered by a floor-length white coverall, knelt at the altar in the chapel of St. Francis. The small chapel was all that remained of the original church. The nave had been converted to an operating theater, but behind it the chancel and altar were preserved intact, and the font had been carefully moved to the small entrance door that led into the amphitheater.

She heard a rustle beside her and smelled Shiloh's clean scent of pine soap, now combined with the antiseptic smell of carbolic acid. Though her head was bowed and her eyes were closed, she smiled slightly. He clasped her hand firmly in his, and Cheney continued to pray. Shiloh looked up at the stained-glass window behind the altar, a glowing image of Mary and the infant Jesus.

After a while Cheney lifted her head and smiled at Shiloh. "Ready?" she asked quietly.

"Sure, Doc. You?"

"Yes." Taking a deep, determined breath, she rose and walked, followed by Shiloh, to the door that led into the operating theater.

The theater was a relatively small rotunda, but the tiers of surrounding seats rose twelve high, about halfway to the cavernous rafters. About forty people, men and—Cheney was surprised to see—a few women were dotted around. The theater was very quiet. But when Cheney entered, she was greeted by a loud rustle of clothing and wood creaks as all the people in the theater rose to their feet. Cheney looked around, bewildered.

Shiloh whispered in her ear, "The nurses and students are all required to stand when a doctor enters the room. The doctors are just standing up to get a better look at you, 'cause you're beautiful."

Surreptitiously Cheney pinched his arm. Hard.

From the operating floor Dr. J. E. Baird announced sonorously, "Dr. Cheney Duvall."

Most of the men sat back down.

Shiloh whispered urgently, "Don't forget! You'll have to give the ladies permission!"

Smoothly Cheney said, "Thank you, and be seated."

In the center of the operating floor was a waist-high rectangular table, swathed in clean white sheets. Mr. Sanford was lying on it, covered by a sheet. He was still unconscious, lying on his back. Shiloh had not been able to confirm that he had not sustained a spinal injury, as he had not regained consciousness; but both he and Cheney knew that if this operation was not done, he would die of the hemorrhage anyway.

Sanford's head was completely shaved and tinted a lurid orange by iodine. Shiloh had carefully positioned his head to the right. Both Dr. Baird and his son, Walker, were standing by the patient. Walker was gently dabbing at Mr. Sanford's nose and ear and continually monitoring his pulse. On a three-tiered wheeled cart beside the operating table were laid out various gleaming surgical instruments, a neat stack of dressings and bandages, and a basin of yellowish liquid. On the second and third tiers were supplementary instruments, extra basins, several bottles, blankets, and more bandages and dressings.

Cheney and Shiloh walked to the operating table, and Cheney assessed the placement of the instruments. She looked at Shiloh and nodded her thanks; they were laid out exactly as Cheney would have done it. He smiled at her reassuringly.

"Dr. Baird," Cheney said quietly, but her voice echoed round the cavernous room, "I've never done a surgery for students or for demonstration before. I'm not certain I can operate and discuss it coherently at the same time. Would you be so kind as to lecture on this procedure as I perform it?"

"Walker will do that," the older man said shortly, folding his arms. "I'm just here to observe, Dr. Duvall."

Cheney swallowed hard but nodded calmly. Turning to Shiloh, she asked in a low voice, "Have you given him anything?"

"No, Doc. Better not. We don't know what kind of effect anesthesia would have on this kind of injury."

Cheney was acutely aware that everyone in the room could hear every word, every inflection. Then stubbornly she thought, *My main purpose here isn't to put on a show . . . I'm here to save this man's life. If I concentrate on that, I'll be fine. If I say something that someone can later criticize, or if I fumble something . . . well, they can just come down here and do it themselves . . . if they dare.*

Squaring her shoulders, she moved closer to Mr. Sanford. In a reassuring tone Walker Baird said, "Dr. Duvall, his respiration has stabilized, but it's very slow. His pulse is slow but steady. Heart rate steady."

Cheney studied the younger Dr. Baird, and he smiled brilliantly at her. It was the first time she'd really looked at him, instead of just seeing the uninjured carriage gentleman.

He was young, perhaps twenty-five. Compact but muscular, he gave the impression of barely controlled energy and sparkling vitality. He had the widest, most delighted smile Cheney had ever seen; his teeth were white and perfect. His eyes, Cheney could now see in the glaring gaslights of the amphitheater, were an unusual dark royal blue, wide, and continuously lit with enthusiasm and interest in whatever he was doing. His movements were quick, hurried, but deft. He had a glowing tan and shiny ash brown hair with blond streaks. He seemed athletic, outdoorsy, oddly out of place in such a sterile and controlled environment. Cheney briefly wondered exactly how capable a doctor he was.

"Thank you, Dr. Baird," she replied. "Will you allow Mr. Irons to assist me? And if you'll just come stand right here by and slightly behind me, I think that will be your best vantage point to see what I'm doing."

"Certainly, Doctor," he said respectfully and stationed himself just behind Cheney's left elbow.

Cheney checked Mr. Sanford's eyes, pulling up on his lids. "Left one is completely dilated," she murmured.

Across from her Shiloh replied, "He's still stable, though, Doc. I think you can do this quick enough so I won't even have to do a local."

She stared at him. "Are you sure, Shiloh? If he wakes up, he'll panic."

Shiloh shook his head confidently. "You don't worry about him, Doc. I'll take care of him. You just concentrate on this here—" Shiloh sketched a square in the air, right in front of and above Sanford's left ear.

"You're right," Cheney whispered half to herself as she stared at Ethan Sanford's head. After that moment she didn't hear anything else except her own and Shiloh's voice. She wasn't aware that anyone else was in the room. She never heard Walker Baird's quiet but thorough lecture as she operated.

Thrusting her hand toward Shiloh, it was steady and sure, as was her voice.

"Scalpel."

Walker Baird's voice was boyish, but his vocabulary and his comprehension of the procedure were expert.

"Dr. Duvall is making a semicircular incision in the left anterior cranial area. The incision is undercut so as to form a smooth seam to facilitate stitching and healing of the dermis and epidermis.

"Now she is peeling the flap of skin back to expose the skull. As the blood vessels of the head are minute and numerous, Mr. Irons will first suction a small area of the incision—what is that, Shiloh? An infant aspirator? Excellent idea!—suction a small area of the incision with an infant aspirator, and then pack it closely with small strips of bandages to clear the exposed skull."

Baird was silent for a few moments as Shiloh worked to stop the bleeding and to clean the skull area. Cheney checked Sanford's vital signs as Shiloh did this. Softly—to Shiloh—she quoted them, and Walker Baird repeated to the observers: "The patient's pulse is fifty-nine. His respiration is twelve, heartbeat regular and steady. The patient has a slightly elevated temperature, which often occurs with intracranial hemorrhage. It's essential that he be kept cool and not get overheated. Mr. Irons will monitor the patient's temperature throughout the procedure, and should his temperature spike, alcohol compresses will be applied to pressure points."

Shiloh had straightened, and Cheney bent low over Sanford's head. "Good. Clean," she murmured. Resuming a strong stance she held out her hand. "Drill. Half-inch."

It was in her hand before she finished speaking.

Baird said, "Now Dr. Duvall will drill a half-inch hole in the skull. The goal is to cleanly cut the skull, and then to pierce the first meninges without breaching the second. After trauma to the head, blood most often accumulates in the potential space between the outermost membrane—the dura mater—and the second layer—the arachnoid membrane."

He waited silently while Cheney drilled very slowly, her hands making strong, sure, repetitive circular motions, the drill bit absolutely still against Sanford's skull. Shiloh stood perfectly motionless, but his stance was relaxed, one hand kept on Sanford's wrist. Sweat began to accumulate on Cheney's forehead, and twice Shiloh dabbed it unobtrusively. Cheney never stopped drilling.

"I'm through the skull," she murmured. "And now—yes—the dura is pierced."

Shiloh moved fast. With one hand he placed a thickly folded dressing by Sanford's left shoulder; with the other he smoothly tipped Sanford's head to the left.

He and Cheney watched closely; but no bloodstain showed on the dressing. Their eyes met over the table.

"Clotted?" Cheney whispered.

"Yeah," Shiloh replied. "Here. Tissue forceps. See if you can pull it out."

Cheney's brow wrinkled for a moment, then cleared. She took the small pointed forceps and Shiloh gently turned Sanford's head back so the opening in the skull was upmost.

Cheney bent over him.

Baird cleared his throat. "Dr. Duvall has successfully drilled the hole in the skull plate and has pierced the dura. Since there is no exsanguination, Dr. Duvall will now explore the opening and see if a blood clot has formed that is preventing the hemorrhage from draining."

Everyone waited breathlessly while Cheney probed the small opening with tiny, patient movements. Finally she breathed, "I've . . . got it, Shiloh."

He pulled Ethan Sanford's head around again, while Cheney slowly extracted the closed forceps from the hole.

The operation was over. Ethan Sanford would live.

3

Odd Hours, Unusual Topics

"Mrs. de Lancie, a carriage is coming up the drive."

Victoria looked up from the letter she was writing. "Thank you, Mrs. O'Neil. Do you have the drawing room ready?"

"Yes, mum."

"Receive Dr. Duvall and the guests, and bring them into the drawing room. Please remain for a few minutes to see if I'll need you to serve. If I see that Dr. Duvall and our guests are content to help themselves, I'll signal you to withdraw."

"Yes, mum." Mrs. O'Neil turned to leave.

"One moment, Mrs. O'Neil," Victoria said quietly. The housekeeper turned and Victoria studied her. She stood quietly, enduring the close scrutiny with a curious absence of expression.

That's it . . . Victoria reflected. *She's so . . . blank. She never shows any expression, any feeling . . . it's like talking to a porcelain doll.*

Clara O'Neil's references listed her as thirty-six years old, but she looked younger. She was tiny, delicately framed except for her hands, which were muscled with hard work and chafed red. She was Irish, with a pretty cream complexion and hints of rose in her cheeks. Her hair was a glowing reddish blond, but she pulled it back tightly into a small, unattractive bun at the nape of her neck. Her gaze was always direct and her hazel eyes were clear, but they held no hint of joy or sadness or anything in between.

"I realize it's very late, Mrs. O'Neil, but it's been my experience that Dr. Duvall keeps irregular hours," Victoria said, more to gauge the housekeeper's reaction than for conversational purposes.

"Yes, mum."

Faintly they heard sounds coming from the front veranda—mostly men's boots thumping loudly on the steps—and Victoria gave up trying to figure out Clara O'Neil . . . for the moment, at least.

"That will be all, Mrs. O'Neil," she said, rising. The housekeeper hurried out of the music room, where Victoria had been writing her letter. Quickly Victoria went to the French cushion mirror in one corner and checked her hair and face. In the dimly lit room she looked rather ghostly, with her white-blond hair and her narcissus complexion. She was wearing a smoky gray satin dinner dress with white Cluny lace at the throat and wrists. The bodice and hem of the dress were trimmed with rare matched black pearls, and her maid Zhou-Zhou had done her fine-spun hair up in three layers of long ringlets with strings of the black pearls adorning the crown.

I don't blaze with vitality and energy and health like Cheney does . . . but I suppose I have a certain glow.

With a final pat of her hair Victoria went from the music room through the archway into the connecting drawing room. With satisfaction she saw that her instructions to the housekeeper had been meticulously followed. The food was attractively arranged on the parquet pearwood console table, with French doré gilt candlesticks on each side. The entire room was lit by candlelight, a trick Victoria had learned from Cheney's mother, Irene Duvall.

Gaslight is a wonderful convenience, and much more efficient than candles . . . but to make a room seem warm, intimate, inviting, candlelight is perfect.

After one last assessing look around the room, Victoria hurried to the door that led into the drawing room from the vestibule to greet her guests as they entered.

Cheney came in first, and Victoria looked her up and down in astonishment. The skirt of Cheney's peach-and-chocolate tea dress was filthy. Two of the ruffles were torn at the knees, and the ribbon trim was hanging by a thread in several places. The sleeves were carelessly shoved up to her elbows, and her hands were stained yellow from carbolic acid.

Victoria's eyebrows shot almost to her hairline. "Cheney! Is that actually *dirt*? Is it *dirt*? All the way up to your shoulders? How in the world did you manage to do that?"

Startled, Cheney looked at Victoria's immaculate elegance, then down at her bedraggled condition, then, woefully, back at Victoria. "Oh, horrors! I suppose I must go bathe and change—"

"Oh . . . oh no, dear! Forgive me! That's nonsense!" Victoria said remorsefully, throwing her arms around Cheney in a quick hug and then leading her to the fireplace. "Cheney, darling, you're freezing! Out without even a shawl! Sit down here by the fire right now."

Grandly Victoria swept back to the vestibule. "Mrs. O'Neil, these gentlemen can attend to their own coats and hats. Go upstairs to Zhou-Zhou and tell her to give you my cashmere shawl for Dr. Duvall. No, Nia, you look as wet and cold and pinched as Cheney does. Go into the kitchen right now, have some hot soup, and go to bed. Zhou-Zhou can attend Cheney tonight."

She turned and resumed greeting her guests.

"Good evening, Mrs. de Lancie," Dr. Baird said as he kissed her hand. "I fear that Walker and I are almost as disheveled as Dr. Duvall. And since the hour is so late, we will take our leave now and call upon you at a more precipitate time."

"No, sir, you will not," Victoria replied spiritedly. "I am indebted to you, Dr. Baird, for sending the messenger boy with word of what occurred. And I am so relieved to see you and Walker unharmed, and it was kind of you to see Dr. Duvall home. So please, do come in. I have food, drink, and a fire, and I decided to wait and dine with Cheney. We are very informal tonight, but it would give me great pleasure if you would join us, Dr. Baird. And you, too, Walker."

"Mrs. de Lancie, it's my great pleasure to see you again." He grinned engagingly and impudently looked her up and down, his eyes wide with admiration. "My goodness, you've grown into a beautiful woman!"

"Thank you," Victoria said coolly, offering him her hand. "I should hope I am better turned out than when I was twelve."

"I don't know," he replied as he pressed a kiss to her hand. "I recall that I liked those long blond ringlets."

"And I recall that you were seven years old and horrible," Victoria retorted. "You put a spider in my hair."

"Am I forgiven?"

"Do you have any spiders on your person?"

"No, ma'am."

"Then please come in. I forgive you, and I'm really very glad to see you again, Walker."

Shiloh was the last of the company, and gallantly he offered Victoria his arm to escort her into the reception room. Cheney and Walker were already hovering over the sideboard; Walker was fixing himself a steaming cup of coffee and Cheney had creamy warm cocoa. Simultaneously they each filched a chocolate ladyfinger arranged on a silver tray. Exchanging guilty glances, they stuffed the sweets into their mouths and chewed quickly.

Dr. Baird was fixing himself a cup of tea. He gave no sign that he'd seen them, but Cheney thought she saw the corner of his mustache twitch.

The doctors and Shiloh gulped down their hot drinks and then began to help themselves to mugs of creamy potato soup and bite-sized cubes of smoked ham with diced apples. Mrs. O'Neil came in with the shawl for Cheney, but quickly Victoria signaled her that she might leave.

After the party had fixed their plates, they arranged themselves around the white marble fireplace. The Bairds settled down in the solid leather club chairs while Cheney and Victoria sat on the elegant Venetian sofa. Shiloh attended to the fire, which was a stack of three hefty oak logs, blazing cheerfully above a glowing three-inch bed of scarlet embers. Cheney was especially grateful for the comforting heat; April nights in San Francisco were cool.

"I must know, how are the men who were injured in the accident?" Victoria asked.

Shiloh, Cheney, and Walker looked expectantly at Dr. Baird. After taking a cautious sip of hot soup, he answered, "The driver of the coal cart sustained a serious—no, I must say deadly—head injury. But Dr. Duvall operated on him, or performed a miracle on him, depending on your point of view, and saved his life."

Cheney began to demur, but Dr. Baird ignored her and went on, "The other man in the coal cart had a bad splinter in his leg, but Walker took it out, and he'll be all right. Odd. It will take him longer to recover from that minor surgery on his leg than it will take Mr. Sanford to recover from that head surgery. Anyway, my driver, Mr. Watts, sustained some abrasions and contusions, and his shoulder was separated. Mr. Irons remedied that faster and more efficiently than anyone I've ever seen." He gave Shiloh an appraising look. "You must be very strong."

"No, sir, strength isn't that important in those cases," Shiloh replied easily. "You just gotta be fast. Real fast. Even grown men can pass out on you in a flat two seconds if you don't get that ball back in the socket quick."

"Yes, I know," Baird said gruffly. "The last time Mr. Watts dislocated his shoulder he passed out twice while I was trying to replace it." He shook his head irritably. "Never did get the hang of it. Finally had to get one of the medical students. Embarrassing, that. And Watts just keeps on doing it."

"Dislocating his shoulder," Walker carefully explained. "Not passing out."

"Well, I assume that means that the men are going to be all right," Victoria commented. "So, Dr. Baird, were you able to salvage your carriage?"

"Yes. The front axle is broken, but somehow the frame remained intact, even though it turned over."

"But how on earth did this happen?" Victoria asked.

Dr. Baird grimaced. "Walker and I were on our way to call on you and Dr. Duvall. A coal cart with two men in it was coming down the hill. We met coming around a curve."

"Quite a meeting it was, too," Walker put in.

"I heard it," Victoria said. "I'm very glad I didn't have to see it."

"Ah, but it afforded me such a wonderful opportunity to observe a prospective staff physician," Dr. Baird said dryly.

"Dr. Baird, now that we are not in an emergency situation, I would like an opportunity to explain," Cheney said hurriedly.

Baird raised his eyebrows. "Explain what?"

"Um . . . well, I . . . I suppose that . . . perhaps I should apologize," Cheney stammered.

"For what?" Baird demanded.

Cheney was taken aback by the man's abruptness, and she stared at him for a moment. Beside his father, Walker was trying very hard to keep from grinning. Cheney suddenly relaxed. "For ordering you and Dr. Baird—Dr. Walker Baird—about like footmen, I suppose," Cheney answered with a small smile.

"Humph. If you'd known who we were, what would you have done?" Baird asked, his already direct gaze growing very intent.

Cheney considered her answer, then shrugged slightly. "The same thing, I suppose, only I probably would've said 'please' and 'thank you' more."

Walker and Shiloh exchanged grins, and even Dr. Baird looked faintly amused. "Maybe you would have, Dr. Duvall," he said, "and maybe you wouldn't. Doesn't matter anyway. You're a fine doctor, and I want you at St. Francis. You've got the job. We'll talk terms tomorrow, but I can tell you right now I don't like to barter. I'll be fair with you if you'll be fair with me."

Cheney's eyes shone. "Thank you, sir. I assure you I'll always give you my best work and a fair accounting."

"Good enough." He turned to Shiloh. "What about you, Irons? Would you consider coming to work at St. Francis? My nursing staff is in a worse tangle than my doctors. I'm short of doctors, you see, but I have plenty of nurses—most of them not worth an ounce of fool's gold."

Shiloh opened his mouth to answer, but Walker burst out eagerly, "Irons, you'd make a lot more money in a shorter time if you'd fight!"

"Yeah?" Shiloh said with interest.

Dr. Baird barked, "Walker, you are not a boxing promoter! You are a doctor! Remember?"

"But, Father, he's The Iron Man! And he could—"

"Shiloh doesn't fight anymore," Cheney interrupted rudely and much too loudly. The three men looked at her with various measures of surprise, and she added lamely, "Do you, Shiloh?"

Shiloh relaxed, leaning back in his chair, stretching out his long legs and crossing them. "Dunno, Doc. Hadn't really thought much about it since the last time—when was it—last year?"

"James Elliott," Cheney said between gritted teeth. "July 23, 1866. He almost blinded you."

"But you won, didn't you, Irons?" Walker said excitedly. "We knew all about it! Elliott was here last winter, you know, and tried to tell everyone at the club what a poof you were, but I told him it was a matter of record that The Iron Man had beaten him the summer before in New York. Seventh round. A clean, fast knockout. So I asked him who it was that was the poof."

"What'd he say?" Shiloh asked with interest.

"Nothing. He just hit me," Walker said mournfully. "Hurt like blazes, too, and I fell down. Guess I showed him who was the poof."

"He hits hard," Shiloh agreed, grinning. "And he knocked me down, too. Which is why I'm not too interested in fighting anymore." He took a long sip of coffee. "It hurts."

Cheney visibly relaxed, while Victoria took a sip of tea to hide her smile. Gracefully she rose and went to the console table to get the tray of ladyfingers, and then served everyone. As Shiloh helped himself, she asked, "So, Shiloh, are you going to take Dr. Baird up on his offer?"

"Don't decide right now, Mr. Irons," Baird said comfortably. "It's late, and we're all tired. Why don't you escort Dr. Duvall and Mrs. de Lancie to the hospital tomorrow when they call? I'd like for you and Dr. Duvall to see something besides the inside of Ethan Sanford's head."

"Dr. Duvall, that surgery was magnificent," Walker declared. "I hope I get an opportunity to try it soon."

Cheney roused herself from a deep reverie, and her eyes began to glow. "You mean you haven't done the surgery before? Shiloh told me that you seemed very familiar with what we were doing. How did you know about the particular nature of cerebral hemorrhage, the location and so on?"

Firmly Victoria set her china cup in the saucer, making a definite attention-getting clink. "Cheney, you have been talking about brain insides all day. I should like to have a different topic in my drawing room, darling."

"I can't believe you're going to try to get this crowd to talk about something besides dislocated shoulders and brain insides, Mrs. de Lancie," Shiloh said lazily.

"I shall use all of my social skills to do so," Victoria said firmly. "As a matter of fact, Shiloh, I've been wondering how you joined this company. You weren't with the Bairds in the carriage, were you?"

Cheney's eyes grew round. "That's right! I'd forgotten! Where did you come from, Shiloh?"

"I was just out riding, looking around," he drawled, "so I thought I'd trot on up here and come see you, Doc. And of course you, too, Mrs. de Lancie. I saw Walker down on Leavenworth Street, almost to the hospital." He slid a devilish grin in Cheney's direction. "His hair was standin' on end, and he was ridin' down that hill like a lunatic man, on a horse with no saddle. So I figured he'd been to see you, Doc."

Everyone chuckled, except Cheney, who made a face at him and helped herself to her second or—if anyone was counting—her third ladyfinger.

"So I rode along with him to help get the ambulance ready, and then I came back up here with him," Shiloh finished.

"Wait a minute," Cheney said, frowning. "How did you know Walker? I mean, Dr. Baird?"

"Please do me the honor of calling me Walker, Dr. Duvall," he suggested. "Everyone has to, or my father answers them. And if they call me 'Mr. Baird,' I think they're talking to my grandfather."

"All right, Walker," Cheney relented. "So how did you two meet?"

"At the Olympic Club," Walker answered enthusiastically before Shiloh could speak. "He came right to the club yesterday, just walked in! Didn't tell anyone who he was! And we have two of his advertising boards on the wall—the fight with Mike McCool and that fight with James Elliott!" At Cheney's look of surprise, he went on vigorously, "Oh, Dr. Duvall, perhaps you don't realize how famous Mr. Irons is among pugilistic enthusiasts. At the Olympic Club we arrange for runners in the city where a high-profile fight is held to telegraph us the results of each round!"

"I didn't know that," Shiloh commented.

"I did," Victoria said with a small smile.

"That fight between Irons and Elliott was a kicker!" Walker declared. "And, Shiloh, what was all that about the Dark Angels of the Mystic Rose? Your advertising board and the New York newspapers were full of mysterious references to them!"

Cheney's eyes turned a venomous green as she gave Shiloh a look of warning that would have withered any rose, mystic or otherwise. Victoria looked coolly amused. Walker Baird looked quizzically at Shiloh, then at Cheney, then at Victoria.

"So what's the line on that, Shiloh?" he demanded. "Your Mystic Roses?"

Shiloh dropped his voice and made melodramatic gestures as he told the story. "They weren't mine, you know. No one can own the Dark Angels of the Mystic Rose. They are for the victor, you see.

"At those two fights in New York, two mysterious, heavily veiled women attended. I won those fights, and the Dark Angels showered me with white roses. Then they disappeared, like ghosts in the mists.

"But it's still told on the docks and in the back alleys of Manhattan that one of the Dark Angels was a healer. They say she cured the Iron Man—that's me—of some mysterious injury when James Elliott almost killed him. Uh . . . me. Then"—he puffed out his chest and raised one fist—"with inhuman strength, the Iron Man rose and knocked James Elliott out cold.

"And it's said that the other Dark Angel's beauty was so great that she was obliged to wear the veil, or the fighters wouldn't fight because they couldn't stop gazing at her."

"That," Cheney said scornfully, "is the biggest bunch of hooey I ever heard."

"Cheney, really. 'Hooey'?" Victoria pronounced delicately. "Who taught you that word?" With silky elegance she brought her teacup up to her lips, surreptitiously winked at Shiloh over the rim, and took the tiniest, most ladylike sip. "And besides, I thought it was a lovely romantic story."

Cheney turned to Victoria wrathfully, but saw that the corners of her mouth were turned up slightly. She looked accusingly at Shiloh, but he was suddenly completely absorbed in something up close to the ceiling. She studied Dr. Baird, who actually looked amused. Desperately she turned to Walker, who met her gaze with an ardently admiring one of his own.

Cheney suddenly regained her sense of humor and turned back to Victoria. "Why, yes, dearest Victoria. I'm certain you do find the story compelling. Especially the part about the heartbreakingly gorgeous Mystic Rose, the one whose beauty blinds you if you look at her face. The short one."

"Yes, the tiny, delicate one," Victoria parried.

"Personally, I thought the tall, willowy one was interesting," Cheney mused. "The one with the long, sharp knife."

"Which one was your favorite, Shiloh?" Walker asked impishly.

"Huh?" Shiloh asked, faintly alarmed.

"Yes, which one was, Iron Man?" Victoria repeated, her blue eyes widening.

"Yes, which one?" Cheney demanded, her green eyes narrowing.

"Uh . . . neither," he said, then hastily amended, "I mean both. Both of them. All of them."

"Smart man," Dr. Baird rasped under his breath.

"Thank you," Shiloh said quickly. "I could use some more help here, Dr. Baird."

"Haven't the foggiest notion what you young people are talking about," Dr. Baird solidly maintained. "Don't want to know, either. I stay away from the Olympic Club. Men there are always doing silly things like swimming and boxing and throwing one another around, or throwing metal balls and spears and such. Grown men, I'm telling you!"

Cheney smiled at Dr. Baird. "The Olympic Club, yes. The athletes.

I have read about it. It's quite famous. Are you going to stay there, Shiloh?"

"No," Shiloh answered.

"Yes," Walker answered.

"I'm not sure I want to start fighting again, Walker," Shiloh protested.

"You don't," Cheney muttered under her breath.

"You don't have to fight, Shiloh," Walker insisted. "I know everyone expects you to, but that's up to you. I'll sponsor you to join the club. But we'd be honored if you'd consider doing a little training, and maybe just some light sparring. Nothing serious. And at least you can stay at the club until you decide what you want to do."

Shiloh thought for a few moments, then nodded. "Okay. It's a real nice place, and that swimming pool is something. I've never gotten to swim for a workout. I hear it's really good for you."

"Oh, it is! It's terrific! Gives you stamina and energy!" Walker enthused.

"As if you needed any more," his father commented grumpily.

Walker was too excited to pay attention. "I'll teach you how to get the optimum benefits out of swimming, Shiloh. It'll be great!"

"And I'll be your sparring partner, Walker," Shiloh generously offered.

Walker's boyish face suddenly grew alarmed. "Um . . . no, thanks, Iron Man. I don't want what few brains I have left leaking out of my ears onto the floor of a ring."

"Walker, I cannot believe you are talking about leaky brain mush again," Victoria said stiffly.

"That reminds me," Cheney said, her brow furrowing. "When the hole in Mr. Sanford's head wasn't draining properly, Shiloh, how did you—"

"Cheney," Victoria said in a quiet but menacing tone.

"Oh," Cheney said in a small voice. "I'm sorry, Victoria."

"So you should be."

Dr. Baird rose and lumbered over to the sideboard to help himself to more coffee. "It's your own fault, you know, Mrs. de Lancie, for keeping company with medical people. We're all arrogant and overbearing and incorrigible, and we *will* talk about the most gruesome things we can think of. Preferably during a meal."

"I know," Victoria sighed. "And I suppose I must get accustomed to it. All of it. The odd hours and the . . . unusual topics. After all, I am engaged to a physician."

"Are you, now?" Dr. Baird said and sketched a little bow before he sat back down. "Your father hadn't written me of this! May I offer my sincerest wishes for your happiness, Mrs. de Lancie."

Walker rose to take Victoria's hand and brush a kiss on it. "I'm delighted to hear this wonderful news, Mrs. de Lancie, and I hope you will be very happy."

"Thank you," Victoria replied, her eyes shining. "I know I shall be."

"Who is this lucky man? A doctor, you said?" Dr. Baird asked.

"Yes, his name is Devlin Buchanan," Victoria answered with a lilt in her normally fashionably bored tone. "He's in England right now, on a fellowship at Guy's Hospital. We haven't set a date yet, actually. He has six more months on his fellowship."

"Wait—Buchanan? At Guy's? Yes, he's the one who wrote that fantastic thesis on the cholera epidemic in New York last year!" Walker declared. "You remember, Father? And . . . and . . . wait a minute! Dr. Duvall, didn't he credit you in that thesis?"

"Yes, he was kind enough to cite me, because I did some laboratory studies for him," Cheney answered, her eyes glowing. Walker noticed that Shiloh was watching Cheney intently, almost obsessively. She went on, "He's an old friend of our family's; in fact, Dev's been almost like a brother to me. He's a brilliant physician"—she smiled at Victoria—"and a fine man. He and Victoria are perfect for each other."

Victoria smiled gratefully back and reached over to give Cheney's hand a light squeeze.

Walker noted these signals with interest, and he also noted that Shiloh visibly relaxed back into his usual careless grace.

Dr. Baird suddenly yawned prodigiously and took out a gold pocket watch. Squinting at it, he growled, "Almost midnight. I'm tired. Ladies, thank you for your gracious hospitality, but I must get home. I'm old and cranky when I don't get enough sleep."

"Cranky? Surely not you, Father!" Walker said mischievously, then helped him to rise. Dr. Baird, Walker, and Victoria all went into the vestibule, while Cheney and Shiloh lingered behind.

Shiloh rose and stretched, almost touching the ceiling, and smiled warmly at Cheney. "I don't wanna go yet, but I guess I better."

"Come back. Anytime," Cheney said quietly.

"How 'bout all the time?" he asked, his eyes glinting.

"How about tomorrow?" Cheney asked. "Bring us a hansom cab about ten o'clock? You're going to the hospital with us, aren't you?"

"Sure, Doc. You know I never get far from you. Don't guess I'll start now." He offered her his arm.

Cheney, smiling contentedly, took it and they went into the vestibule, where Victoria was helping Dr. Baird with his greatcoat. The three men made their good-night salutes, and Cheney and Victoria walked onto the veranda to say good-bye.

Dr. Baird turned as he was leaving and smiled at Cheney. It was the first time she'd seen him smile. He was an attractive man in a rough, craggy sort of way that was completely unlike Walker's well-scrubbed, athletic looks. Cheney wondered if Walker was like his mother.

"I shall see you tomorrow at St. Francis then, ladies?" Dr. Baird asked.

"We're looking forward to it," Victoria replied.

"As am I," he said, bowing in an old-world courtly manner. "And, Dr. Duvall—"

"Yes, sir?"

"I think that today I had an opportunity to observe one of the most capable, most expert, most dedicated physicians with whom I've ever had the pleasure to work," he said formally. "Having you on the staff will honor St. Francis de Yerba Buena."

Cheney could hardly sleep all night.

4

House of the Good Herb

"I can't believe you refused to ride in a hansom cab, Victoria," Cheney scolded.

"As I explained before, Cheney dear, there is no need for me to ride in a hansom cab," Victoria replied complacently. "Here is the landau. We are in it. It is taking us to the hospital. Why should I—or you, for that matter—ride in one of those public conveyances?" She gave a very slight shudder.

Shiloh grinned down at Cheney. "Yeah, Doc. Why should you ride in one of those disgusting things?"

"You be quiet," Cheney ordered him. "You're just as bad as she is."

"The lady was in distress," Shiloh said with a shrug, casually laying his arm along the back of the seat. Wholly unconsciously, Cheney leaned closer to him, and he looked as quietly pleased as the infamous cat that had managed to do away with all remaining evidence of the canary. "When I got that message from Mrs. de Lancie this morning, she sounded so scared! How could I possibly refuse to come to the rescue?"

"I thank you, sir, for your kindness," Victoria said. "I was, indeed, in great distress when Cheney told me you were actually coming to call for us in a hired cab! Imagine!"

"Imagine," Shiloh repeated solemnly, pinching Cheney's shoulder lightly. She retaliated by elbowing him in the ribs.

"Well, I think it's disgraceful, Victoria. A hansom cab wouldn't hurt your reputation. Everyone in America knows you're as rich as King Solomon," Cheney grumbled.

"Hansom cabs," Victoria pronounced grandly, "are likely very dirty."

"I saw some dirt on one once," Shiloh offered helpfully.

"Victoria, dear, have you ever had a piece, an iota, a speck of dirt on you? Ever? In your life?" Cheney asked with brittle brightness.

"Dirt?" Victoria whispered the word as if it were obscene. "On me? Why on earth would I have ever had dirt on me?"

"My point exactly," Cheney said triumphantly, though Shiloh and Victoria weren't sure exactly what she'd won. But Cheney ranted on, "And how on earth did you two manage to buy a landau, two horses, a driver, and two footmen—all before ten o'clock this morning?"

"I didn't do it, Shiloh did," Victoria said with painstaking slowness. "And as I told you, Cheney, we already had the landau. In our carriage house."

"We have a carriage house?" Cheney asked, bewildered.

"The driver, Mr. Yancey, and his family are already living in the caretaker's cottage. His two sons are the footmen."

"We have a caretaker's cottage?" Cheney wondered.

"So all Shiloh had to do was to buy the horses," Victoria finished.

"Yeah. All I had to do was find four matched grays before ten o'clock on a Saturday morning. And it's a good thing you've got sackfuls of money, Mrs. de Lancie, because Mr. Fain sure made you pay for this team." Shiloh brightened. "But, Doc, I met this Mr. Fain at the Olympic Club. He's also got some really good-looking saddle horses."

Cheney sat up straighter and looked at Shiloh with interest. "He does?"

"I think I'm going to buy this chestnut two-year-old," he told her excitedly. "Well . . . you saw him. That quarter horse I was riding yesterday. Mr. Fain said he'd let me try him out, and he's a good horse. Tough and strong."

"Oh, I miss Sock and Stocking terribly," Cheney sighed, "but I know they're happy with Tante Elyse." Cheney and Shiloh had left their horses with Cheney's great-aunts on their indigo plantation in New Orleans.

"Happy?" Shiloh echoed. "They're probably living in the dining room of Les Chattes Bleues by now!"

"Not if Tante Marye is still alive," Victoria said.

"Anyway, perhaps I should—could—buy a horse," Cheney said half to herself. "I could ride . . . yes, I could ride to the hospital! I brought my saddle, and—" She looked up at Victoria quizzically. "Does Steen House have stables?"

"Of course."

"Would you mind if I stabled a horse, Victoria?" Cheney asked. "I don't know what I'll do about a stable boy—perhaps I can take care of it myself—"

Victoria rolled her eyes. "Cheney, my dear. You are the most wonderful friend I've ever had, and I am so happy you're here with me. The house is yours. The stables are yours. The servants are yours. Mr. Yancey and his sons are there to take care of the carriage and the horses of Steen House. That includes your horse, too."

"Why, thank you, Victoria," Cheney said with a small measure of surprise at Victoria's vehemence. She was not normally so outwardly emotional. "And I'm glad we got to come here together, too."

Victoria smiled. "Buy her a horse," she told Shiloh.

"Okay," Shiloh said with satisfaction.

"Wh-what?" Cheney stuttered. "I beg your pardon—what did you say?"

"I said okay," Shiloh explained.

"Not you! Her!" Cheney said rudely and pointed.

"Cheney, don't point," Victoria said mildly.

"But—"

"We'll talk about it later, darling. Shiloh, knock on the window and signal Mr. Yancey to stop here, please."

"But, Victoria, I want to know—"

"Look, Cheney. It's the hospital. I thought you'd want to see it from this vantage point."

"Oh yes, I do, but we will talk about this later, Victoria," Cheney said with all the sternness she could muster.

The carriage door swung open, one of the footmen lowered the steps, and the two young men stood respectfully on either side to assist the ladies down.

Victoria, Shiloh, and Cheney stood on the crest of one of the city's forty-two hills and looked to the south. To the east, the dunes of San Francisco were covered with houses, shanties, shacks, mansions, and businesslike brick buildings, all contained in a neat patchwork of geometric squares that seemed rather absurdly precise, considering that they took no account of the topography. In the distance they could see the bay, although a heavy fog was veiling it and rolling inland quickly.

Directly below them the line of the city was clearly drawn. The buildings seemed impossibly close together from Hyde Street to the bay; west of Hyde Street was an endless vista of sandy hills and meager valleys. Dotted here and there in the western wilderness were dairy farms, but the only real landmark, directly below them at the very edge of town, was St. Francis de Yerba Buena.

"What does *yerba buena* mean?" Cheney asked, staring down at the neat little hospital.

"Good herb," Victoria answered. "When the Spanish first came here, a wild mint grew everywhere that the Indians used for healing purposes. It's scarce now, but Dr. Baird grows it in the hospital gardens. He says it does make a wholesome sweet tea."

The four-acre grounds were a square of green in a dusty valley. The mission building, which now held offices, the operating theater, and the chapel, gleamed a clean and pure white in the weak morning sun. L-shaped wings extended to each side of the mission, red lines drawn against the green lawn, for all that could be seen of the low-lying one-story extensions were the red tile roofs. To the rear, forming a square similar to a city square, were three outbuildings, also made of adobe with red roofs. Behind them were neat geometric squares of the gardens. Farther back were two large wooden structures, obviously the stables and barn, which served as a carriage house for the two ambulances.

"It's actually been plastered over, you know," Victoria told them. "All of the outside of the adobe buildings. Adobe lasts a long time, but the whitewashing doesn't weather well. The walls of all of those structures are three feet thick. The mission was built in 1799, and all of the buildings retain the original walls. The wings used to be cloisters for the monks and quarters for the Indians. There were several adobe outbuildings, workshops, and stables and barns. As you can see, all of them were torn down but those three. The stables and the barn are new."

"You know so much about it," Cheney said in surprise. "I didn't think you had much interest in such things."

Victoria made an elegant gesture with one tiny white-gloved hand. "It's part of my family's concerns, both business and civic. I'm really here to represent my father, so I try to be as informed as I can. That way I can advise him knowledgeably."

"I'm impressed."

"It's a responsibility that I take seriously," Victoria said quietly. "The Lord has blessed me and my family so much. We must be good caretakers of everything that comes under our area of influence."

Cheney smiled at her. "*Noblesse oblige.*"

"Something like that," Victoria agreed, her eyes sparkling. "Only the nobility part is in our hearts only. My poor mother"—and she sighed dramatically—"has never forgiven me for not marrying someone with a title. But I told her that 'Dr. Devlin Buchanan' was going to have to do. That name is noble enough for me."

"I want to go to the hospital," Cheney decided, "and so does Shiloh. Yes, you are ready to go. So, Victoria, are you going to stay up here on this windswept hill and picturesquely moon over Dev all day, or are you coming?"

"I," Victoria announced haughtily, "am coming."

★ ★ ★ ★

The facade of the mission was unassuming, topped by a roof with projecting eaves, crowned by a modest cross. High above the carved wooden doors was a wrought-iron balconet. In openings in the gable were housed three solemn bells.

The heavy double doors opened, and Dr. Baird came out to greet them. Dressed in a dark frock coat, blindingly white shirt with a stiff white collar, and an elegantly simple black tie, he was much more imposing and intimidating than he had seemed the night before. Cheney felt a moment's trepidation but reminded herself of his warm and gratifying words when he'd taken her leave.

"Good morning, Mrs. de Lancie, Mr. Irons, Dr. Duvall," he greeted them in a businesslike tone. "Thank you for being so prompt. I've decided to take you all on a tour first. After that we'll have tea in the doctors' hall and discuss business. Please come with me."

He offered his arm to Victoria, and Shiloh and Cheney followed.

"As you can see, the vestibule is the original narthex of the mission," he explained. "The hand-carved screen and the two statues were brought here on mules from Mexico in 1800. This is St. Francis, and the other is St. Luke. I've always thought it a good sign that, although the statues were brought here while this was still a Franciscan mission, they chose St. Luke the physician as a patron saint."

"I suppose all doctors feel a special affinity for him," Cheney murmured. "I certainly do."

Dr. Baird gave her an approving look and went on, "We sectioned off four offices and the operating theater, of course. This is my office, that's Dr. Werner's—you'll meet him—and this one is Mrs. Tilden's. Right now she is the nursing supervisor. The other one is vacant."

Following a passageway that circled the operating theater, Dr. Baird said, "This is the men's general ward." The long, low room was painted a pleasing cream color. Arched windows were spaced evenly down both sides of the room, their white wooden shutters open to the gentle morning sun. On each side of the room were iron beds, each with a simple wooden crucifix centered on the wall behind. Cheney saw Ethan Sanford and Ike Trimble. When Mr. Sanford had woken up, it was easily determined that he'd sustained no spinal cord injuries. Cheney wanted to stop and talk to them, but Dr. Baird was hurrying along, and she only had time to smile and nod.

Walking quickly down the row of beds, Dr. Baird told Cheney, "You'll have a chance to review all of the patients when you come to work, Dr. Duvall. Right now I'll just introduce you to Dr. Werner."

A man wearing a white coverall with the St. Francis mark embroidered on the left breast was bending over a patient about halfway down the room. As the group neared him, he straightened, then came to meet them.

He was tall, over six feet, and of such a military bearing that he marched rather than walked. As he neared them, he assessed each of them carefully; first Victoria, then Shiloh, lastly Cheney. His eyes were winter blue, and his jaw and mouth looked carved.

"Dr. Werner, may I present to you Mrs. Victoria Steen de Lancie, Dr. Cheney Duvall, and Mr. Shiloh Irons. This is Dr. Carl Werner."

"How do you do, Mrs. de Lancie," he said with a stiff bow. "I have met your father and know him slightly. I hope I have the pleasure of making your acquaintance during your stay here in San Francisco."

"Certainly you will, Dr. Werner," she replied with a queenly nod of her head. Dr. Werner hadn't offered her his hand. "Dr. Duvall and I plan on giving a dinner party for everyone here at the hospital, and we hope you will attend."

"Ah yes, Dr. Duvall," he said, turning his arid gaze on her. "The female doctor."

"It's a pleasure to meet you, Dr. Werner," Cheney said stiffly, offering him her hand. He gazed at it for a moment, then gave it one barren up-and-down handshake.

"Pleasure," he muttered, then turned to Shiloh. "You're the medic? In the war?"

"Yes, sir," Shiloh replied, and Dr. Werner shook his hand firmly, with something like relief.

"Has Dr. Baird persuaded you to come to work here?" he asked, narrowing his eyes in an assessing gaze. "We need you, Irons. None of the nurses or attendants have any training, except for Mrs. Tilden. And she, of course, can't train the male attendants. It's difficult for physicians to work with unskilled assistants."

"It's true I have experience, sir, in the war, and I've been fortunate to be Dr. Duvall's assistant for the last two years," Shiloh said steadily. "But I've never tried to train or supervise anyone else. I'm not certain that I'm the man St. Francis needs."

Werner's gaze never shifted to Cheney; it was obvious he had dismissed and forgotten her. "Dr. Baird thinks, and I think, that you are exactly the man St. Francis needs," Werner replied with spare grace. "It was a pleasure to meet you, but you must excuse me, ladies, Mr. Irons, Dr. Baird. I must go back to work."

"This way, please," Dr. Baird instructed, and they moved down the room to a hallway that led directly off to the left. "This is one of the experiments that St. Francis is conducting," he said with a measure of pride. "This first wing has been converted into seven private rooms."

He threw open the first door to reveal a small but pleasing room with a plain wooden bed, a three-drawer chest, and two armchairs with needlepoint embroidery. Over the bed was centered a pleasing oil painting, a summer landscape with a quiet river. Two windows on either side of the room looked out onto courtyards; one the center square of the mission complex and one a smaller private courtyard that was between the two wings that ran perpendicular to the general ward.

"We have five more rooms just like this. At the end of the hall is a more luxurious suite with a bath, finely furnished. It is occupied right now by Mr. Benjamin Nash, who is having a particularly bad turn with gout," Dr. Baird said with barely contained pride. "I don't want to disturb him, but the women's private rooms are identical to these—except for the furnishings—and the suite in that wing is unoccupied. I'll show you that one."

"And how are the private rooms working out?" Victoria asked politely.

"We've had a fair occupancy in the women's wing," Dr. Baird replied. "Several of the ladies of good family in San Francisco have begun to recommend St. Francis' private rooms for their lying-in, and it seems to be getting a favorable reception. The men's wing has not had quite the same success yet, but in my experience, if the wives approve, the men will follow along."

"So they are expensive?" Cheney asked.

"Yes, they are," Baird admitted. "But believe me, Dr. Duvall, no one is getting rich from the private room fees."

"What we are trying to accomplish, Cheney, is to offer better hospital accommodation for those who can afford it," Victoria explained. "And we hope that the private room fees will, first of all, pay for themselves, and then we hope that they will be in sufficient demand that they will help support the hospital overall."

They returned to the men's general ward, and Cheney looked down at the end of the long room. "There's another wing down there, isn't there? Are those private rooms, too?"

"Not yet," Dr. Baird answered. "As Mrs. de Lancie explained, we will add more private rooms if we can get the patients. But right now that wing—we just call it the east wing—and the west wing, which is at the end of the women's general ward, are empty. We use them for storage. When the mission was renovated, we cleaned the wings up, plastered the outside, and put gas and water lines in them, but we haven't added any interior walls."

They returned to the main building and toured the women's general ward and the luxurious private ladies' suite. It was furnished with an oak full tester bed with embroidered linen sheets, two matching night stands, and a matching armoire. By the window looking out onto the main courtyard was a small sitting area, with a French daybed and an ottoman that was large enough to set serving trays on.

"What is the charge for this room?" Cheney asked curiously.

"Five dollars per day," Baird answered sturdily. "The other private rooms are three dollars per day. Yes, I know it sounds outrageous, but you'll find San Francisco is an expensive place, Dr. Duvall. And I may say that wages are commensurate with prices. Have been ever since Sun Mountain money started flowing into San Francisco."

"The silver mines?" Shiloh asked. "That's over a hundred miles away. I figured Virginia City was getting all of that money."

Baird shook his head as he led them out a door onto the grounds, which were actually too big to be called a courtyard. It was more like a town square, with a carriage drive encircling the hospital and outbuildings. "The saloons and theaters and hotels and restaurants and . . . um . . . other entertainment establishments in Virginia City get all of the miners' money," he told Shiloh with a furtive look at the ladies. "But San Francisco has two things that draw the investors' money, and that's the big money: banks and the stock exchange. Virginia City can't compete with either."

The courtyard was lovely. In the center stood a stone fountain twelve feet high, merrily splashing water from a small bowl on the top to a smaller one in the middle and finally cascading into a huge bowl that sat on the ground. The pool that was the bottom tier was big enough to be called a pond. Cheney wandered over to it and, sure enough, there were fat goldfish swimming in it.

Today Cheney had decided on a dress of bright yellow tartan glacé with tartan squares of deep brown and hunter green. It was the new "walking dress," which meant that it only reached to her ankles, instead of the hem sweeping the ground. Her brown kid boots matched perfectly the dark brown of the dress and had hunter green velvet bows attached along the row of buttons. Her hat was a saucy little brown casquette set low on her forehead, with a yellow feather and yellow ribbon that encircled her curly coiffure in the back instead of tying under her chin. She carried a yellow parasol, and in the morning sun her face seemed to glow from the golden tint.

Shiloh watched her standing at the fountain, smiling down at the goldfish, and missed whatever Dr. Baird had been saying to him. "I'm sorry, sir, I was admiring the fountain. What did you say?"

Baird squinted toward the cheerily bubbling fountain and at Cheney, who was returning to the little group. "Humph, so I see," he muttered knowingly. "I was just saying that this first building is the pharmacy, which we keep fully stocked at all times. That's the kitchen and laundry, and that last building is the doctors' hall."

"Oh yes?" Cheney asked, rejoining them. "I've never heard of such an amenity for hospital staff physicians. Dev told me most of them just sit down in a hallway or something when they have a chance."

"Not good for the doctors, not good for the hospital," Dr. Baird maintained. "The hall has a sizable sitting area, a very small kitchen for making tea and coffee, and the beginnings of a library."

Cheney looked at the neat little adobe cottage and smiled brilliantly at Dr. Baird. "When can I come to work?"

He nodded approvingly. "Tomorrow, I hope."

"Not today?" she asked with disappointment.

Dr. Baird shot Shiloh a cunning glance, then lowered his voice as if he and Cheney were conspirators. "Your assignment today, Dr. Duvall, is to secure Mr. Irons, here, for my hospital."

Cheney never lagged behind. With candy sweetness she trilled, "Shiloh, dear, you will be coming to dinner with Victoria and me tonight, won't you? I have a very special meal planned, and I won't take no for an answer."

Shiloh groaned. "Boy, do I know that tone of voice. I know when I'm down for the count. Dr. Baird, I'd like to apply for a job on your medical staff." He stuck his hand out.

Dr. Baird shook it heartily. "That's good, Irons, that's capital! Come on into the doctors' hall—there are several things I need to ask you. I have no military experience, you know, and I think that possibly the army has already figured out how to handle some of the problems that I'm encountering, and—"

Repentantly he turned back to the ladies, as he had taken Shiloh's arm and begun hustling him toward the doctors' hall . "Er . . . um . . . Mrs. de Lancie, Dr. Duvall, would you care to join us? I mean . . . er . . ."

"Thank you, Dr. Baird, but I would like to sit out here in the gardens for a while." Victoria spoke politely, but her blue eyes were flashing dangerously. "Certainly you need to interview prospective employees in private. I'm sure you'll want to speak with Dr. Duvall when you are finished with Mr. Irons. Perhaps, Dr. Duvall, you would care to wait here with me?"

"Yes, that would be fine, Victoria," Cheney said with a tinge of amusement. "Please, Dr. Baird, you gentlemen may take your leave of us. I already know that Shiloh will be a valuable addition to your staff, and I'm sure you have much to discuss."

With relief Dr. Baird turned and resumed hauling Shiloh toward the cottage. Shiloh ventured one small rueful look at Cheney behind his back, then with resignation returned his full attention to Dr. Baird.

When they had disappeared into the doctors' hall, Victoria fumed, "Well! Cheney, that man seems to have no conception of what an asset you will be to his staff—and he seems to think that Shiloh is some sort of miracle worker!"

Cheney smiled at her friend. "On the contrary, Victoria. I have found Dr. Baird to be the most respectful and appreciative physician I've ever met. Besides Dev, of course." Entwining her arm with Victoria's, she led her to one of the benches that were placed around the fountain. "He's been very fair with me, Victoria. And, after all, he did give me a job."

Victoria sniffed daintily. "Probably because my father asked him to."

"He doesn't strike me as the sort of man who would compromise in that way," Cheney said thoughtfully.

Victoria was silent for a few moments. She stared at the fountain, and her profile showed lines of disapproval and stubbornness. "I suppose not. No, from what my father told me—he did say that he couldn't promise you a position here. He said that Dr. Baird ran this hospital, and he would only do what's best for St. Francis. Father said he is a just man, but sometimes the men who are completely just and always fair are also harsh."

"Yes, I think that's true," Cheney agreed. "So you must apply it to this situation, Victoria. Dr. Baird already told us that his main problems are with his nurses and medical attendants. He seems to understand that Shiloh is capable of setting the standards for physician's assistants, and that he likely will be able to supervise men. Therefore, he views Shiloh as an extremely valuable addition to his staff. Therefore, it follows that he would have much more to discuss with Shiloh than with me."

Victoria admitted, "Fair, I suppose. But harsh. Just as Father said."

"Not really," Cheney responded mildly. "It only makes sense. And, Victoria, dear, this is a man's world. If I were a man, likely I wouldn't feel snubbed by Dr. Baird's actions. You only were tiffled because you're a lady, a beautiful lady, an elegant and much-sought-after lady, and you're not used to men just charging off and leaving you standing out in the yard."

"*Tiffled* is not a word, Cheney," Victoria scoffed. "And in any case, I am never tiffled."

"I've seen you tiffled," Cheney remarked mischievously. "Extremely tiffled."

"Only in private," Victoria grandly maintained, "because it would be vulgar to be tiffled in public."

"And that, Victoria Elizabeth Steen de Lancie, soon to be Buchanan," Cheney declared vigorously, "is something that you would never do."

★ ★ ★ ★

The doctors' hall was, logically, essentially masculine. A brown leather sofa, comfortably cushioned but not overly stuffed, with clean lines and massive ball-and-claw feet, dominated one wall. Two black leather club chairs, with a reading lamp on a small table in between, were arranged at the back of the parlor. The entire back wall was covered with bookshelves from floor to ceiling, and a motley collection of enormous dusty books, small slim paperbound books, and assorted piles of publications were haphazardly arranged in the half-empty shelves. On a tea table was a shabby tea service with two partially full cups.

"Sorry," Dr. Baird said unrepentantly. "Mr. Irons and I had tea. I believe there are some more cups in the kitchen—would you care for some?"

"No thank you, sir," Cheney replied comfortably, settling herself on the sofa. Cheney had a spare elegance about her, much in contrast to Victoria's fragile demeanor and manner. Cheney never made graceful, rather exaggerated gestures with her hands. As a matter of fact, she made it a point to discipline herself to sit very still, but to retain a calm composure, as she had a tendency to fidget. As Cheney sat, she crossed her ankles to the side and rested her hands together in her lap, consciously arranging them in a relaxed pose. Her back was straight, but her shoulders were relaxed. Her back never touched the back of a chair or a sofa in public.

Dr. Baird picked up his half-drunk cup of tea and regarded Cheney gravely. "I've already made it clear that I'm glad to have you here at St. Francis, Dr. Duvall."

"Yes, sir, you've been very kind."

"Not really," he replied. "You're a good doctor. So I want you to understand that your position is not dependent upon this interview. But there are some things I'd like to know about you, and I would appreciate candor."

"I understand. I'll be glad to tell you anything, sir, and I will be honest."

"Yes, I believe you are," he said firmly. Settling more comfortably into his chair, he stared at Cheney with his most piercing gaze. "Why do you want to work here, Dr. Duvall?"

Cheney considered her answer before she spoke, and Dr. Baird patiently waited. Finally she said in a clear and positive voice, "I've always wanted to work at a hospital. I applied to several as soon as I got out of medical school. None of them would hire me; some of them wouldn't even consider me. So I moved on to other fields."

"Yes, I know your history," Baird said quietly. "An impressive list of accomplishments. The voyage with Asa Mercer to Seattle, with a hundred women. Six months in the hills of Arkansas. Your work in New York during the cholera plague." His eyes grew more assessing and he asked carefully, "I believe you established a viable private practice in Manhattan last year?"

"Yes, sir, and the practice is still viable," Cheney told him. "Before I left—to visit Charleston, South Carolina, on some family business, and then to visit my great-aunts in New Orleans—I took a new medical student as a partner. From all accounts the practice is still growing and strong."

"Your partner—a man or a woman?" Dr. Baird asked bluntly.

Cheney answered evenly, "A man. I interviewed two women doctors but found them unsuitable. The young man appeared to be dedicated, intelligent, and hardworking; evidently my patients like him, because he has retained almost all of them and has added more."

"Why did you find the two women doctors unsuitable?" Dr. Baird asked.

Cheney knew this point was important, and she knew why. She smiled. "The two ladies were from the same medical school I attended, the University of Pennsylvania. They were both well-educated and dedicated. But they were too conscious of being *female* physicians and not concerned enough with just being good doctors. I think you understand my point, Dr. Baird."

One eyebrow raised sardonically, he answered, "Certainly I do. I applied the same test to you, Dr. Duvall, and be assured that if you had shown signs of medical suffragettism, I wouldn't have hired you."

"I know that, sir," Cheney said, her eyes sparkling, "and I wouldn't have hired me, either, were that the case."

His quick grin flashed under the bushy mustache, then he again grew somberly businesslike. "To return to my original question, then, Dr. Duvall, it would appear that you wanted St. Francis because we're the only hospital that would hire you."

"That's not exactly true," Cheney replied. "I received an offer from New York City Hospital last spring just before I left, but I declined it. What I really am interested in is proprietary hospitals, Dr. Baird. Just like St. Francis. I think it's wonderful."

"Why?" he asked with his customary bluntness.

Again Cheney took time to study her thoughts before forming them into words. "I have found that, although I do love the practice of medicine, I would like to find a way to help more people. I try to be the best physician I can be to each patient, no matter how trifling or serious the illness or condition. But somehow, I'd like to be part of a larger picture, I suppose you'd say. Does . . . does that make sense?"

For the first time that day Dr. Baird smiled, easily, openly, and his dark eyes lit up. "Perfectly, Dr. Duvall. In fact, that is precisely how I feel, what I want, and what I'm trying to do. The only difference here is that you're a very skilled doctor, and I'm not. No, don't indulge me or flatter me. I care about my patients, and I try, but I just don't seem to have a . . . healing touch, I guess you'd say. Walker has it. Dr. Werner has it. You have it. I don't.

"But I'm really good at running this hospital, Dr. Duvall, and I'm good at it because I care so much about the patients. I'm going to spend my life figuring out how to make the highest quality medical care and treatment as kind, as benevolent, as helpful, and as affordable as possible. That's why—even though I can't set dislocated shoulders and I forget the difference between chamomile and comfrey—I'm still a good doctor."

"Yes, sir, I believe that you are," Cheney agreed quietly. "I'm honored to be working for you, Dr. Baird."

"Thank you," he said with dignity. "But there's one thing here that I think I can see about you, Dr. Duvall, that I don't even think you've realized yet."

"Oh? What's that, sir?"

"That the main reason you want to work here is because you feel the same way I do about medical care and treatment," he answered shrewdly. "And I think that you'll learn everything there is to know about this hospital, and one day you'll head back to Manhattan and open up a hospital of your own."

Cheney blinked several times with surprise. "Why . . . why, Dr. Baird, do you know that I never quite formed the thought in my mind, but now that you've outlined it—"

"Yes, just so," he said dryly. "And that's why I want you to sign a contract for six months. I want to keep you here at least that long, Dr. Duvall. And then, if you feel that you are ready to leave, I'll let you go, with my blessing."

"I'll sign a six-month contract gladly, sir," Cheney said gratefully. "And, Dr. Baird, I must tell you one more thing."

"What's that?"

"You can't know how wonderful it is," Cheney said in a low tone, "to be treated with respect, to be listened to, to be taken seriously, to be—" She searched for the word.

"To be needed," he finished for her. "Dr. Duvall, I assure you, you are needed."

PART TWO

Better Than Rubies

For wisdom is better than rubies;
And all the things
That may be desired
Are not to be compared to it.

Proverbs 8:11

5

The Most Dangerous City

Cheney's horse, Eugènie, snorted in terror, rolled her eyes, and sidled to the right, almost into the ditch. She pawed the air, puffing dramatically, and snipped and stamped and generally made a dramatic fuss.

"Oh, horrors, no!" Cheney shrieked in a high falsetto. "It's a *rock*!" Throwing back her head, Cheney laughed while snappily guiding Eugènie back into the middle of the road with a tap of her blunted spur and a nominal flick of her riding crop. "You're not fooling me a bit, young lady! You just settle down, because I'm telling you I'm not going to get out of this saddle, and you will take me to Chinatown!"

"You like her, don't you," Shiloh observed, watching Cheney fooling with the little bay thoroughbred mare. Eugènie required constant attention.

"She's a challenge," Cheney replied. "She's so fidgety!"

" 'High-spirited' is what you call it, Doc," Shiloh told her solemnly. "In ladies of good breeding."

She glared at him. "We're talking about Eugènie, right?"

"Sure. Who else?" he said guilelessly. "And Eugènie Le Fain sure is well-bred, in a direct line from Darley Arabian. She's fiery, and Mr. Fain said she loves to race. But she's so little, and she passed on her small size to her foal. So Mr. Fain says she'd make a perfect lady's saddle horse—if the lady can be found who can make her behave. I told him I knew just the lady."

"She is wonderful," Cheney said a little breathlessly. "But I can see that long rides on her would be tiring. She doesn't just walk along, does she?"

"No," Shiloh said in a low tone, his eyes alight. "She dances." He was staring directly at Cheney, and she lowered her eyes and blushed. He went on in his normal lazy drawl, "Y'know, Doc, Mrs. de Lancie's going to buy her for you if you like her. For your birthday."

Cheney sighed. "Yes, I know. Victoria told me at church this morning that you'd be bringing my birthday present for me to ride this afternoon. I tried to tell her that buying a horse for me was much too extravagant a gift . . . but she's stubborn. She just smiled in that demure way of hers and asked whether I'd rather have a horse or something in the way of diamonds. Isn't that ridiculous?"

"No," Shiloh responded quietly. "I'd give you both, and more, if I could."

"Eugènie, stop that this minute!" Cheney fussed and tightened up on the reins firmly but not sharply. The mare was tossing her head so energetically that Cheney's leg had loosened from the leg-lock on her sidesaddle. "I beg your pardon, Shiloh, what did you say?"

"Nothin'. So I see you and Eugènie are hitting it off. Whaddya think about ol' Balaam, here?"

"Balaam?" Cheney repeated doubtfully. "That's his name?"

"Uh . . . well, not his full name," Shiloh hedged. "Mr. Fain called him something else, but Mrs. Fain objected to it in polite company."

"Ah," Cheney nodded, her eyes crinkling with amusement. "He's named after Balaam's famous steed? The talking one?"

"Yeah. You know. The one who kept arguing with Balaam," Shiloh explained. "Mr. Fain said that's really why he was named just plain . . . well, you know. He argues."

"He does?" Cheney looked at Shiloh's horse doubtfully. He was a handsome quarter horse, full-chested, muscled, a chestnut of dark reddish brown with a slightly lighter mane and tail. He had what was called a "white face," which meant that it was more than a blaze; the white patch covered his eyes and mouth. His expression was surprisingly intelligent, almost cunning, Cheney thought.

"He's sly," Shiloh went on. "And he's real smart. Mr. Fain said when they first started working him, he let them have their way for two days, and then he got sick of it. The third day he started limping, and they figured he had a stone bruise, so they pulled him from the workout. The next day he seemed fine, but after about five minutes of working he started limping again—only it was a different foot. But you know—and Balaam knew—that if a horse starts limping, you have to pull him and check it." Shiloh grinned. "He won. He's never done a full quarter horse workout in his two-year life."

"But he looks in such wonderful shape!" Cheney exclaimed. "He's so muscular, so healthy looking!"

"Yeah, Mr. Fain says when they put him out to pasture he'll run and cut and show off for hours. Can't put any of the other quarter horses in with him, 'cause he drives 'em crazy, wanting to play." Shiloh spoke almost with pride, patting Balaam on his rippling shoulder.

"You really like that horse, don't you?"

"Sure do."

"All right, then. He's yours. Happy birthday, Shiloh," Cheney said smugly.

"Huh? It's not my birthday!" Shiloh protested.

"How do you know?" she retorted. "I have decided that you may share my birthday, April 21. So, technically, no, your birthday is not until Friday."

Shiloh couldn't argue. He was an orphan; in fact, he was a foundling. He'd been placed on the steps of the Behring Orphanage in Charleston, South Carolina, in the middle of the night of November 2, 1843. For years that was all he'd known of his past.

But in the last two years, through fortuitous—Cheney believed miraculous—circumstances, Shiloh had found out quite a bit more about his history. He'd found out that a man, an old sailor named Navvy Wingo, had found him on the beach of James Island off the coast of South Carolina after two ships, the New Orleans freighter *Ahava* and the clipper ship *Day Dream*, had wrecked during a storm. The *Day Dream*, they'd learned, had listed its home port as San Francisco. The trip to California had been the next inevitable step in his search.

With the infant Shiloh, according to Navvy Wingo, was an Oriental girl, young, delicate—and dead. She'd died saving the child, who was in a crate marked "Shiloh Ironworks"—the owner of the *Ahava.* In the crate was a fish made of very thin worked metal. Shiloh and Cheney had never been able to identify exactly what the fish was, whether it was simply an odd sort of decorative item, or if it had some purpose that they were unable to comprehend.

The baby Shiloh had been wrapped up in a long scarf, or tapestry, that was intricately embroidered and appeared to be Oriental. Hidden in the scarf were a quantity of gold and a single perfect pearl. The gold Shiloh had never seen, because someone had taken it; but Shiloh didn't mind, because he loved Linde Behring very much and readily forgave her when she confessed her theft to him before she died. The pearl he had given to Cheney.

Now Shiloh and Cheney were going to Chinatown, on the off chance that someone there might be able to explain or identify the only clues that Shiloh had to his past and his family.

Cheney went on stubbornly, "And I'm buying that silly horse for you for your birthday."

"You can't do that, Doc," Shiloh argued. "It's too expensive a gift."

Cheney smiled at him as demurely as she could. "Would you rather," she asked sweetly, "have that silly horse or something in the way of diamonds?"

He stared at her. "Rubies," he whispered.

"What?"

"Rubies," he said softly. "You're more like rubies. So I'd rather have Balaam than diamonds."

Confused, Cheney stammered, "What . . . what are you talking about, Shiloh?"

He turned back to face forward. "I can't believe you're going to buy me this horse. That's real generous. I shouldn't accept it, but I think I will, with thanks, Doc."

By the ease with which he'd surrendered, Cheney knew that Shiloh didn't have the money to buy the horse. So she made certain she gave him good justification for accepting the gift from her. "Well, I've known you two years, Shiloh, and you've given me birthday presents every year. And I really hadn't thought about it until this year, that you never claim a birthday! So we'll share mine, until we find out when yours is. And we will, you know, somehow, someday. Anyway, I figure Balaam will do for the last three birthdays. Even though I don't think you'll ever get him trained!"

Shiloh flashed her a grateful smile, then shrugged carelessly. "I don't want to race him, or work horses with him. I just want him to take me around, you know, lazin' along like this. And besides, he does talk. I like it, except mostly he just gripes."

"Shiloh, that horse does not talk."

"Sure he does. You just wait. When he gets tired of dawdling around town, you'll hear him."

"Um-hmm. I hope I do, for your sake," Cheney teased. "So where are we? And which way is it?"

They'd reached the foot of Russian Hill, and Shiloh had reined in

Balaam at the intersection of Broadway and Leavenworth. "Uh, I'm trying to figure out the best way, Doc. It's over there"—he waved to the southwest—"but . . . uh . . . we might need to go farther south and kinda circle around."

"Circle around what?" Cheney demanded suspiciously.

Blowing out an exasperated breath, Shiloh answered, "Pacific Avenue. I don't really think you'd enjoy Terrific Pacific, Doc."

"The Barbary Coast?" Cheney said brightly. "And why not? I might want to um—see how terrific it really is. Let's go."

"No, Doc, you do not want to see how terrific it is," Shiloh stated flatly. "Really. You really don't."

Now Cheney looked exasperated. "You're just talking about going that way on Broadway, and then due south, aren't you? On Dupont Street? So we'd just be crossing Pacific Avenue, right?"

"Well, yes, but listen, Doc, on Broadway—"

"I mean, we don't have to parade down the entire avenue, do we?" Cheney said impatiently, then spurred Eugènie very lightly. But, of course, that meant that Eugènie took off down Broadway as if she were shooting out of the starting gate at Ascot. Shiloh and Balaam plodded along resignedly behind them.

"Isn't she a kicker?" Shiloh told the horse. "I'm telling you, that riding do-up looks great on her!"

Balaam tossed his head slightly, then chewed on his mouthpiece, making brassy smacking noises.

"No, I'm talking about the Doc," Shiloh told him. "But, yeah, that Eugènie's a fine lady too."

Cheney was wearing a new riding habit with a cocky new hat and daring Wellington boots. The riding coat was of black velvet with satin lapels, man-cut, with an open corsage. She wore a fine cambric blouse with a man's black silk cravat and a diamond stickpin. The deep cuffs of the jacket were embroidered with lace. Her skirt was full, with both sides of the overskirt gathered up to the hip to reveal the underskirt, which was layers of white embroidered flounces. Her hat and boots were actually men's articles, which was why Cheney felt so daring. The hat was a snappy silk top hat with a red satin ribbon band. Nia had attached a ruby and emerald pin on the left side, anchoring a spray of pheasant's feathers. Her Wellington boots were actually boys' boots, finely made of the softest kid leather. Cheney had splurged in New Orleans and bought a spur; the ankle band was of silver with gold insets in a diamond pattern, and the spur itself was solid gold in a diamond shape. She did, indeed, look stunning on the proud but delicate horse.

Cheney got far ahead of Shiloh. Finally she turned her horse, and Eugènie galloped back to them. Cheney had to allow Eugènie to circle Shiloh and his mount twice before she would slow down to a prancing trot.

"Y'all are makin' me and Balaam tired," Shiloh groused with a fake yawn. "You wanna stop and rest?"

"I don't think I can get this horse to stop," Cheney retorted, "much less rest."

The western end of Broadway was residential, with mostly shabby houses and shacks, their hurdy-gurdy appearance on such rolling terrain contrasting oddly with their precise lineup in tight military rows. Occasionally there were more substantial-looking houses of two stories, sometimes with gingerbread trim and a small turret, and always with at least one bay window. But even the finer homes were on tiny little lots.

"This is the funniest-looking city planning I've ever seen," Shiloh mused. "This city's laid out like it's in the middle of the plains of Nebraska Territory or something."

Cheney laughed. "Yes, a man named Jasper O'Farrell drew it up in 1847. It appears he just drew the outline of the peninsula, took his ruler, and started blocking it off. You see these houses? Every lot north of Market Street is twenty-six feet by ninety-eight feet. Evidently Mr. O'Farrell and the city planners hadn't noticed that San Francisco is just a bunch of hills, some small, some not so small. Some of those lots are probably straight up, like walls!"

"Vertical lots," Shiloh explained gravely. "I've already had three people try to sell me one."

"I wouldn't doubt it," Cheney commented. "It looks to me like you can buy—or sell—anything you want to in this town."

Coming to a stop again in the middle of the intersection of streets, Cheney gazed ahead with narrowed eyes. Even Eugènie either sensed something or objected to the smell, because first she sidled that way, then this way, and finally started trying to back up.

"See, Doc, I tried to tell you," Shiloh said uneasily, reaching out and taking hold of Eugènie's bridle. "It's not like the Barbary Coast is in a fenced area around Pacific Avenue. It kinda spills over onto Broadway, too."

"Oh," Cheney said in a small voice.

Ahead of them, for the three blocks they could see, there were no houses. There were buildings of all kinds, from the two-story brick "Belle's Salon and Emporium" to a ramshackle three-sided structure that had bottles of whiskey piled on crates from the dirt floor up to the ceiling behind a rough wooden counter. Faint strains of ribald music came from a windowless adobe square building with a hand-painted sign that read "Jenny's Cabaray." There were a few horses standing patiently at hitching posts, and Cheney saw one cart pulled up to Belle's Emporium. Mostly there were people just walking, or staggering, up and down the street.

"This doesn't look too bad, Shiloh," she finally said calmly. "And after all, it is one o'clock on a Sunday afternoon. I'm well-escorted. What can happen?"

"Anything," Shiloh retorted. "But this is Stockton, I think, so the next street should be Dupont. Take a right, cross Pacific and Jackson . . ." He gave Cheney a questioning look. "You sure you wanna go this way? We can go back."

"No, no, that would be ridiculous," Cheney argued. "Let's go."

"Wait!" Shiloh reached out and yanked hard on Eugènie's bridle. Cheney had made a movement to spur her, but Shiloh almost pulled the little mare down to her knees. "Don't do that, Doc!" he said roughly. "You stay right here close by me, you hear? Don't you let this little butterfly dance off with you, not in the Barbary Coast! If you do, someone will be eating Eugènie for supper, and you'll be serving it in your knickers!"

"Shiloh!" Cheney was shocked, both at his tone and his crudity.

"You wanted to come down here, woman," he said with a grimace. "You better know what you're getting into. Now, you go—slow!—a little ahead of me. But I'm going to try to keep Balaam right next to Her Highness, here. Don't talk to anybody, don't even look at anybody. If anyone says anything to you, I'll answer them."

In spite of the absurdly uncomfortable situation she was in, Cheney smiled. She'd been in awful situations before, with Shiloh escorting her. Most men didn't dare to accost her in any way with Shiloh Irons at her side, and the ones who were stupid enough to try had paid dearly.

They went down Broadway slowly, for the foot traffic was dense, and if they tried to hurry, no doubt they'd knock down some staggering drunk. Catcalls and whistles began to sound, and Cheney straightened her shoulders and looked straight ahead, her color high. Eugènie tossed her head disdainfully and made a rude noise with her lips.

They turned on Dupont Street, and Shiloh and Balaam crowded Cheney and Eugènie even more. Cheney understood what he was trying to do, which was guide them right down the center of the street, and even Eugènie meekly allowed herself to be prodded. As far ahead as they could see, there was no carriage or horse traffic. Only people, and all of them were men. All kinds of men: short, tall, drunk, sober, dressed in rough and filthy clothing, and finely dressed with frock coats and beaver top hats. Some of them walked purposefully, but many of them simply milled around, holding bottles or flasks.

As they passed Pacific and headed toward Jackson, Cheney stole a look down "Terrific Pacific." She couldn't believe the squalor or the smell. Even though they were out in the open air, the sour reek of whiskey was strong, as if the streets had been watered with it. The buildings she could see were much the same combination of rude shanties and brick buildings that they'd just passed on Broadway. But one building on the block of Dupont and Pacific stood out; it was a three-story clapboard, and on the corner of each story was an open porch. Women were crowded on all three stories. They began calling out to Shiloh and Cheney, who were, naturally, quite a sight on the streets of the Barbary Coast.

"Hey, luv! You lookin' for a job, princess? C'mon, let's see some o' your charms! You gotta advertise, you know, and not dress like a little nun!"

"Ooh, Bridgette, looka him! Hey, you, pretty boy! Me an' my friend Bridgette here would dance with you for free, sweetie! Bet Her Nibs there don't dance! How 'bout it, sweets? Free now, both of us!"

Many of the comments from the women were crude, and Cheney even heard a few graphic obscenities shrilly screamed at her. She couldn't keep herself from stealing a glance at the brothel and saw that most of the women were half-naked. In fact, on the top floor, one woman who was obviously blind drunk was completely naked from the waist up, and she was the one who was shouting slurred obscenities.

Oh, Lord, forgive me for being so stupid and so stubborn! she thought, gritting her teeth. *How could I be so dumb?*

Grimly Shiloh rode on, now so close by Cheney's side that the two horses occasionally grazed each other. Every muscle in Shiloh's body was tensed, and he was ready to grab Eugènie's bridle at any second and spur them both to a gallop in case of trouble. If they ran over somebody, well, that didn't look like the worst thing that could happen to a man on this street.

Down Pacific Avenue they occasionally heard gunshots, and once they heard a dull boom that could only have been a twelve- or twenty-gauge shotgun. They passed a group of men who were singing and dancing around a bonfire in the street. They appeared to be burning a piano and the remains of the wooden frame of a bed. Cheney saw one man lying half-in and half-out of an alley between two saloons and wondered if he was passed out or dead. Men swarmed around them now, so close that they brushed against Cheney's skirts. She resisted the almost overwhelming urge to pull her leg out of the stirrup and cower into a little ball in the saddle. There was not a single woman on the street—except Miss Cheney Duvall.

Swallowing hard, she concentrated on controlling Eugènie and gazed straight ahead into the distance. Occasionally she stole a comforting glance at Shiloh's hands. He had good hands, strong hands, capable hands. At the moment they looked relaxed, as he held Balaam's reins in a deceptively casual pose. But Cheney could see the veins and tendons in his wrists, tracing up to the rolled-up sleeves of his shirt, and she knew that he was ready to spring. She sighed. She'd gotten him into this ridiculous and embarrassing situation too.

Suddenly a man's face loomed up directly in front of Eugènie's nose, followed by another man and then a third. The mare came to a stumbling halt, as it is true that a horse will try very hard not to actually run into or over a person. The first man, who had a mangy yellow mustache, fumbled and stumbled till he got hold of the mare's bridle.

Squinting up at Cheney, he said in a cotton-woolly, singsong voice, "Hey there, pretty girl, pretty girl, whassa matter wid ya? Yer little horse here, this here horse 'most ran over me an' my buddies!"

With morbid fascination Cheney saw that the man was so drunk that his eyes were crossing. Staring at him as he spoke, she could hardly believe it, but his eyes actually moved lazily back and forth toward his nose in oddly tranquil waves.

Shiloh grabbed Eugènie's bridle and yanked her close, as if she were a tiny little terrier. He leaned over the poor mare's head to look straight into the man's face. "No!" he said loudly. "Just no! You understand that, little man? No matter what you're thinkin', just no!"

"Whew!" the mustachioed man exhaled, letting go of the bridle as if it had suddenly turned into a hot branding iron. "Whoa there, big feller. I was jis'—"

"No," Shiloh repeated. Leaning back into his saddle and keeping his hold on Eugènie's bridle, he led the horses forward again.

"But . . . but . . ." In his earnestness the man staggered backward. His two buddies caught him and set him upright. "But I wanted to—"

"No," Shiloh said again as they rode past him. "You understand now?"

"Yeah," he said, nodding with that peculiar intensity the very intoxicated have. "Yeah, I unnerstan'. Ya mean 'no.' I unnerstan', big feller. No."

It seemed as if the rows of squalid bars, dance halls, gambling dens, and brothels would never end, but finally, after they got past Jackson Street, the buildings began to look a little more respectable, the street was cleaner, and the foot traffic more orderly.

"Shiloh, I'm so sorry," Cheney said contritely. "I'm . . . I . . . just didn't know."

"That's right," he said grimly. "You didn't know, and you never should have. But once you got it into that head of yours to tour the Barbary Coast, I wanted to be sure and be with you. Scared me to death to think of you and Mrs. de Lancie puttin' on some fool costume and comin' down here for a lark."

"We wouldn't have done that," Cheney scoffed.

"Oh no?" Shiloh snapped. "Blamed fool know-it-all women, think you can just flounce along anyhow and go anywhere and have a little tea party! And I'm tellin' you right now, those two young'uns aren't like those bulls Mrs. de Lancie had in Manhattan! Tim and Eddie Yancey are okay for dressin' up in silk britches and flappin' in the breeze on the back of that fancy carriage, but they're not bodyguards! They're just kids!"

"The footmen?" Cheney said, bewildered. "But . . . Shiloh . . . listen to me—"

Rudely Shiloh pulled the horses to a stop, then turned to face Cheney squarely. His eyes were a cold wintry blue, his jaw was like stone, and his voice was ominously calm. "No, you listen to me, Doc. Did you know this city has a reputation as the most dangerous in the world? You just saw one reason why—the Barbary Coast. But it's not just those two streets. San Francisco is a young city, a brawling city that wasn't built by blue-blooded families that have some sense of honor and nobility and community. This city was built by men, rough men, who gnawed gold out of those hills and then built themselves one big saloon and brothel to spend it in. That's San Francisco."

"All right, Shiloh," Cheney said meekly. "I'll be careful, I promise. I won't go wandering around by myself. I'll be responsible."

Shiloh started the horses again. By now Eugènie, much subdued, seemed content to follow Balaam's lead.

With ill humor Shiloh grumbled, "Well, I'll be coming to get you every night to take you to work. I'll be bringing you home too. And I don't want to hear anything about it, either."

"But . . . but . . . how did you know I'd volunteered for the night shift at the hospital?" Cheney stammered. "I was going to tell you today!"

"I knew," he muttered. "Which is why I volunteered for it too." His face softened back into his easy smile, and he added with a superior air, "In fact, I volunteered for it first, before you did. And I told Dr. Baird you would. And you did."

Cheney sniffed. "You think you're so smart, Mr. Big Feller Iron Man. Don't forget, you'll be working with me, and doctors get to boss nurses."

"Okay, Doc," he said mildly. "Next time two or three drunks try to climb up into the saddle with you, I'll let you boss them."

"No, that's all right," Cheney said hastily. "You do that kind of bossing very well. And, Shiloh, I really am sorry. And . . . and . . . thank you."

He shrugged. "Welcome."

Chinatown was a study in contrasts: busy, yet quiet; drab, but with riotous touches of color; clean and orderly, yet with a mysterious air.

Cheney and Shiloh dismounted at a hitching post that had a red scarf tied on to one end. It was typical of the surroundings. The buildings were ramshackle, poor, shabby, but buntings in bright colors hung in odd corners and on the outsides of the windows, and the plank sidewalks were draped with canvas awnings painted scarlet, bright yellow, emerald green.

An old Chinese man came trotting over and bowed obsequiously. "Speak English, yes. Watch horses, yes?"

Shiloh flipped him a coin, which he deftly caught, bit, then tucked into some unseen pocket of his loose tunic. He grinned sunnily at them. "Watch horses, yes."

"Yes, these are our elephants," Shiloh told him gravely. "We're just going down here to Queen Victoria's ball to waltz the night away. When we get back, we want the elephants washed, the tigers tamed, and the peacocks put to bed. Yes?"

"Yes, sir, yes, sir, you betcha," the man agreed vigorously.

Cheney and Shiloh turned, and Cheney giggled. "He speaks such good English."

"I figured. Hope our horses are still here when we get back. But I think they would be, even if we'd just left them somewhere. From what I understand, the Chinese don't dare court trouble by messing with white people. They have trouble enough as it is, even when they aren't guilty of anything but being Chinese."

"Goodness, they're . . . diminutive, aren't they?" Cheney noted. She towered over everyone, and of course Shiloh looked ten feet tall.

"Yeah. And they're built smaller than us, too," Shiloh replied, the corners of his eyes crinkling. "But look around, Doc. What do you see?"

She concentrated on the people on the street. Men hurried by, holding large lumpy bundles that smelled sunny, of clean laundry. A few women, some of them dressed in the same loose pantaloons as the men, walked quickly down the very edges of the sidewalk, carrying bundles of food or neatly folded stacks of clothing. Some women crowded the narrow streets, balancing bamboo poles on their shoulders, from which hung baskets heavy with vegetables and fruits. Several children ran up and down the street, the smallest most often holding the hand of an older child.

"Most of the adults are older people," Cheney observed. "That's it. They all look like grandparents. And little children. No young people."

"The men are all gone. They're all working on the railroad."

"But what about the young women?"

Shiloh gave her a sidelong look, then merely shrugged. "Look here, Doc. This is a shop, sorta. Isn't it?"

It was difficult to tell which were shops and which were homes. All of the buildings were two- or three-story structures with few windows, and none of them had large display windows as did the retail stores to which Cheney and Shiloh were accustomed.

He had stopped in front of a three-story building with a red canvas awning shading the front stoop. The front door was open, and an Oriental tapestry was hanging on it. By the door was a blue and white porcelain vase, a delicate little cage, and a woodcarving of a bird.

"It does appear to be some sort of display," Cheney agreed. She stepped closer to examine the hanging on the door. "You know, Shiloh, this isn't what I'd call similar to your scarf, but the—I suppose you'd call it the stylization—is something like it."

He stepped closer and stared at the tapestry. "Yeah, I see what you mean. Like this background design, whatever it is. It swirls and curls like some places on my scarf."

Silently a man and a little boy appeared in the doorway. The man was old, ancient, with a snow-white pigtail and a long wispy mustache and beard. The boy was perhaps four and very solemn. His round face was upturned toward Cheney and Shiloh, and he regarded them with delicate almond eyes rounded with awe. The man and the boy were dressed identically, in black tunics with black satin frogs anchoring the seam in front, loose black trousers, white stockings, and soft black slippers.

"Good afternoon, sir," Shiloh said courteously. "We were just admiring this tapestry. Do you speak English?"

"Yes. Two dollars," the man said, equally courteously.

"Well, actually, we'd like to know a little something about it," Shiloh went on. The man and little boy watched him intently, their eyes alive with interest. "Where was it made? Is it Chinese?"

"Yes." The old man nodded firmly. "Two dollars."

Shiloh and Cheney exchanged amused looks and Shiloh asked in the same polite tone, "And was this made by mermaids at the bottom of the China Sea and brought here on sea horses by Neptune?"

"Oh yes, sir," the man said, beaming. "For two dollars."

"Thought so," Shiloh commented.

Cheney knelt so that she was eye level with the little boy. He looked like a toy, with his moon face and golden skin and tidy costume. "You're a doll," she said with delight. "My name is Cheney. What's yours?"

He stared at her solemnly. Cheney smiled at him, and after long moments his somber expression split into a hearty grin. "That smile is worth two dollars," Cheney breathed and pulled a gold piece out of her reticule. She held it out to him. The little boy reached for it, then stopped and looked uncertainly up at the older man.

A shadow of a frown crossed the older man's creased face, and then he smiled again, took the tapestry down, and held it out to Cheney.

"No." She shook her head. "I just want the little boy to have the money."

He pushed the tapestry toward her.

"But—"

"Doc," Shiloh said softly, "I don't think the old man wants the little boy to take charity. It'd be like he's a beggar. You see?"

"Oh, horrors," Cheney muttered, her cheeks flaming. "Have I had several stupid attacks today? Sir, I beg your pardon," she told the man. "I didn't mean to insult you or your grandson. At least, I assume he's your grandson. Please pardon me. I . . . I . . . really like this birdcage," she said, again kneeling to touch the tiny little cage. "How much is this?"

The man bowed, smiled, and said, "One dollar." With dignity he rearranged the hanging back on the door.

The little boy watched Cheney avidly, then picked up the cage. It was very small, really too small for a bird. And it wasn't wrought iron. It was made out of some kind of thin reeds, with a tiny pagoda at the top. The little boy held up the cage, pointed to it, and made a shrill whistling noise with his teeth.

"Yes, a birdcage," Cheney smiled.

His earnest brown eyes fixed on her, he kept repeating the whistle over and over at regular intervals. Cheney was puzzled.

"A cricket!" Shiloh exclaimed. "Doc, it's a cricket cage!"

"Yes," the older man said with relief. "Click-it."

"Why, how enchanting!" Cheney declared. "Here, sir, are two dollars. Do you, by chance, have a cricket that I might buy?"

Amazingly, the man seemed to understand. Gently he took the cage inside the house, while the little boy remained where he was, staring up at Cheney and Shiloh.

"We must look like great scary monsters to him," Cheney murmured. "Especially you."

"Thanks a lot, Doc."

"No, I mean, because you're such a big man, and also because of your light hair and those icy blue eyes," Cheney explained. "Don't you know we look like something out of nightmares to them?"

The man came back out holding the cage. In it were a cricket and a green plant—Cheney thought it was probably just a weed—arranged in a very small teacup with no handles. The weed was planted just so, with three small white stones arranged on top of the soil. With great ceremony the man bowed and presented it to Cheney.

"Thank you," she said.

"Yes," he said. He and the little boy disappeared back into the shadows of the house.

Cheney and Shiloh walked on. They saw several more places with a few items meticulously arranged outside the front door. One place had vegetables and fruit: Chinese lettuce, radishes, carrots, snow peas, bamboo shoots, plums, and mandarin oranges. Shiloh bought a dozen of the small, bright fruits, and as they walked he peeled one. He and Cheney shared the succulent, tart quarters, and Cheney put a piece of it in her cricket's cage, which Shiloh was gallantly carrying for her.

"Whatcha gonna do with this cricket?" Shiloh asked. "You really going to keep it?"

"Well, I don't think so. Not for long, anyway. But I can't wait to see Victoria's face when I show her my new pet."

Shiloh grinned at the thought of Mrs. de Lancie's ice maiden features crumbling in horror when Cheney announced she was bringing a bug into the house. "Doc, can I be there? Please?"

"Of course," she laughed. "I may need your help to bring her around when she has the vapors."

They walked past anonymous shanties and the occasional shop. Once they saw another couple, Westerners, passing down the other side of the street, also obviously sightseers. Other than that, the only people on the streets were Chinese. Shiloh and Cheney smelled the heady, heavy smoke of incense, the bleach and soap smell of laundries, and exotic, spicy cooking smells.

Once when they passed a small house, better appointed than the others, with draped windows, the door opened and a well-dressed man came out. He looked slightly dazed. With difficulty he comprehended that Cheney was walking along the sidewalk. As if he moved in a sea of honey, he slowly reached up, felt for his hat, tipped it, then wandered in the opposite direction as if he weren't certain where he was. Cheney stopped at the doorway of the house and sniffed. "What in the world is that scent?" she muttered. "It's like—what is it like?"

"Like nothing you've ever smelled, Doc," Shiloh muttered, taking her arm firmly and hustling her quickly down the walk.

"But . . . it . . . was it camphor? Camphor smoke? No, that's not right," she worried, then insisted, "Just tell me, Shiloh. What was it?"

He sighed, rolled his eyes, and answered, "Opium, Doc. That was an opium den."

"But . . . but . . . is that legal?" Cheney exclaimed. "That's not legal!" She stopped and half turned, but Shiloh stubbornly pulled her along.

"So whatcha gonna do, Doc? Arrest them?"

"Well, no, of course not," Cheney said indignantly. "I just . . . wanted to see, that's all."

Shiloh took a deep, long breath. "Doc," he said in a cajoling voice, "please don't tell me that you've decided you need to see an opium den. Please?"

"Well . . ." she dawdled, glancing at him with half-closed eyes, "no, I guess not. Unless you want to."

"No, that's okay," he said hastily. "No. No opium dens today. We'll save that for our next fun Sunday afternoon outing."

"All right," Cheney said impertinently. "Next Sunday afternoon. Opium den outing. Put it on my calendar."

"I'd laugh," Shiloh intoned, "if I was sure you were joking."

"Mmm," Cheney hummed noncommittally. "Wait! What's this? Shiloh, look at all this stuff!"

They had come to what looked like a "real" shop. At least, it had a wide display window. But the wares were like nothing Cheney and Shiloh had ever seen.

Hung from the ceiling were deer's antlers, incense sticks, dried flowers and herbs, kites, streamers, paper dragons, odd bits of bleached bones, tied bundles of feathers, and bunches of dried vegetables. Set tidily in rows in the windows were jars, some small, some enormous. In the jars were pickled whole toads; sea-horse skeletons; ginseng root whole, sliced, and powdered; sharp stalks of bamboo; other herbs of green, saffron, and brick-red hue; many jars of powders of different shades of brown that could have been anything; long needles; whole stretched lizard skins. The door was ajar, and odd smells, each too distinct to mix together, floated out. Cheney and Shiloh smelled the sweet cloying smell of fruity incense, the hypnotic scent of sandalwood, the odd flat smell of dried animal skins, and herbs, some pure, some noxious.

"What is this place?" Cheney murmured.

Shiloh said thoughtfully, "Looks to me like an apothecary, Doc. Betcha this is the doctor's house."

"Doctor?" Cheney repeated. "But . . . look at all of these . . . things! They're—"

"Chinese," he said flatly.

She looked up at him, her eyes growing somber and thoughtful. "I wonder—do these people have any access to medical care and treatment? I mean, can they go to the hospitals?"

"Dunno." Crossing his arms, he gave her a speculative glance. "Uh . . . Doc?"

"Um-hmm?"

"D'ya think we could maybe work a day or two at St. Francis—you know, the place where we have jobs—before we start thinking about opening a Chinese hospital?"

"I wasn't thinking about opening a Chinese hospital," Cheney replied indignantly.

"Not today?"

She smiled. "Not today."

"Someday, maybe?"

"It seems that you know about our somedays better than I," she said dryly.

With a half-smile he turned to study the exotic wares in the window. "Hope I do, Doc. Hope I do."

6

Houses and Stuff and Papers and Stuff

"It's entirely too frivolous," Cheney scolded. "Do something, Nia." Nia raised the silver brush to Cheney's hair.

"It looks very feminine, but modest," Victoria argued stubbornly. "Leave it alone, Nia." Nia dropped the brush.

"Nia," Cheney said in a warning tone. The brush came back up.

"No, Nia," Victoria said clearly.

Slowly and carefully Nia laid the brush on Victoria's dressing table. Raising both her hands in a defensive gesture and backing away slowly, she announced, "I just remembered I need to brush Miss Cheney's wool cloak. It's cool this evening."

"Fine. You may brush Cheney's cloak, because you certainly don't need to brush her hair," Victoria said with satisfaction.

Cheney turned on the padded bench seat to face Victoria, who was reclining lazily on a chaise "fainting couch" behind her. "You are so bossy," she declared.

"As are you, Cheney dear."

"That may well be, but I don't tell you how to wear your hair."

"No, but that's because I wear my hair in fashionable and ladylike coifs," Victoria replied smugly. "I am obliged to check you every time you leave the house to make certain you don't have your wonderful, luscious hair tied back with a rawhide thong or all pushed up into a man's droopy hat."

"You're exaggerating. I've never worn a man's droopy hat," Cheney retorted. "But if you don't let Nia fix my hair," she continued slyly, "I'm going to wear a mob cap to the hospital."

Victoria sat up straight and stared at Cheney. "Oh, horrors, Cheney! A mob cap? You'll be mistaken for the charwoman!"

"I probably will be anyway," Cheney muttered, turning back to scrutinize with narrowed eyes her reflection in the mirror. "Evidently women doctors are only myths in California. It's not just a prejudice against me, apparently. First I have to break the news to them, and they go through this stunned disbelief stage before they enter the critical phase—"

"But the mob cap," Victoria protested, changing the subject back to the more important topic. "You're joking, aren't you?"

Cheney shook her head, her eyes brightening with mirth. "No."

"Nia, come here and fix Cheney's hair this instant," Victoria ordered.

Nia, who was in the corner of the boudoir brushing Cheney's cloak and whispering with Victoria's maid Zhou-Zhou, sighed with resignation. "Yes, ma'am."

Cheney settled back on the seat and faced the gilt mirror mounted over the rectangular draped and swagged table that was serving as Victoria's dressing table.

"I can't imagine that you have the effrontery to order my maid around," Cheney remarked, her eyes still glinting. "Not to mention deciding how I'm going to wear my hair."

Victoria settled back on the chaise and with a languid movement waved her maid over to her, then handed her a bottle of pink lotion. Zhou-Zhou was a young French girl, tiny and sassy, with crisp brown curls, sparkling brown eyes, and a heavy accent encouraged and even carefully cultivated by Victoria. "Rub some of this on my shoulders, Zhou-Zhou," she ordered, then continued, "Well, you are in my boudoir, Cheney."

"So your territorial rights extend to my hair?"

"Something like that. Mmm, this new Roses of Heaven lotion smells so lovely. Zhou-Zhou, apply some to Miss Cheney's hands and neck."

"No, Zhou-Zhou," Cheney ordered, shooing away the lively little maid as if she were an offending gnat. Again she turned around to face Victoria accusingly.

Zhou-Zhou and Nia exchanged covert exasperated glances. Then Nia put the brush down again, and Zhou-Zhou corked the top of the lotion bottle and placed it carefully among the litter of toiletries and cosmetics on the dressing table.

"Victoria, dear, you really must make an effort to concentrate," Cheney said with a long-suffering air. "I know it's difficult, but please try. I'm going to *work*, not to a dinner party. I am a doctor. I am going to a hospital. To go to work. You're an intelligent woman. You can comprehend that."

Victoria sniffed daintily. "You're right, it is difficult for me to comprehend a lady such as you going to work in a hospital at ten o'clock at night. And it seems to me the least you could do is look your best. And wear a light, delicate fragrance."

"The only light, delicate fragrance I want to be scented with for work is carbolic acid. And as for my hair—" She scooted back around on the seat and said impatiently, "Hurry, Nia, whatever are you thinking? It's almost time for Shiloh to call for me!"

Rolling her eyes, Nia muttered, "Yes, ma'am," and continued trying to tone down Cheney's coiffure, which—considering how Cheney fidgeted—was something akin to giving castor oil to a naughty five-year-old.

"Anyway, Victoria, dear, I was just teasing you," Cheney went on. "Honestly, I can't have these long ringlets flopping over my shoulder and into people's faces, can I? And as for wearing perfume, many asthmatics and people suffering from catarrh have a sensitive reaction to them. It's just not becoming for a doctor."

"How tiresome," Victoria said in a bored tone. "And I suppose you'll be wearing that drab clothing all the time, too."

"Yes. Gray, navy blue, or black skirts. White blouses. No jewelry," Cheney answered with perverse enjoyment. "Speaking of clothing, are you finished dressing? I'm not going to make you late, am I?"

"No, the Westins are sending their carriage for me at about ten o'clock, and I'm already finished with my *toilette.* Except for my gloves. Where are—oh yes, thank you, Zhou-Zhou." Briskly she pulled on the over-the-elbow white gloves, and Zhou-Zhou knelt beside the chaise to button up the eighteen tiny buttons on each one. Victoria went on idly, "Cheney, you really are going to be obliged to attend as many of these social events as possible. Every invitation we've received is for both of us, you know."

"How can I do that, when I'm working at night?"

"You can go to the opera and the theater, and you can accept some invitations for dinner. You're not going to work *every* night, are you?"

"No," Cheney answered reluctantly. "As this is an experiment and a new concept for the hospital, Dr. Baird said I may pretty well decide on my own schedule. The other doctors seem to just come and go as they please. Anyway, Shiloh and I were planning on working quite a bit until we're familiarized with the hospital and how it works. But I was planning on sleeping some."

"I know that, Cheney, and of course you must try to rest as much as you can. But although I'm going to make certain that everyone of consequence knows that the Steens are sponsoring the hospital—still, everyone will need to meet you."

Cheney sighed. "They will? Victoria, you and your family name are more of a reference for the hospital than I could ever be!"

"Maybe," Victoria said softly, "but how did you contact your patients in Manhattan, Dr. Duvall?"

Cheney half smiled. "By going to the opera and the theater and as many social events as I could. Oh, well, I suppose I'll just have to make that sacrifice again."

"Exactly," Victoria agreed. Standing, she maneuvered around to check her face in the dressing table mirror.

"Oh, dear, I am bothering you, Victoria!" Cheney said regretfully. "Hurry up, Nia! Can't you push this poof on top of my head down some more?"

"She can smooth down that lovely bouffant, Cheney," Victoria corrected her severely. "And take your time, Nia. It's my fault that this house is so insufficiently furnished that you don't have a dressing table," she added irritably. "I've made arrangements for suitable furniture to be shipped, but you really must accompany me to buy some accessories, Cheney. We need linens, too, and some dinnerware and flatware. The draperies are most unsuitable, and I'm not certain about two or three of the rugs."

Cheney groaned. "Sounds like a lot of thankless work to me."

"Oh, really?" Victoria said coolly. "This, from a person who is going to work in a *hospital* at ten o'clock at night?"

A giggle escaped from Zhou-Zhou, which made Cheney and Nia laugh, and finally even Victoria smiled faintly. Cheney said tentatively, "You may have something there, Victoria. Perhaps I should go shopping for house furnishings with you. I've never undertaken such a task before, and it . . . might be enjoyable, I suppose."

"Spending money is always enjoyable, Cheney," Victoria declared, her blue eyes sparkling. "You'll see."

★ ★ ★ ★

"What I can't believe," Shiloh said with a melancholy air, "is that she liked the cricket. That was just no fun at all."

Cheney smiled. "Victoria insisted that it's a lady cricket, and she named her Yi. It's true, she was no fun. But you didn't hear Zhou-Zhou when Victoria handed her the cage and told her to cover the bottom with suitable scraps of silk or satin. Zhou-Zhou shrieked so loudly that Mrs. . . . Mrs. . . . the housekeeper came running, thinking that the house was on fire or people were being murdered!"

"Mrs. O'Neil," Shiloh said airily. "That's your housekeeper's name. And I think I heard Zhou-Zhou. I was only a few blocks away by then, you know."

"I have a hard time remembering her name," Cheney muttered. "In fact, I have a hard time remembering she's alive. Anyway, Victoria said that Yi's cage will go well with the decor she's planning. She says that Oriental accessories are very fashionable right now. And we're going to furnish the house."

"Furnish it?" Shiloh asked, bewildered. "What's all that stuff we've been sitting on?"

"Stuff that's not suitable, apparently. So we're going to buy more . . . stuff. Other stuff."

"Oh," Shiloh said uncertainly and glanced at Cheney quizzically. "You don't sound too sure about it, Doc. Haven't you ever bought house stuff before?"

"No. I've never had a house before."

"You want one?" Shiloh asked. His tone was careless, but he shot a penetrating glance at Cheney's face. In the half darkness it was hard to see her features, but he could tell a lot from the set of her shoulders, the angle of her head, the slight unconscious gestures she made with her hands.

"Mmm . . . someday," she answered carelessly. "Right now Steen House is going to be enough of an undertaking for me."

Shiloh was satisfied and relaxed back in the saddle. They rode for a while in an easy silence. Cheney breathed deeply and pulled her gray cloak closer around her shoulders. "The air here is so odd. It's damp and close when the fog comes in from the bay. But when it's not foggy it's so dry and arid."

"All kinds of humors and miasmas," Shiloh said gravely. "No telling what kind of patients we'll get at the hospital."

"In this town," Cheney agreed dryly, "there is no telling. But I do think that Dr. Baird is trying to do something unique, and workable, with St. Francis. Now, if I can just figure out how to include a charity ward or maybe a clinic for the Chinese—there are so many poor immigrants here—Armenians, Chileans—"

"Doc, don't you think you might better work for an hour or two before you take over the hospital?" Shiloh ventured.

Cheney laughed. "Yes, good idea. I'll give it a day or two. It's just my sanguine humor, you know. Dominated by the blood. I get carried away."

"I think you've got the pretty humor," Shiloh decided, "with the beautiful miasma."

"What nonsense!" Cheney exclaimed, ducking her head, although she knew that Shiloh couldn't see her blush in the night.

"No, it's not," Shiloh argued. "Just like I've got the handsome humor, with the smart miasma."

"We're here," Cheney stated firmly, "so you'd better straighten up. You're supposed to be the supervising attendant, not Mr. Iron Head."

"Okay, Miss Physician," Shiloh said meekly. "I'll put my medic's hat on my iron head. But first it looks like I better put my stable boy's hat on." He dismounted, then assisted Cheney to dismount. She didn't require it, of course, as she was an expert horsewoman, but Shiloh was always careful to help her. "Guess I'll take the horses back to the stables, Doc. You go on in. And . . . uh . . . you know that empty office?"

"Yes, the last one on the right?" Cheney asked.

"Uh . . . yeah. Well . . . uh . . ."

Shiloh's stammering was interrupted by the creaking of the front doors of the hospital. Walker Baird hurried out and down the steps, followed closely by a young Chinese boy. "Good evening, Shiloh, Dr. Duvall. Sorry I didn't hear you—meant to meet you, and all that—"

He took Cheney's hand and kissed it, which caught her a little off guard. Kissing a lady's hand—particularly an unmarried lady's—was unusual for American men, even upon first introduction. At meetings after that it was not a gesture that many men could make comfortably. Still, she said smoothly, "Good evening, Dr. Baird. What finery! Are you just leaving?"

Walker Baird was in full evening dress: a black suit with tails, white silk waistcoat with pearl buttons, a white linen shirt with a tucked front, a white cravat, black patent leather shoes, and a silk top hat. "No, I just got here. I was at the opera, but it was boring, so I decided to come be with you for a while, Dr. Duvall. And you, too, Shiloh, of course."

"Of course," Shiloh repeated pointedly, but Walker seemed not to notice.

"Dr. Duvall, may I present to you Li Shen," Walker said, stepping aside to introduce the Chinese boy standing subserviently behind him. He was a short, husky boy of about sixteen with beautifully modeled features, wide-set eyes, clear bronze skin, and jet-black hair pulled back into the inevitable braided pigtail.

Walker laid his hand on the boy's shoulder affectionately. "Li Shen and his brother, Li Bai, work here at the hospital. They are the gardeners, do the laundry and cleaning, and attend to the horses. Li Shen, this is Dr. Duvall." He pointed to Cheney, and the boy stole a shy look at her face. "And this is Mr. Irons." Li Shen glanced at Shiloh when Walker pointed to him. "Please accept my apologies for pointing, Dr. Duvall," Walker explained, "but Li Shen has only learned a little English."

"I understand, it's quite all right," Cheney said dismissively. "It's a pleasure to meet you, Mr. Shen." She held out her hand.

"The Chinese say their family names first," Walker explained.

"Oh, I see. Then it's a pleasure to meet you, Mr. Li." The boy hadn't looked back up at Cheney's proffered hand. He stood, his head bowed, his hands at his sides, the palms turned behind in a curiously subservient stance.

Walker took her hand and held it lightly between his. "He'd be frightened to shake your hand, Dr. Duvall. It's just not done."

Cheney sighed. "Yes, I know. But I keep trying, anyway." Gently she withdrew her hand from Walker's grasp, as he seemed to be content to hold it. In a businesslike tone she asked, "I'm ready to report for work, Dr. Baird. Shall we go in?"

"Of course," he agreed. "Li Shen, will you take care of these horses, please? Thank you. Shiloh, shall we go to your office?"

"Shiloh's . . . office?" Cheney repeated, staring up at him with raised eyebrows as they entered the hospital vestibule.

"Uh . . . that's what I was trying to explain to you, Doc," Shiloh ventured. "Dr. Baird said I'm going to have papers and stuff, so I'm going to need an office. That's what Dr. Baird said."

"Papers and stuff," Cheney repeated in a muffled tone. Her face was averted, so Shiloh couldn't see the smile tugging at the corners of her wide mouth.

"Yeah," Shiloh said uneasily as he held the office door open for her. "You know. Papers and—stuff."

"Yes, of course. And did Dr. Baird mention to you where my office might be?" Cheney asked innocently, now gazing up at Shiloh wide-eyed.

"Uh . . . you can have this one, Doc," Shiloh finally managed to get out.

Finally Cheney laughed. "I couldn't resist, Shiloh. I so rarely get to tease you. I don't care if you have an office and I don't."

"You don't?" he asked tentatively.

"Of course not," she insisted, her eyes beginning to take on a certain stubborn glint. "You didn't really think that I'd be angry, did you?"

"Huh? Oh no, huh-uh, not you, Doc," he stammered.

Walker Baird grinned mischievously. "I don't have an office either, Dr. Duvall, if that comforts you. Guess we know who the important people are around here. Guess that means that you sit behind the desk, huh, Shiloh?" he continued airily. "Don't worry, Dr. Duvall and I will just sit in these two uncomfortable straight-backed chairs in front of the desk. It's all right, don't worry about us. We're only doctors, after all."

Shiloh slumped into the padded leather armchair behind the plain oak desk. "I think I'm tired of having this office already," he grumbled. "More trouble than it's worth."

"That's the way I feel about offices," Walker declared with feeling. "You get one, next thing you know, you're just sitting in them doing papers and stuff."

"Yeah," Shiloh grunted.

Cheney declared, "Oh, Shiloh, that's enough. I think it's wonderful that you have an office, because I'm certain you'll need it. And I know you'll do a good job, whether it's nursing or doing administrative or supervisory work."

"Thanks, Doc," he said, obviously pleased. He sat up a little straighter in his chair and looked around. "Not too bad, is it?" As the office had never been occupied, it was completely bare except for the desk, the chairs, and the bookshelves on one wall. "Maybe Mrs. de Lancie will help me put some things in it, kinda make it look more personal."

Cheney frowned fleetingly, but Shiloh saw it and looked curiously pleased, while Walker looked back and forth between them shrewdly. But the instant passed, and Cheney turned to Walker in the chair beside her. "I have about a hundred questions, Dr. Baird. Your father and I spoke at length in our interview, but we only talked about the hospital in very broad terms. I'm not certain of the scope of my responsibilities—or authority—here."

Walker leaned a little closer to her and looked directly into her eyes as he spoke. Both he and his father did this with great intensity, no matter how inconsequential the conversation. It was a compelling trait, for it made the people they were speaking to feel as if they were important and deserved full attention.

"Simple questions, Dr. Duvall, but the answers aren't so easy. You see, my father and I have discussed this at great length, because this is an unusual situation. You are aware, of course, that each of the doctors who is connected with the hospital has his own patients? That is, each patient was admitted by one of us—I, my father, Dr. Werner, or Dr. Tasker—and each of us is considered to be the primary physician for each patient."

"Yes, I understand," Cheney told him. "So I am the first staff physician, as such."

"Exactly," Walker responded with relief. "You are, of course, directly responsible for the welfare of each patient when you are on duty. You have full authority over all the nurses. But you have no authority over the other doctors."

"I see. So that means that I'm responsible for giving each patient the particular care that his physician has ordered. What about emergencies? Do I send for the primary physician?"

"Each doctor has given specific orders concerning that," Walker replied. "Dr. Tasker and I prefer to be summoned if there's even a minor change in one of our patients. Dr. Werner and my father leave different instructions for each of their patients."

"All right," Cheney said thoughtfully. "Dr. Baird—"

"Walker, please."

"Even at the hospital?"

"Especially here," he replied dryly. "If you try to address me as Dr. Baird, everyone will be looking around to see where my father is."

"All right, Walker," Cheney relented. "I assume that the prescriptives are made up during the day and are readily available?"

"Yes. Our apothecary, Mr. Indro, works during the day. His last duty in the evening is to make up the prescriptives required for the night and issue them to the nurses' stations."

"What if I should need a prescriptive?" Cheney asked.

"Um, a prescriptive?" Walker asked with some confusion.

"Yes. A prescriptive," Cheney repeated impatiently. Shiloh sat forward, tensing a little, but he couldn't catch her eye.

"Well, Dr. Duvall," Walker finally answered slowly, still meeting her gaze, "what prescriptives did you think you might need? In the case of an emergency, perhaps?"

"Not necessarily," Cheney replied shortly.

For a long moment Walker hesitated. Then he asked quietly, "Dr. Duvall, may I ask you a question?"

"Certainly."

"We took the liberty of assigning Mr. Sanford and Mr. Trimble to you as your patients. Tonight you will leave instructions for them, will you not?"

"Certainly."

"Suppose I came in tomorrow and changed or supplemented your instructions. How would you view it?"

Cheney's expression changed from slight pique to wry amusement. "Why, Dr. Baird, I would take great exception to your actions. I would, most likely, make a formal complaint to you."

"Probably kinda loudly," Shiloh offered helpfully.

"Exactly," Walker agreed, although it was unclear whether he was agreeing with Cheney or Shiloh.

Cheney ignored both comments. "Point taken, Dr. . . . I mean, Walker. I'll be conscientious in observing all doctors' instructions."

"I know you will," Walker said, his unusual royal blue eyes gleaming. "And I know you'll understand, of course, that there may be times when you'll be obliged to make a judgment call. The only unbreakable rule here is the same as it is in every situation for a doctor: you must act in the patient's best interests. I believe you will always do that, too. I'm very glad to have you here at St. Francis, Dr. Duvall."

"Thank you. I hope that I'll fulfill your expectations, and your father's too, Walker," Cheney said fervently.

"You will," Walker said confidently. "As a matter of fact, I should like for you to be my physician, Dr. Duvall. Am I your first, besides our accident victims?"

"Why . . . yes. How kind of you, Walker."

"Yes, how kind of you, Walker," Shiloh repeated, his left eyebrow raised sardonically. "You don't get sick much, do you?"

"Unfortunately not," Walker answered him mischievously. "But I might get lucky."

Shiloh grinned crookedly. No one could regard Walker Baird as a threat. He was a rare person: a man's man, and one whom women liked and trusted. Rather like Shiloh himself, though he didn't realize it. "Yeah, lucky," he muttered, then brightened. "Or, hey, Walker, we could do a little sparring. I could ring your bell, you know, and the Doc could take care of you for days."

"Maybe weeks," Walker readily agreed. "I don't think I want to get that lucky. Not even for Dr. Duvall."

Cheney looked back and forth between the two men and said firmly, "You two can sit here and talk nonsense all night." She rose and swept grandly to the door, then turned and dramatically announced, "I have patients waiting."

★ ★ ★ ★

The two nurses on duty were Sallie Sisk and Bethena Posey. Mrs. Sisk was a cheerful, red-faced, red-haired woman of about fifty. Miss Posey was a quiet girl of eighteen, pretty in a delicate sort of way, Cheney thought, though she was really too thin and her skin, while striking, was as white as virgin snow.

The other male attendant on duty with Shiloh was a boy with the quirky name of Jesty Tukes. "My mother had a strange sense of humor," he explained. Small and studious-looking, he told Shiloh and Cheney that he wanted to be a doctor. "But I can't afford Toland Medical College, so I'm learning everything I can here at St. Francis, and my mother and I are saving every penny. One day I'll get to go. Anyway, when I heard that you were going to work at night, Mr. Irons, I switched to this shift. I've heard you have a lot of experience—with the war, and everything—and that you were in New York last year during the cholera epidemic and were on the Metropolitan Board of Health—"

"Hold on, Mr. Tukes," Shiloh said, not unkindly. "Dr. Duvall, we're going to go back to the men's ward. Will you excuse us, ladies?" He nodded politely to Cheney and the two nurses. Mrs. Sisk grinned widely at him, and Miss Posey's sharp cheekbones flushed a pale rose as she ducked her head.

Cheney sighed. *Both of them are already smitten,* she thought, watching Shiloh's wide shoulders and easy, long stride as he and the young man went toward the door. Jesty Tukes was still talking. *Too bad there's no prescriptive for broken hearts. . . . Shiloh usually manages to leave a few in his wake, wherever we go.*

"Dr. Duvall?" Mrs. Sisk asked politely. Cheney came out of her reverie and realized she'd been staring at Shiloh as he walked down the ward toward the door.

"Um, yes, Mrs. Sisk. Now, would you please walk the ward with me and give me a synopsis of each patient?"

"Surely, Dr. Duvall."

Cheney looked around. "First, though, I should like to have an apron. Yes, like yours, Mrs. Sisk. I prefer aprons to the coveralls."

"But, Dr. Duvall, only the nurses wear aprons," Mrs. Sisk said hesitantly. "The patients will think you're just another nurse, I'm thinking."

"Oh," Cheney said uncertainly. "Then I suppose I'll wear one of the coveralls. Yes, that would be best, at least for a while. Thank you, Mrs. Sisk. Now, where is the carbolic acid?"

Mrs. Sisk and Miss Posey exchanged blank glances. "The . . . what, ma'am?" Mrs. Sisk asked, her brow furrowing.

"Carbolic acid. The disinfectant." Cheney looked impatiently up and down the ward. "Surely you're familiar with carbolic acid. It's strong-smelling. There should be washstands, with basins—"

By the mystified looks on the nurses' faces, Cheney could see that further explanation was futile. With a quick indrawn breath, she searched the neat rows of beds. On just a cursory examination she could see at least four pregnant women. "Do the doctors here do dissections?" she demanded.

"Dissec—? Well . . . yes, Doctor," Mrs. Sisk stammered.

"And you don't know what carbolic acid is? Do you have chloride of lime solution? To wash in, somewhere? The bathrooms? Do you have liquor chlorina?" Cheney's growing agitation was confusing Mrs. Sisk and frightening Bethena Posey, she could see. But her consternation was so great she couldn't attend to them at the moment. With angry steps she swept down the row of silent beds into the hallway that circled the operating theater and led to the men's ward.

Shiloh and Jesty Tukes were sitting at the nurses' station, a long table with a gas lamp at either end, positioned about halfway down the ward. Cheney hurried to the table, and both Shiloh and Jesty Tukes looked up at her quizzically, then got to their feet. As soon as he saw Cheney's face, Shiloh stepped around the table and hurried to her. Taking her arm, he spoke quietly. "Come with me, Doc . . . we can talk over here without waking any of the patients."

Or without Jesty Tukes hearing her. . . . Shiloh mentally added. He could see that she was angry, and Cheney Duvall, M.D. could be pretty rough when she lost her temper. She was always sorry for it immediately afterward—both for her anger and for the loss of her dignity—but Shiloh didn't want the staff to get that kind of first impression. Quickly he walked her to the far corner of the ward, by the hallway. "What's the matter, Doc?" he asked calmly.

"There's no carbolic acid, Shiloh," she fumed in a quiet but strained voice. "There's no chloride of lime solution. There's no liquor chlorina. There's only soap and water."

Shiloh moved close to her and put his hands on her shoulders. Looking down into her face, his calm, warm blue eyes met her stormy green ones squarely. "Okay, Doc, calm down. I already knew they weren't using it because I had to use mine for Mr. Sanford's operation. But don't worry, we'll find some. There's bound to be something in the apothecary. If not, I've got some in my medical bag. You do, too, don't you?"

"Of course, but that's not the point," Cheney replied. Her shoulders were tense under Shiloh's light touch. "They do dissections."

"I know," he said soothingly.

"And there are maternity cases here—"

"I know, Doc, but listen—"

"Listen?" she snapped. "I'm not the one who needs to listen!"

"Well, sometimes you do," Shiloh said mildly. With a delicate movement, he gently massaged her shoulders.

Cheney wasn't even aware of it, but she did relax, shut her eyes tightly, and took a deep breath. "You're right," she murmured.

"I know," he agreed.

Stormily she narrowed her eyes and pursed her mouth.

He made a face at her.

Cheney couldn't help but smile. "Okay, I'm listening. What?"

Shiloh dropped his hands to his sides and then took both of her hands in his. Without realizing it, Cheney clung to his hands tightly. "Doc, you're the best doctor I've ever seen. So don't . . . don't get everyone here upset first thing, okay? I know how important this hospital, this job, is to you. But you've got to give people a chance."

"But, Shiloh, we're talking about real people here," Cheney asserted stubbornly, although it was in a calmer tone. "We're talking about the difference between making patients well and strong, and a horrible death. We're talking about—"

"No, we'll talk about all that in a minute, Doc," Shiloh said lightly. "And we'll take care of it. I'll help you. But, Doc, you've got to realize that the best way for you to teach someone something—especially doctors," he added cynically, "is to treat them with respect, to reason with them, to give them the chance to make the right decision themselves. Okay? Not to burn them at the stake and then explain it to them."

Cheney actually smiled; it was weak, but it was a smile. "All right. I won't start piling up the brush and sharpening my stakes yet."

"Good," Shiloh said approvingly.

"But you do know—"

"I know, Doc. I know this is something you can't live with."

"Not to mention—"

"The patients," Shiloh finished agreeably.

"Yes. So—"

"I'll go with you to talk to Dr. Baird about it," Shiloh offered, his eyes sparkling.

"Stop that," Cheney ordered.

"Can't," he murmured and moved close to her.

Cheney yanked her hands free and whirled away. She stopped at the door and turned back to him. Her eyes sparkled, her cheeks were flushed, but now she looked vivacious instead of angry. "Nurse Irons, come with me immediately. We've got to go to the apothecary. I'm going to find something sanitary to wash my hands with, even if it's pure grain alcohol!"

"Great," Shiloh muttered to her as he followed her, "and after we wash our hands, and everybody else's in the place, we can all have a good stiff drink."

"What'd you say?" Cheney asked accusingly.

"I said, 'That's a great idea, I think.' "

"Oh. And, Shiloh—"

"You're welcome."

7

By First Intention

The fog-leadened sunrise made the women's ward look a sad dingy gray. Cheney threw open a window that faced the main courtyard and breathed deeply, even though the air was chilly and damp. She could barely see the outbuildings.

"What time does Mr. Indro usually arrive, Mrs. Sisk?" she asked the nurse.

"He should be here anytime now, Dr. Duvall. He's usually in before seven."

Cheney was exhausted, so fatigued that she was having difficulty focusing her vision. Her thoughts were sluggish. Her hands and feet were cold, while the rest of her body felt warm and clammy. Leaning wearily against the window frame she brooded. *I hope I can adjust to working all night better than this! I had no idea it would be so tiring. . . .*

Consciously straightening her sagging shoulders, she turned to watch Sallie Sisk and Bethena Posey as they worked, waking up the patients, assisting the ones who could to get out of bed and to the bathroom, briskly serving juice from a wheeled cart. *They seem to feel fine. . . . If they can adjust, then I certainly will!*

Cheney found Sallie Sisk to be cheerfully helpful and an efficient and kind nurse, though she was obviously uneducated. In fact, she couldn't read or write, but she remembered a patient's name, condition, and doctor's orders to the letter after being told once.

Bethena Posey, on the other hand, had some formal education and was a fairly knowledgeable assistant. Miss Posey double-checked the doctors' instructions and made notes for both of the nurses when appropriate. She was intelligent. Unfortunately, she was coltish and awkward—Cheney hoped it was her age, as she was only eighteen—and very clumsy. In that single night she had spilled a patient's medication, bumped into a bed and waked up a patient, and torn a hole in her apron.

Cheney thought Miss Posey would be terribly embarrassed at these accidents, since she had seemed so shy upon first acquaintance. Indeed, at each unfortunate occurrence she had given Cheney a swift frightened glance, then quickly smoothed her features back into her wide-eyed innocent expression. When Cheney said nothing to her, she relaxed, cleaned up the mess, and went about her work. During the night Cheney overheard Mrs. Sisk teasing Miss Posey about "somersaulting over bed and patient and all." To Cheney's surprise, Miss Posey answered her with amused composure, "You'd think with thirty beds in here I wouldn't do it *every* night, hmm?"

"No, no, Mrs. Sisk, please don't give Mrs. Brandon orange juice," Cheney said, hurrying to the patient's bedside. "Good morning, Mrs. Brandon. I am Dr. Cheney Duvall. Since you suffer from ulcers, you should have apple juice."

Nurse Sisk looked uncertainly down at the glass of orange juice she was holding. "But . . . but Dr. Duvall, Dr. Werner—"

"Yes, Dr. Werner ordered juice for this patient," Cheney said shortly. "But she shouldn't have acidic drinks."

Mrs. Brandon was the housekeeper for a prominent San Francisco family; she had sustained a broken hip from a fall down a staircase. She sniffed and pursed her lips. "I've drunk orange juice all my life, Miss Duvall. And Dr. Werner himself has been here when it's served to me."

"I am a doctor, Mrs. Brandon, accredited by the University of Pennsylvania. Orange juice aggravates your ulcers, does it not?" Cheney asked evenly.

"No, it does not," the patient replied spiritedly.

"Very well, Mrs. Brandon, here is your orange juice. Are you comfortable this morning?" Cheney took the woman's left wrist and checked her pulse. "Did you sleep well last night?"

Slightly mollified, Mrs. Brandon replied, "I slept very well last night, Dr. Duvall. And I'm fine this morning, thank you, now that I have my juice."

Cheney smiled. "Good. You are progressing very well, Mrs. Brandon. In a few days you should be able to go home." She returned to the nurses' station.

Shiloh was standing by the nurses' desk, his arms crossed, watching her. "You look awful tired, Doc. Why don't you let me take you home? It's been too long for your first night."

He followed Cheney as she went back to the window, which Miss Posey had closed. Cheney pushed it open again irritably. "No, I want to wait and talk to Mr. Indro, and then I want to ask Dr. Baird about the carbolic acid."

"Okay. There are a couple of things I want to ask him about too."

"Good morning," a cool voice said behind them. "Mr. Irons, I'm certain that if you have any questions I can answer them."

Cheney turned to see a woman of about thirty-two or three, with neat tawny brown hair and assessing brown eyes, watching her, though she had addressed Shiloh. She was a small but well-built woman, with a pleasing symmetry of figure. Her features were distinctive, with a strong jaw line, prominent cheekbones, a Roman nose, and wide, full lips.

"Dr. Duvall, may I present to you Mrs. Ionia Tilden, the supervising nurse here at St. Francis. Mrs. Tilden, may I present to you Dr. Cheney Duvall," Shiloh said with unusual formality.

"How do you do, Mrs. Tilden," Cheney said, nodding politely. "It's a pleasure to meet you."

"I'm pleased to meet you, Dr. Duvall." Mrs. Tilden folded her hands primly in front of her apron. "I prefer to be addressed as Nurse Tilden, Dr. Duvall. I attended St. Ambrose Training School in Boston." At Cheney's blank look, she explained, "St. Ambrose's is based on the Nightingale Training School at St. Thomas' Hospital in London. All of the precepts and principles as defined by Florence Nightingale are taught there, and I graduated at the top of my class."

"I see. With that caliber of training, I'm sure you are a valuable addition to the nursing staff here at St. Francis," Cheney commented. "I'm looking forward to working with you, Nurse Tilden."

"It appears that we shan't be working together, Dr. Duvall," she responded coolly. "I don't work at night. However, as I was saying, perhaps I may be able to help you if you have questions. I'm certain that you wish to go home and rest, and it may not be necessary for you to disturb Dr. Baird."

"I'm not going to disturb him," Cheney answered with weary curtness. "It's just that I must speak with him about some matters of importance."

"I see." Ionia Tilden met Cheney's bleary gaze with a seamlessly bland expression.

Easily Shiloh said, "I think I saw Mr. Indro go into the apothecary just a few minutes ago, so if you'll excuse us . . . Dr. Duvall?" He offered Cheney his arm.

Gratefully she took it, and she and Shiloh went out into the courtyard. "What was I going to ask Mr. Indro—oh yes, the carbolic acid. But it seems there was something else. . . ." Impatiently Cheney shook her head to try to clear her murky thought processes. "Oh yes, Mr. Nash. How did he rest after the two o'clock check last night?"

"That poor man's hurtin' pretty bad," Shiloh answered. "Gout must be awfully painful. Jesty told me he's usually a pretty good patient, kind and grateful, but when he's in a lot of pain he gets cranky. I finally rigged up a kind of cradle for his foot so it wouldn't have to rest on the bed and tucked a sheet and coverlet all around his ankle. He couldn't even stand for the sheet to touch him."

"I just wonder if he's tried colchicine," Cheney muttered.

Shiloh felt uneasy; Mr. Benjamin Nash, the wealthy widower in the private suite, was Dr. Werner's patient. Nothing was prescribed for him except laudanum in doses that were so small as to be useless. Twice a day he received a borage foot soak. Shiloh considered whether to say something to Cheney but decided not to. She was tired, she needed to rest, and he felt that he'd made the point last night that she needed to soften her fighter instincts.

The apothecary was a sizable adobe cottage with a bell on the front door, as if it were a shop instead of a hospital's private store. The bell jangled lightly, and a man nimbly hurried around the plain wooden counter as they entered. He was of medium height, rotund and balding, and behind his thick spectacles his faded blue eyes held a mixture of shrewdness and inquiry. "Good morning. Permit me to introduce myself. I am Lawrence Indro, the apothecary for St. Francis. You must be Dr. Duvall. I'm charmed. And Mr. Irons? Pleased to meet you, Mr. Irons."

He shook hands briskly with Cheney and Shiloh, then waved in an encompassing gesture around the room. "Isn't it wonderful? Whatever you need, Dr. Duvall, I'm certain I can provide."

The pharmacy was certainly impressive, but Cheney reflected with amusement that it didn't inspire in her the same gleeful admiration that Mr. Indro seemed to feel. He was like a boy in a roomful of expensive toys.

The counter was situated about three feet from the door and spanned the width of the room. Behind it, lining the three walls, was an assortment of *materia medica* such as Cheney had never seen. Lined neatly along the floor were casks, large bottles, and crates. Above them were shelves spaced unevenly—to allow for differently sized containers—all the way up to the ceiling. Filling them were hundreds, perhaps thousands, of twinkling colored bottles; clear ones filled with colored substances; empty ones waiting to be filled; cans with somber labels; prepared mixtures with eye-catching labels; jars of myriad shapes and sizes filled with herbs, powders, rolled pills, dried flowers, and small mineral rocks.

"We wanted to come in last night to get a couple of things, Mr. Indro, but the door was locked," Cheney told him with faint exasperation.

"Yes. Dr. Baird's orders, ma'am," Mr. Indro said respectfully. "I'm so sorry. I should have met with you yesterday to inquire of your needs and have any prescriptives prepared before you came to work. It's just that I'm not accustomed to anyone generating new orders during the night."

"It's quite all right, Mr. Indro," Cheney said hastily, as he seemed so contrite. "First, do you have colchicine?"

"Oh yes. Colchicine, a poisonous alkaloid extracted from the corms or seeds of the meadow saffron. Marvelous for gout."

"Yes, it is," Cheney replied. She looked thoughtful, then stormy for a few moments. Shiloh watched her changing expressions anxiously, and Mr. Indro watched her gravely. Finally she sighed deeply and went on, "Actually, all we needed last night was some carbolic acid. You do have it, don't you?"

"Yes, of course," he said eagerly. "Please, come this way." He hurried around the counter, and Cheney and Shiloh followed him. Kneeling on the floor, with an effort he pulled out a sizable wooden cask and took off the close-fitting top, averting his head as he did so. "Here you are. Phenol. How much do you require, Dr. Duvall?"

Cheney and Shiloh exchanged mystified glances. Cheney leaned over to closely stare into the cask. It appeared to be filled with a grainy white substance. Suddenly a stultifying odor assaulted her nostrils, burning them, and made her see dizzily dancing black spots. Jerking upright, she stumbled back and took a gasping breath. Her eyes filled with smarting tears. "Uhh—" she groaned.

Immediately Shiloh's arms were around her waist. "Doc? What the

. . . what. . . ?" he muttered in alarm, then turned to look at the little apothecary accusingly.

Mr. Indro replaced the round wooden top carefully on the cask. "Phenol," he said dryly, "also called carbolic acid. A poisonous white crystalline compound derived from coal tar. Caustic fumes." He stood and wiped his hands on his black apron carefully. "You're not supposed to sniff it, Dr. Duvall," he added sorrowfully.

Cheney coughed.

Shiloh pulled her closer. With one hand he took a clean cotton handkerchief out of his pants pocket and dabbed at her tearstained cheeks. "Don't cry, Doc," he said with thinly veiled amusement. "Makes men nervous when ladies cry."

"I'm not a lady, I'm a doctor," she managed to get out between hoarse coughs and pushed him away. "Mr. Indro, what in the world is that poison?"

Mr. Indro exchanged a long-suffering glance with Shiloh over the rims of his thick spectacles. Clearing his throat, he recited, "Phenol, also called carbolic acid. A poisonous white—"

"I know, I heard that," Cheney interrupted and immediately perceived the rudeness in her tone. "I beg your pardon, Mr. Indro, it's certainly not your fault I stuck my nose in your poison barrel. Please forgive my discourtesy. It's just that I thought carbolic acid—what I've always used—that is, the carbolic acid I'm familiar with . . . is . . . is . . ." She was making absurd gestures, as if Mr. Indro could read what her carbolic acid was from the signs. Dropping her hands and sighing, she looked up at Shiloh helplessly. Mr. Indro looked up at him with a helpless expression too.

"It's a yellow liquid," Shiloh said.

"Ah," Mr. Indro said with relief. "You mean the prepared commercial mixture. Carr's Carbolic Compound?"

"Yes, that's it," Cheney said eagerly.

"I believe I do have a small bottle of that back in the storeroom," Mr. Indro declared. "One moment—" He started toward the door in one corner of the back wall.

"No, wait, Mr. Indro," Cheney said dully. "Never mind. I just wanted to know if the hospital kept it in stock." She started toward the door, her shoulders rounded with lethargy.

Shiloh hesitated, and Cheney turned to him questioningly. "Mr. Indro, what do you use the phenol for?" he asked.

"Li Shen and Li Bai use a dilute solution of it to mop the floors and clean the walls," Mr. Indro explained. "I understand that it has decisive sanitizing properties."

"I'm glad you understand it," Cheney muttered blackly.

Shiloh gave her a reproachful look, then took her arm. "Thank you, Mr. Indro. It was a pleasure to meet you. Could I come talk to you sometime? I'm not much on medicines and stuff, and I'd like to learn."

Lawrence Indro's doleful round face brightened considerably. "I'd be pleased, Mr. Irons," he exclaimed. "Anytime, anytime. And, Dr. Duvall—"

"Yes?" She turned to face him.

"I'm . . . I . . . apologize for your . . . disappointment," he said contritely.

Cheney sighed. "No, Mr. Indro. It's I who must apologize. And, Mr. Indro—"

"Yes?" he responded hopefully.

"With your permission, I'll be back with Mr. Irons. I need to review my pharmacopoeia, too. And I promise I'll be in a better humor when I do."

"Oh, thank you, Dr. Duvall," he said fervently.

With a rueful smile Cheney turned to leave.

★ ★ ★ ★

Shiloh insisted that Cheney have a cup of hot tea before they talked to Dr. Baird. Cheney met the head cook, Mrs. Raymond, a neat, chubby, crisp woman of about fifty, and her assistant, Angelina Cassavettes. Angelina was eighteen, Sicilian, sultry, and outrageously flirtatious with Shiloh. A sure sign of Cheney's fatigue was that she paid scant attention.

After taking a few sips of the scalding tea, Cheney marched to Dr. Baird's office. Outside his office door she looked up at Shiloh to tell him calmly, "I'll be nice."

"Okay," he said with resignation.

Cheney knocked on the door, and Dr. Baird's gruff voice answered instantly, "Come in."

Cheney and Shiloh entered. Walker was lounging in one of the chairs in front of his father's desk, but he hurried to his feet as Cheney entered, as did Dr. Baird. This was the largest and most luxuriously appointed office, with two leather wing chairs and a Chesterfield sofa at one end of the room, with Dr. Baird's fine mahogany desk and two visitors' chairs at the other.

"I'll go ahead and start morning checks," Walker excused himself after cordial greetings were exchanged.

Cheney noted with envy that in spite of Walker's late evening—he had stayed at the hospital until after midnight, and then was going to the Westins' party, the same one that Victoria was attending—he looked fresh and energetic. Cheney was certain that she looked dull, pasty-faced, and work-grimed. She looked down at herself; sure enough, she was still wearing her coverall and it was smudged. Still, she was determined not to let her discomfiture with her appearance affect her.

"Dr. Baird, there are several matters—" With a quick guilty glance at Shiloh she cleared her throat and began again. "Dr. Baird, I hope we're not intruding upon your morning routine?"

"Quite all right, Dr. Duvall," he said evenly. "Naturally, I'm interested in how the night shift progressed. I wouldn't have imposed upon you to report to me this first morning, however. In fact, I'm a little surprised to see you still here."

"Well, there is a matter of some importance that I—that Mr. Irons and I—wished to discuss with you," Cheney explained.

"Very well." Dr. Baird waited.

Cheney hesitated; again she was feeling woolly-headed from losing a night's sleep. Now that she was in Dr. Baird's presence, she was intimidated and couldn't recall exactly how she had planned to broach the subject.

Smoothly Shiloh began, "Dr. Baird, Dr. Duvall and I use carbolic acid as an antiseptic, both to cleanse our hands while dealing with patients, and to treat open wounds or sores. Are there any rules at St. Francis for prevention of sepsis?"

Dr. Baird stared at him steadily, then transferred his severe gaze to Cheney. "St. Francis is the cleanest hospital you'll ever see," he asserted. "The floors are mopped twice a day. The walls are thoroughly cleaned once a week. The sheets are changed every other day. Nurse Tilden checks each attendant's fingernails when they report for duty, and they are required to wash their hands anytime they handle unclean things like bedding or bandages or waste. I never use donated sheets as other hospitals do. I buy bolts of linen that the nurses make into dressings and bandages."

"Yes, sir, I've seen that St. Francis is clean and well tended in all particulars," Cheney said carefully, regaining her composure after Shiloh's matter-of-fact introduction. "But there have been studies that have shown that simple cleanliness is not enough. Certain substances prevent sepsis and seem to be a preventive for some communicable diseases. For instance, extensive use of carbolic acid prevents the spread of cholera."

Dr. Baird countered, "We've never had a cholera plague here, Dr. Duvall."

"Sir," she went on quietly, "there was a study in 1847, proven by Dr. Ignatz Semmelweiss and published in the *Vienna Medical Journal*, establishing that puerperal fever is in most cases a cadaveric infection, but it is sometimes an infection by means of putrid exudation or discharge from a living organism—"

"Are you telling me that one of the mothers has child-bed fever?" Dr. Baird demanded, sitting bolt upright and gripping the arms of his chair tightly.

"No, sir—"

"Then . . . someone has a cadaveric infection?" he snapped with growing impatience. "No, no, that means they're dead—is someone dead?"

"No, sir," Cheney said desperately. "It's just that this study proved that puerperal fever can be prevented if the doctors cleanse their hands with carbolic acid before they examine the postpartum women. It's vital, especially, after they've done a dissection."

Still Baird looked irritably confused. "We've never had a case of puerperal fever either, Dr. Duvall. And I can assure you that all of the doctors here are men of wholesome habits."

Cheney answered in a low voice, "Sir, I'm not questioning their personal hygiene. What I'm trying to say is that soap and water are not enough. Sepsis prevention is required. That takes carbolic acid. Or a chloride of lime solution. Or liquor chlorina. Soap won't do it."

Dr. Baird sank back in his chair and rested his chin on his chest, regarding Cheney and Shiloh with narrowed eyes. "So what you're asking me is if you can have some carbolic acid to wash your hands in? And to treat open lesions?"

"Sir, I believe that this is an important enough medical discovery to warrant a change in hospital procedure," Cheney insisted. "I think that all hospital personnel who handle the patients should be required to cleanse their hands with carbolic acid."

"The doctors, too," Baird stated in a slow, slightly stunned voice.

"The doctors especially," Cheney said firmly.

Dr. Baird dark gaze tracked to Shiloh, his expression incredulous. "You subscribe to this . . . obsessive washing, Mr. Irons?"

"Uh . . . yes, sir, I do. Once you get in the habit, sir, it's really not that . . . uh . . ."

"Bizarre?" Baird suggested sarcastically.

"Intrusive," Cheney said stubbornly, her eyes now flashing green fire warnings. "And certainly not obsessive, Dr. Baird."

"I really learned about it mostly during the war," Shiloh said in a matter-of-fact tone that appeared to distract Dr. Baird from Cheney's mounting temper—as Shiloh had known it would. "I've read the study Dr. Duvall just mentioned, and I had some trouble making it fit real life, if you know what I mean," he continued in a "man-to-man" voice that Cheney found acutely irritating.

But she had lost Dr. Baird's audience, as his full attention was now on Shiloh. "So how did you reach this same conclusion about hand-washing in poison, Mr. Irons?" he asked with no hint of rancor.

Shiloh shrugged, leaned forward, and crossed one booted foot over his knee. "Over and over again I saw men with open wounds. After they had already gotten inflamed and filled with pus, then the doctors would try to clean them out with carbolic acid. It just never worked."

"What do you mean?" Dr. Baird asked intently.

"They died," Shiloh said shortly. "And they died badly. Worse than dying from a gunshot wound, I thought. Worse than bleeding to death. Anyway, to me it just seemed like those wounds that got all septic like that were just . . . dirty. That's all. They looked dirty, and they especially smelled dirty. So I tried just cleaning them out with carbolic acid before they got septic."

"And?"

Shiloh shrugged and leaned back in his chair. "Most of the time it kept them from getting that killing fever and pus. I didn't keep exact numbers on it, but I could sure tell a difference."

Baird, in his turn, leaned back in his chair and stared into the distance. "You know, Hippocrates said something I've never been able to forget. . . ." he said in an oddly distracted voice. "He wrote about 'healing by first intention.' He tried to figure out why some wounds healed without all that nonsense about 'the irritative period' and 'laudable pus' . . ." Suddenly he straightened in his chair. "All right, Mr. Irons. What do you want?"

"I'm not too sure about the procedures," Shiloh said smoothly. "Dr. Duvall has studied all the published research, like that one by Dr. Semmelweiss and that new one by Joseph Lister. In fact, she and Dr. Devlin Buchanan wrote a paper on antisepsis themselves. You know Dr. Buchanan? Mrs. de Lancie's fiancé?"

A smile lurked in J. E. Baird's dark eyes, and the uncompromising line of his mouth twitched. He turned back to Cheney. "You have a fine champion in Mr. Irons, Dr. Duvall."

"Yes, I suppose I do," Cheney agreed with a lingering trace of irritation. "So you will consider decreeing the use of carbolic acid for antisepsis, Dr. Baird?"

"I will consider it, and I will speak to the other doctors about it. In the meantime, Mr. Irons may require the nursing staff to use it. And I will provide—what is it you need? Washstands with basins?"

"Yes," Cheney answered quickly. "Stationed at both ends of the wards."

"Fine. I'll see to it." He glanced at Cheney astutely. "You seem exhausted, Dr. Duvall. Are you certain you wish to continue working at night?"

Cheney made an effort to compose herself. Smoothing her skirt nervously, she replied, "Oh yes, sir. I beg your pardon. I hope I'll . . . adjust soon."

"I think you will, if that is what you want," Baird declared. "You seem to be a lady who knows how to get what she wants." Before Cheney could think of a reply, he grumbled, "Now, who the blue devil is this man Semmel-something? And who's this Joseph Lister I'm supposed to be so impressed with? You'd better bring these studies to me, Dr. Duvall. Though some people seem to doubt it, I can read. And write. Fluently."

"I have no doubt, sir," Cheney said gratefully. "And I'll be glad to bring you the studies. And, sir, thank you very much for your attention."

"You're welcome, Dr. Duvall," he grunted, leaning over his desk and shuffling papers irritably in a clear dismissive gesture. "But next time you have a question for me, bring Mr. Irons. He's good at interpreting for you."

Cheney and Shiloh stared at each other. Shiloh grinned. Insufferably.

Cheney looked thunderous—for a brief moment.

Then she made a face.

8

COMMONERS FIRSTHAND

Cheney's later recollections of the first week of night work were always stark contrasts of light and dark, sound and silence. She envisioned long hours in shadow on the wards, with the nurses and male attendants always speaking to her in hushed reverent tones. In her remembrances were cries of pain. She recalled the quiet questions she and Shiloh asked as they made their twice-nightly checks, and the sleepy answers of the patients. She remembered hours of sitting at the nurses' station in a pool of amber light from the small gas lamp on the table, reading the doctors' notes on each patient. Long discussions with Shiloh, and sometimes Bethena Posey and Jesty Tukes, often took place in his office. Mrs. Sisk would make pots of hot yerba buena tea, and they talked about prescriptives and various treatments and the patients. During the week Cheney slept odd hours during the morning and afternoons, and often awoke not knowing if it was day or night.

Walker Baird checked in with Cheney and Shiloh every night. Twice he stayed late with his patients, one of whom was Mrs. Archibald Caplan, who was expecting her first child. Strong in Cheney's memory was the night young Mrs. Caplan had a long and difficult labor, and finally gave birth to a healthy baby boy. Cheney's visions of those hours were of stark garish gaslights, the weakening cries of the mother, Walker Baird's calm voice, Shiloh's white and strained face, Sallie Sisk's stolid assistance, and Bethena Posey's composure with the terrified Mr. Caplan. Dr. Walker Baird was solicitous with Mrs. Caplan in her hours of agony, but unfailingly confident. He never showed signs of weariness.

The washbasins and stands Dr. Baird had promised Cheney were on the wards the very next night. Cheney and Shiloh trained the nurses and attendants in the use of carbolic acid and insisted that the attendants all use them according to strict rules of sanitation. Nurse Ionia

Tilden accepted Shiloh's authority on this matter and agreed to enforce the use of the solution during the day. Some mutterings about cracked dry skin and the astringent smell were overheard by Cheney and Shiloh. Cheney ignored them, but Shiloh repeatedly and patiently explained the theory of antisepsis to all of the nurses and attendants.

At ten o'clock Friday night Shiloh and Cheney reported for work as usual. Walker Baird met them at the door dressed in evening clothes. "I was attending the Laskers' dinner party," he said accusingly even before greetings were exchanged, "and Mrs. de Lancie told me that today is your birthday, Dr. Duvall. And you celebrate yours today, too, Shiloh. Why don't you take the evening off and go celebrate?"

"We wanted to work," Cheney answered as she breezed in the front door of the hospital and crisply removed her gloves, hat, and cloak.

"Some of us did," Shiloh mumbled.

"Dr. Duvall," Walker went on reproachfully, "this hospital does not condone the use of slave labor."

Cheney went into Shiloh's office to get her coverall. Mrs. Sisk had gotten in the habit of putting a clean one there for her each night. Shiloh had installed a small gilded mirror on the wall above one bookcase, and Cheney always did a perfunctory check of her face and hair before she went to work. "I haven't worked a week yet, Walker," she replied as the two men crowded into the small office behind her. "Four nights in a row is hardly slave labor."

"But you must take some time off," Walker insisted.

"We will."

"When?" Shiloh asked brightly.

"Sunday," Walker declared before Cheney could answer. "I'm inviting you both to Cliff House for luncheon for a belated birthday celebration. And when I go back to the Laskers', I'll bully Mrs. de Lancie into accepting my invitation too."

"Well . . ." Cheney said, staring into the mirror and fidgeting with her hair.

"Yes," Shiloh said. "She said yes. I say yes. Thank you, Walker."

"You're welcome, Shiloh. And, Dr. Duvall, I'll call on you and Mrs. de Lancie in the morning and leave my card, just so I'll be proper," Walker said with satisfaction. "Otherwise Victoria—I mean, Mrs. de Lancie—will say I'm vulgar and bourgeois."

"She says that about everyone," Cheney laughed. "But you know, I do believe I'll accept your invitation, Walker. Thank you so much."

"You're welcome. Shall I see you in the morning, then?" Walker asked, his midnight blue eyes shining.

"If you're too early Victoria won't be 'at home,' " Cheney warned. "And if you're too late I'll be asleep."

Walker took her hand and brushed a quick kiss on it. "Then when I return to the party I shall ask Mrs. de Lancie at what time one might be fashionably late for morning calls without being so late as to miss the company of the hardworking Dr. Duvall," he said with a gallant air. "Good night, then, Dr. Duvall. Good night, Shiloh."

"Good night," Cheney said.

Shiloh muttered, "Good night, Walker."

Cheney hurried out toward the wards without looking back.

★ ★ ★ ★

Cliff House was perched on a rocky promontory on a distant northwestern point of the peninsula, brooding over the Pacific Ocean in splendid isolation. Victoria's landau traveled through what seemed like miles of deserted dunes with only straggling shrubs and lofty rocks for decor. A straight road cut through the sand across the Outside Lands, as the northwestern barrens of the peninsula were called, and Cheney, Victoria, Shiloh, and Walker saw several carriages, carts, and riders coming and going.

"I'm surprised at the amount of traffic," Cheney remarked.

"Cliff House is very popular for luncheon and promenades on Sunday afternoon," Walker explained. He was sitting by Victoria and smiled smugly down at her. "Don't worry, Mrs. de Lancie. I know that Cliff House has acquired somewhat of an unsavory reputation for being a haunt of the undesirable elements. I believe that some late nights there are particularly rowdy. But Sunday afternoons are traditionally more genteel."

Victoria's left eyebrow peaked slightly, and she said with mock severity, "I should hope so, Walker. Cheney and I would never keep company with undesirable persons. Particularly Cheney."

Cheney looked uncertain at this declaration, while beside her Shiloh grinned, his even white teeth gleaming and the "V" scar beneath his left eye crinkling. "No, the doc would never be involved with unsavory persons. Like feuding clans in the back hills of Arkansas . . . or General Nathan Bedford Forrest . . . or pugilists—"

"Victoria made me go to your boxing matches!" Cheney exclaimed indignantly.

"Nonsense," Victoria replied coolly. "And besides, even if I did, we were in the Marquess of Queensberry's party. Hardly unsavory persons. Stop that laughing, Walker. You are still a troublemaker."

"Yeah, Walker," Shiloh put in. "Quit making trouble."

"You're just glad I'm here to take some of the heat," Walker grumbled to Shiloh. "It's not fair."

"Life is not fair," Cheney told him, her eyes sparkling with mischief. "You're too young to know that yet."

"I beg your pardon?" Walker retorted with righteous indignation. "I happen to know, Dr. Duvall, that we are celebrating your twenty-sixth birthday today. I, too, am twenty-six years old."

"Walker Baird!" Victoria scolded. "You most certainly are not. You are twenty-two years old. What impertinence."

Grinning easily, he leaned back in his seat and crossed one leg over the other. "What difference does it make? Shiloh lies about his age, too. He says he's twenty-three, but I think he's about twenty-one or two."

"Shiloh doesn't lie," Victoria retorted. "He just doesn't know."

"Actually I think I'm prob'ly 'bout eighteen or nineteen," Shiloh drawled, casually sliding his arm along the back of the seat and shifting so he was a little closer to Cheney.

"Sometimes you seem even younger," Cheney commented innocently.

"Thanks, Doc."

Walker studied them with narrowed eyes for a moment, then his boyish features smoothed. "So, Shiloh, have you been able to find out anything about your family? About the clipper?" Shiloh had told Walker about his history—or rather, the lack of it.

"No, 'fraid not," Shiloh replied. "I went down to the Embarcadero early Monday morning, but they laughed when I asked to see the harbormaster's records from 1843."

"I'm not surprised," Walker said sympathetically. "My father says that sea traffic was sparse until forty-nine, of course. Before the Gold Rush there were just military vessels and a few commercial ships bringing supplies. But the population of San Francisco was only about three hundred people. One commercial vessel twice a year was about all it took to bring supplies to little old Yerba Buena. And there weren't any shipbuilders here, you know. I'm surprised that the *Day Dream* listed San Francisco as its home port."

Shiloh shrugged. "Could've been a mistake in the Lloyd's of London report after the shipwreck."

"That's kind of unlikely," Walker scoffed. "You ever dealt with them?"

"No, Lloyd's of London only assures my jewels," Shiloh said in a stuffy voice, assuming a snobbish expression. Cheney giggled and poked him in the ribs. "Ow," he mumbled.

Walker laughed. "Well, they insure the hospital. And they're as thorough as an army of ants. Particularly when there's a sizable claim."

"So why would a private yacht list San Francisco as its home port?" Cheney asked rhetorically, furrowing her brow. "Maybe the ship was built here? No, wait—you said the population was only three hundred people? Walker, are you lying again?"

"No, Dr. Duvall, I'll never lie to you again," Walker said solemnly. "Up until January of 1848—when gold was discovered at Sutter's Mill—the population of San Francisco was about three hundred people."

"Was your father here then?" Cheney asked with interest.

"Yes, he was." Walker grinned. "He was at Sutter's Mill. That's right, he was just a carpenter working at that old sawmill. As soon as they started finding those glittering rocks in the mill race, he knew exactly what was going to happen. He took every cent we had and went out and staked a claim. He knew every one of those hills, had walked 'em all, knew every trickle of every stream of water. He had been looking for a homestead, you see. By 1850 he'd already cashed out his rocks and sold his mine."

"Fascinating," Cheney murmured.

Walker saw a hint of a wistful expression on Shiloh's face and went on quickly, "Anyway, what about the *Day Dream*? What the devil was your yacht doing here in 1843, anyway, Shiloh?"

"Walker—" Victoria said hesitantly, "isn't it traditional to list the nearest well-known seaport as the home registry for a ship? I mean, you might purchase a yacht in Scotland, for example, and live in Pittsburgh. Wouldn't you list your home port registry in New York?"

Shiloh sat up a little straighter and became intent.

"Yes, that's right," Walker agreed, "but that doesn't help Shiloh much. In 1843 . . . where would a family who can afford their own clipper live out here? San Francisco was really the only sizable settlement. And that was mostly *hidalgos*, and monks, Ohlone Indians, and a few frontiersmen who'd wandered this far west. Certainly there was no shipbuilding here—every piece of wood has to be imported." He made a sweeping gesture toward the sandy, barren view outside the landau's glass windows.

Shiloh nodded, then eased back in his relaxed posture, assuming a careless expression. "Think they live in Mexico? Think maybe I'm an eighteen-year-old Mexican?"

Everyone laughed, and then Victoria appraised Shiloh's six-foot-five Nordic looks. "I think you're a Prussian soldier."

"I think you're a British captain of a man-of-war," Walker offered.

"Maybe a Viking jarl," Victoria decided.

"Roman gladiator?" Walker mused.

"I think you're all silly," Cheney grumbled, though she moved closer to Shiloh and began to wave her fan over him in exaggerated gestures of obeisance. "Everyone knows Shiloh is the long-lost King of Simbalingadoriman."

"Simbaloringadum," Shiloh gravely corrected her. "And could you fan a little more to the right?"

Agilely Cheney whipped her fan shut and tapped his knuckles with it.

"Ow," he mumbled.

"There's no such place as Simbalingamoridan," Victoria declared.

"Simbaloringadum," Shiloh patiently repeated. "And me and the Doc are going to go find it someday."

"We are?" she asked, her eyes brightening to emerald stars.

"Yeah, Doc. You promised. Back in New York, in the park, after the plague. Laura Blue heard you," he insisted.

"I did no such thing," Cheney said, haughtily turning away from him. "Victoria, these two men lie. We have found ourselves in unsavory company after all."

Victoria gave an exaggerated sigh. "I should have Robert and James toss them out of the carriage."

"Tim and Eddie," Shiloh told her. In an aside to Walker he said, "She calls all her footmen Robert and James. And they let her."

"So would I," Walker said firmly. "And so would you, Robert."

"Yeah, guess I would, James."

The carriage drew to a halt. Walker gave Shiloh a mischievous look, and they jumped out of the carriage at the same time. Shiloh hurried around to Walker's side, and they opened the door and lowered the little steps for Cheney and Victoria. Then they bowed in unison as the ladies stepped out. Poor Tim and Eddie stood behind them, resplendent in their black and gold livery, looking at each other and at the two men uncertainly.

Victoria came out first and quickly opened her parasol. She looked cool and immaculate in the benevolent afternoon glow, wearing a taffeta carriage dress; the bodice and pannier overskirt had stripes of icy mint green and wintry blue. The underskirt and small train were a dark kelly green trimmed with white Alençon lace, cord, and tassels. Her kelly green carriage mantle was short, trimmed with velvet ruching, with insets of the same lace down the back and around the front openings. Smiling slightly, she nodded to the confused footmen. "You and your father may walk down the promenade if you'd like, Tim, Eddie. I expect we shall be about two hours."

"Yes, ma'am," they said in unison with great relief. They scooted around to the driver's box and clambered up while Cheney was still coming out of the carriage.

She glowed in a carriage dress of Caledonian silk, which was cream-colored and patterned with thin stripes of a deep coppery-gold color and a deep chocolatey brown. The overskirt was small and gathered to a small bustle in the back, accentuating Cheney's small waist. The bodice was tight, with a V-shaped insert of rows of Maltese lace. Instead of a mantle or cloak, Cheney carried an ecru Delhi shawl with a delicate raised pattern in copper-colored silk. Her hat was of straw with a one-inch brim that dipped down to her eyebrows in front. The crown was trimmed with a wide satin ribbon that matched the copper color in her carriage costume, with the ribbon and an arrangement of small yellow chrysanthemums centered in the back of the hat.

Walker bowed and held her hand a little longer than was strictly necessary as she came down the carriage steps. "You look lovely today, Dr. Duvall. Your dress becomes you; the colors glow almost as much as you do."

"Why, thank you, Walker," she said, smiling. "I suppose I do look different from my usual hospital style. And . . . oh! . . . the first time you saw me. At the accident . . ."

"You looked like an angel," he said. "A fiery one, perhaps."

The plank walkway into the back of Cliff House—the front was practically hanging out in thin air—was wide enough to accompany all four of them abreast. But, of course, the ladies must be in the middle, so Walker naturally fell into step by Cheney, and Shiloh took Victoria's arm.

Cliff House was a single-story shingled building built in 1863. It rambled along a sizable rocky promontory that overhung dramatic cliffs and great rocks where sea lions played. The dining room of the restaurant was presentable, mainly because of the breathtaking view of the wild Pacific and the crashing surf below. As the building had many rooms, it also had three saloons—one supposedly for "ladies only," but that was a rather loosely enforced rule—two gambling halls, and other rooms that once were used as private dining rooms by the society patrons. As the small private rooms did not afford the excellent view of the common dining room, however, the wealthier patrons had begun to request tables alongside the great windows in the larger room, so many of the smaller rooms appeared to be empty. Although Cheney and Victoria or any other lady would never admit to knowledge of it, the other rooms were rumored to be used by prostitutes at the more rambunctious parties at Cliff House at night. However, on this Sunday afternoon most of the patrons were families with children or young couples, the lady often chaperoned by a maid. One small anteroom adjoining the dining room was filled with these chaperones, knitting and gossiping and glancing eagle-eyed through the archway into the dining room.

As they stood at the open double doors of the dining area, Victoria impatiently searched the room, her icy blue eyes studying each hurrying waiter. They were dressed in short black jackets and black serge breeches with long white linen towels tied around their waists. Every waiter who scurried by had his hands full of either steaming plates or dirty dishes, and each one had a harried "I'm too busy to stop and talk to you" look on his face.

"Where is the majordomo?" Victoria demanded. "We really must be announced—perhaps that would clear a way to our table."

Walker rolled his eyes, then with a muttered apology to Cheney hurried to take Victoria's arm. "Mrs. de Lancie, I'm afraid Cliff House has no majordomo," he explained.

"No majordomo?" she repeated. "Then how is one announced? Isn't that how this is done, when one dines in a common dining room?"

Walker looked around the lively confusion of Cliff House. Children laughed and tried to escape from their parents' tables, many of them with large balls or sticks and hoops. The clinking of glasses and taps of pewter upon crockery joined in a discordant jangling song. The conversation level was only slightly below shouting. There were several well-dressed people there, men in fine broadcloth morning suits or severely cut black business suits, and ladies in Sunday promenade finery. But most of the people were not as splendid, though they were obviously dressed in their Sunday best. Always obvious to an observer was that baffling demarcation of appearance, mannerism, and expression that separated the middle classes from the upper.

"My dear Mrs. de Lancie, have you ever dined in a public dining room?" Walker asked doubtfully.

"Why, no, of course not," she answered, but her eyes were roaming over the controlled pandemonium of the dining room with avid curiosity. "It's rather . . . invigorating, is it not?"

Behind Victoria and Walker, Cheney and Shiloh exchanged grins. Walker cast a questioning look behind, and Cheney stepped up slightly to speak to Victoria. "Yes, it could be exhilarating to observe commoners firsthand, hmm, Victoria?"

"Why, yes, I should think so," she replied, straightening her slim shoulders. "Do you think we might sit over there?" As Victoria Elizabeth Steen de Lancie would never point, she merely glanced at a table set for four in the center of the dining room, directly beneath a window with a panoramic view.

At that moment a little man with a mustache and an exasperated air hurried up to them. He was bald, except for a fringe of black hair encircling a shiny pink pate, and he had slim white hands that gestured busily and dramatically. His recognizable badges of honor were an unused monocle hanging from one buttonhole and a long black dress coat. He had the inevitable apron tied on, however, even though he was the maitre d'. "Oh my, oh my, it's Dr. Walker Baird, isn't it?" he fussed. "We thought your father was reserved today!"

"Sorry, Elders. But I do have a distinguished guest—may I present to you Mrs. Victoria Elizabeth Steen de Lancie? Mrs. de Lancie has graciously consented to join my party today," Walker recited formally.

Victoria gave the maitre d' a frigid nod.

"Oh, dear, Mrs. de Lancie? Mrs. *Steen* de Lancie? Please, madam, allow me to escort you to your table . . . so honored by your patronage,

Madame de Lancie . . . will this be adequate? . . . honored . . . your waiter, yes, I shall send him over promptly. . . ."

Victoria merely nodded at the man. As Cheney and Shiloh walked behind them, Shiloh whispered to her, "What's the story here, Doc? I thought I had this society introduction stuff down, but it looks like Walker missed a step."

Cheney whispered back, "No, Shiloh, dear. You see, the maitre d' is not someone who would be properly introduced to Victoria. Walker was merely making him aware of who she is."

He sighed. "Y'all's rules are confusing."

"Not my rules," Cheney lightly remarked.

"Sure they are," he muttered.

Cheney gave him a sharp look, but he stepped around her neatly to hold her chair. "Hey, Robert, aren't we supposed to stand behind them?" he asked Walker mischievously.

"I'm James," Walker insisted. "You're Robert."

"Doesn't matter," Shiloh shrugged, grinning down at Victoria.

Mr. Elders, who was hovering over Victoria, looked up at him with wide eyes.

"Anyway, I think us footmen are supposed to wait in there, Robert," Walker answered, nodding toward the maids' anteroom.

Mr. Elders blanched as he sized up Shiloh's lean, muscular frame; his denim breeches, clean but worn; his knee-high cavalry boots; plain black muslin shirt; and the long canvas duster he often wore. "You . . . James? Are you the footman? Um . . . er . . . yes, this way, please . . ." Mr. Elders started trying to shoo Shiloh toward the anteroom.

"Uh . . . Doc . . ." he mumbled, trying to evade the maitre d's flapping hands.

Cheney and Victoria looked disinterestedly out the window. "Fabulous view, is it not, Mrs. de Lancie?" Cheney remarked.

"Quite," Victoria replied. "But it is difficult to enjoy it with the servants making such a fuss."

"Oh dear, oh dear," Mr. Elders muttered, still trying to corral Shiloh away from the table. The image was something like a small bantam rooster trying to corner a bemused wolf.

Walker finally managed to hurry around the table and take Elders' flailing arm. "Elders," he said a little breathlessly, "this is Mr. Irons. Mr. Shiloh Irons. He's a member of my party. The ladies were just . . . er . . . having a little joke."

Elders stopped waving his arms in Shiloh's face and peered up at him suspiciously. "Mr. Irons? You are a member of Mrs. de Lancie's party?"

"Whew," Shiloh muttered with relief. "Yes, sir. Really, I am. Really. Doc . . . c'mon."

Cheney took pity upon him. "Yes, Elders, he may join us. If he promises to behave himself."

Still Elders was not sure. With a dark look he went back to hover obsequiously in Victoria's vicinity. "Mrs. de Lancie, this Mr. James Irons wishes to join your party. With your permission. . . ?"

Willing herself to keep a straight face, Victoria replied, "Yes, Mr. James Irons is a member of our party, as is Mr. Robert Baird. They may join us, of course."

Elders took a deep breath, partly of relief and partly of exasperation. His expression clearly communicated that society's sense of humor was certainly odd, and their jokes were a little difficult for plain folk to find amusing. "Yes, ma'am," he murmured, then bustled off.

Finally Shiloh sat down—rather hurriedly, before anyone tried to stop him—and Walker took his seat. The table was circular, so they were seated Shiloh-Cheney-Walker-Victoria, which was satisfactory to everyone.

"Sorry, Shiloh," Walker said, though his eyes sparkled with merriment. Victoria and Cheney both returned their gaze out the window; Cheney's shoulders were shaking slightly.

"Yeah. Y'all think it's so funny," he grumbled.

"Well, we are the ones who started about the footmen and all," Walker admitted.

Shiloh looked around guiltily. "Don't even say that out loud. Mr. Elders might come haul me off bodily."

Everyone laughed at this absurd image. Cheney teased, "Why, Shiloh, no one would ever mistake you for a footman, not really. You're too . . . too . . ."

"I know, I know," he said darkly. "Too tall. Can't have a matching pair, huh, Mrs. de Lancie? Scandalous to have unmatched footmen. I'm like odd gloves, or two left boots."

"Shiloh? You're not really offended, are you?" Victoria asked, her eyes softening to a sweet pastel blue. "Please forgive me. I never meant to hurt you."

"Hurt?" Cheney repeated, bewildered. "Shiloh—"

Shiloh glanced down at her; for a moment his gaze was stony, distant, but then his eyes softened and he grinned. "Hurt? Naw. But that Elders has a mean right hook. Maybe I should ask him to be my sparring partner."

Walker laughed and Victoria smiled. But Cheney's and Shiloh's eyes locked, and his expression sobered again as he studied her face. Cheney suddenly thought, *We all see it as a big joke . . . but perhaps it's not so funny if you're not . . . not . . . what? I see Shiloh as just like me, in my . . . my social class, my equal. But . . . he has no money, he has no family, he has no prospects—does it bother him? Well, of course, you ninny, it must! But he . . . doesn't show it. And I . . . after two years, this is the first time I've ever considered it from his point of view!*

"Doc," he said gravely, still staring down at her. "Look at it from my point of view."

"Wh-what?" Cheney was jarred from her reverie. She realized she'd been staring deeply into Shiloh's eyes, while Victoria and Walker were carrying on a conversation. "I . . . I . . . beg your pardon?" she said in confusion.

"Don't you think," Shiloh said slowly, with a secret smile, "that we should have oysters for a starter?"

Knowledge of

Part Three

Witty Inventions

I Wisdom dwell with prudence,
And find out knowledge
Of witty inventions.

Proverbs 8:12

9

Of Pertinence and Impertinence

April sauntered into May without Cheney's notice or permission. In the complex evolution required to change one's night into day and day into night, she triumphed; but all of the dreamy days and the stirring nights ceased to be identifiable with other artificial time periods, such as the day of the week or the month. To Cheney it was simply midmorning, which meant it was time for her first sleep; or late afternoon, which was time for her second sleep; or night, which was time to go to work.

Mrs. Victoria Elizabeth Steen de Lancie appeared at operas, theaters, and countless dinners and luncheons and parties. It was reported in the society pages of the *Alta California* that the charming and dedicated Dr. Cheney Duvall, of late from a private practice in Manhattan and currently on staff at St. Francis de Yerba Buena Hospital, had joined the beautiful Mrs. Steen de Lancie at the Tivoli Opera House for the premiere of *A Midsummer Night's Dream* performed by the Royal Shakespeare Company. They were joined in the Steens' box by Dr. Walker Baird. A week later readers of the *Alta California* were made aware that the lovely Dr. Cheney Duvall and Dr. Walker Baird were at the Old California Theater for *H.M.S. Pinafore*, and were joined by the beautiful Mrs. Steen de Lancie in the second act.

In the next two weeks, Mrs. Victoria Elizabeth Steen de Lancie was accompanied by Dr. Cheney Duvall and Dr. Walker Baird to three dinner parties. One of them included on the guest list the "Railroad Kings"—Collis P. Huntington, Charles Crocker, Leland Stanford, and Mark Hopkins. Another dinner party was given for the members of the Royal Shakespeare Company. Victoria's close friends, Mr. and Mrs. Gray Westin, gave a dinner party for the four "Silver Kings"—John W. Mackay, James C. Fair, James L. Flood, and William S. O'Brien. The beautiful Mrs. Steen de Lancie was escorted by Dr. Walker Baird and accompanied by the charming and gracious Dr. Cheney Duvall.

During this month Cheney didn't see Shiloh at all, except at work, and on one Sunday when they again toured Chinatown. Once when she asked Walker what Shiloh was doing with himself, he replied that Shiloh was teaching the pugilistic art at the Olympic Club for long hours each day. With curiosity Walker asked Cheney why she hadn't asked Shiloh himself, but to that Cheney could give no answer.

★ ★ ★ ★

"Shiloh!" Cheney scolded. "Just look at your hands!" Whipping around, her elbow caught the small mirror in Shiloh's office. It exploded on the floor.

"Aw, man," Shiloh muttered, staring down at the twinkling piles of shards. "Why don't we bring a coupla black cats in here? Put up some ladders to walk under? Maybe spill salt all around?"

"I'm . . . I'm sorry," Cheney said, kneeling. "How clumsy of me! Shiloh, I'll replace your mirror. And what are you grumbling about?"

"Never mind," he said, taking her arm and lifting her to her feet. "Don't try to pick that up, Doc, you'll just cut yourself. I'll get Jesty to sweep it. And don't worry about the mirror, you're the only one who uses it."

"I believe you were primping right behind me, which is when I saw your hands," Cheney retorted. Shiloh had bent down to glance in the mirror and smooth down his shiny blond hair. He had let it grow long, but he couldn't bear for it to be untidy. Now Cheney took both of his hands in hers and studied them disapprovingly. "Shiloh, just *look* at these knuckles. Open lesions."

"Will you bandage them for me, Doc?" he teased. "Please, Doctor Cheney?"

Dropping his hands, she folded her arms and gave him a narrow-eyed, ill-humored stare. "You've been fighting. Walker told me."

"Sparring." He shrugged.

"You're going to ruin your hands."

"Naw, I'll be careful."

"Yes, I see," she said sarcastically. "You're so careful you only got three knuckles abraded instead of six or seven. Shiloh, why are you fighting, anyway?"

His face became guarded, and his voice was expressionless. "For the money."

"Oh," Cheney said uncertainly, "oh yes. Well . . . well . . . anyway, you know—*you know*—it's not just skinned knuckles. In your profession, it's dangerous to have open sores on your hands."

He looked down at his boots and sighed faintly. "Sorry, Doc. I guess I do need to always wear Broughton's mufflers, even for just knockin' around."

"Yes, you do. Will you?"

"Yes, ma'am," he said meekly. "Now will the charming and lovely and dedicated Dr. Cheney Duvall please doctor 'em up and bandage 'em?"

"Of course I will." Cheney slipped on her coverall and demanded as she was leaving Shiloh's office, "But why haven't you done it yourself? Carbolic acid, at least, or iodine?"

Close behind her he breathed, "I wanted you to. You are my doctor, aren't you, Doc?"

Glancing back quizzically over her shoulder she replied, "Well, of course, Shiloh." In the hallway leading to the women's ward she stopped and stared up at him with misgiving. "Shiloh, there's nothing wrong, is there? You—you're not sick, are you?"

He stared down into her eyes, and a warm, gentle smile turned up the corners of his firm mouth. "No, Doc, I'm great. I just wanted to make sure you're still my doctor. You were my doctor first, you know."

Cheney was puzzled and tried to frame a question, while Shiloh merely looked down at her, his eyes lazily traveling over her face, from her sparkling green eyes, to her small nose, to her generous mouth.

"Oh, here you are, Dr. Duvall," Sallie Sisk said with relief, hustling around the gently rounded hallway. "Mrs. Irby's time's a-comin'. Early."

Cheney hurried after the nurse, but Shiloh hesitated. Cheney looked back at him and saw the reluctance in his posture. "Shiloh—?"

He shifted to the other foot and made a curiously ungainly gesture with one hand. "Doc, I don't like nursing pregnant ladies. Makes me nervous. Do you really need me?"

Cheney stopped midstep and whirled around to face him. "It does?" she asked in astonishment. "I didn't realize."

"I know," he said uncomfortably. "Anyway, I do need to get my hands seen to before I do anything. I'll go get Jesty Tukes to bandage the right one . . . can't do it too good with my left hand." He hurried around the hallway toward the men's ward.

"Well, gracious me!" Cheney exclaimed to herself as she watched him almost running away. "I didn't think anything bothered him! Of all things, deliveries! I must ask him about it later. . . ." She hurried after Mrs. Sisk's round and bustling figure.

"Who is Mrs. Irby?" she asked as they almost ran down the ward. Cheney had taken the previous day off, and Mrs. Irby had not been a patient the last night she'd worked.

"Mrs. Brookshear Irby," Sallie Sisk answered breathlessly. "Mr. Brookshear Irby is the king of some bank, I gather, and Mrs. Irby is some other king's daughter and granddaughter. She's in the private suite."

They reached the hallway to the private rooms, and Cheney stopped to wash her hands in the washbasin of carbolic acid. "Just a moment, please, Mrs. Sisk. I'd like for you to give me a little more information about the patient before I just walk in there."

The nurse, her ruddy color heightened even more by exertion and by anxiety, turned to Cheney and blew out a long breath. "Whew! Now, I know you're like that, don't I, Dr. Duvall? She's just got me and Miss Rees all a-flitterin' and a-jitterin'!"

"It's all right," Cheney said soothingly. "We'll take good care of her. But . . . did you say it's Miss Rees tonight?"

"Yes, ma'am," Mrs. Sisk intoned. She gave Cheney a deliberately bland face, her head cocked saucily to the side. "Miz Edith Rees herself," she repeated in an uncanny echo of the querulous nurse's voice.

"Mmm," Cheney said noncommittally. Miss Edith Rees was an adequate nurse, but a melancholy woman. At thirty-five she was unmarried and bitter about it. Her grievance clearly marked her already plain features and distorted her morose communication into sullenness. She was Cheney's least favorite nurse, for even with the cold and distant Ionia Tilden, Cheney had been able to establish a basis of pure professionalism that governed their rare meetings. At any rate, Cheney certainly wasn't going to gossip with Mrs. Sisk about the other nurses, regardless of her personal feelings about them, so she continued rather severely, "And about the patient?"

Mrs. Sisk looked slightly miffed, then recited in an injured tone, "Mrs. Brookshear Irby. She was admitted yesterday with labor pains, but she's naught yit in her seventh month. The pains stopped this morning, and she's been free of 'em all day. 'Til about an hour ago, and no doctor's been here since early evenin'."

Cheney frowned. "Whose patient is she?"

"Dr. Werner's."

Careful to keep her face and voice neutral, Cheney asked, "And his instructions?"

"Dr. Werner ordered complete bed rest, patient to be as still as possible, eat soups and puddings only, small glasses of angelica wine during the day, two at night."

"All right, anything else?"

Mrs. Sisk's round red face wrinkled.

"It's all right, Mrs. Sisk," Cheney said briskly. "I need to know everything you feel is pertinent about this patient."

"I ain't impertinent, Dr. Duvall," Mrs. Sisk maintained solidly, "but seein' as how you don't much like to talk about personals, is all—" She waited, eyeing Cheney with scarcely concealed triumph.

Cheney got a stern hold on her temper. Sallie Sisk was a good woman, plainspoken and hardworking. But all of the nurses tended to treat Cheney with much more familiarity than they would dare show a male physician. It was difficult to create a satisfactory working alliance with them while trying to maintain a professional demeanor demanding respect. That was one reason that Cheney had finally seen the advantages in the hospital rule that nurses always rise when a doctor entered the room. It was a tangible reminder that there was, and must be, differences in authority and responsibility between nurses and doctors.

"Mrs. Sisk, I certainly wouldn't want to intrude in anyone's personal life for amusement," Cheney said in a carefully mild tone. "But anything that affects a patient's well-being must be made known to the doctor. You understand that."

Sallie Sisk was a jolly woman, generally happy with her lot in life and not too dissatisfied with her station, either, so she smiled at Cheney and said in a conspiratorial tone, "Mrs. Irby is forty-eight, Dr. Werner says *in confidential*, seein' as how Mrs. Irby tells she's thirty-nine. And she didn't want this wee baby at thirty-nine nor forty-eight, neither, and she's kinda embarrassed by it, too, if you're askin' me, and then at the same time, there you are, a woman's going to feel guilty about it, no mistake. And *that's* made her nerves all a-bangle, and *that's* made her go into labor, I'm thinkin', for what it's worth, and she is that nimby-pimby, like them hairy little yappin' dogs with bows in their ears, that she won't stay alone for a minute, not even for a person to go fetch 'em some tea or summat." This passionate speech was ended by Sallie Sisk squeezing her mouth into a ruler-line and bobbing her head once emphatically.

"Thank you, Mrs. Sisk," Cheney said, her voice even but tinged with mirth. "I feel much more prepared to deal with this patient now. Just one more question—did Dr. Werner leave instructions about calling him if Mrs. Irby should get ready to deliver?"

"Why . . . why, I dunno," Mrs. Sisk said with some confusion.

"Would you check for me, please?" Cheney asked, moving to the door of the suite.

"But . . . but . . . Dr. Duvall . . ." the nurse said in an vaguely pleading tone.

Suddenly Cheney recalled that Mrs. Sisk could not read, and Miss Rees was the other nurse on duty; Miss Rees didn't help Sallie with the doctor's instructions as did Bethena Posey. Nurse Rees only answered direct questions she was asked. "Never mind," Cheney said lightly. "I'll ask Miss Rees to fetch Dr. Werner's notes for me. Would you please make a round to check on the other patients, Mrs. Sisk? I can see that both you and Miss Rees have been greatly distracted by Mrs. Irby."

"Thank you, Dr. Duvall," the nurse said gratefully and hurried back out onto the ward.

Cheney took another few seconds to smooth her skirt, take a deep breath, and deliberately relax her shoulders and expression. She opened the door and went to the patient's bedside. Miss Rees sat in a chair close by the bed, her hands primly folded in her lap, her expression severe as she watched the patient.

Viola Irby did appear younger than forty-eight, but she was not a convincing thirty-nine. Her hair was her best feature; dark brown, lustrous, and wavy. Now damp tendrils clung to her forehead and neck. Her features were pleasing, her brow smooth, but crow's-feet had entrenched themselves in the corners of her eyes, and petulant lines between nose and mouth had replaced the smoothly full skin of youth.

"Good evening, Mrs. Irby. I am Dr. Cheney Duvall. Tell me how you are feeling," Cheney said quietly. Taking the woman's overly warm hand in hers, she subconsciously registered a slightly elevated pulse.

"You? A doctor? Where is Dr. Werner?" Mrs. Irby demanded. She had a pleasant voice, a soft alto, but now it was overlaid with spikes of tension.

"Are you feeling any pains, Mrs. Irby?" Cheney prodded her gently.

"Are they regular or uneven? Have you timed them?"

"Yes, I'm feeling labor pains," she replied shortly. "They're uneven and mild, but they are labor pains. I should know, I have three children."

"And they were all normal deliveries? No complications?" Cheney asked.

"Where is Dr. Werner?" the patient asked again, her nostrils distending with anger. "He knows all of my history—my entire family's history."

"I'm not aware of Dr. Werner's whereabouts at this time," Cheney said evenly. "At the moment I'm concerned with doing everything we can to stop this premature labor. Mrs. Irby, I assume you know that there is no prescriptive that stops the onset of labor. Your best course is to remain as calm as possible and keep your mind as restful and peaceful as you can. Have you had your angelica wine tonight?"

"Yes." She leaned back on the satin pillows and closed her eyes, making a visible attempt to relax. "Two small glasses."

"Would you like more? And perhaps some honeyed pears?" Cheney asked.

Mrs. Irby's distraught brown eyes jumped to Cheney's face. "I thought I was to have nothing to eat—except curds and whey."

Cheney was amused and smiled. Mrs. Irby almost smiled back. "Nothing heavy, nothing that will tax your system," Cheney told her. "But I personally think honeyed pears are very relaxing. Our apothecary, Mr. Indro, is kind enough to keep the night staff fully stocked with them. Miss Rees? Would you go prepare a tray for Mrs. Irby—a small bottle of angelica wine, some honeyed pears, and some soda crackers? And also bring Dr. Werner's notes on Mrs. Irby to me."

Without a word, and with only a minuscule disapproving glance at Cheney, the nurse left the room. "Now, Mrs. Irby, I want you to eat all you want—within reason—which I am sure you'll do since you are so trim, and therefore must not be given to overeating. I believe that if you don't feel hungry, you'll be much better able to relax."

A wave of pleasure smoothed out her strained features at Cheney's small compliment, and Cheney felt satisfaction. She went on, "Now, about these pains—"

"Doc? Sorry to bother you—"

Cheney turned to see Shiloh timidly peeking around the door. "Come in, Shiloh. Mrs. Irby, this is Shiloh Irons—"

"Oh, we've met," Mrs. Irby said in the closest thing to a normal tone Cheney had heard yet. "Good evening, Mr. Irons. I'm so glad you're here tonight. I did enjoy your reading last night. Would you be so kind as to read more of Mr. Hawthorne's *Twice-Told Tales* to me?"

"It'd be my pleasure, Mrs. Irby, except I believe Mr. Irby just arrived. I think he'd probably like to read to you," Shiloh answered, taking her hand. Cheney saw with satisfaction that his knuckles were bandaged, and his hands and the white linen strips were tinged slightly yellow by carbolic acid.

Mrs. Irby sighed, then made a small face. "Yes, he will, and although Brookshear does have nice diction, he doesn't put as much feeling into it as you do."

"Then I'll have to give him some hints," Shiloh said, winking at her. She blushed with pleasure.

Cheney stiffened a little, then asked, "Did you need me? Or were you just checking up on Mrs. Irby?"

"I need you, Dr. Duvall," Shiloh answered. "Will you excuse us, Mrs. Irby?"

"Well . . . I . . . don't much like to be left alone," she hedged. "But since you say Brookshear's here—and that dismal nurse is bringing me a tray—"

"You won't be alone for more than a few moments, Mrs. Irby," Cheney assured her. "And I'll be back to check on you shortly."

When she and Shiloh had gone some way down the hallway Shiloh asked worriedly, "She gonna have her baby tonight?"

"I don't know," Cheney replied. "I haven't had time to do an examination or assess her pains yet."

"Well, I think you need to come take a look at Marlett Fair," Shiloh stated.

"He's worse?"

"Yeah."

Marlett Fair was eighteen years old, slight, blond, with finely modeled features and aristocratic hands. A relative of the "Silver King," James C. Fair, the young man was an only child and was doted upon, particularly by his mother. When he became ill and had not improved after three days of home nursing, Mrs. Fair insisted that Dr. Baird admit him to St. Francis. The young man was of a delicate constitution and was ill and weak. Dr. Baird had diagnosed severe catarrh and prescribed coltsfoot infusions, mustard poultices, and brandy at night.

Mrs. Fair had insisted upon only Napoleon brandy and stayed with her son at night to minister to him.

Mrs. Fair fluttered.

"Oh, Mr. Irons! He's so ill! He's having so much trouble breathing! Can't you do something? Can't anyone do something?" Mrs. Fair's delicate hands were like a bird's feathers ruffling in a strong wind. She was porcelain blonde, much like her son, and her eyes were wide, blue, and filled with fear.

"Now, Mrs. Fair, would you please be seated right here on this comfortable chair?" Shiloh said in a voice one would use when speaking to a small frightened child. "Dr. Duvall will take good care of Marlett, you know. And aren't you a little chilled? Where's your lap robe? No, I'll get it for you, you just sit down." Shiloh busily began tucking the lap robe around Mrs. Fair, and she calmed down considerably. As Cheney examined the young man, Shiloh, by much cajoling, persuaded Mrs. Fair to sample a bit of the fine Napoleon brandy. She would only consent to take it by teaspoonfuls—as it was a medicinal aid, after all—but she did manage to choke down three, or four, or five doses.

"Hello, Mr. Fair. Tell me how you feel tonight," Cheney said, smiling reassuringly.

Dull blue eyes barely focused on Cheney's face under heavy, swollen lids. "My throat hurts, Dr. Duvall," he answered thickly.

"Mmm. What else?" Cheney took his wrist and held it for a minute, frowning down slightly at the gold watch she kept in the pocket of her coverall. She timed his pulse for thirty seconds; it was elevated to ninety per minute, which was too high to be merely the result of his fever. For the next thirty seconds she surreptitiously counted his respirations. Many people stopped breathing normally when they were aware that someone was counting. Marlett's was at eighteen per minute, which was all right for an adult at rest, but his breathing was labored. His nostrils distended slightly as he inhaled, and he was using his diaphragm and neck muscles to pull the air in.

"I . . . can't eat," Marlett recited weakly. "My throat feels tight, and . . . and . . . like it's full, or something. . . . And I'm cold. Even with the poultice and the brandy . . . I'm cold."

"Shiloh, would you go get Mr. Fair's records for me, please?" Cheney asked lightly, and Shiloh hurried out of the room. Mrs. Fair's intense worried gaze fixed on Cheney's face, and Cheney smiled briefly at her, then turned back to the sick man. He was ghost-pale, his skin felt hot, but he shivered occasionally. Cheney took a thermometer from a tray on the bedside table and shook it up and down vigorously. "When was the last time your temperature was taken, Mr. Fair?"

"This afternoon, by Dr. Baird," his mother answered anxiously. "It was normal then."

Cheney placed the thermometer in his mouth, warning gently, "Be careful, Mr. Fair, and don't bite down on that when you shiver. You can keep it steady under your tongue, can't you?"

He nodded.

Cheney untied the neck of his linen bed shirt and pulled it open down to his waist. "Just relax, please, I'm just going to check you over a little more carefully."

The door opened and Cheney turned, expecting to see Shiloh; but it was another attendant, Baltimore Florey, who entered the room with Marlett Fair's records. "Good evening, Dr. Duvall, Mrs. Fair, Mr. Fair. Dr. Duvall, Mr. Irons was needed by another patient. May I have the honor of assisting you?"

He stepped closer and looked Cheney straight in the eye, while she darkly assessed him. Baltimore Florey, an intelligent, educated man of forty, was a good nurse—when he was sober. He appeared to be tonight, Cheney saw with relief. He was balding, scholarly looking with weak eyes and thick spectacles, short, and asthmatic. Tonight his gaze was clear, his face was not flushed, and his cultured voice was steady.

"Certainly, Mr. Florey," she replied, turning back to Marlett Fair. "I was just about to palpate Mr. Fair's chest. Would you please remove the pillows so we may lay him down flat?" Cheney reflected regretfully that Shiloh always knew to do these things without instruction, but she hadn't yet seen another medical assistant who could anticipate a physician's needs without being asked. And Shiloh always assisted her personally. Someone else must be gravely ill, indeed, if he had sent another attendant.

Gently Cheney placed her thumbs on the xiphoid—a small piece of bone at the bottom of the sternum—and rested her hands lightly on each side of Marlett's thin chest, spreading her fingers wide. He breathed—once, twice, three times—and Cheney nodded with satisfaction. Both of the lungs were working equally well; her hands moved symmetrically with his respirations. Mr. Florey was watching her with open curiosity, but Cheney didn't like to instruct students or assistants while she was making a preliminary assessment. Later, if he asked, she would explain chest palpation to him.

Cheney took the thermometer out of Marlett's mouth and said calmly, "One-hundred-one point two. Would you make a note of that, and the time, in Mr. Fair's notes, please, Mr. Florey? Now, Mr. Fair, can you sit up?"

He said yes, but he needed help. Cheney pulled her stethoscope out of the coverall's voluminous pockets, but at that moment the door opened and Shiloh stepped in. "Doc, would you please come with me?" he asked politely.

Cheney needed to finish her examination of Marlett Fair, but she knew that Shiloh didn't ask her to leave any patient unless he had good reason. "Excuse me for a moment, Mr. Fair. Mr. Florey, perhaps you could give Mr. Fair some sips of cool water while we have him sitting up? Drink as much as you can, Mr. Fair, but slowly."

She stepped outside in the hallway, followed by Shiloh, and he closed the door firmly, then walked to the end of the hallway to automatically wash in the antiseptic. "Doc, listen, I've got Mr. Dibley over there, and I was thinkin' he's got a good start on pneumonia. And then Mrs. Sisk came hoppin' in and told me she thinks little Molly Costanza has it too."

"Pneumonia?" Cheney asked, frowning. "But she just had a mild case of measles, didn't she?" Molly Costanza was a precocious eight-year-old, the daughter of a favored servant of one of the fine San Francisco families.

"Yeah, and she's pretty much over them," Shiloh answered, "and she's been running around all over both wards yesterday and today."

"All right," Cheney said calmly. "You go and auscultate and percuss Marlett Fair. I need to know the results as soon as you finish."

Shiloh nodded. "Listenin' and thumpin'. I can do that. But what's the deal? You think Fair's got pneumonia, too?"

"I don't think so," Cheney said with a touch of unease. "But I don't want to say just yet. I need to know how his lungs sound—and, oh, Shiloh, when you auscultate, pay careful attention to the upper anterior airways. Listen for stridor. You know what that is, don't you?"

"Yeah, it's that kinda rough, high-pitched whine when they breathe in." His eyes crinkled with puzzlement. "But you can usually hear that without a stethoscope, can't you?"

Cheney washed her hands quickly. "Not when they first start, it's very faint, but you'll be able to catch it. Come find me as soon as you finish."

She hurried out to the ward and saw Jesty Tukes bending over a patient about halfway down the row of beds. Mr. Dibley's wet, throaty coughs were audible all over the ward. Almost all of the other twenty-six male patients were awake, though they were uncomplaining, merely lying in bed, some of them watching Mr. Dibley anxiously. He was a slight elderly man, a butler, and he drew little caricatures of people to amuse everyone.

Before Cheney reached Mr. Dibley, she heard quick footsteps behind her and turned to see Sallie Sisk running to catch up with her. "Dr. Duvall—" she said in a hoarse, urgent whisper, "Mrs. Irby . . . I think she's going into real labor. And that little Mrs. Callister? You know, she's only eighteen, and a tiny little whiff of a thing? She's in labor, and—I'm no doctor, mind you—but her stomach looks funny."

Cheney stopped, sighed, and asked calmly, "Funny? Funny how, exactly?"

Sallie Sisk's round, honest face screwed up with concentration. "Well, lumpy-funny. I'm thinkin' she's a-gonna have that little one upside-over, or sideways, if you know what I mean."

"I'm afraid I do," Cheney answered. "A breech birth." She bit her lower lip, then counted on her fingers. "Shiloh, Mrs. Sisk, Miss Rees, Mr. Florey, Mr. Tukes. Is anyone else here tonight?"

"Just Li Bai. And it's startin' to look like we're in a bit of luck there—at least he speaks a little American," Mrs. Sisk said dourly.

"Go look in on Mrs. Irby, and then go to Mrs. Callister. I need to give Mr. Tukes some instructions, and then I'll be right there," Cheney told her hurriedly. "Meanwhile, for Molly, have Miss Rees isolate her at the far end of the ward, start a menthol vaporizer, put on a hot mustard pack, and get her bundled up."

"Miss Rees is with Mrs. Irby, and I'm thinking she—or someone—is gonna have to stay with her," Mrs. Sisk declared.

"Wonderful," Cheney muttered. "Then you forget Mrs. Irby, go check on Mrs. Callister, and then go tend to little Molly. Can you do that?"

"Of course, Dr. Duvall, I remember everything you said," she replied indignantly, then swept off toward the women's ward.

Again Cheney turned toward Mr. Dibley's bed, but again she was halted—this time by a raucous commotion coming from the vicinity of the vestibule. Some man banged the heavy double doors open and started yelling for a doctor. Cheney, with a last regretful glance at Mr. Dibley, was reassured that Jesty Tukes was still with him and hurried down the ward and through the hallway toward the voice.

"Halloo! I need a doctor!"

"Sir! Please! I'm right here," Cheney said as calmly as she could while she skittered around the hallway to face the young man. With a start she realized that she recognized him; he was Joe Ryman, a medical student from Toland Medical College. He often attended operations and dissections at St. Francis, and he and some of the other students sometimes observed interesting cases, mostly under Dr. Werner's tutelage. Joe Ryman, along with three or four other unruly young men, had attended Cheney's operation on Jerry Sanford. They had been respectfully silent during the surgery, but as soon as Dr. Baird and Walker had withdrawn, they had made crude jokes and called out raucous and sometimes suggestive comments to Cheney. Shiloh had lost his temper and started toward the young men, but Cheney had stopped him and asked him to finish stitching Mr. Sanford. He had reluctantly agreed, still muttering black threats, and Cheney had rather hastily withdrawn to the solitude of the chapel to wait for him.

"Calm down, Mr. Ryman," she demanded. "You of all people should know that you'll disturb the patients."

He was regretful, because he was not a bad sort, really; but he ran with a rowdy crowd and often took on their habits and mannerisms. He was about twenty, and though he was average-looking and unremarkable, he had a great deal of self-assurance, an engagingly crooked smile, and a commanding, gravelly voice.

"Sorry, Dr. Duvall. You the only doctor here tonight?" he asked anxiously.

"Yes, I am. For now, at least."

"I need an ambulance—maybe two. Is Mr. Irons here?" Craning his neck, he searched both hallways anxiously for Shiloh's tall form.

"Yes, he is. But you're going to have to tell me what you need."

He focused back on her face, looking up at her a little, as he was only five ten, and Cheney was a little taller in her heeled shoes. "It's Guy," he said in a worried growl. "Guy Fain. And four of our buddies. We all got into a tiff, down on Pacific. Everyone got hurt but me, and I rode like the devil to come fetch the ambulance carts."

"How hurt?" Cheney asked bluntly.

"Knife wounds, gunshot wounds, blows. You name it."

"All right. Stay here," Cheney ordered him severely. "And don't shout anymore! I'll be right back."

She started toward the men's ward, but Sallie Sisk hurried around the hallway, and from the other side Shiloh rounded the gentle curve.

"Dr. Duvall, Mrs. Callister—she's having real and true problems," Mrs. Sisk panted.

"Doc, I dunno about Marlett Fair," Shiloh put in as he and the plump little nurse reached Cheney at the same time. She was surrounded, and Mrs. Sisk, Shiloh, and Joe Ryman all started talking at once.

"Be quiet," she said in a normal tone, and everyone grew silent in the space of a second. "Mr. Ryman needs an ambulance. Shiloh, I want you to go—you're best at field injuries, and we have knife wounds, gunshot wounds, and blunt trauma."

"I'll need someone else to help carry stretchers," Shiloh said instantly.

"Mr. Ryman will assist you," Cheney replied, turning to the medical student and giving him a severe once-over. "Listen to me, Mr. Ryman. I understand that you are almost a doctor—but right now you're not, you're just a student. Mr. Irons has more experience, more scientific knowledge, and better instincts than you and your busy little student friends have all together. Do you understand what I'm trying to tell you?"

"To do everything Mr. Irons says, ma'am," Ryman answered humbly.

"That's the first smart thing I've ever heard you say, Mr. Ryman," Cheney commented acidly. "Now go."

Shiloh and Joe Ryman hurried toward the front door. In passing Shiloh told Cheney, "Mr. Florey noted everything about Marlett Fair. I'll be back as soon as I can."

"Hurry," Cheney said evenly.

"Okay," he grinned and winked impudently at her. "For you."

10

Full o' the Moon and Likewise Thirteen Friday

"Dr. Duvall—" Sallie Sisk began insistently after the door closed behind Shiloh and Joe Ryman.

"Please." Cheney held up her hand, a clear stop signal. Mrs. Sisk shut her mouth. "I want you to go back to the ward and get Miss Rees. Yes, I know she's with Mrs. Irby, but Mr. Irby is here now, is he not? She can be without a medical attendant for a few minutes. Then go out and find Li Bai. All of you go to the nurses' station and wait for me." Before Mrs. Sisk had a chance to reply, Cheney hurried around the hallway in the direction of the men's ward.

"Humph! Doctors and the like! Never a please, let alone a thank you!" Mrs. Sisk grumbled, but she picked up her skirts and scampered to do Cheney's bidding.

Cheney went straight to Jesty Tukes, who was still hovering over Mr. Dibley, patting him ineffectually on the back as he coughed. Cheney saw with relief that Jesty had propped him in a half-sitting position, but he seemed at a loss to know what else to do.

"Good evening, Mr. Dibley. I hear you're causing us some trouble tonight," Cheney gently teased him.

"Yes, ma'am, I was hoping to get some attention from you," he replied with a tremulous smile. He was a dignified-looking gentleman, thin and angular, with the meticulous grace that good butlers always seemed to have.

"And so you shall," she assured him, picking up his hand and squeezing it warmly. "But just now I must take Mr. Tukes and bawl him out. You don't mind, do you?"

"No, ma'am, certainly not. Unless you'd like me to do it for you? I've had years of experience with upstart footmen and sassy scullery maids," Mr. Dibley replied, leaning back on his pillows and fighting for air. Cheney knew he had pneumonia just from the sound of his breathing.

"You may have your turn as soon as I'm finished with him," Cheney replied, smiling and stroking his limp hand. "As for me, I need a little more experience intimidating sassy nurses and upstart medical students. Come along, Mr. Tukes."

Jesty Tukes followed Cheney, though the look on his face clearly showed that he considered Dr. Duvall quite expert in intimidating nurses and medical students, and he dreaded whatever was lying in wait for him. Cheney hurried to Marlett Fair's private suite, opened the door, and said lightly, "Mr. Florey? Would you come with me? Don't worry, Mrs. Fair, Mr. Fair. We'll be back in a few moments."

Mrs. Fair looked distraught, while Marlett looked pale and exhausted, but Cheney firmly pulled Mr. Florey from the room and started toward the women's ward without another word. Scurrying behind her, Mr. Florey made motions, pointing to Cheney's figure hurrying ahead of them, and raising his eyebrows inquisitively. Jesty Tukes shrugged elaborately, raising both his hands, then pressed them together as if in prayer. Mr. Florey didn't dare laugh out loud.

The normal night silence of the women's ward was not to be on this night. From Mrs. Callister's bed came cries of pains, now about twenty minutes apart. Molly Costanza, still in a bed in the middle of the ward, coughed constantly. Low moans sounded from other beds. Some women tossed uneasily as they dozed, sighing restlessly.

Miss Rees and Mrs. Sisk were seated at the nurses' station desk, with Miss Rees thumbing through doctors' notes and Sallie desperately whispering questions to her. Behind them stood Li Bai, subservient in shadow, waiting, just as he was told. When Cheney came to the station, Mrs. Sisk rose quickly, while Miss Rees took more time and arranged her plain features into an unpleasant frown that made her look even less attractive.

Cheney deliberately didn't give the nurses permission to sit. "Come close, Mr. Tukes, Mr. Florey. I don't want to speak up too much; the patients have been disturbed enough tonight as it is, and the night isn't over yet." Jesty and Baltimore Florey obediently moved closer to Cheney.

"We have several patients who need constant care tonight, and Mr. Irons is out in the ambulance right now. He'll be bringing back four or possibly five injured men." She paused and took a deep breath.

Mrs. Sisk took advantage of the pause to mutter darkly, "It's allus this way, in the full o' the moon."

"Full o' the moon?" Cheney echoed blankly.

"Thirteen Friday too," Mrs. Sisk continued in a graveyard voice.

"Thirteen Friday?" Cheney couldn't help but say.

All of the attendants—except Li Bai—nodded solemnly.

"That's why Bethena won't work," Mrs. Sisk informed the astonished Cheney. "She allus hurts hersel' in the full o' the moon, anyways. And it bein' a Thirteen Friday too—tch, tch, tch. She'd likely cut offen a leg, or fall and break her head."

"Dr. Duvall broke a mirror tonight," Jesty intoned. Everyone looked appalled, even the sour Miss Rees.

"Oh, dear, I did." Cheney was distracted, then distraught for a moment; then she shook her head impatiently. "Never mind all that. It's—just superstition, and we are all professionals and—and—of a scientific turn of mind here."

The nurses and attendants looked at her doubtfully.

"Aren't we?" Cheney asked hesitantly. "Oh . . . blue thunder! Just . . . listen to me, everyone, and stop worrying about the lunar cycle and the broken mirror. I—we—need some help tonight. Another doctor, certainly, and at least one more attendant. Li Bai, can you ride?"

"Yes, ma'am," he said eagerly.

"Good. Take my horse—you know Eugènie?"

"Yes," he said, grinning widely, his straight teeth gleaming white in the shadows. "Pretty lady, high lady. Fast."

"That she is," Cheney agreed. "Take her and ride as fast as you can. I want you to go try and find either of the Dr. Bairds. Do you understand?"

"Yes, Dr. Duvall," he said, stepping forward slightly. He was a fine-looking, strong young man, a larger and slightly older version of his younger brother, the sturdy Li Shen. "I understand. Find Walker or Dr. Baird." His English accent was excellent, with only a little flattening of the "r's" and "l's."

"Good. And . . . another assistant . . ." Cheney stopped to consider, her brow furrowing.

"Mr. Venable lives just over there," Li Bai volunteered, nodding toward town. "At bottom of hill."

Cheney hesitated; she'd never worked with Hack Venable. He was about twenty, handsome in a dramatic, roguish way, with rather coarse manners. He always worked during the day. Shiloh had told her that he was a fair nurse, though not a dedicated one. "No, we need another female nurse," she decided.

"Nurse Tilden does not work at night," Miss Rees said stiffly. They were the first words Cheney had heard her say in this already-long night.

"Thank you, Miss Rees," Cheney said dryly. "What about Bethena?"

"Superstition or no," Sallie Sisk said firmly, "the patients and us and wee Bethena hersel' are better off if she don't try to nurse in the full o' the moon and likewise thirteen Friday."

Cheney sighed. "And Lana Sharpless?" Miss Sharpless, eighteen years old, shy and nondescript, was the only other female nurse on staff.

"She's in Sacramento visitin' her auntie all week," Mrs. Sisk said. "Won't be back 'til Thursday next."

Cheney bit her lower lip for a moment, then told Li Bai, "I want you to go get my maid. Her name's Nia. Do you know Steen House?"

"Top of Russian Hill?" he asked eagerly. "I know."

"Good. Go, Li Bai, and please hurry."

He bowed, a curious up-and-down quick-quick bob, and then glided down the aisle toward the door, silent in his soft slippers.

Before he reached the door into the hallway, however, two people came stumbling into the ward. A small woman, crying, was trying to hold up a man who shuffled along painfully, unable to put any weight on, or indeed barely move, his leg. Cheney and the attendants looked up at the noise, and immediately Cheney whispered, "Stay right here, all of you." Then she almost ran to the couple making their painful way down the aisle. Li Bai had stopped and automatically had gotten under the man's other arm, helping to hold him upright.

"Mr. Trimble?" Cheney asked when she neared him. "What's wrong?" Ike Trimble, the man who'd been injured in the carriage accident, had been discharged after a week in St. Francis. His head had healed nicely, and his leg was on the mend. Cheney hadn't seen him since his discharge, though she'd encouraged him to come back for a check of his still-healing leg.

"Good evening, Dr. Duvall," he said quietly with a touch of shame. "This here's my wife, Elaine."

The small weeping woman cried, "His leg! It's goin' bad, Dr. Duvall!"

"All right, all right, Mrs. Trimble, please don't worry. We'll take care of it," Cheney said soothingly, though her eyes were anxious. "This is Li Bai, and he's helping us out tonight. I must take a few moments to speak to the attendants on duty"—Cheney nodded to the tense little group at the nurses' station behind her—"but Li Bai will help you to the men's ward and get you settled in. Would you like your old bed, Mr. Trimble?"

"Anywhere's fine, Dr. Duvall," he mumbled with unmistakable relief. The three turned awkwardly and headed back toward the door. Elaine Trimble looked back over her shoulder, her woebegone childlike face covered with tears, and called softly, "I'm so glad you're here, Dr. Duvall. Ike says you're the best doctor anyone, man or woman, could ever hope for."

"Thank you," Cheney said with real pleasure. "I promise you I'll take good care of Mr. Trimble. So you try and cheer up for him a little, hmm?"

"Yes'm," the young Mrs. Trimble tremulously promised.

Cheney hurried back to her group of assistants. "This," she muttered, "is getting unmanageable."

Miss Rees looked disagreeably satisfied, so Cheney bristled, "Everyone listen closely because it seems I'm only going to have time to give instructions once. Miss Rees, look in on Mrs. Irby for a few moments only, and then go to Mrs. Callister. Move her into the private room next to Mrs. Irby."

Miss Rees pursed her stingy mouth tightly. "Mr. Callister is only a clerk, and they cannot pay the private room fee. That is why Mrs. Callister is on the public ward. Ma'am," she added reluctantly.

"Ma'am," Cheney repeated ominously, her green eyes flashing, "that is not your concern. You will obey my orders without question. Do you understand the instructions I've given you?"

The nurse's sparse eyebrows shot up in alarm, and she appeared unable, or unwilling, to answer Cheney for long moments. Finally she said sullenly, "Yes, I understand."

Cheney stared hard at her and waited.

Miss Rees took a deep breath, then said in a stronger voice, "Yes, I understand your instructions, Dr. Duvall."

"Thank you," Cheney said blandly. "After you get Mrs. Callister moved, make a quick check of the rest of the patients, please."

"Yes, ma'am," Miss Rees replied, appearing slightly mollified by

Cheney's even tone and courteous words.

"Mrs. Sisk, I want you to move Molly Costanza down to the far end of the ward, right by the door into the west wing. I know you remember the instructions I gave you before—before—something else happened?"

"Before everything else happened," Mrs. Sisk declared, "and yes, ma'am, Dr. Duvall, I remember everything."

"You know how to do it?"

Mrs. Sisk nodded her head vigorously.

"Good. Then Mr. Tukes, you go with Mrs. Sisk and see how she sets up a menthol vaporizer and makes a hot mustard plaster. Then you do the same for Mr. Dibley. All right?"

"Yes, ma'am," he said eagerly.

"And give Mr. Dibley two fluidrams of laudanum, and give Miss Costanza two minims of brandy," Cheney ordered. Mr. Tukes looked surprised, while Mrs. Sisk looked scandalized. "I know it's unorthodox," Cheney added quietly, "but you must understand that neither of them is in imminent danger tonight. The best thing for them—and for us, considering how understaffed we are—would be if they can sleep."

"Certainly, Dr. Duvall," Jesty Tukes said quickly. "Do we dose them before or after the plaster?"

"Good question, Mr. Tukes," Cheney said encouragingly. "After. Immediately after. Any more questions? Good. Now, Mr. Florey, do you have any surgical experience?"

Mr. Florey's weak eyes went down to his shoes. "Not much, ma'am," he admitted in a low voice. "I've observed several surgeries, but I'm rarely asked to assist."

"Well, you may need to assist tonight, Mr. Florey, and I believe you'll be fine. Right now I need you to come with me and check on Mr. Fair, and I'll give you some instructions about him. Then I need you to try, as best as you can, to prepare an emergency surgery cart for me."

He looked up, and his sad eyes glimmered with some hope and a touch of determination. "I . . . I believe I can do that. As I said, I've observed some operations, and I think I know what's needed."

"I've assisted Dr. Werner twice," Miss Rees said frigidly. "Perhaps I would be a better choice."

"No, thank you," Cheney said firmly. "Mr. Florey will assist me until Mr. Irons returns."

At this, Baltimore Florey's rounded shoulders were thrown back, and his head was held higher than it had been in years. Cheney, who was already leaving to go to Marlett Fair's room, noticed but gave no sign.

★ ★ ★ ★

"Good evening, Dr. Duvall," Mr. Indro said as calmly as if he were greeting her at the theater.

"Oh! Mr. Indro, I'm so happy you're here," Cheney said with more relief than she realized. "How does it happen you're here at"—she squinted down at her pocket watch—"good gracious, one-thirty in the morning?"

His spectacles glinted weirdly in the dim light of the private wing hallway. "I heard the ambulance and hurried to look out my window to see if it was St. Francis'," he explained carefully. "It was. And as I am aware of the inexplicable fact that many injuries occur, and people appear to get more ill, on—"

"I know, I know," Cheney sighed. "The full o' the moon, and likewise Thirteen Friday."

"Precisely," he said with a spare smile.

"You might as well know that I broke a mirror tonight," Cheney added with dark amusement.

"Ominous," he sighed. "And I'm afraid that Beebee has a terrible time of it on nights such as these. Jokesters, pranksters, and some of the medical students seem to get particularly cruel on these nights. I must admit that I wanted to check up on him, along with all of the extra patients I'm sure you've already admitted."

"I'm almost afraid to ask," Cheney said, "but may I venture a guess as to exactly who Beebee is?"

"Of course."

"Black cat?"

"The apothecary's cat, and he does have the misfortune of being solid black," Mr. Indro said with quiet glee. "As I mentioned, he does have a difficult time of it on All Hallow's Eve, and on the . . . er . . . full o' the moon? Is that correct? Ah yes. And Thirteen Fridays," he added with relish. "Embellishments of the colorful Mrs. Sisk? Yes, just so. Now, what may I do to assist you, Dr. Duvall?"

The moments of lightness over, Cheney demanded, "I need ephedra. Do you have it?"

"*Ephedra sinica*, or the Chinese shrub *ma huang*. Yes, certainly."

"Form?"

"Decoction, powder, or rolled pills." Cheney hesitated, frowning.

"May I ask the patient and his or her condition," Mr. Indro ventured. "Perhaps I may help you with dosage, Dr. Duvall? If you should have any questions, that is."

"Oh yes, thank you," Cheney said with relief. "It's Mr. Fair." She nodded toward the door to the private suite at the end of the hallway where they stood. "I think he has diphtheria."

Mr. Indro's face wrinkled with uncertainty. "Diphtheria? Isn't he a young man?"

"Yes, I know it's primarily a childhood disease, but he seems to have some of the symptoms . . . and it's not pneumonia, and it's much more serious than simple catarrh," Cheney said, unconsciously allowing her uncertainty to show to this older and wiser man.

"Hmm. Have you, by any chance, ever used an autolaryngoscope?" Mr. Indro asked.

Cheney's eyes lit up, and she cocked her head slightly with interest. "Why, no, I haven't, and I didn't even think to ask. We have one? And so I could see if the false membrane is forming in his upper air passages?"

"Oh yes, certainly," Mr. Indro said with unmistakable pride. "I made it myself, and though it's only been utilized once, it works perfectly. I could assist you, Dr. Duvall," he added hopefully.

"That would be wonderful," Cheney said gratefully. "Will you please go get it right now? And also bring ephedra—so you can advise me on the dosage?"

Mr. Indro nodded vigorously, and his glasses bobbled. "Certainly, especially if we can see if the false membrane is there, and if it is, to what degree it is blocking his airway."

"Yes, yes, of course." Cheney considered for a moment. "I also need some cocaine powder and some morphine sulphate. You have rolled pills? That would be fine. Mrs. Sisk and Jesty Tukes are concocting black mustard packs. If you have time to assist them, I would be grateful. Also, Mr. Florey is setting up an emergency surgical cart. Would you help him? Thank you, Mr. Indro. I—I—can hardly express to you how grateful I am, and relieved I am, that you are here," she added in a low voice.

"Certainly, Dr. Duvall. I'm honored to be of assistance to you." He whisked down the hall and out of sight.

Cheney, alone for the first time since she'd stepped in the door that night, pressed her fingertips to her temples. She felt assaulted by the fast-moving events of the night, confused by the life-and-death priorities, and frightened by the decisions she was making so quickly, with so little time to consider. She felt buffeted, as if strong riptides pulled her this way and that.

"Dr. Duvall?" Jesty Tukes came tentatively into the hallway, his voice regretful at the intrusion.

"Yes, it's all right, Mr. Tukes," Cheney said, straightening herself. "What is it?"

"It's Mr. Irons, Dr. Duvall. He's just arrived and pulled the ambulance around to the side entrance of the East Wing."

"All right, I'm coming."

"But . . . but Dr. Duvall . . ."

"Yes?" Cheney said a trifle impatiently.

"There's a carriage. A fine carriage just pulled up in front."

"What?"

The front doors banged open—this hollow booming was getting to be very unwelcome to Cheney—and a man called loudly, "Here! I need a doctor!"

Cheney gritted her teeth, then ordered, "Mr. Tukes, go see to Shiloh and the ambulance. I'll go see about this gentleman."

"Yes, ma'am," he said and skittered off.

Cheney again went to the vestibule with dread.

A gentleman in fine evening clothes stood just inside the gaping front doors. In his arms he held a young, beautiful Chinese girl. Blood flowed from her simple white skirt onto the highly polished floor of the vestibule of St. Francis de Yerba Buena, and grimly pooled at the foot of the statue of St. Luke the Physician.

11

Fear and Fever

"What can I do?" Jesty Tukes asked Shiloh, fidgeting with embarrassed ineptitude.

Shiloh frowned darkly and jammed his hands into the deep pockets of the white coverall he wore. None of the hospital's coveralls fit him, so he was obliged to wear it open, as a coat. The sleeves were too short, the shoulders cut into him and were irritatingly tight across his shoulders and back, and it flapped around his knees. Still he considered it important that he wear it, as all of the male attendants and doctors were obliged to do by hospital regulations.

"There's five of 'em, and they're all drunk and noisy," he grunted. Narrowing his eyes, he looked up and down the deserted, darkened corridors of the east wing.

"Twenty-eight beds in the ward tonight," Jesty told him. The ward only had thirty beds.

"Twenty-eight? I thought there were twenty-seven."

"Mr. Ike Trimble came in. His leg's going septic."

A mist of worry darkened Shiloh's light blue eyes and then was gone. "Okay. We'll have to put these boys in here. What about beds? We have any extra?"

"Yes, sir," Jesty answered eagerly. "In two of the private rooms. All of the hospital's beds are made to stack double, you see, for bunk beds. The frames of the top tiers are stored in one room, and some extra mattresses in another."

"Good. I'll go get Ryman, and you two get five beds set up and made up."

The door from the ward opened, and Baltimore Florey came in, wheeling a noisy cart. "Dr. Duvall said to bring this, Mr. Irons."

"Yes, good," Shiloh said, hurrying to help the small man wheel the cranky cart and running his sharp eyes over the contents quickly.

"Looks real good, Mr. Florey. Here's what I want you to do. Put some scalpels, some needles, and a lot of catgut in a basin of carbolic acid. Can you go find a bucket? Yeah, just a bucket—even the ones Li Bai and Li Shen use to mop will be fine. Then wash it out good with carbolic acid, throw that solution out, and fill it with clean solution. You'll use that to wash your hands after you touch each patient, before you go to the next one. Got it? Good. Now, I'm gonna go talk to the boys in the ambulance, tell 'em it'll be a few minutes before we can get them into bed. Come get me when you've got the beds set up, Jesty."

Shiloh went back out the side door of the east wing to the waiting ambulance. It was a large enclosed wagon, six feet wide and eight feet long, drawn by four massive horses that were built for power to negotiate the hilly streets of the city.

Inside the wagon on each side were two wooden racks, one three feet above the floor, one six feet. The racks were grooved to hold the wooden poles that formed the sides of the stretchers, which were then simply hung in the racks to serve as hammocks. Between the four hammocks, in the middle of the wagon, was a space about two feet wide, and the ceiling was exactly six feet high. Shiloh was obliged to turn sideways and stoop painfully to get access to the patients, and it was impossible to keep from jarring the hammocks on one side or the other. The four hammocks held the most seriously injured men, while the fifth patient was huddled on the floor.

Li Bai was fussing with the horses. Shiloh had driven them hard, and one of them had a broken harness trace. After their reckless gallop they snorted and pawed and arched their necks impatiently. In the cool night air their powerful bodies steamed as if they were creatures from the underworld.

"Li Bai! Go inside and help Mr. Tukes. He'll tell you what to do," Shiloh ordered. Obediently the Chinese boy double-checked the knot tying the horses to the iron hitching ring, then ran inside.

Joe Ryman had opened the double doors at the back of the ambulance and had lowered the ramp in preparation for unloading the patients. He stood in the open doorway, his face anxious. "Shiloh?"

"Mr. Irons," Shiloh corrected him sharply. He had found that most of the medical students—particularly the ones like Guy Fain, who were specializing in surgery—were long on arrogance and short on manners. Joe Ryman was one of the better-behaved ones, but still, it was a good place to start. "It's going to be a few minutes before we can move them in. Turns out it's busy around here tonight."

"All right," Ryman nodded, then carefully added, "Mr. Irons. Is there anything we can do right now?"

"Yeah, I need to help that boy with the gunshot to the leg. Keep pressure on that entrance wound. The others will be all right for a few minutes." With a grimace Shiloh started up the ramp, dreading the close ambulance with the hurt men crowded so close to him, the air filled with the smell of cheap whiskey and blood.

Joe Ryman hurriedly moved aside to let Shiloh pass, but he swallowed hard and said, "I . . . I can do that, Mr. Irons. His name's Laban Smith, and he's a friend of mine. If you need to do something else. Inside, that is," he finished nervously.

Shiloh stared down at him, and though he was unaware of it, he looked like an angry giant to the slight young man. "All right. Just hold that dressing over that entrance wound, not hard enough to make his leg numb, but hard enough to keep it from bleeding."

Shiloh turned and started back down the ramp.

In a weak voice Ryman called, "Uh . . . Mr. Irons?"

Impatiently Shiloh stopped and turned around. "Yeah?"

Ryman gathered his courage to ask: "Shouldn't I do a tourniquet?"

"No." The word was sharp, and Shiloh hurried toward the door. Then he stopped and looked back at the young man who hovered uncertainly in the back of the cart. "The bullet didn't come out, Ryman. No exit wound. There's no tellin' where it is in his leg. The extreme pressure of a tourniquet might shift it around—and then it might hit an artery."

"Yes . . . yes, I see. Thanks, Mr. Irons," Ryman said thoughtfully.

"Welcome," he said and went back inside the east wing.

In under four minutes Shiloh, Jesty Tukes, and Li Bai had the beds set up and made with crisp, clean linen sheets. Shiloh and Jesty brought in the hammocks, while Joe Ryman and Mr. Florey helped the patients get into the beds. Shiloh dispatched Li Bai to take care of the wet and overexerted horses. The welfare of the ambulance horses—particularly on nights such as these—was as important as that of the patients. Shiloh then sent Jesty to the ward to take care of Mr. Dibley.

"Mr. Florey, did Dr. Duvall give you any other patients to see to?" Shiloh asked the studious little man.

"No, Mr. Irons."

"Good. I know you're a good dresser—can you stitch?"

"Well . . . well . . . have before," Florey stammered. "I . . . it's been a while. . . ."

"Can you do it?" Shiloh asked without rancor.

Florey stared up at him, squared his shoulders, and nodded with finality.

"Yeah, you can," Shiloh said, assuring him. "First, come here. This is Mr. Guy Fain."

"We're acquainted," Florey said dryly.

Guy Fain was a sultry-looking young man with dark hair and flashing dark eyes and arrogance sharpening his dramatic looks. He had a knife wound, a deep laceration in his side, just under the rib cage. "You're not going to let this ol' rummy sew me up, are you, Shiloh?" he demanded. Though he was pale, and his forehead and upper lip were sweating, a cruel smile played on his full mouth.

"Mr. Irons," Shiloh corrected him. "Mr. Florey's gonna do it. Take it or leave it."

"Leave it," Fain retorted hotly. "And you have no authority to order stitching done, nurse. I want a doctor."

"Fine." Shiloh shrugged. "Dr. Duvall will be here as soon as she can, I know."

"Dr. Duvall? That female? No!"

"Then you can wait until another doctor comes in the morning," Shiloh said quietly. "But you're going to lose a lot of blood by then."

Fain lay back on his pillow and closed his eyes in defeat. "Let the rummy do it, then. But your hand trembles once, old man, and I'll—"

"If my hands were shaking, I wouldn't volunteer to do it," Baltimore Florey said with an echo of lost dignity.

Shiloh gave him an approving look. "Give him a fluidram of laudanum, wash the wound out good with carbolic acid, rub the edges with cocaine powder, then stitch. Got it?"

"Yes, sir," Florey replied steadily. He had taken a small book out of his pocket, and a stub of pencil, and he took copious notes.

Shiloh moved him along to the next bed. "This is Mr. Wesley Nance. Grazed by a .22 on the arm. He'll be all right for now, I've bandaged it up. Just give him a fluidram of laudanum."

The next bed, the next pale young man. "This is Mr. Daniel Van Toll. Cracked ribs, but not broken. We'll bandage him up tight later. Right now he just needs to lie still. He's got a blow to the head, doesn't seem to have a skull fracture, but we need to check him every five minutes. You know how to check his state of consciousness, Mr. Florey? Get him to answer some simple questions, check his extremities to see if he's got pain sensation, test the strength in his fingers. Check his pupils to see if one or both of them dilate. If you notice anything odd, no matter how small, you come get me or a doctor real quick, okay? And no laudanum for him, not right now."

Baltimore Florey nodded with assurance, and Shiloh moved on.

"This is Mr. Hudson Kramer. He's got a broken nose, a broken hand, and a knife wound, through-and-through, in his right foot. Keep him quiet. I see his foot's stopped bleeding, but you'll need to check it every few minutes—yeah, check it when you examine Mr. Van Toll. I'll come back and set his nose; meanwhile, keep him propped up in that position. Just leave the hand alone, don't let him move it. Give him two fluidrams of laudanum."

Florey scribbled confidently, so Shiloh went on, "And this is Mr. Laban Smith. He's got a .22 shot in the leg. It's going to need surgery. Mr. Ryman, you doing all right?"

Ryman was sitting on the side of Smith's bed, holding a blood-soaked dressing to the unconscious man's thigh. "Yes, Mr. Irons," he said quietly, though he was pale and sweating with the effort of sustaining a continuous strong pressure on the injury.

"Change that dressing when it gets soaked like that," Shiloh ordered. "But you need to push harder, Mr. Ryman. The idea is for the pressure to close off the blood vessels so it stops the bleeding, right? And don't wash out the wound yet. We'll do that when we ready him for surgery, which I'm going to go try and get set up right now. You men carry on; I'll be back as soon as I can."

Shiloh went to the door leading into the men's general ward, noting that Baltimore Florey looked confident and determined, while Joe Ryman looked uneasy. *Best I can do right now*, Shiloh told himself, pushing down the doubts that plagued him. Even if Mr. Florey was quick and sure, he needed another pair of hands. *I'll get Li Bai to help*, Shiloh decided. *He's real steady, and I think he's pretty smart. He can check the head trauma and relieve Ryman on that leg . . . Fain won't like having a Chinaman nursing him, but he'll just have to take it like a man.*

Since Shiloh was the Supervising Attendant, the performance of each nurse and each attendant was his responsibility. Dr. Baird had insisted upon this, even though Shiloh had felt that it would cause problems with Ionia Tilden. It had, although she was too reserved to display her resentment openly. But Shiloh had been able to sense it and was wary of the nurse. Still, his job was to supervise each medical assistant, and he took his responsibilities seriously.

He went straight to the bed by the door into the east wing. Jesty Tukes had moved Mr. Dibley there and had set up a screen on the ward side, both to afford the patient some privacy and to mute his deep coughing.

As Shiloh came through the door, Jesty looked up with relief. "Mr. Irons, will you help me for a minute? I'm . . . I'm just not too sure about this mustard pack."

Shiloh sniffed appreciatively and inspected the vaporizer: a tall rack holding a basin, with a candle burning close underneath. "Smells good," he said approvingly. "That's not just menthol water, is it?"

"No, Mr. Indro's here, and he gave me some mint to put in it," Jesty replied.

"Makes it a lot more palatable," Mr. Dibley said gamely, but almost inaudibly, between throaty coughs. "Good evening, Mr. Irons." His sunken cheeks had scarlet streaks, and his eyes were dulled with fever.

"Good evening, Mr. Dibley. We're tryin' to cook up a pack for your chest here," Shiloh said quietly, adjusting the man's pillows, gently sponging his forehead, and feeling of his pulse. "Help break up that cough, I think, and maybe sweat out that fever. You know, don't you, Mr. Dibley, that you need to spit out the stuff you're coughing up?"

"No, I guess I didn't," he said wryly. "Seems very poor form, does it not?"

Shiloh grinned. "Yeah. Only time a man's excused for spittin', I reckon. Here. You just spit into this little basin, okay? You comfortable? 'Cause you need to stay kinda propped up like that. Good."

He turned back to Jesty, who was wrestling with a large mortar and pestle and staring down into it mournfully.

"Okay, Jesty, what's the trouble? Yeah, that looks kinda like yesterday's grits, doesn't it?"

Jesty agreed sadly. His poultice looked nothing like Mrs. Sisk's had. It was mealy looking and kept balling up into big lumps around the sides of the pestle.

Shiloh squinted down at the concoction and muttered, "You got a little too much flour, I think."

"Mrs. Sisk told me to add four tablespoonfuls of flour to a tablespoon of mustard," Jesty sighed. "I thought I did that, but . . . well, you see."

"Doesn't matter," Shiloh assured him. "Just add some more hot water, a few drops at a time, and then stir. If it's still gummy, add some more. But don't add too much hot water all at once. You can put it in, but you can't take it out. If you get too much, you'll have a porridge plaster."

Mr. Dibley grunted a laugh, and Shiloh turned to wink at him. "Bet you know about cookin' up one of these, huh, Mr. Dibley?"

"As a matter of fact, I do. Here, young man, let me see that. Oh, dear, yes. Add four drops of hot water. Four, mind you. And you can run along, Mr. Irons. Mr. Tukes and I will make out quite nicely, I think."

Shiloh said quietly, "I'll be back in a few minutes. If you get too tired, Mr. Dibley, you just rest."

"No, I can attend to this," the butler said with a trace of gratitude. He actually felt better, now that he could do something.

Shiloh understood perfectly.

He went next to Marlett Fair's room. The young man was working hard, his neck muscles tensing slightly, and his nostrils flaring with each painfully slow inhalation. He was exhausted, sunken back on his pillows like a thrown-away doll, but his eyes glittered with fear and fever. Mr. Indro was leaning over a table by his bed, his hands moving quickly over a curious-looking wood and steel apparatus. He didn't look up when Shiloh entered the room.

Mrs. Fair was pacing about the room like a nervous cat, wringing her hands, tears streaming down her face, sniffling loudly. Shiloh went straight to her and took both of her nervous hands in his. Looking straight into her swollen eyes he said calmly, "Mrs. Fair, this behavior won't do. If you can't sit down over there and be calm and quiet, I'm going to have to take you to the doctors' hall."

"But my son . . . but he . . . he . . ." she cried in anguish.

"I know," Shiloh said in a soothing, deep tone. "He's very ill. And you are probably making him worse."

She drew in a sharp, rough breath, and a hint of anger tensed her doll-like features. Shiloh met her eyes, calmly, not unkindly. Finally, after long moments, she nodded dumbly. He led her back to the chair, seated her, and bent down to speak closely in her ear. "We can help him, you know. But he needs to see that you have confidence in us. Do you?"

Her mouth tightened, then she gave her son a tiny smile—he was watching them with his fear-filled eyes—and nodded firmly to Shiloh. "I apologize, Marlett," she said in a tremulous voice that strengthened as she spoke. "I know I've made you nervous. I'm worried about you, but Mr. Irons tells me you're going to be all right." She smiled reassuringly at her son. It was a difficult thing for her to do, and tears still stood in her eyes, but Shiloh could see that she was using all her frail strength to keep them back.

"Thank you," Shiloh whispered, straightening and hurrying to Mr. Indro. "You have that set up for Dr. Duvall?"

"Yes, Mr. Irons," he answered. "It's all ready. Perhaps you would step outside with me for a moment?"

Shiloh and the apothecary went outside the room. With determination Mrs. Fair started talking to her son about how much she liked the landscape painting above his bed. Marlett was lethargic and seemed not to be listening, but his hands and mouth had lost some of their strain.

"I've had the autolaryngoscope set up for some time now," Mr. Indro said worriedly. "But Dr. Duvall has not yet come."

"Have you examined him?" Shiloh asked quickly.

"Yes . . . although I had no authority to do so," Mr. Indro fretted.

"That's okay, I've been shovelin' out prescriptives and handin' down diagnoses and bossin' attendants around like I'm Dr. Carl Werner or somebody," Shiloh said with deliberate nonchalance. "Let's just say that we're all on emergency status tonight and let it go at that. What about Fair?"

"Dr. Duvall was right, he does have diphtheria," Mr. Indro said gravely.

"Diphtheria?" Shiloh was surprised but wasted no time speculating on Cheney's diagnosis. "So he's got that thing in his throat? That's why his breathing's so off?"

"Yes, exactly. Dr. Duvall and I had discussed giving him some ephedra, but I haven't seen her since, and I have no doctor's orders," Mr. Indro said helplessly.

Shiloh folded his arms and frowned, deep in thought. "She's not on this ward," he muttered. He gave Mr. Indro a sharp look. "Do you think you could give him the right dosage, Mr. Indro? Do you feel confident of it?"

"Yes, I do," he answered instantly. "I would recommend an ephedra and hawthorn decoction. The ephedra would open his air passages, while the hawthorn will regulate his heart."

"Do it," Shiloh said, "on my authority. Dr. Duvall approves."

The apothecary looked doubtful for a mere second, then said firmly, "Yes, I believe she does. Or will. Or did."

"All of that," Shiloh said with a tense smile. "And, Mr. Indro, better keep some digitalis on hand in there. That boy's frail, and his heart's working hard already, pushin' air in and out."

Mr. Indro drew a small glass vial out of his vest pocket and displayed it proudly, holding it up between his thumb and second finger. "Digitalis," he said reverently. "The dried leaf of the common foxglove serves as a tonic for heart arrhythmia or failure."

Without another word he turned and went back into Marlett Fair's room.

Shiloh's next stop was Ike Trimble's bed. To his surprise, Nia was calmly wrapping his leg with a wet dressing and explaining how to do it in her soft little-girl's voice to Elaine Trimble, who hovered over her. "Good evening, Mrs. Trimble, Mr. Trimble. Hullo, Nia," he said with real pleasure. "I'm sure glad to see you here tonight."

"Me too," Ike Trimble said. "Glad to have my favorite nurse back."

Shiloh stared at his face hard for a few moments in the semidarkness; the lamp by his bed was out, as Nia had no need of it to simply soak and change the dressings. As he spoke, he casually laid his hand on Trimble's forehead. "Glad to see you, too, Mr. Trimble, but I'm sorry your leg's giving you some trouble." He felt feverish, and Shiloh took his pulse, this time counting it carefully with his pocket watch and noting his respirations. Both were fine—but there was the fever.

"Nia, lemme see that leg," he said. "Light the lamp for a minute, will you?"

Nia removed the dressing, and Shiloh bent over Trimble's leg. Nia held the lamp close, and they exchanged quick grave looks, unseen by Mr. Trimble and his wife. The tissue around the wound had not yet blackened, but directly around the edges the skin was darkening to an ominous bronze. A very faint sickening-sweetish smell drifted up to Shiloh's sensitive nose. "Has the doc examined him yet?" Shiloh asked Nia casually.

"No, sir. She's got an emergency and hasn't been able to make rounds." Nia spoke carefully, for Mr. Trimble's benefit.

Don't we all, Shiloh thought grimly. Aloud he said, "Mr. Trimble, when did you notice this wound not healing properly?"

"It ain't healed proper since he got out of the hospital," Mrs. Trimble said in a shaky voice. "Just today I saw how bad it was getting."

"Does it hurt?" Shiloh asked Trimble.

"Yes," he answered stoically.

"Did you eat today?"

Mutely he shook his head.

"Sick? Vomiting?"

"Yes. Yesterday," Trimble answered, showing the first signs of apprehension.

"An' he still went to work. Dr. Duvall told us not to let that sore get all dirty. But I ast you, how can a man stay clean, haulin' coal?" Mrs. Trimble clasped a thin shawl about her shoulders, her fingers worrying the cheap felt border.

"Don't worry, Mrs. Trimble," Shiloh murmured. "Nia's taking good care of your husband. We're going to do just a short surgery tonight—probably won't take half an hour—"

"Oh no, oh no!" Mrs. Trimble wailed.

Ike Trimble blanched, collapsed back onto the thin pillow, and pleaded in a hushed, frightened voice, "You . . . you ain't gonna have to take off my leg, are you, Mr. Irons?"

Consciously Shiloh arranged his expression into polite concern and easy confidence. "No, Mr. Trimble. You're a lucky man. Dr. Duvall has devised a new treatment for—"

"Don't say it," Trimble hissed fearfully, and a convulsive sob was wrenched from his wife.

"—for this condition," Shiloh went on blandly, wisely understanding Mr. Trimble's fear of hearing the dreaded *gangrene.* "It's a short operation and a disinfection remedy."

Mr. Trimble closed his eyes and panted, obviously trying to control his fright-filled breathing. Mrs. Trimble's frantic gaze stayed honed in on Shiloh's face as if she would find truth written plainly on his forehead. Shiloh stood still, at rest, allowing her to stare wretchedly at him for long moments. Finally he saw her girlish features begin to grow composed.

Ike Trimble opened his eyes and stared at his wife, stricken. She awkwardly searched for his hand, as if she'd been struck blind, but when she found it, she didn't cling to it in desperation, she stroked it softly. "You said she's a good doctor," she said in a thin, breathy voice. "I . . . I . . . don't think Mr. Irons would lie to us."

"I wouldn't," Shiloh stated flatly.

"No, he wouldn't," Nia put in quietly, "and Dr. Duvall will be able to take care of this, just as she promised you, Mrs. Trimble."

"Yes," she agreed thoughtfully. She and her husband were staring at each other, and it seemed that an invisible mantle of calm now enveloped the couple.

"Okay," Shiloh said with relief. "So Mr. Trimble just needs to rest right now, and, Mrs. Trimble, you and Nia need to work on cleaning out that wound as thoroughly as possible."

"All . . . all right. Nia, she's showing me what to do, and I'd like to do for my husband as much as I can," Mrs. Trimble said with determination.

"Good. You listen to Nia, she knows what she's doing." Shiloh took Nia's arm and pulled her down to the foot of Trimble's bed. "Listen, Nia, that wound needs to be irrigated. Have you ever done that before?"

Nia shook her head.

"Easy. All that means is washin' it out with strong streams of carbolic acid. What you need to do is get a stack of towels, a wide basin, and an irrigation tube. All of that stuff will be in the closet, down at the end of the ward. Mr. Tukes is down there—you met him?—okay, he'll show you where it is and what an irrigation tube is. All it is, is a hollow tube, with a plunger, to squirt out liquid kinda hard. Sit Mr. Trimble in the chair, and prop his leg up on another chair. Put the basin underneath his leg. Put the nipple of the tube right against the wound, then plunge, ten times, using the full tube. Then put a wet dressing on it. Fifteen minutes later, irrigate it again, ten times. After that, every half hour, irrigate it five times. Got it?"

"Yes, sir. Ten times, fifteen minutes, ten times, fifteen minutes, five times every half hour after that. I got it, Mr. Shiloh," Nia said, her wide doe-eyes focused intensely on his face.

"Yeah, you got it. Don't worry, Nia. You're a good nurse, quick and smart. You'll make a good doctor." Shiloh turned on his heel and hurried off before he saw the pleasure make the young Negro maid's face glow.

As Shiloh left the men's ward, he noted with satisfaction that most of the other patients were asleep. The ones who were awake didn't stop him or call for him. They merely stared at the ceiling or watched Nia and the Trimbles. They didn't seem restless, merely awake and curious.

Crazy night, Shiloh reflected. Licking his lips, he suddenly realized how dry they were, and that he was very thirsty. A rueful smile crooked his firm mouth. *I've talked more tonight than I have in a whole month. . . . Knew it'd be this way, shufflin' papers and tellin' people what to do and how to do it instead of doin' it myself. Don't like it much. . . . I'd rather be working on those shot-up boys or taking care of Ike Trimble's leg.* With a shrug he dismissed his ire. It was his job. He'd agreed to do it. He'd do it, and do it to the best of his ability.

He had to.

12

Dramatic Lighting and Poorly Staged Plays

The women's ward, in contrast to the men's, had an atmosphere of tension and unease, and was filled with noise that was oddly hushed. Some of the women talked from bed to bed in stage whispers. No words could be heard, just an undulating hum and the soft susurration of s's. Two women were walking up and down the wards restlessly, stopping to talk to this patient or that one. Loud cries of a woman in labor sounded clearly, beginning as a low moan and rising to a frantic scream. Shiloh sighed. Either Mrs. Irby or Mrs. Callister was having a tough time of it.

At Mrs. Irby's door, he squared his shoulders, then opened the door only a crack to stick his head in.

Miss Rees sat by Mrs. Irby's bed. Her expression was bland, but she was speaking, and Shiloh was surprised to hear how reassuring she sounded. "The pains are still thirty minutes apart, Mrs. Irby. So we have time for me to sponge your back. Would you like that?"

"Why . . . yes, I think I would. I have some lotion in my bag, and it smells quite refreshing. Would you please rub my arms and shoulders too? That would be marvelous. Go on, Brookshear, I know you want to go outside and smoke one of those awful cigars. I suppose it'll be another half hour before I shall be screaming at you again. "

"Thank you, m'dear," he said with an awkward bow. A stately looking gentleman with fine thick gray hair and sideburns and a dignified mustache brushed past Shiloh with open relief. Already his hand was fumbling in a breast pocket for the infamous cigar.

"We're doing fine, Mr. Irons," Miss Rees said with cool courtesy. "Unless you require me somewhere else?"

"No, that's all right. Just checking on you, Mrs. Irby. Are you feeling all right?"

"No, I'm not," she said petulantly. "Being in labor is not a joyful, fulfilling experience, as some women try to make it out to be." Impatiently pushing a damp brown curl back from her face, she blew out an exasperated breath and composed her voice back into its pleasing contralto. "Never mind me, Mr. Irons. At least I'm not having as much trouble as that poor girl next door."

"I'm sorry for the disturbance," Shiloh said rather lamely.

"Nonsense," she retorted. "Believe me, I know she can't help it. Don't you think you'd do better to see if you can help her, rather than baby-sitting me?"

"Yes, ma'am," he said meekly. "Well . . . if you'll excuse me . . ."

He shut the door and steeled himself, then went straight into Mrs. Callister's room. Walker Baird looked up, and his boyish face was finely drawn into lines of strain. But his voice was neutral, even a bit careless. "Good, here's Mr. Irons. Mrs. Callister, I need to speak to him for a moment. Have you met him?"

Mrs. Callister, a slight girl of eighteen, grimaced and clutched her swollen abdomen. Tears started from the outer corners of her eyes, then seemed to spring out as if they rose from an angry ocean wave. She clenched her jaw, her mouth turning bloodless white with the strain. Then a cry of pain burst from her as if it were a loosed wild animal.

Walker squeezed his eyes shut for a brief moment, as if he, too, felt her agony. Then quickly his face returned to its normal warm expression with just the right touch of concern. He patted her hand, though she was obviously unconscious of any sound or gesture, and hurried to Shiloh's side. "Go get Mrs. Sisk, I want her to assist me. She left just a moment ago to check on Molly Costanza and then Dr. Duvall. Tell her to bring the obstetric kit and to set up an emergency surgery cart."

"She gonna need a cesarean section?" Shiloh asked in a worried tone.

"I hope not," Walker said grimly. "But this baby's an incomplete breech—you know what that means? It means he's almost standing up. His feet are coming out first. And that means that, because of this odd delivery, her cervix won't be dilated enough for the head. It takes special forceps—and a steady hand and a steel heart—to deliver a baby this way."

The two men glanced at the girl in the bed. She was in agony, exhausted almost to the point of unconsciousness, and she didn't have the strength of a kitten.

"Uh . . . Walker . . . is that baby almost delivered?" Shiloh asked tentatively.

"Well, sort of. One foot is," he said blackly.

"Then . . . uh . . . maybe she could have some nitrous oxide?" Shiloh asked, almost pleaded. "It might help just a little, and if that baby's almost here, it shouldn't hurt him. Or her."

"Her," he said absently. "Yes . . . yes . . . very light concentration. Just enough to give her a few moments of peace, free from pain. Thank you, Shiloh, you're absolutely right!" He reached up and clapped Shiloh solidly on the shoulder. "Can you get—never mind. Send Mrs. Sisk, first thing. We've got two inhalers and canisters around here somewhere, she'll know."

"Okay," Shiloh said with relief and left Mrs. Callister's room. He didn't think he could bear to be in the room much longer; although her cries were audible all over the ward, being in the same room with her actually made him feel pain—in his shoulders, in his arms, in his hands. He knew it was from tension. He'd automatically steeled himself, drawing in his muscles until they felt as tight as a longbow's draw, when she cried out. He couldn't help it. All he could do was get away from it.

His strides long and harsh, he went to the curtained cubicle at the end of the women's ward. Mrs. Sisk was bending over the sleeping Molly Costanza, who was breathing evenly, though with occasional snorts. Impatiently he gestured for the nurse to follow him, and Shiloh led her far enough away from Molly's curtained cubicle so as not to wake her.

"Nitrous oxide inhaler and obstetrics kit to Dr. Walker," he said brusquely. "And be sure and wash your hands, and wash each instrument first."

"Yes, Dr. Irons," Mrs. Sisk said nervously.

Shiloh didn't correct her; it was a sign of his distraction that he didn't even notice. "Where's Dr. Duvall?"

Dramatically Mrs. Sisk pointed across the aisle to another bed that was completely obscured by two screens. Shiloh had thought the screens were just being stored there. "She's there," Mrs. Sisk answered in an ominous whisper, "with that poor and wee Chinee."

Without another word Shiloh turned and slipped between the two screens.

Bent low over the bed, Cheney looked up as he appeared. Her face was fixed in an expression of clinical warmth and polite concern, but Shiloh could detect the strain that didn't show. Her fingers, strong, lissome, as white as gardenias, rested on the patient's hand.

Slowly Shiloh's gaze fell to the girl in the bed. Her face was a small moon, her eyes wide dark wedges under straight thin brows, her mouth a tiny cupid's bow. She was covered neatly with a sheet and two blankets, and the form underneath was small. Shiloh took a step closer. She couldn't have been more than sixteen or seventeen years old.

"This is Little Wren," Cheney said in a low, conversational tone. "She doesn't speak English."

"Hello, Little Wren," Shiloh said quietly. His casual gaze sobered, and his mouth tightened. This girl was specter-pale, and her lips were blue.

She closed her eyes, and Shiloh was again fascinated by the construction of the Oriental eye; there was no fold in the eyelid, so when the girl's eyes closed, they were two perfect smooth dark crescents. Long thin lashes, as proportioned as if they'd been drawn with ink, rested against her cheeks.

She whispered something. Cheney bent lower over her, close to her face, and murmured an interrogative sound, but the girl didn't try to speak again. Shiloh could see that her breathing was rapid and much too shallow. Soundlessly he slipped to the other side of the bed and laid his hand on her forehead; he was appalled to see how brown, how strong, how vital his hand looked against her sickly rice-paper skin. She was clammy and cold. His hand went to her other hand, which was posed on her abdomen as if it were a dead white leaf that had fallen to the ground. Her pulse was feeble, almost undetectable.

With an obvious effort, summoning her failing strength, she opened her eyes and whispered again. Shiloh could have sworn that he saw a glimmer of a smile somewhere behind the dull black of her eyes.

Cheney looked frustrated; she couldn't make out the words.

"She said 'Ren Xandou,' or something like that," Shiloh said in a dull voice. "Guess it's her name."

This time the corners of the girl's cherub mouth did turn upward, just a little bit. She closed her eyes again.

Cheney gave a directing glance outside the screens, and Shiloh followed her out into the aisle. "A—*gentleman*"—Cheney spat the word—"brought her in. By the time I got her into bed and the bleeding stanched, he was gone."

"What happened to her?" Shiloh asked, his voice steady but the tone distorted, so deep it seemed to come from his gut.

Cheney's eyes flickered. "She had an abortion, sometime late tonight, I think. It was butchery. Massive hemorrhage, shock."

Their eyes locked; they stood motionless. Slowly Shiloh's jaw tightened, while Cheney's green eyes grew into great pools of pity and sorrow.

When Mrs. Sisk's voice reached Cheney's ears—she sounded as if she were very far away—Cheney started and saw that the woman was standing right by her, speaking in a hoarse whisper. Behind her in the gloom stood a man, an older man he seemed by his stooped posture and thin vulnerable outline. Cheney ignored him. Shiloh never moved; his gaze just went from focusing on Cheney's face to a lost-beyond-the-horizon stare.

"Yes, Mrs. Sisk, what is it?" Cheney demanded.

"It's Mr. Fair, ma'am. Mr. Indro says you have to come. Now." She was twisting her rough red hands back and forth over her white apron.

"Can't Dr. Walker see to it?" Cheney asked harshly.

"No, ma'am," Mrs. Sisk replied, almost flinching. "He's took up with Mrs. Callister and can't leave her. Mr. Fair . . . Mr. Fair, he's almost not breathin', Dr. Duvall."

Cheney's vision sharpened and her brow cleared. She plucked at Shiloh's sleeve. "Shiloh, please come with me, right now."

He looked at her as if she were a stranger. "Now? But that girl—no one should die all alone, Doc."

Behind Mrs. Sisk, the gentleman stepped forward slightly, and his face came out of the shadows. It was a good face, patient and kind. The skin was like cured and tanned leather stretched over bare bones, but his eyes were bright and warm. "Excuse me, please. My name is Reverend Justice Merced, and that's why I'm here. To stay with Ren Xandou."

Shiloh and Cheney stared at him blankly, while Mrs. Sisk nodded vehemently.

Still Shiloh hesitated, staring at Reverend Merced with unfocused, impersonal anger.

"Mr. Dare Dunning came to my house," Reverend Merced continued in a reasonable tone. "He told me that Little Wren was dying and he brought me here. He's waiting outside." He nodded lightly toward the west wing exit.

Shiloh jerked as if he'd been stung. Before anyone could move or say anything, he'd disappeared through the door into the empty west wing.

He reached the exit out of the west wing and wrenched it open. Outside, standing by a fine curricle hitched to the iron hitching ring, a man stood, smoking and looking up at the stars. Shiloh appeared in front of him as fast and silently as if he were an avenging angel. "You Dunning?" he demanded.

The man considered Shiloh—his height, his taut stance, his bunched hands—coolly. Dunning was much smaller, slightly built, finely dressed, with sensitive, almost feminine hands. "That's right, I'm Dare Dunning. And you?" he asked in a carefully neutral voice.

"Irons," Shiloh said softly. "Shiloh Irons." He stared angrily at Dunning, and the smaller man bore it well. Casually Dunning made eye contact, and then with negligent ease drew on his cigarette, blew out a thin stream of pale smoke, and again seemed to study the weak stars that paled in the phosphorescence of the bloated moon.

Shiloh's thoughts were in turmoil for long moments; his mind seethed and raged. But his instincts, sharp and insistent, finally dominated his finely honed anger.

He's a gambler, Shiloh realized, *and a good one. He's bluffing, and it's a good bluff . . . but he's scared. Not sure if it's of me, or about the girl . . . doesn't matter, really. For sure he didn't have to bring the girl in. He's scared, but he's getting ready to take whatever I dish out, pay the price. . . .*

The perception dissipated Shiloh's anger like Dunning's cigarette smoke that disappeared in the chilly night breeze. Moving to stand to the side, instead of in his challenging stance right in front of the man, Shiloh asked in a more normal, but still persistent, voice: "You the father?"

With slow deliberation Dunning threw the half-smoked cigarette down and stepped on the tiny glowing coal, grinding his foot back and forth, back and forth, in a precise military movement. "I don't know," he said slowly. "No way of knowing." He risked a quick glance at Shiloh's profile. He saw an angry man, a man saddened, his fine features hardened into molten metal. "After all, she is a—"

"Don't say that," Shiloh growled. "Don't call her that."

Dunning shrugged almost imperceptibly, then crossed his arms and stared up at the sky. Shiloh was staring at the moon, the eerie light making the two men, the curricle, and the pale horse look like actors and props in an ill-lit play.

"She was so young," Shiloh said, harsh accusation roughening his voice again. "She was just a kid."

"Is she dead?" Dunning asked, his bored tone sharpening.

"Not yet."

Dare Dunning's head drooped just a bit, then he straightened, and his voice was again the carefree gambler's voice. "She was at M'lady Maxine's. Maxine's no lady, but she's smart. She dresses the Chinese girls up in Oriental finery—their hair all fixed up so intricately, with those ivory picks with gold tassels . . . sometimes fresh flowers . . . rice powder and kohl-darkened eyes . . . satins and silks and brocades . . . red veils . . ." Dunning started slightly, jerking himself out of his reverie. "I really didn't know how young Little Wren was. Couldn't tell, until I saw her tonight, when she was . . . was . . ."

"Bleeding to death from a botched abortion?" Shiloh said tightly.

Dunning sighed, then reached into his vest pocket and pulled out an elegant ebony cigarette case. Popping it open, he made a slight gesture toward Shiloh, who ignored him. "Guess not," he muttered dryly and lit a cigarette, drawing deeply from it.

"She's dying," Shiloh said suddenly, his voice deep with sadness. "Don't you think you should be with her?"

Dunning hesitated before answering. "No. I doubt very much that she would want me with her."

A long silence reigned.

"No . . . no, guess not," Shiloh finally muttered.

"That's why I brought her here," Dunning told him resignedly. "And that's why I went to get Reverend Merced. People like you and Reverend Merced should be with her."

Shiloh was confused by this simple declaration of faith and suddenly wondered why in the world he thought he was any better than Dare Dunning, anyway. But his thoughts were interrupted by sounds behind them, and Cheney stepped in front of him. Ignoring Dunning, she stared up at him sternly and laid both her hands lightly on his arms. "I need your help, Shiloh. Please."

Shiloh watched Dare Dunning, who was still looking for something in the impersonal night sky. "I'll stay until she dies," he said calmly. "Then I'll take her to her people. She has no family, but the Chinese will want to bury her."

As if suddenly awakened from a nightmare, Shiloh wiped his brow and blinked several times. When he spoke, it was in his normal easy tone. "Okay, Doc. Let's go."

Cheney and Shiloh went back into the hospital. Shiloh only cast one quick glance at Little Wren's screened cubicle as they hurried toward Marlett Fair's room. Mrs. Sisk followed, almost running on her stubby legs to keep up with Cheney's and Shiloh's long loping pace. Over her shoulder Cheney ordered, "Mrs. Sisk, I know you have to go back to Walker and Mrs. Callister. But the one thing I insist that you do first is to get Mrs. Fair out of that room. I don't care if you have to toss her over your shoulder and carry her out. Get her out of my way."

Shiloh smiled grimly at this vision, then asked, "Tracheotomy, Doc?"

"Only thing I know to do," she told him resignedly. "Have you ever assisted at one?"

"Nope. You ever done one?"

"Nope."

Now Shiloh truly smiled at Cheney's unconscious echo.

She asked, "Does anyone know if there's a surgical cart handy?"

Behind them Mrs. Sisk panted, "Mr. Indro . . . he's got one ready."

"Good man," Shiloh muttered.

They stopped at the basin of carbolic acid, and both of them plunged their hands into it at the same time. Mrs. Sisk scurried by them and hurried into Marlett Fair's room. Mrs. Fair's hysterical voice sounded like a scared cat wailing.

Shiloh searched Cheney's face. "You're all right with this, aren't you, Doc? It'll be a cupcake for you."

She smiled tensely. "I'm fine. You all right?"

"Sure." He shrugged and thought how much it hurt his shoulders and neck. They felt as if someone were pushing large dull needles into them. He tried to loosen the knotted muscles and gave no sign of the pains shooting through him.

As they hurried down the hallway, Marlett Fair's door was wrenched open and Mrs. Fair came out—or rather, popped out. Close behind her was Mrs. Sisk, who hurried to her side and encircled her waist with one beefy arm. Mrs. Fair looked up hopelessly and helplessly at Shiloh and Cheney as they passed in the hallway, but Mrs. Sisk was propelling her so quickly she didn't have time to say a word.

Mrs. Sisk was muttering in a soothing monotone, "Now, you just come along wi' me, Missus Fair, that's right, and let Dr. Duvall see about Mr. Marlett. You'd just be in the way, you know, and you shouldn't mind a whit—I'm always in some doctor's way, it seems, and they sure and certain don't mind tellin' you to skitter off, e'en when you're just trying to help, or e'en when you're doin' your best to get outer the way in the first place—"

Cheney and Shiloh ran into Mr. Fair's room. Mr. Indro looked up, his face twisted with distress. "He's just about closed up, Dr. Duvall. In one or two more minutes—"

Cheney bent over Marlett Fair. Shiloh moved to the surgical cart set up by the bed, grabbed a bottle and a roll of cotton bandage and cut a strip about six inches long, then folded it three times to make a small absorbent pad. His hands moved quickly as he rearranged this scalpel and that one. Deftly he selected three needles and a roll of cat-gut and threw them into the basin of carbolic acid on the second tier. "Cannula," he muttered to himself, then looked up at Mr. Indro. "Cannula? And rubber tubing?"

Mr. Indro wrung his hands. "Cannula? I don't . . . don't . . ."

"It's all right, Mr. Indro," Shiloh said calmly. "You couldn't have known. I need a tube, fixed, about three inches long—small diameter. Small. Just . . . um . . . about like a pencil. I need another flexible tube—rubber—about twelve inches long. Can you get those in a hurry?"

"Yes." Mr. Indro's childlike features settled into stern determination, and he rushed out of the room.

"How's he doing?" Shiloh asked, still bent over the cart. He was rifling through the instruments on the lower tier. Mr. Indro had, correctly, put the scalpels and rolls of bandages and a basin of carbolic acid on the top tier, but the rest of the instruments and extra bandages and basins were piled rather haphazardly on the second and third tiers. Shiloh had to find some small forceps, tiny forceps, and though his fingers shifted steel instruments this way and that, he made no sound. He knew Cheney was irritated by clanking surgical instruments.

Clinically Cheney answered, "Extreme strain in inhalation. Pallor, bluish lips. Pulse—can't get it. He's restless, Shiloh, getting combative."

Shiloh looked up alertly. "You need help?"

"No, I've got him," Cheney said confidently. "He's so weak—Mr.

Fair? Listen to me," she went on, lowering her voice to a soothing, quiet timbre.

Shiloh thought, when she spoke to patients like that—the ones who were almost overcome by their fears—that her voice sounded as soft and reassuring as a warm summer rain. He smiled with satisfaction as his nimble fingers touched on some tiny forceps, just like a delicate insect's pincers.

"You're going to be all right, Mr. Fair. I know you're having trouble breathing, and I know you can't speak. But I can help you. Mr. Irons can help you. We'll take care of you. That's it . . . that's it . . . please try and relax and save your strength."

The thrashing in the bed and the animal panting groans subsided somewhat. But Mr. Fair's inhalations were sticky-sounding, with a harsh, high-pitched moan, almost a bark. Shiloh reflected that a tracheotomy was going to be the boy's only hope, but it was going to be tough to do, since he couldn't be sedated. There was no way to give him a pill or a drink of laudanum, as the false membrane of diphtheria was blocking his throat. Shiloh mentally shrugged. He'd held down bigger, stronger, more hysterical men for operations much, much worse than a tracheotomy.

"Okay, here we go," Shiloh muttered to himself. With light grace for such a big man, he moved to the other side of the bed, pulling the cart after him. Cheney remained where she was, grasping Marlett Fair's hand, looking straight into his wild eyes, speaking softly.

"Now, Mr. Irons is going to swab your throat with iodine first. Then he's going to apply a local anesthetic—" She paused briefly, her eyebrows raised slightly, and looked at Shiloh. He looked surprised, then nodded. He had cocaine powder, certainly. But rubbing it on the skin wasn't going to deaden all the way through to the trachea. Still, the doc knew what she was doing. Shiloh speculated that this was just another tool she was using to calm down the patient down.

"—you will still feel some pain, Mr. Fair," she was saying quietly. "But it will be brief. Then you'll be able to breathe easily again. Can you be calm and listen to me and help me?"

He managed to croak, "Yes."

"That's good," she said encouragingly, then cast a worried glance at Shiloh. He shrugged, quickly swabbing Fair's throat with iodine, but his anxious eyes were on the door.

Shiloh finished with the iodine; now Marlett Fair's throat was a ghastly orange hue. He rubbed cocaine powder thoroughly, with gentle circular strokes, over the small bony lumps of the tracheal tube, and about an inch on both sides. When he finished, Mr. Indro still had not arrived, so he did it again. *May be best thing, anyway . . .* he speculated. *The longer this stuff is applied, the more it soaks in . . . he'll be numb at least down to the muscle. . . . Wonder if muscles feel pain?* He almost smiled at his idle mental question. *Sure muscles feel pain. My neck's killin' me.*

Mr. Indro burst into the room, his fringe of gray hair cowlicked straight up on one side, his chubby cheeks pink, his spectacles wobbling. "Here! Cannulas, all sizes! And rubber tubing, all you want! Extra stethoscope tubing, you see! Will this do?"

"That's wonderful, thank you so much, Mr. Indro," Cheney said warmly. "We're ready to proceed, so would you please assist Mr. Irons and me? Yes, over there, and give the jar and the tubing to him." Cheney spoke again to Marlett Fair, reassuring him, as Mr. Indro moved to the other side of the bed. He and Shiloh conferred in rough, hurried whispers.

Shiloh squinted at the jar Mr. Indro carefully placed on the cart. "Got 'em soaking in carbolic acid—"

"Carr's carbolic compound," the apothecary corrected him breathlessly.

"Yeah, right, good deal, man! And the tubing? No, just swish it in this basin once, that's all right."

Deftly and quickly Shiloh snipped off about a twelve-inch length of tubing, then took the smallest scalpel and poked a hole in it, penetrating through the tube to the other side. Picking up the jar of yellow liquid, he stared at it, grinning. Inside were about a dozen tubes, all of different lengths and sizes.

"*Angelica archangelica*," Mr. Indro whispered proudly. "The roots and fruit furnish a fragrant flavoring oil, the fruit makes a fine confection, the leaves distill into a sweet wine. And the stems are hollow—they make whistles."

"Excellent," Shiloh murmured, selecting a small reed and snipping it off to a three-inch length. Then he inserted it through the hole he'd made in the length of rubber tubing. "Mr. Indro, I'm going to be busy. Do you think you can help Mr. Fair be still?" He gave Indro a stern look that meant *hold him down.*

"Certainly, Mr. Irons," the meek apothecary said confidently. He took Mr. Fair's hand in one of his, then lightly laid his other hand on the young man's shoulder. He gave Shiloh a single sure nod.

"We're ready, Doc," Shiloh said and held out a scalpel, far down the bed so Fair couldn't see it.

Cheney took it, careful to hold it beyond Mr. Fair's gaze, then put her other hand on his forehead. "Tilt your head back, Mr. Fair. That's right. Just as far as you can."

Mr. Indro replaced Cheney's hand on Fair's forehead, his mouth tightened into a grim straight line.

Quickly, lightly, Cheney reached up and gently felt for Fair's Adam's apple, then positioned the scalpel directly beneath. Quickly, lightly, she drew the scalpel down about two inches. Blood welled up. Shiloh stanched it before it could dribble down Fair's neck. The boy didn't move a muscle; Cheney noted that he was still breathing, with as much difficulty as before. He had arched his back, and he was as rigid as if he were convulsing—but Mr. Indro gave no sign. He was looking straight down in the boy's eyes with a compassionate expression.

Cheney handed the bloody scalpel back to Shiloh. With one hand pressed against the opening in the boy's neck, he took the scalpel with his other hand, selected another smaller, more pointed one, and slapped it firmly into Cheney's hand. She bent over the boy and delicately made a minute opening through three cartilages covering the trachea.

Again she shoved the scalpel toward Shiloh. He grabbed it, then handed Cheney the tubing, with the inserted cannula. Cheney waited while Shiloh picked up the tiny forceps he'd found and held open the hole she'd made in the trachea. He managed to staunch the bleeding, hold the incision open, and still keep his big hands out of Cheney's way as she bent down and maneuvered the tube into the opening. "Got it," she breathed.

Immediately Shiloh threw the forceps back on the cart, picked up the thin rolls of cotton he'd trimmed down to about a half-inch width, and with tiny delicate movements, tucked them around the cannula, arranging and packing them as closely around the tube as if they were embroidery. No blood seeped through the third layer, and Shiloh nodded to Cheney with satisfaction. Gently she pulled the rubber tubing around Fair's arched neck and tied it in a simple twist behind, just tight enough to stabilize the cannula but not so it was uncomfortable to the patient.

Cheney bit her lip, and Shiloh knew that she was now concerned about the trickiest part of a tracheotomy: teaching the patient to breath through an opening in his neck instead of through his nose. "Mr. Fair?" she said lightly. "We're finished, and I must say you were the best patient I've ever had. Now, lie down . . . get comfortable . . . and listen to me."

His eyes were wild and unseeing; he still fought for breath. Odd hollow gasps sounded through the tubing, but Fair's nostrils were pinched in panic.

"Listen to me, Mr. Fair," Cheney said more sternly and raised her voice just a note. "I told you that we were going to insert a breathing tube in your throat. It's done. All you have to do is use it. Close your eyes. That's it, close your eyes, Mr. Fair."

Finally, after long frantic moments, he closed his eyes. His hands stopped flailing desperately and his shoulders stopped writhing.

"That's very good. Now concentrate. Listen. Just to me, just to my voice." Cheney's voice rose and fell in rhythmic, soothing waves. "Very good. What I'm going to do—just be still—is gently pinch your nostrils shut. When I do, you think about your throat—think about the tube, and the way the air is coming through it—that's it . . . that's it . . . that's fine. Mr. Fair, you're breathing."

★ ★ ★ ★

As if some evil gnome, unseen, was watching them, timing them, gauging just when they might take a moment to breathe easy, a tap sounded on the door of Mr. Marlett Fair's room. "Mr. Irons? Mr. Irons?" came Jesty Tukes' inquiring whisper.

Shiloh and Cheney, still on either side of Mr. Fair's bed, exchanged resigned glances. "Will you excuse us, Mr. Fair?" Cheney asked as politely as if they were at high tea. "Don't worry, you're doing just fine. I'll talk to your mother, and then I'm sure she'll want to come back in and be with you."

The young Mr. Fair began making weak frantic signals. "What?" Cheney asked, mystified.

"Yeah, I'm sure Mr. Indro will be glad to stay with you, Mr. Fair," Shiloh said reassuringly.

The apothecary patted the boy's thin shoulder and said lightly, "Of course, I shall be glad to stay with you, Mr. Fair. And I'll be even gladder if you should allow me to sample a drop of that wonderful brandy over there on the table." He mopped the top of his shiny head theatrically. "This is considerably more exacting than rolling pills."

Marlett Fair almost smiled and weakly gestured toward the table that held the fine old Napoleon brandy. Then he closed his eyes in weary contentment.

Cheney and Shiloh stepped outside the room. Jesty Tukes waited for them, his brown eyes wide with distress. "Mr. Irons, I . . . I . . . wasn't too sure about interrupting you, and I didn't know you were in there, Dr. Duvall—"

The boy was obviously distraught, the strain of the night beginning to tell. "Mr. Tukes," Cheney said briskly, "the first thing you must learn as a medical student is to always sound sure of yourself, even—or perhaps especially—when you're not."

"Huh? I . . . I mean, I beg your pardon?" Jesty was mystified, and a little appalled that Dr. Duvall appeared to be advising him to be impudent. Only Shiloh's half-grin made him understand that she was teasing.

"Oh yes," she went on, completely aware of his confusion. "You must bang on the door and shout, 'Mr. Irons! Dr. Duvall! Your presence is required with another patient!' "

With a trapped look on his face, Jesty opened his mouth wide and took a deep preparatory breath. Hastily Cheney went on, "No, not . . . really shout, Mr. Tukes. I just mean that you must develop a stern voice and a commanding demeanor."

Jesty clamped his mouth shut, cleared his throat, and lowered his tenor to a comically deep and artificial baritone. "Mr. Irons, Dr. Duvall!" he grunted. "Your presence is required with another patient!"

Cheney and Shiloh exchanged amused looks, and Shiloh clapped the boy so soundly on the shoulder he almost staggered. "That's much better, Jesty," he declared. "But you'll need to practice, you know, polish it up a little. Now, which patient is it that's about to croak now?"

Jesty's freckled face positively sagged at this irreverent sally, but he noted that Dr. Duvall seemed unmoved. In fact, she muttered something under her breath about "lining them up, like ducks in a shooting gallery," but Jesty just had to ignore it.

"Er . . . ah . . . er . . ." he stammered, his face flushing deeply.

"It's all right, Mr. Tukes," Cheney said kindly. "Mr. Irons has a rather unsettling sense of humor. Don't pay any mind to him."

"Me? What about you and the ducks?" Shiloh retorted indignantly, but Cheney grandly ignored him.

"Who is it, Mr. Tukes?"

"It's . . . I think . . . somebody had better see about Mr. . . . um . . . the gunshot wound to the leg," Jesty finally sputtered desperately.

Shiloh's face became grave and he quickly recited, "Mr. Laban Smith, twenty years old, .22 gunshot wound to the inner thigh, right above the knee. No exit wound. Not massive bleeding, but steady."

"Tourniquet?" she asked quickly.

He shook his head. "No, Doc. Joe Ryman, you know, was unhurt. He's been applying steady pressure, keeping the bleeding down."

"Good, Shiloh," she murmured, staring down at the floor, deep in thought. "Surgical removal . . . I'll need you to assist, of course."

Shiloh blew out an exasperated breath. "Listen, Doc, why don't we just go ahead and get set up in the operating theater? I've got those five injuries stashed in the east wing, 'cause we didn't have the beds in the men's ward. We can't do a surgery in there, it's dark and musty. And besides, I think you're gonna want to do Ike Trimble's leg as soon as you finish the gunshot wound."

"Tonight? Is it that advanced?" Cheney asked worriedly.

"No, it's not. But that's the point, right? For us to try what we talked about on the ship?" Shiloh challenged her.

"Shiloh, that concept is completely experimental. We were just talking, just . . . exploring the idea," Cheney argued. "No one's ever tried it, that I know of."

"What?" Jesty Tukes couldn't contain his curiosity, even if Dr. Duvall fried him for interrupting.

But she merely answered him in a thoughtful voice, as if she were reviewing the procedure herself. Which, indeed, she was—and Shiloh knew it. "Copious irrigation of the necrotic tissue. Surgical incision, then decompression and drainage. Extirpation and debridement of the secondary involved tissue, followed by copious irrigations."

Jesty Tukes had not one lame clue as to what she was talking about, but he summoned all his courage and asked excitedly, "Dr. Duvall, can I observe?"

"No," she said.

"Yes," Shiloh said. "He's my nurse, Dr. Duvall."

"We're too short on the wards," Cheney argued. She didn't notice that the decision had been made, and now they were merely working out the logistics.

"I think I can get it covered by then," Shiloh said firmly. "And besides, Doc, I want Jesty and Baltimore Florey to set up the operating theater. Mr. Florey did a bang-up job with the emergency cart, and Jesty can help him."

"No," Cheney said coldly. "You're my surgical assistant, Shiloh, and I want you to do it. You may have Mr. Tukes assist you, if you insist, but you're the one who knows exactly how it should be done. I believe Mr. Florey and Mr. Tukes are conscientious attendants, but they can't possibly know how to set up for two consecutive emergency surgeries—particularly one that no one's ever heard of," she added dryly.

"I know," he said patiently, "and I'll come back and see that they've done it right, Doc. It'll all be in perfect order before you set foot in the theater, I promise."

She stared at him suspiciously. "What is it, Shiloh? What's so pressing that you can't attend to this yourself?"

His eyes fell, to Cheney's amazement. Normally Shiloh always looked a person straight in the eye as he was speaking to them. "I . . . I just wanted to go see that little Chinese girl," he said in a muffled tone. "I thought someone ought to." He didn't sound embarrassed, merely uncomfortable.

Cheney's face immediately softened. "Well, why didn't you say so, you great ninny?" His head shot up, and he gave her an exasperated look, so she went on with feigned impatience, "Well? Go on, Shiloh. What are you loitering about here for? You—Mr. Tukes, come with me. We're going to get Mr. Florey right now so you two can start getting that theater set up. And mind, you turn on and turn up all those gas lights! I cannot abide doctors who operate with dramatic lighting, as if they're great actors on a stage!"

★ ★ ★ ★

Shiloh hesitated outside the screens that shielded Ren Xandou. He heard Reverend Merced, his voice a pleasant rumble, speaking insistently. With a start he realized that the pastor was speaking Chinese. Shiloh slipped between the cubicles and stood still.

The elderly man looked up and nodded but kept speaking quietly to the girl. Shiloh caught two English words: Jesus Christ. The girl nodded once, twice, and Reverend Merced patted her dying-flower hand.

She was almost dead, Shiloh knew instantly. No blood colored her face. Even the attractive golden hue of the Orient had drained away. Her lips, too, had no color; they were merely faint outlines done with a child's palest blue chalk. Her hair was the only thing about her that looked alive. It shimmered with rich life, fanning over the pillow, onto the bed, and down past the mattress, in glorious ebony waves. Shiloh wanted to touch it.

"Son? Did you come to say something to Miss Ren? I know—and she knows—that no doctors can help her now," Reverend Merced said quietly.

Shiloh swallowed hard. "No, sir. I . . . I guess I just came, to . . . to be with her. Maybe it's kinda selfish of me, but . . . but . . ." He almost choked.

"It doesn't seem a selfish act to be with a stranger in her last moments," Reverend Merced commented in such a strong and sure voice that Shiloh was able to draw from it. "I think it is a kind and noble act."

Shiloh stared at the girl, and very slowly she turned her eyes to him. They weren't dead eyes, not yet; the candle of life still flickered faintly.

"You wanted to tell her something, perhaps?" Reverend Merced asked Shiloh mildly. "I could translate for you."

Shiloh moved closer to her so he could see her face and remember it. She watched him, without curiosity, without emotion, only with the slightest hint of inquiry. Before he could restrain himself, he reached out and touched her hair with feather-light fingers. She almost smiled. He was encouraged, so he picked up a few of the black satin strands and gently caressed them. Staring down at her hair, he spoke as if he were in a trance, but he paused after every few sentences to allow Reverend Merced to translate for him. The girl kept her eyes on Shiloh's face.

"A girl—I think she must have been like you—young and so pretty, with such beautiful, glowing hair, saved my life once when . . . when . . . I was just a little baby," he said haltingly. Reverend Merced translated.

"I'll always remember her, even though I never met her, didn't even know about her until just a few months ago. But she lives on . . . in my memory," he said softly. "I can see her . . . I can see her face, like yours, with those unforgettable eyes. . . . I can see her hair, like this, like a rich, glowing river. . . ."

Reverend Merced translated, the Chinese interpretation seeming to take much longer than Shiloh's simple words.

"I couldn't thank her. But I'll never forget her," Shiloh finished in a hoarse whisper. "And, Little Wren, I think I'll never forget you."

She listened to Reverend Merced's words—they sounded unreal, alien, a singsong nonsense to Shiloh—but she smiled. Then she whispered something, and the pastor nodded. Later Reverend Merced gave Shiloh three strands of Ren Xandou's hair . . . fulfilling her last wish.

She closed her eyes and sighed gently. She took a breath—as light as a spring's playful breeze—then another, and another.

Reverend Justice Merced and Shiloh Irons stood on either side of Ren Xandou's bed, holding her bloodless hands and watching her in silence. She never opened her eyes or spoke again. The two men stayed like that until she died.

He that is slow to anger
Is better than the mighty;
And he that ruleth his spirit
Than he that taketh a city.

Proverbs 16:32

13

RENAISSANCE AND BAROQUE

Steen House, on the inside, was a sprawling manor house. The outside, however, had a different aura. Modeled after the English architect Richard Norman Shaw's radical new designs, Steen House, like other Queen Anne style buildings, appeared to be neither classical nor medieval. It was highly eclectic, ornate, and rather whimsical.

The first floor was of narrow clapboards, the second floor was of intricately designed and laid shingles. Twin gables, very steep, were prominent on either side of the double entrance doors, which formed a single arch. Two corner turrets, borrowed from the French *chateaux*, rounded the sides of the house. Long banks of tall narrow windows adorned the front, while wide low bay windows jutted from both sides. The chimneys were massive, the roof was steeply gabled, the moldings and trim were highly stylized decorative woodwork. The house was painted a mild sky blue, and the trim was a creamy yellow.

As Cheney and Shiloh rounded the last curve of Russian Hill before turning into the circular drive of Steen House, Cheney yanked Eugènie to an abrupt halt. "Oh no," she muttered. "Morning callers!"

Two carriages were pulled up close to the front door. The one in front was a landau with two footmen, one of whom was already walking up on the veranda to ring. The other carriage—a barouche with a driver only—sat patiently, the driver waiting a decent interval before ringing the bell to leave his master's or mistress's card.

"We could go back down the hill and take the bridle path to the stables," Shiloh suggested, "then come up through the gardens."

"Excellent idea," Cheney declared. "I just can't face callers right now, after the night we've had. Gracious! Calling at this time of the morning!"

Shiloh and Cheney turned their horses, and Shiloh led the way back down the hill through an opening in the tall hedges that encircled the grounds of Steen House onto a dirt pathway that followed the inside of the hedge.

"What time is it, anyway?" Cheney asked peevishly.

"Ten-eighteen," Shiloh answered, checking his pocketwatch. Four sad notes of *When Johnnie Comes Marching Home* filtered out but were quickly smothered as Shiloh snapped the gold cover shut. Cheney had given him the watch two years ago for Christmas. He had bought a plain brass pocketwatch, which he kept in his medical bag and used for work, but he was always careful to keep Cheney's watch with him and use it all other times. It was the most expensive item he had ever owned and he treasured it, though not solely for that reason.

"So rude to make such early calls," Cheney complained. She was exhausted but was at that peculiar stage where she felt irritating surges of nervous energy coursing through her. Her eyes, though shadowed slightly with fatigue, glittered brilliantly. Her neck and shoulders ached, but she was unable to command them to loosen.

"Yeah," Shiloh agreed indignantly. "Making morning calls in the morning! What can they be thinking?"

"I can't imagine," Cheney grumbled, oblivious to the irony.

They followed the path downhill, catching occasional glimpses of the wide stone walkway that led up to the house through the trees. When they were about halfway down, Shiloh suddenly whistled, making Eugènie start and rear. Cheney scolded her sharply. Shiloh gave Cheney a penetrating look, but Cheney didn't see, as she was struggling to control the mare, who was evidently reflecting her mistress's disquiet.

Tim and Eddie Yancey had been walking down the main garden walk, but at Shiloh's whistle they turned and hurried through the terraced flower beds toward him. "Hello, boys," Shiloh called. "Would you mind taking the horses down?"

"No, sir," Tim, the older boy, replied. He was eighteen, and Eddie was sixteen. They were nice-looking boys, with identical sparkling brown eyes and crisply curling brown locks. Tim was perhaps the more attractive of the two, for he was bright and confident, while Eddie was shy and reserved. "We're going down to the stables, anyway, Mr. Irons. Good morning, Dr. Duvall," Tim continued. "Mrs. de Lancie's going shopping, so we're going to help Dad get the carriage ready."

Cheney and Shiloh dismounted and handed the reins over to the two young men with relief. Though the gardens behind Steen House were ingeniously staggered, and the wide path leading up to the house was gently terraced, it was still quite a climb from the bottom of the hill.

The pathway was of square gray flagstones laid in a diamond pattern. It was the main avenue through the gardens and was a full six feet wide. Since the gardens had been so cleverly built up along the hill, the path was more like a series of terraces, with only one or two gentle steps to ascend to the next level.

Shiloh looked around with interest. He liked the grounds of Steen House, which were modeled after English country gardens. The trees were mostly bishop pines, with occasional oak trees dotted here and there. The gardens, though carefully landscaped, were predominantly planted with ferns and ivy, along with some plantings of flowers that grew wild on the peninsula: yellow bush lupine, manzanita, cream bush, toyon, coffee berry, chamise, monkeyflowers. The effect was of lush woodland green, with the gentle colors of the wildflowers only incidental. As they neared the house, the sides of the path were planted with more cultivated species: pink and blue hydrangeas, azaleas, camellias, rambling roses. These, however, served merely as colorful borders to the walkway and were pruned to grow low to the ground, in keeping with the woodland atmosphere.

Cheney, however, saw no hydrangeas nor wildflowers nor indeed even the flagstone walkway, though she had her head down, appearing to study the path. Her eyes were narrowed to slits, and her steps were quick and impatient.

"Hey, Doc, wait for me," Shiloh muttered, widening his stride to catch up to her. "You're steamin' on like you're marchin' to Georgia or somethin'."

"Hmm? Oh, sorry, I was just thinking," she replied absently, though she did slow down to a more leisurely pace.

"Well, I'm not," Shiloh declared.

"What? That's silly! Of course you're thinking! You can't help thinking!" Cheney said.

"I can."

"You can," Cheney repeated icily. "How?"

"I dunno. Can't think." His eyes, a bright blaze of blue, cut toward her.

"Oh, you!" Cheney pinched him, and he caught her hand, tucking her arm through his securely. She walked closer to him, laughing at his silliness, and he smiled.

The back of the house was spanned by a screen-enclosed loggia on the first floor and a wide balcony on the second. The entire length of the house had a generous terrace, which held brightly blooming roses in great stone urns formally placed. Four wrought-iron dining tables, each with four chairs and a generous umbrella, lined the terrace. Victoria sat at one, which was covered with a snowy white linen tablecloth. Behind her Mrs. O'Neil stood subserviently in front of another square table on which a bright silver tea service and three platters with silver covers gleamed.

Victoria, Cheney reflected, looked like the subject of a soft watercolor. Her silver hair, as yet undressed, fell loose about her shoulders and gleamed brightly in the cool morning light. She was wearing blinding white, a loose sacque jacket and matching skirt, trimmed with airy white lace and inset with pink ribbons. As Cheney and Shiloh neared her, she slowly raised a teacup to her lips, her grace and elegance pronounced even in private repose. On the table was a silver bowl with a simple arrangement of pears and grapes. Victoria was reading the morning newspaper, relaxed in the cushioned chair, resting against the back, her legs crossed but still angled to the side in a most refined manner. She looked up, smiled, and unconsciously straightened into a more formal posture.

"Good morning, you two. Truants, are we?"

"Aren't we all?" Cheney asked, sinking into a chair. Shiloh courteously held it for her, then made a little bow to Victoria.

"May I join you, Mrs. de Lancie?" he asked.

Pleasure lighted Victoria's normally distant expression, for she appreciated Shiloh's lack of presumption toward her; he never treated her with uncomfortable familiarity, even when their meetings were informal—even intimate—such as this. Since this made her trust him even more, she was more comfortable with Shiloh than she was with almost anyone, except, of course, Cheney and Devlin Buchanan. Relaxing back into her previous, less formal pose, she answered with pleasure, "Please do, Shiloh. I'd welcome your company, and I'm sure both of you would like some breakfast." She made a slight gesture to Mrs. O'Neil, who unobtrusively set tableware and napkins for Cheney and Shiloh, and then served them coffee, two sugars and heavy cream for Cheney and black for Shiloh.

"Thank you, Mrs. O'Neil," he murmured. "You remembered I like it black in the mornings."

She nodded, then began to prepare plates for them.

"You look exquisite," Cheney said wearily, eyeing Victoria's daintiness with a jaundiced eye. "And I, as usual, am rumpled."

"Difficult night, was it?" Victoria asked sympathetically. "But, Cheney, you are not *rumpled*, not strictly, not in the sense that you are disheveled."

"I," Cheney insisted stubbornly, "am rumpled. And I am starving. I know you're not having anything for breakfast, either. All you ever eat is . . . honey and flowers and . . . and . . . mead."

Victoria looked amused, while Shiloh looked mournfully down at the tidy brown egg in the delicate porcelain eggcup that Mrs. O'Neil placed in front of him. "And hummingbird's eggs," he added sadly.

"Mrs. O'Neil, please go prepare a more substantial breakfast for Dr. Duvall and Mr. Irons," Victoria said. "Their favorites are, I believe, steak and potatoes and eggs fried with runny yellows, topped with sharp cheese." Shuddering delicately, she asked them politely, "If you would care to wait, I'm certain Mrs. O'Neil can make you some biscuits."

"No, I'm too hungry," Cheney declared.

"I am too," Shiloh agreed. "Just bread and butter and jam. Lots of it, please."

"Lots of bread and butter and jam," Victoria obediently dictated to Mrs. O'Neil.

"Very good, mum," she said in a low voice and glided into the house.

"She talks," Cheney observed. "I wasn't too sure of it."

"Yes, but so far all I've heard her say is 'Yes, ma'am,' 'Very good, ma'am,' and 'Thank you, ma'am,' " Victoria declared. "Limited vocabulary, but adequate for a servant, I suppose."

"She's got a secret," Shiloh said airily, popping a grape into his mouth and crunching with enjoyment. "And she's also got a son."

Cheney's and Victoria's gazes honed in on his face. "Secret? What secret?" Victoria demanded.

Shiloh shrugged. "I dunno. It's a secret."

"He's full of pithy wisdom today," Cheney told Victoria with ire. "Don't pay any attention to him."

"Well, is the son a secret?" Victoria persisted, ignoring Cheney.

"Don't guess so," Shiloh answered, picking four more grapes off the bunch and lining them up neatly in front of him to be demolished methodically. "She told me he's sixteen, his name is Ennis, he's handsome like his father, and he's a troublemaker like his father."

"Why do people tell you these things?" Cheney demanded with exasperation.

Victoria's face changed just the slightest bit; a light of knowing, of understanding, crossed her delicate features. She dropped her eyes and sipped her tea. Shiloh glanced at her, then stared at Cheney's openly puzzled expression. Finally he answered dryly, "Doc, servants talk. They don't talk to you, and they wouldn't talk to Mrs. de Lancie. But they talk to each other all the time."

"But you're not a servant," she protested. "You're . . . you're . . ."

"What?" he challenged her.

Now Cheney looked confused and distraught. Victoria watched her, then said to her, "I perceive Shiloh to be in a class all by himself—well, perhaps I should include your father with him, Cheney. You see, everyone is comfortable with Shiloh, and that is a very special standing, indeed."

"Why, thank you, Mrs. de Lancie," Shiloh said, obviously pleased. "That's a real nice thing to say."

"Truthful," Victoria corrected him briskly. "Cheney, you seem overwrought this morning. Was it because of last night? Was it truly difficult at the hospital?"

"It was horrible," Cheney answered with a tinge of anger. "I've never felt so . . . disorganized and . . . inadequate in my life."

"You did a really good job, Doc," Shiloh put in quietly. "No one could have done any better."

"What happened?" Victoria asked.

"Everything," Cheney asserted stiffly. "Pneumonia. Emergency surgeries. One young girl with an acute hemorrhage. She died. Two very difficult births. One of the babies was fine, though the mother had a terrible time of it. The other . . . the other . . ."

"We lost a baby," Shiloh went on, as Cheney had to stop to swallow hard several times, her face working painfully. "It just couldn't be helped. It—"

"He," Cheney said in a thick voice.

"He was too early, and no one can stop that or change it," Shiloh explained. No grief sounded in his voice, but his jaw tightened.

To Shiloh's consternation, Victoria's eyes filled with tears. He was still searching for something to say when she pulled herself ramrod-straight and impatiently, quickly swiped at her eyes. Cheney's head was bent, so she didn't see. "So tragic," Victoria said softly, but her voice was strong. "Even though we know that the baby is with our Lord Jesus Christ now—and that should be the greatest comfort of all—it's so hard not to grieve for babies."

Cheney seemed not to hear. "And all of those boys, stuck in that dark and deserted wing . . . and the nurses! They've had absolutely no training in emergencies! Even though they meant well—even Miss Rees—they were almost useless! I'm going to make a report—yes, that's it! I shall make a report on the unreadiness of the hospital for emergency care, and I'll make recommendations for changes in staff training and supply inventory. Shiloh, you'll help me, won't you?"

Reluctantly Shiloh replied, "Well, sure, Doc, but listen, you—"

"And Dr. Baird should set aside at least part of one of the wings for an emergency . . . um . . . area, to process the patients when the ambulances come in!" Cheney frowned, deep in thought. "How do the ambulances get called out? Someone just comes running, don't they? Isn't that rather inefficient? Why can't we have a telegraph station, like City and County Hospital?"

"Whoa, there, Doc," Shiloh said with an attempt at lightness. "You're gallopin' off again. All that reportin' and recommendin' sounds like a lot of work to me. Didn't I—and you—just get off work? D'ya think we could leave it for at least an hour or two?"

"Yes, Cheney, you really should," Victoria insisted. "You work much too hard, anyway. Why don't we just enjoy this lovely morning and talk about something fun?"

"Fun?" Cheney echoed quizzically.

"Yes, fun," Victoria repeated darkly. "I'm sure you recall having fun? You know, those times when people smile and laugh and say witty, rather meaningless things? They go places to look at things and do things that aren't of grave importance?"

Suddenly Cheney softened. "Oh yes, I dimly recall something like that. For example, would one such instance have something to do with lots of money and stores and purchases of goods?"

Victoria was suddenly animated. "Shopping! Oh, would you—but you're too tired, aren't you, Cheney, to go shopping with me?"

Cheney smiled. "I may fall apart in an hour or two, Victoria, but right now I feel as if I'm bursting with energy. I believe it would be good for me to go out today and forget last night. For a while, anyway."

"Right," Shiloh said with satisfaction. Both women looked speculatively at him, and suddenly his firm mouth drooped. "You . . . you don't need me to escort you, do you, ladies? I mean, I . . . it . . . I . . ."

Cheney and Victoria exchanged sly glances, then laughed at Shiloh's woebegone expression. "No, Shiloh, dear, we shall be fine," Victoria said. "But thank you for offering—I think."

Suddenly he narrowed his eyes and looked stormy. "Wait a minute. You two aren't going someplace you don't need to be going, are you?"

"Why, whatever do you mean?" Victoria asked angelically.

"You never did take me to see that opium den, Shiloh," Cheney said thoughtfully.

"I know where one is," Victoria told her brightly. "That wild girl, Lily Hitchcock Coit, was at the Watermans' party last night, and she told all of us which of the dens in Chinatown is where the very best people all go."

Now Shiloh's eyes widened, and his mouth tightened to a ruler-straight line. "Now, listen here, Doc, Mrs. de Lancie—"

Cheney and Victoria both tried very hard to keep their faces innocently bland, but neither of them could manage when they saw Shiloh's outrage. They burst out laughing.

"Some joke," Shiloh said, not at all amused. "You two better stay out of Chinatown. And the Barbary Coast. And South of Market. And the Embarcadero—Meigg's Wharf, especially. And—"

"Shiloh, we'll be fine," Cheney scoffed. "And we'll be good, I promise."

"Yes, Shiloh. Today we are just going to Gump's and then to the City of Paris. Perhaps to Ghirardelli's," Victoria added, smiling dreamily, "for chocolate."

"Mmm, Ghirardelli's chocolate," Cheney repeated softly. "Do we have any right now? Any of those thin little wafers?"

"No, and you may not have any for breakfast," Victoria scolded. "Your plow hand's feast will be here soon."

Cheney sighed. "Well, I'm not a delicate fairy-tale princess like you, Victoria. I can't live on love and mead and flowers. I need food."

"And if I could eat as you do," Victoria said enviously, "I would. Only I should look like one of those fat, sassy sea lions at Cliff House."

Severely Shiloh studied first Cheney, then Victoria. "Both of you," he finally said firmly, "are beautiful and gracious and elegant ladies. So stay out of Chinatown."

★ ★ ★ ★

Persons of consequence in the city of San Francisco shopped in Portsmouth Square, which was bordered by DuPont Avenue, the first street laid in the little city of less than three hundred people. But as the number of people and streets grew, and DuPont Avenue came to be known as *Du Pon Gai* by the Chinese who lived there, San Francisco's members of high society slowly drifted southward.

Then for a time many elegant ladies, usually escorted by finely dressed men, could be seen promenading along Kearny Street. In the wake of such persons fine retail stores always appeared, so that they could promenade right into them and spend some of their gold. But still, the plain working people and plain working buildings inexorably followed them too, so the quality drifted even further south, followed by their inevitable retinue.

Around the end of The War between the States, in 1865, wealthy and fashionable persons began to be seen and noted promenading in the small park known as Union Square. Miraculously, elegant stores soon surrounded that square, and now not only glittering gold dust but gleaming chunks of silver were the basis of the steady flow of exchange.

"What's at Gump's?" Cheney asked as the grand landau clattered over the still-rough plank streets.

"All sorts of wonders," Victoria replied merrily. "Jade—green-fire jade and milky-white jade of purity. Wondrous pearls from the mysterious depths of the China Sea. Magical silks spun by lovely butterflies. Fragrant incense, the smoke of the heavens. Strange, mythical creatures made of precious stones who come alive at midnight, if you can convince them you aren't watching them."

"Would they take mythical money, do you think?" Cheney asked mischievously.

"I doubt it very seriously," Victoria replied, her blue eyes sparkling aquamarine. "The two Gump brothers are German, and very down-to-earth, considering they deal in such fanciful goods."

"So what fanciful goods are we buying today?"

"I don't know. I haven't seen what I want at Gump's yet."

"But you will see something you want," Cheney predicted.

"I'm sure. We still need something for the drawing room. I don't know what, but I will when I see it—and also accessories for the music room, to enhance the piano—"

"We have a piano in the music room?" Cheney asked, bewildered. "I thought it had the Louis XV parlor suite and the cushion mirror."

"It did, but I moved them into the great hall when the piano arrived," Victoria said impatiently. "Do you mean you haven't seen our exquisite piano in the music room? It's a Gaveau grand made of kingwood, with gilt bronze mounts."

"Oh," Cheney said uncertainly. "I guess I haven't been in the music room . . . lately."

"Ever?" Victoria sternly asked.

"I must have been, sometime," Cheney muttered, her brow wrinkling. "I knew about the parlor suite."

"That's only because I asked you if I should move it into the great hall, in the corner, for a focal point," Victoria said with exasperation. "You said yes."

"I did? Oh, I did. Well, how does it look in the great hall?"

"You haven't been in there, either."

Cheney smiled, the corners of her eyes crinkling. "I was sometime, I think. It seems I remember what it looks like."

"Do you? What does it look like?" Victoria demanded accusingly.

"It's . . . uh . . . big. And empty. Except, of course," Cheney added mischievously, "for the lovely Louis XV parlor suite and the matching cushion mirror in the corner."

"Just as I thought," Victoria declared. "You haven't been in there, either. Cheney, how are you supposed to help me choose furnishings and accent pieces if you haven't even seen the house?"

"I don't know," Cheney ingenuously admitted.

The two women stared at each other, Cheney with such bewilderment and Victoria with such indignation that they both started giggling.

"It doesn't matter," Victoria finally admitted. "You have good taste. I will value your opinion, anyway."

"You will?" Cheney asked with some surprise. At Victoria's quizzical look she went on, "It's just that we're so different, Victoria. Our tastes are almost completely opposed."

"Perhaps our preferences are different," Victoria stated, "but we both have good taste." She smiled warmly. "It's just that you, Cheney love, are Renaissance. I, on the other hand, am Baroque."

"What on earth does that mean?" Cheney asked.

"I haven't the foggiest notion," Victoria replied, her eyes dancing. "But a gentleman said that of us once, and I thought it sounded so lovely and romantic."

They both laughed, and Victoria thought, again, how wonderfully unselfconscious her friend was. *No, that's not right . . . she's completely unconscious of how compelling, how exotic, she is . . . any other woman would immediately have demanded to know who this gentleman was that was making such romantic observations of the two of us . . . but it never even occurred to Cheney . . . and likely never will.*

The landau came to a stop, and immediately Tim and Eddie appeared at the side to open the door, lower the stairs, and assist Cheney and Victoria out. They were stopped in the middle of the street, oblivious to traffic both behind and in front, so that the ladies could go straight into Gump's.

"We're going just down to the City of Paris, on Stockton, after we finish here, Tim," Victoria told him. "You may take the carriage over to the square and park it. When we're ready we'll just walk over there and find you."

"Thank you, ma'am," Tim said, then hopped up on the driver's step to relate the instructions to his father.

Cheney and Victoria entered Gump's, one of the most elegant and expensive stores in San Francisco. As the trade in Oriental goods had prospered, and the demands for all notions from the mysterious Far East had increased, Gump's had prospered exceedingly since their establishment only two years before. They sold mostly Oriental goods, but they had added imports from other faraway lands, disdaining more prosaic American items.

The Gump brothers had proven to be shrewd in retailing. Instead of the wall-to-wall-to-ceiling clutter that most retail stores displayed, they had chosen instead to follow the dictates of Oriental culture in arranging their fineries. The large open ground floor room was painted a simple muted blue-white, with spotless white marble floors, delicately veined with blue. The room was cleverly sectioned off into squares, with a certain type of good displayed in each area: pearls and other jewelry in one, silks in another, statues and vases and urns in yet another, and so on. Instead of having an immense warehouse room to display furniture pieces, the furniture was incorporated into the displays of other goods, so that each section formed its own tableaux, with one exquisite piece the focal point.

Cheney and Victoria both paused just inside the front door, and with identical assessing expressions, they studied the glittering grandeur laid out in front of them. Then in the same instant Cheney went left and Victoria went right.

The older Mr. Gump—neither of them ever made his first name known—hurried to Victoria's side. His brother, having observed closely Mrs. Victoria Elizabeth Steen de Lancie's companion, followed Cheney. Both men were tall and stern, with hawk noses and far-seeing blue eyes. The older brother was about fifty, with graying and thinning hair, while the younger was about thirty. His hair was an indifferent blond, and he kept it severely plastered down.

Stepping to Cheney's side, he bowed with military precision and announced stentorially, "I am Mr. Gump. I am honored by your patronage today, madam. May I have the great pleasure of assisting you?"

"Good afternoon, Mr. Gump," Cheney said, offering him her hand, which he bent over but did not kiss. "I am Dr. Cheney Duvall, and I like this secretary. Will you tell me about it, please, and name a price?"

"Ah yes, this is a very fine piece," he agreed gravely. "It is unique, is it not?"

"It's certainly different," Cheney said with a tinge of humor. "I imagine it's not to everyone's taste. But I do like it."

The "very fine piece" was, tactfully stated, unique. It was, not strictly, a secretary, for it had no knee-space; it was not a cabinet, for it was built too low; and it was not a chest, for the drawer space was negligible. The frame was made of bamboo, and the insets were of plain black lacquer, with mirrors in six of them: two round mirrors, two square ones, and two diamond-shaped ones. Two tall, thin drawers were on each side, but the middle piece and the bottom tiers were open shelves. The top had a rather peculiar structure as a back, made of steamed and shaped bamboo, partly geometrical squares and diamond shapes, and partly curlicues and arches.

With a smile that was mostly a cool gleam in his eyes, Mr. Gump recited: "This is a fine cabinet, made in Kiao-chow, of the Shantung province. The lacquer panels, framed mirrors, and the high quality of its architectural elements make it of special interest. But the superiority of the frame construction is why this piece is in Gump's. You will note that there are no other bamboo pieces here? That's because we have found that, generally, bamboo is a structural disaster. It resists glues, splinters at the approach of a saw, and cracks when nailed. But this piece—please, madam—test the sturdiness of construction—you see? It's not at all rickety, and you hear no creaks when you shake it. You may search this fine cabinet, and you will find no cracks, no splinters, because there are no nails. Yes, it's glued together, but it's seamless work. My brother and I tried to find out what kind of glue the craftsman used," he said wryly, with the hint of the smile lightening his eyes once again, "but the gentleman's English appeared to get suddenly worse. In fact, it became, at that point, almost unintelligible."

"I'll take it," Cheney said, smiling.

"Wonderful, madam," Mr. Gump said, rubbing his long, strong hands together.

"Oh no," Victoria murmured, suddenly appearing at Cheney's side. "This?"

"Don't you like it, Victoria?" Cheney asked mischievously.

"Um . . . it's quite . . . unique," Victoria hummed.

"Quite," Cheney said happily.

"Quite," Mr. Gump agreed, also happily. "Madam Duvall—"

"Doctor," Cheney politely corrected him.

"Please accept my sincerest apologies, I misunderstood you, madam," Mr. Gump said gallantly. "Dr. Duvall, this piece is indeed unique—by that, I mean that it is hand-crafted by—"

"Yes, the little Chinaman who doesn't speak good English when asked about his methods," Cheney said crisply. "And I know that that means it's a one-of-a-kind."

"It most certainly is that," Victoria ardently agreed.

Ignoring her, Cheney went on, "So kindly give me a price, Mr. Gump, and we shall see if I can take this lovely cabinet home."

"Eighty-three dollars and seventy-nine cents," Mr. Gump said plainly.

"I believe fifty dollars would be a fair price, Mr. Gump," Cheney said firmly.

"I'm afraid I couldn't let this lovely piece go for that little, madam—pardon me, Dr. Duvall," he said with sad regret. "I could, perhaps, come down a bit—"

"Sixty-seven dollars and eighteen cents," Cheney said gaily.

Mr. Gump's stern face crumpled into high mirth. "Dr. Duvall, in recognition of your shrewd bartering instincts, I will allow you to have this piece for seventy-one dollars and four cents."

"Sold," Cheney said with satisfaction.

"Now, Mrs. de Lancie, how may I be of assistance to you today?" he asked immediately, seizing the opportunity of the moment.

"I am purchasing that four-partitioned screen over there, and that lacquer cabinet over there, Mr. Gump," Victoria replied, smiling. "But Mr. Gump has already assisted me with these purchases."

"Madam de Lancie, we have some lovely pearls that I purchased in Italy last summer," he said quickly. "I thought I should keep them, for they are exquisite; but as I've not been blessed with a wife, I decided just yesterday to display and sell them. May I be so bold, Mrs. de Lancie, to inquire if you would be interested in them?"

"Perhaps," Victoria said, her eyes shining. "Italian, you say?"

"Yes—they are Venetian," he said reverently. "Very old, and unlike precious stones, pearls only grow more lustrous with age. If you will forgive me, Mrs. de Lancie, these pearls are exquisite, a superb, glowing ecru, and they would complement your beauty as no vulgar glitter ever could."

"Ah yes," Victoria said with barely concealed amusement. "I do see the point you are making. And these pearls—old, you say? Are they antiquities?"

"Indeed they are," he answered eagerly. "The collection—it is a necklace, earrings, and a magnificent comb—are set in gold and have a signature mark that was used from 1580 to almost the turn of the seventeenth century."

Cheney and Victoria looked at each other wide-eyed. "Baroque," Cheney whispered.

"I'll take them," Victoria instantly announced.

This unsettled even the somber Mr. Gump. He swallowed, then gulped, "Sight unseen? Price unknown?"

"Yes," Victoria said firmly. Cheney nodded eagerly.

For the first time in two years, both Mr. Gumps left their store early—immediately after Madam Victoria Elizabeth Steen de Lancie and her companion, Dr. Cheney Duvall, left. Their celebration at the Oriental Palace Restaurant lasted until long past midnight.

14

That Shiny Foolery

Two gentlemen, young and dashing and dapper, sauntered up Stockton Street toward Tasker's Sartorial Salon. Jauntily they stepped, nimbly making their way through a gauntlet of wares, as many of the stores, lacking display windows, placed their goods outside right on the sidewalk. The tall, cheerful gentleman swung an ebony cane, while the shorter, handsome one gestured with an ivory one. They passed a dry goods store with cans and jars and bottles stacked along the frontage; a clothing store with piles of ugly brown and gray woolen items untidily folded and strewn on the walk; a market with baskets of fruits and vegetables piled helter-skelter. Great grisly chunks of unidentifiable meat, emitting thick odors of blood and tripe, hung from hooks suspended from a simple rack over the front door of a butcher shop. They were passing just in front of the Washoe Safe Works when their avid searching eyes lit on a vision—or rather two visions.

Two women appeared to float toward them. One was tall, stern, with the sinewy allure of a naiad, and she wore a fiery coral dress that seemed to the two dazzled young gentlemen to shimmer with heat. The other was airy, ethereal, with the crystalline, untouchable loveliness of a sylph, and her clothing was of such icy, translucent blue satin that it seemed it would melt at a man's ungracious touch. Fair, haughty, neither of them appeared to see the two young men stepping hastily aside to allow them to pass.

The comely gentleman with the ivory cane elegantly pirouetted to his right, sweeping off his silk top hat with alacrity and tucking his cane securely under his left arm out of the ladies' way. Unfortunately, as he took a small steadying step behind in order to make a flourish of a bow, he stepped off the sidewalk, lost his balance, and crashed to the street, landing in a most undignified sprawl directly in the middle of a healthy horse's leavings.

The other tall gentleman, who was more athletic, swept up his cane, doffed his hat, and performed a gallant sweeping bow, but the mischievous fates amused themselves with him too. One of Washoe's sturdy safes squatted directly behind him. With surprising speed he sat down on top of the safe, then vaulted backward over it, his legs obediently following his head. Tragically, Washoe's Safe Company was located right next to Larkin's Hardware, and the gentlemen's lost feet knocked over a tripod stand of shovels, which knocked over four plows, which knocked over a phalanx of picks, of which the last one in the row fell on Mr. Larkin's toe.

The visions sailed past, majestically unaware of the commotion in their gentle wake. Their eyes searched straight ahead, far beyond the clownish mortals who groveled—however unintentionally—at their satin-shod feet. Languorously they glided past the lurid meat, the array of bright vegetables, the drab clothing, the prosaic bottles and jars, and disappeared into the glitter of the City of Paris.

As soon as the ten-foot-high entrance doors silently closed behind them, Cheney and Victoria glanced at each other. Cheney, unable to contain her mirth a moment longer, burst into laughter, while Victoria daintily opened her fan in order to stifle her giggles behind it.

Victoria Elizabeth Steen de Lancie was never long unattended in any retail establishment, and the illustrious City of Paris was not to be excepted. Monsieur Félix Verdier hurried up the long main aisle.

Long, bony, with a prominent hook nose and heavy-lidded sad eyes, Monsieur Verdier dressed impeccably and spoke English with a liquid French flavoring. In 1850 Monsieur Verdier came to sprawling, gold-swollen San Francisco, and his modest trunkfuls of fabrics and lace were snatched up so fast that he returned to Nîmes immediately for more, and more, and better. Upon his return he founded the City of Paris—named after the blessed ship that brought him to this El Dorado—and the grand four-story retail store had prospered magically ever since. Monsieur Verdier's trips to France were now leisurely and expensive, and he made vast purchases from Paris and Nîmes and Lyon, and also from grateful little villages such as Limoges, Aubusson, and Sèvres.

By the time he reached Cheney and Victoria, they had regained their composure. In spite of his angularity he kissed their hands with fluid grace and with a flourish entreated them to follow him to a showroom especially set up just that morning for Madame de Lancie's perusal.

As they followed the so-busy Frenchman toward the rear of the store, Cheney struggled to look at the clutter and jumble of goods crowding each side of the generous red-carpeted main aisle. Countless bolts of rainbow fabrics, jungles of rolls of fabulous laces, glittering glass, gleaming porcelain, shoes, ribbons, gloves, jewels and jewelry, headless hats, abundant reticules, parasols, shawls, feathers, beads, ruffles, linens, forests of pillows and cushions, paintings, mirrors, dinnerware, tapestries, a magnificence of perfumes. Cheney's senses were assaulted. Her eyes darted here, then there; she heard the echoes of ladies' voices, querulous, inquiring, dissenting; she smelled flowery perfume, the acidic odor of new dye, the dusky scents of old tapestries.

"You've made arrangements for a private showing of some goods?" she asked Victoria curiously.

"Yes, Monsieur Verdier contacted me when he received a shipment from Bordeaux," Victoria answered as they hurried to keep up with the Frenchman's long stalking gait. "He bought two estate lots and inquired if I would be interested in some fine Sèvres porcelain."

"And I gather that you are."

"Oh yes, I love Sèvres," Victoria replied, glancing at Cheney. "Do you?"

"As a matter of fact I do. Particularly the blue," Cheney answered enthusiastically. "Blue is my favorite color, and I think Sèvres is the most heavenly shade."

Monsieur Verdier led them to the back of the store. A generous space had been cleared of more common merchandise, so that the empyreal porcelain of the small village in France might be showcased in a lofty manner.

"*Voila*, Madame de Lancie, Mademoiselle Duvall," Monsieur Verdier announced dramatically. "The splendid Sèvres."

An ancient Flemish tapestry had been suspended from the ceiling with golden ropes and fat tassels in order to set off a cubicle from the rest of the busy floor. A handsome Aubusson rug anchored the tableaux. Two Louis XV commodes with jewel-like marble tops held an array of the collection. To one side loomed a magnificent Empire ormolu-mounted *bibliotheque*, with the golden double doors opened, and more translucent porcelain glowed inside. Beside it was a Louis XV ormolu-mounted chair covered in heavy silk damask, with matching enormous urns on either side colored in dreamy colors of cream, rose, and peach.

On the other side a spindle-legged round marble Louis XV occasional table stood, displaying a richly hued seven-piece dinner setting of royal blue trimmed in gold. Victoria's eyes gleamed, and she nonchalantly moved to the table to study the setting. "Do you have a full dinnerware collection of this, Monsieur Verdier?"

"*Mais oui, madame,*" he answered gleefully. "One hundred fourteen pieces."

"I shall take it all. And the table," Victoria decided, and Monsieur Verdier's droopy features were ecstatic.

"Exquisite," Victoria murmured, moving slowly to marvel at the collection of small items on one of the commodes: a mantel clock with a sculpture of cupids mounted on top; two stately bronze *doré* candelabra; two candlesticks, small and intimate; a covered urn; a pair of cachepots; a bronze *doré* box; a footed truffle dish. Each had the typical Sèvres pastoral scenes in soft-focus pastels of seventeenth-century maids and gentlemen surrounded by flowers upon a creamy blue background.

"Ah yes, the exquisite clock," Monsieur Verdier murmured appreciatively. Victoria had touched one delicate gloved finger to the finely crafted sculpture on top of the clock. "This clock is a Louis XVI mantel clock, and the sculpture is by Boucher."

Behind Victoria, Cheney delicately cleared her throat. "Um . . . *pardonnez-moi,* monsieur, but I believe you are mistaken. François Boucher was court artist to Louis XV, not his son, whose reign began in 1774. Boucher died in 1770, you know."

"Eh? What do you say, mademoiselle?" Monsieur Verdier asked stiffly. "You tell me the sculpture is not a Boucher?"

"*Mais non,* monsieur," Cheney replied hastily. "Obviously it is a Boucher. It's just that that would make the piece a Louis XV, not a Louis XVI, *n'est-ce pas*?"

"Harumph," Monsieur Verdier throatily answered.

One of Victoria's perfect eyebrows winged slightly. "I, for one, simply cannot learn to tell the difference between Louis XV and Louis XVI. The styles are so similar, and one doesn't remember which it is, anyway, even when the truth is known."

"They are very similar, almost identical," Cheney remarked with a tinge of amusement, eyeing the Frenchman's eloquent pique. "But one difference is that the fires of revolution had only just begun to smolder during Louis XV's reign, and the peasants had not yet picked up their scythes and sickles and sticks to beat aristocrats. It was in poor Louis XVI's reign—I do feel sorry for anyone who is beheaded, don't you, monsieur?—that ormolu, that shiny foolery, came in vogue. Since the court was still sinfully ornate during Louis XV's reign, it is likely that the Boucher is gold instead of glazed with some base metal. But I'm certain you were aware of that, were you not, Monsieur Verdier?"

"Er . . . hrm . . . *Mais oui, mademoiselle! Très bien! C'est ça!*" Verdier agreed enthusiastically, his ire dissipating in the realization that Cheney had just alerted him to the mystical presence of gold.

Coolly Victoria reached in her velvet reticule and pulled out a small square of shiny neutral-colored cloth. With small precise movements she pulled the cloth tight over her forefinger, touched the cupid's knee, and made two tiny circles. Then she lifted the cloth to peruse it. A dark smudge had appeared. "Jeweler's cloth," she pronounced. "It is gold."

"But of course, Madame de Lancie," Verdier piously agreed.

Cheney smiled.

Slowly the three moved to the eloquent eight-foot cabinet, the *bibliotheque*, which was commonly used to store books, but which could serve as an ornate linen cabinet. Without speaking, her eyes alight, Victoria studied the porcelains displayed. Then she came to stand in front of the chair that was flanked by the two great urns.

"These urns are over one hundred years old," Monsieur Verdier said, pointedly avoiding reference to any monarch's reign. "But they are in exquisite condition. Not the slightest fault in the workmanship, not a single crack or"—he shuddered dramatically—"scratch."

"Yes, they are excellent pieces, and I believe I shall take them," Victoria said thoughtfully, "but I was really wondering about this chair, Monsieur Verdier?"

With a wary glance at Cheney beneath his half-closed eyes, Monsieur Verdier pronounced carefully, "It is a Louis XV, with ormolu—yes, I believe it is ormolu, and not gold, Mademoiselle Duvall—mountings, and satin brocade coverings so fine you cannot see an individual thread, though—"

Cheney cleared her throat. Delicately.

Monsieur Verdier's drowsy eyelids lifted as he rolled his eyes theatrically. "*Oui, mademoiselle? Qu'est-ce qu'il ya?*"

"Mmm, oh, it's nothing, nothing," Cheney said brightly. "The chair, you are correct, Monsieur Verdier, it is a Louis XV. It's just that I happened to notice the arms—you see how they are set back from the front border of the seat? Naturally, you know this chair is called a *fauteuil à la reine.* It's named for Madame de Pompadour, who made it fashionable to place chairs along the walls, which is why the back is so straight. The inset arms are to allow for hoop skirts, which became fashionable after the . . . um . . . 1720s, was it not, monsieur?" Cheney finished guilelessly.

"O ciel," Monsieur Verdier murmured fatalistically. "I have no idea, Mademoiselle Duvall. I am, however, certain that you must be correct."

Victoria scolded, "Cheney, I thought you knew nothing about household furnishings."

"I don't, particularly," Cheney answered mildly. "I just know a little about French history."

"Family history," Victoria corrected her with a shrewd look from under her lashes at Monsieur Verdier.

He brightened considerably. "You are French, Mademoiselle Duvall?"

"On my mother's side," Cheney replied modestly.

"Yes. Mademoiselle Duvall is the Vicomte de Cheyne's great-niece," Victoria told Monsieur Verdier airily.

Now Monsieur Verdier's shaded eyes grew earnestly wide. "The . . . the . . . Maxime-Louis-Augustin de Cheyne? Vicomte de Cheyne? Of Varennes?"

"Mais oui," Victoria said simply.

At this time Monsieur Verdier embarked upon such a torrent of apology, such a stutter of embarrassment, such a kissing of the hands and such repentant bows, that Cheney was disconcerted.

"Please, monsieur, I am an American. I've never even met the vicomte . . . and . . . my father is Colonel Richard Duvall, and . . . I . . . he . . . is American," she finished with a slight blush of chagrin.

Victoria, amused, brought Monsieur Félix Verdier's raptures to an end by coolly announcing, "*Alors,* monsieur, as my friend Mademoiselle Duvall approves of your Sèvres and your furnishings, I believe I shall take them."

"All of them?" Monsieur Verdier asked, recovering miraculously.

"Yes," Victoria answered firmly. "All of the Sèvres that you have. Also the occasional table, the commode, the carpet, the tapestry, the *bibliotheque.* Now the chair—do you, by chance, have any more? Surely with two estate lots there would be a number of chairs?"

Again the eyes were heavy-lidded, appearing sleepy, but with a light of craftiness brightening them. "Ah yes, Madame de Lancie, but they are not here. I retrieved all the Sèvres, but the furniture I intended for display purposes only. As Mademoiselle Duvall so graciously has illustrated, I am ignorant of the particulars of furnishings. So." He made an expressive gesture of helplessness.

"So," Victoria persisted, "you are saying that you have more chairs? But you have not yet set a price for them?"

"Precisely," he said dryly. "There are many, many items in the lots, and I bought both of them sight unseen. The remainder of the goods are still stored in my warehouse, madame. Perhaps by next week I shall have them catalogued and . . . er, um . . . detailed."

"By next week I was hoping to have my house completely furnished," Victoria said with a pretty sigh, "and I was hoping that the City of Paris would benefit the most from my patronage. But you have reminded me, monsieur, of the brand-new U. S. Bonding Warehouse, which, I believe, has many fine pieces of imported furniture?"

With alarm Monsieur Verdier harrumphed, "The Bonding Warehouse? Madame surely is not contemplating furnishing Steen House from a *warehouse*?"

"Fine furniture is stored in your warehouse, is it not, Monsieur Verdier?" Victoria asked sweetly. "So."

"So," he repeated in defeat. "If Madame de Lancie and Mademoiselle de Cheyne would care to accompany me to the City of Paris warehouse, perhaps madame would see some items of interest."

"I'm Cheney Duvall," Cheney corrected him sternly. "Dr. Cheney Duvall."

"A thousand pardons, Dr. Duvall," Monsieur Verdier said with a trace of weariness. "I am, as always, your most humble servant."

"As always," Victoria agreed cheerfully. "Shall we go?"

★ ★ ★ ★

In 1851 the eastern shore of Yerba Buena was a wooden jungle with quarter-decks forming the jungle floor and masts the surreal trees. About 775 ships lay deserted in the bay; after the anchor was dropped, the crews and passengers abandoned everything, cargo and all, and headed for the golden hills. Just south of the little village of Yerba Buena, in what were ironically to be called Happy Valley and Pleasant

Valley, were encampments, full of tents and shanties built from the disdained hulls and forgotten sails of abandoned ships.

Twenty-six years later, Cheney and Victoria saw a bustle of urban busyness out the windows of the landau. On their way to First and Bryant Streets they saw the wharves two blocks away. Now the masts were in orderly, prosperous lines, disgorging valuable cargoes into the blocks of new warehouses being built as fast as the materials could be grabbed. Brickworks, sawmills, foundries, refineries, ironworks, shoe factories, and flour mills buzzed and roared ceaselessly. Hundreds of hurrying people, distinctive only by the sameness in their drab working clothes, crowded the still-narrow streets. Rincon Hill and South Park, once the enclave of the fashionable, huddled forlornly, crowded to their borders by colorless squares of utilitarian buildings. South of Market was no longer a fit habitation for the noble and affluent, and what prominent citizens were left stared longingly at the cool heights of Russian Hill.

The City of Paris warehouse loomed between two other monoliths: The Oriental U.S. Bonding Warehouse and the Pacific Mail Steamship Company's warehouses and wharves. Monsieur Verdier had hurried to his great storehouse, in which fine furniture lay strewn all about, and collared four stout stevedores.

As the landau neared, Victoria and Cheney giggled at Monsieur Verdier's high frantic calls, passionate and colorful, to the stumping workers as they hauled chairs, commodes, beds, chests, armoires, and hundreds of smaller accessory pieces out through the gaping doors into the bleak afternoon sun. Soon, Cheney thought, a ceaseless fog would come drifting over the city, bringing a disconsolate chill and damp.

"—both of the other bedrooms; one of the turrets needs a console of some sort; some kind of accent pieces for the music room; the drawing room—no, no, I believe the Oriental secretary from Gump's will finish it out nicely—" Victoria was reciting half to herself.

"How can you remember all of it?" Cheney demanded.

"It doesn't matter," Victoria answered, her eyes alight. "I shall purchase the finest pieces, anyway. If they won't go in Steen House . . ." She shrugged expressively. Victoria, Cheney knew, owned four large homes herself. Cheney had no idea how many homes the Steen family owned altogether.

"At any rate, Cheney," Victoria said briskly, "as I knew you would, you have proven to be a most knowledgeable advisor. And besides, Steen House is yours, too, for as long as you care to have it. I want to choose things that you like."

Smiling warmly at her friend, Cheney declared, "Victoria, I have never seen such fine things in all my life. Such grand furniture, for royalty! Personally, it seems to me that Steen House—" Abruptly, with some embarrassment, she cut off her words.

Wisely Victoria nodded. "Of course, I know that these furnishings of the French court are much too ornate for a whimsical little cottage like Steen House. But, Cheney, you see, don't you, why I'm purchasing the best—the absolute finest things I can?"

"Um—no, I really don't understand it, Victoria," Cheney admitted. "You usually display more of an innate sense of what is fitting for a room or a house."

"Cheney dear, you really must understand," Victoria said with a trace of impatience. "Even though it's rather awkward . . . this is not New York. This is San Francisco. It's a very young city, and the most prominent citizens of this city base their hierarchy on one thing, and one thing only."

"Money," Cheney sighed.

"Exactly," Victoria said with satisfaction. "Lineage, history of a family's social standing is never taken into account. But . . . you do see, don't you, that the Stanfords, and the Westins, and the Crockers, and all of the upper classes are *conscious* of this?"

"I think I see what you mean," Cheney said slowly. "Even though they unquestionably have the highest social standing, they know that in New York, for example, they would simply be considered a moneyed bourgeois, while the Steens, for example, are the aristocrats?"

Victoria shrugged with careless *élan.* "When we get ready to sell Steen House, it will be purchased because it is Steen House. It's to be expected that it will only be furnished in the most elegant manner. Even though"—she smiled wickedly—"it's actually just a quaint little cottage."

"So," Cheney said jauntily.

"So," Victoria agreed.

The carriage finally maneuvered to a halt in the narrow alley, Tim and Eddie appeared in the windows, and Cheney and Victoria hurried to the royal accouterments strewn about the wooden planks surrounding the City of Paris' great hiding place.

In the next three hours, while the fog seeped in to mantle them with drizzly gray tatters, Victoria purchased twenty-two Louis XV chairs, one Venetian settee, two Aubusson carpets, one Italian handmade cherrywood bed, an ornately hand-carved and gilded Venetian mirror, two black lacquer Chinoiserie bookcases, two Louis XV commodes, a Baccarat vase, a Baccarat gold epergne, a French giltwood mirror, eight enormous eighteenth-century Italian paintings with rococo gilded frames, and a lyre form ormolu clock in burled wood with matching music stand.

Cheney was exhausted and astounded when she mentally calculated that Victoria, in one afternoon, had spent around four thousand dollars.

When they returned to the carriage, Victoria ordered Mr. Yancey to take a turn about the wharves. Settling back in the blue velvet seat, she said merrily, "Since we've already disobeyed Shiloh's strict orders to stay in Union Square, I think we might as well have a look at the infamous wharves of San Francisco."

"Let's not tell him," Cheney said hastily. "He does fuss so."

"I've observed that it does little good," Victoria commented. "And besides, he only does it because he worries about you."

"Well, he shouldn't," Cheney said ungraciously.

"He must," Victoria said, her voice velvety. "He's in love with you, Cheney. Surely you must know that."

Cheney flushed a deep, wretched red. She turned her head toward the window, but her eyes were empty. She searched the drab gray of the bay, and the ships neatly lined up along the endless wharves, rolling gently in the low tide. For long minutes she didn't speak, and Victoria regretted her invasion, however gentle and well-meaning, of Cheney's—and Shiloh's—privacy.

Suddenly Cheney sat upright, her blank, bleak eyes sharpening. "Victoria—look!" Quickly she called out and tapped the ceiling of the landau with the handle of her parasol. "Mr. Yancey! Stop, please!"

The landau came to a halt, and Tim and Eddie dutifully appeared at the window. Cheney hurried out of the carriage and almost ran to the end of the wharf. Victoria, mystified, followed her at a more sedate pace, while Tim and Eddie helplessly followed.

"What on earth—are you all right, Cheney?" she asked.

"Oh . . . oh yes, of course," Cheney said hastily. "It's just that . . . I saw that ship. That one." She pointed.

With a hint of disapproval Victoria turned to look. The carriage had been driving along a long pier, with the wharves jutting out perpendicular in the bay. Victoria narrowed her eyes, for the light was uncertain and the mists a watery dimness. The ship Cheney was so dramatically pointing to was a clipper, and it was gracefully floating away from the Pacific Mail Steamship Company's jetty.

"Do you see?" Cheney whispered, as if she spoke only to herself. "Can you see? Isn't the name . . . something . . . something . . . *Day Dream*?"

"Yes . . . yes, I believe it is," Victoria murmured. "But—I can't quite make it out."

Beside her Tim said confidently, "That clipper? Oh yes, she's a beauty, ain't she?"

"Can you make out the name?" Cheney demanded impatiently.

"Sure, Dr. Duvall." Tim shrugged. "*Locke's Day Dream.*"

15

YESTERDAY, NOW, AND ALWAYS

"Quiet night," Shiloh commented.

"Mmm," Cheney absently agreed.

"Nice, after Thirteen Friday and bein' full o' the moon," he went on, watching her curiously.

Her face averted, Cheney appeared to be studying Eugènie's mane. Her fingers twirled the coarse strands, then entwined them. Like a gambler shuffling a deck of cards, she deftly threaded the horse's mane through her fingers, then released it and threaded it again backward. "Mmm," she mumbled.

With a crooked smile Shiloh squinted up at the early morning heavens. For once the sky was blue, the air was clear, the sun was friendly. "Warm sunny morning," he idly remarked.

"Mm-hmm."

The corners of his mild blue eyes crinkled with amusement. "Myself, I like a green sun with purple stripes."

Cheney had no comment. Eugènie's mane evidently required her undivided attention.

"Orange sky too," Shiloh went on airily.

"Mm-hmm."

"Good thing you're not watching where Eugènie's goin'," he drawled, "since she's gonna step off that big cliff. 'Course, she can always flap her wings and just fly off, I reckon."

Cheney glanced quizzically at him, but her eyes were vacant, her question brainlessly polite. "I beg your pardon?"

"Never mind, Doc. I was just yammerin'."

"Oh." Again Cheney performed her one-handed braiding of Eugènie's mane.

Shiloh sighed. "Something the matter, Doc?"

"Hmm? Oh. Oh no, not . . . really. Is something the matter with you?"

"Seems like there is."

"What? What's wrong?" Cheney demanded, her eyes becoming alive for the first time since they'd left the hospital.

"Seems like I've turned into an awful bore," Shiloh replied mischievously. "Even Balaam won't talk to me this morning."

Cheney said wryly, "We've come . . . what, half a mile, and I haven't said anything, have I?"

"Been hummin' a lot."

"Sorry," she said. "I'm just thinking about things."

"Warned you about that."

"I know, Mr. Iron Head, but I can't just shut my brain off as you can," Cheney muttered. "I think about things."

"Worry, you mean."

"I suppose."

He gave her a sharp glance, then turned aside, idly watching the early morning scene of workers hurrying by, the occasional drunk staggering around, the street cleaners' toiling. "You worried about the meeting tomorrow, Doc?"

"The . . . meeting? Oh, you mean with Dr. Baird and the others?" Cheney's mouth tightened into a rigid line. "No, I'm not at all worried. I've already organized my observations and suggestions into a coherent outline. There are a few things that I'd like for you to go over with me. I'm off tonight—you are too, aren't you?"

"Yes, ma'am," he answered jauntily.

"Then I need you to help me turn my outline into a complete report."

"I'm really sorry, Doc, but I've got some things to do tonight," he said easily. "Besides, you don't need me to write reports and stuff. You're a lot better at that kind of thing than I'll ever be."

"But . . . but . . ." Cheney stammered. She couldn't recall a single time that Shiloh had refused to help her, no matter what the request. Then she grew resentful, which in turn filled her with confusion—and Cheney Duvall hated being confused. Finally she said coldly, "You're right, of course. I'm ready to give a report and some badly needed recommendations right now."

Shiloh grew intent. "What you're saying is you're ready to give them what-for."

Cheney shrugged carelessly. "That's a crude way to put it. But obviously Dr. Baird is aware that changes need to be made in the hospital's policies and the staff training. I assume that's why he called this meeting—to discuss the breakdowns we had Friday night and what we can do to correct them."

"You assume that, huh," Shiloh said dryly.

"Of course. What else?"

As it was obviously intended as a rhetorical question, Shiloh played by the rules and gave no answer. He was silent for long moments, in deep thought. Then with a half-shrug he brought the subject back to his original question. "So is the meeting what you're studyin' about so much?"

"Well . . . no . . . no, actually I . . . I was thinking about . . . something else," Cheney replied in such a sudden fluster that Shiloh gave her a sharp, discerning look.

"Me?" he asked quietly.

Cheney took a deep breath, then quickly, before she could change her mind, answered, "Yes."

Both of them looked ahead, around, aside.

"Shiloh—" she began, then stopped.

He waited.

"Shiloh—" she tried again, with less inflection.

He waited.

"Never mind," she said despairingly.

He laughed. "Doc, you are one tryin' woman! Are you going to talk to me or not?"

"No," she impishly replied.

He turned back and lifted his chin impudently. "Sure you are," he said with calm assurance. "You always do."

"You are insufferable," Cheney said, but her mouth was twitching and her eyes danced. "I'm never going to tell you anything again as long as I live."

"Sure you will. Like, for instance, about whatever it is that happened yesterday while you and Mrs. de Lancie were shopping that you're wantin' to talk to me about."

"Did she tell you?" Cheney asked sharply.

"Nope," he replied easily. "I haven't seen her."

"Oh. Well . . . it's probably nothing," Cheney murmured. "I've been debating about whether or not to even mention it . . . but it is your life, I suppose. . . ."

"If it's about my life, yeah, I'd appreciate it if you'd let me in on it," Shiloh asserted. "That'd be real generous of you, Doc."

Cheney sighed with exasperation. "It's probably nothing. It's just that yesterday, down at the docks—"

"You were down at the docks yesterday," Shiloh said darkly.

"Yes, I disobeyed your direct orders," Cheney sarcastically retorted, "but that's not what I wanted to tell you—"

"Guess not," he growled.

"Listen, Shiloh, do you want to hear this or not?" Cheney snapped. "It's . . . oh, this is silly! It's just that yesterday we saw a clipper. A fine, elegant clipper, pulling out from the wharves of the Pacific Mail Steamship Company."

"Yeah?" Shiloh's voice was now curious.

"The name of it was *Locke's Day Dream*," Cheney said. After a moment she finished rather lamely, "That's all. I just saw it from the carriage window, and we stopped to . . . to . . . look at it, but it was pulling away."

"Yeah?" Shiloh repeated thoughtfully, his eyes brightening to a clear topaz blue. "*Locke's Day Dream.* Coincidence, maybe . . . but it's an unusual name."

"We made inquiries of the men at the warehouse," Cheney went on, "but they were just stevedores who had unloaded a shipment of raw sandalwood from the clipper. They only had a receiving report from the Pacific. No papers from the ship, I mean. They didn't know anything about it."

Distress colored her voice, and Shiloh looked at her gravely. "Doc, thank you for this."

"For what?" she retorted. "It's nothing. It doesn't help."

"But you do want to. Help me, I mean," he said thoughtfully. "You really do, don't you?"

"Well . . . well, of course," Cheney replied uncertainly. "You're my friend, Shiloh, and I want—I want to help you. Always."

He stared at her, his eyes blazing blue, his mouth suddenly set in a tense line. Cheney tried to meet his gaze, tried to keep her face open and warm, but she weakened and dropped her head. Unthinkingly she began frantically plaiting Eugènie's mane again.

The tension between them pervaded the sweet morning breeze. Suddenly, with visible exertion, Shiloh relaxed his shoulders, loosened his death-grip on the reins, and lounged carelessly in the saddle. "Thanks, Doc," he said lightly. "You're a good friend, always have been to me. I really appreciate you trying to see about that clipper. Maybe I can get some information from the harbormaster. Might be something, you never know."

As he spoke with such undemanding warmth, Cheney's mind eased, her emotions calmed, and her hands stilled. She smiled. "Do you think I might come with you? When you go to see the harbormaster, I mean? I'd love to see the Embarcadero. And of course I need your permission," she added scathingly.

He shrugged and grinned easily at her. "Sure, Doc. But . . . listen. Would you maybe be interested in going to see Reverend Merced with me? You remember, the man who came—"

"To be with Little Wren," Cheney interrupted eagerly. "Of course I remember."

"Well, he was a Chinese missionary for years," Shiloh told her. "And he speaks Chinese and understands their culture, probably more than any other white man ever will. He has close ties with the Chinese community here in San Francisco. I told him a little about Pearl."

"You did?" Cheney was astonished. Shiloh didn't tell many people about his past, and she had found that even when he did, about all he said was that he'd been raised by the three Behring sisters in an orphanage in Charleston. He rarely mentioned the mysterious Oriental girl who had miraculously saved his life. For Shiloh to have said something about it to a total stranger was extraordinary. "What did he say?" she asked eagerly. "Did he know anything about . . . anything?"

"He probably knows something about something," Shiloh replied solemnly. "But probably not everything about everything. Maybe he knows anything about anything. I dunno."

"Oh, Shiloh! Will you just tell me!"

"Naw," he grunted. "But if you'll come with me this afternoon to Reverend Merced's house, maybe he'll tell you something."

"Us," Cheney corrected him. "Tell us. And yes, I'd love to come. Thank you so much for inviting me. I . . . it . . . I . . ." She cleared her throat and forged ahead, her cheeks suddenly flaming, her eyes restless. "I'm flattered, and honored, that you include me in this part of your life, Shiloh," she formally recited. "Thank you."

It was a long time before he answered. Cheney's eyes relentlessly searched ahead, though she saw nothing.

Finally he answered, his voice deep and deliberate. "You're welcome to all of my life, Cheney. Yesterday, now, and always."

Tears started in her eyes, and her throat felt seared. Bowing her head, she took a deep, harsh breath and spurred Eugènie much too hard. Cheney left Shiloh behind and rode home alone.

★ ★ ★ ★

Cheney, Victoria, Zhou-Zhou, and Nia went to church, and on the way home Cheney mentioned that she was accompanying Shiloh that afternoon to visit Reverend Merced. This invoked ladylike outrage from Victoria, much babbling in French from Zhou-Zhou, and plain stubbornness from Nia.

"You ain't—aren't going with no single man to no single man's house," Nia declared. "That's why I'm here, to chaferone you."

"*Oui, oui, mais oui, mademoiselle*," Zhou-Zhou chattered, her brown curls bouncing energetically. "You are a fine lady, and you must not go out without Nia."

"Zhou-Zhou, I'm certainly not going to start taking your advice on acceptable social behavior," Cheney snapped. Zhou-Zhou looked a little embarrassed and a little hurt, but Cheney ignored her. "And it's *chaperone*, Nia, and it's silly for you to start worrying about such niceties now. I've been to Chinatown twice with him, by myself."

"And I shouldn't have let you," Nia retorted, "and I'm not going to let you again. You're not going to be able to use that tired old excuse about me not bein' able to ride for much longer. Mr. Yancey and Tim and Eddie are teaching me. And you sure aren't going to no single man's house with just you and Mr. Irons."

"He's widowed," Cheney argued. "And he's a minister. And after all, if one should start worrying about appearances, it does appear that a single man comes and spirits me away every night, then brings me back home in the morning."

"That is different and you know it," Nia maintained spiritedly. Although her appearance and demeanor were nothing like her strong Amazon mother's, just now she did sound exactly like Dally Clarkson, even with her little-girl breathy voice.

"But that's my point," Cheney scoffed. "I know it. You all know it. Shiloh knows it. Who else matters?"

"That's different and you know it," Nia solidly echoed, grandly negating Cheney's argument.

"She's absolutely right, Cheney," Victoria stated with an air of finality. "As I am your chaperone, also, I won't allow you to go unchaperoned to a single man's house."

"Victoria, you make no sense," Cheney said impatiently. "As I have already pointed out, I go 'sashaying' about with Shiloh every night. Unchaperoned."

"That's different," Victoria grandly maintained, "and you know it."

"I wish everyone would stop saying that," Cheney muttered between gritted teeth.

"Cheney, dear, why is it so important for you to go unchaperoned?" Victoria asked with honeyed sweetness. "Are you that anxious to be alone with Shiloh?"

Cheney blinked several times, as if a rock had been thrown directly at her eyes. Victoria watched her with cool amusement, Zhou-Zhou with wariness, and Nia with a certain comprehension. Finally Cheney said stiffly, "He's calling for me at two o'clock, Nia, so be prompt, please. And I suppose we'll need the landau, Victoria, if you would be so kind."

"I'm not at all kind," Victoria declared airily. "But still, you may use the landau."

★ ★ ★ ★

Reverend Justice Merced lived in a small house on a narrow lot, shoulder to shoulder with other small houses on identical skinny lots. Shiloh and Cheney had, in fact, passed his house on their first trip to Chinatown, as it was on the western end of Broadway. On their second trip to Chinatown, Shiloh had flatly refused to take Cheney through the Barbary Coast, and Cheney had not protested much, so they had taken a more circuitous route. But Cheney recalled Reverend Merced's house, because she had particularly noted it when they'd passed it that first week.

It was very small, but it was newly painted a pretty robin's-egg blue with white trim, shutters, and doll-sized veranda. On the right was the front door, painted pink, and the left side was a generous octagonal bay window. The lacy decorative woodwork and the gentle pastel colors made the little cottage look something like an Easter egg and something like the gingerbread house that Hansel and Gretel discovered.

The Steenses' landau pulled up in front of the house—the carriage and team of four horses were actually longer than Reverend Merced's lot was wide—and after Cheney, Nia, and Shiloh climbed out, Cheney instructed Mr. Yancey to return for them in two hours. She couldn't help but smile as she saw the two small rectangles, bisected by a white rock walk up to the front door, that served as the front yard. Not a single weed, or even a blade of grass, showed. The entire yard was carpeted with pansies, of all hues, all combinations, but all the same delicate size. Thick, healthy, modestly low-growing, they made the most delightful carpet Cheney had ever seen.

Reverend Merced came out onto the veranda, wiping his hands on a white apron, his sun-creased face wreathed with smiles. Through the open door a hotly tantalizing smell of meat and spices drifted.

"Good afternoon, Dr. Duvall. You honor me and my humble house." He took Cheney's hand in both of his and clasped it warmly. "Good afternoon, Mr. Irons. Good afternoon, ma'am."

"This is my maid, Nia Clarkson," Cheney said. "Nia, this is Reverend Justice Merced."

Nia bowed her head. "Good afternoon, Reverend."

"I'm so pleased to have guests," he said pleasantly. "Come in, come in. I'm preparing a treat for all of us; at least I hope it will be a treat for you."

He led them into a small drawing room with a generous fireplace, down a hall with two closed doors on each side, and through the dining room, which held an old work-scarred table. No chairs were visible. The table was littered with books, sheaves of papers covered with spidery handwriting, the *Alta California,* the *Evening Bulletin,* a Chinese newspaper, pens, ink bottles, and paintbrushes of all sizes stuck in a glass jar. As they went through the last room of the house—the kitchen—Cheney was surprised to see that it was orderly and spotless. No litter of whatever was cooking was evident. "I hope you don't mind visiting with me outside," Reverend Merced was saying. "I so much prefer sitting out here in my little garden."

Along the back of the house was an open terrace formed of flat gray stones, irregularly shaped but painstakingly crafted together, with the same small white stones as filler. On one end was a square brick stand with a hearth about waist-high; inside the small square recess a tiny hot fire hissed. By it was a long rickety bamboo table with a threadbare yellow tablecloth and four mismatched wooden chairs.

Reverend Merced's "garden" was not what Cheney pictured a garden to be. The back of his lot was a long skinny expanse of verdant, close-clipped grass. Shielding the terrace on either side, and forming a border all the way down to the end of the lawn and across the back, were dense stands of bamboo. The slender stalks grew thick, and the thin leaves rustled with the slightest stir of air.

Observing Cheney's curious expression, Reverend Merced sighed. "When I was in China, I missed pansies so much," he told her. "And then, when I got here, I missed bamboo. My eyes missed it, for I find it a tranquil sight, and my ears missed its singing."

"It does sound soothing," Cheney agreed. "And it has a certain spare beauty as well."

Reverend Merced turned back to Shiloh and Nia, who were unobtrusively studying the bamboo table. On it was displayed a curious collection: knives, a vicious-looking meat cleaver, a lumpy wad of dough, four small bowls filled with a brown sauce, a green sauce, a black sauce, and a red sauce, some small squares of wafer-thin rice paper, small cubes of cooked pork piled on a square oak cutting board, a head of cabbage, an onion, a porcelain saltcellar, and several small bowls holding dried herbs and spices.

Reverend Merced looked regretfully at the litter. "I intended to have the *jiaozi* finished at exactly the time you arrived, and I did cook the pork. But then I decided to make tea . . . and I started reading the newspaper while I waited for the water to boil. A death notice came to my attention, and I started searching through some of my journals, for I thought I knew something of the bereaved family. In China, you know. I began reading and sipping tea . . . and then . . . here you are." He smiled guilelessly. "Could we visit while I cook?"

Cheney's eyes sparkled. "This is . . . what did you call it, sir? *Jiaozi?* Something already smells absolutely heavenly! Perhaps we could help you?"

"I'll help," Shiloh said hastily.

"No, Miss Cheney, I'll help," Nia said at the same time.

Cheney frowned at the intriguing ingredients that, even in their disarray, were somehow arranged artistically, in a group that was pleasing to the eye. "I'm a physician," she grumbled. "Surely I can understand simple cooking instructions."

Reverend Merced observed, "Dr. Duvall, if I can learn to cook *jiaozi*—even though inefficiently—I know that you can. Are you certain, however, that you wish to help? Seems a bit of an imposition, doesn't it?"

"No, we'll all help," Cheney decided. "I think I will enjoy it. I've never actually tried cooking before."

Shiloh and Nia exchanged resigned glances, which made Reverend Merced smile slightly. "Very well, then, Dr. Duvall, would you be seated here? Yes, Mr. Irons there—and Miss Clarkson, would you sit there?"

Nia looked uncertain—servants were never asked to sit with their employers—but Cheney nodded, so she gingerly sat in the chair Reverend Merced had held out for her, her eyes wide and cautious.

He instructed them, "Now, *jiaozi* is a meat-filled dumpling, a traditional north China dish served on special occasions—such as this, when you have honored guests in your home. Miss Clarkson—perhaps you would like to make the dumplings? You shape this dough, you see, into a roll. Then you cut it into pieces about an inch long. Squash it down—like this—and shape it so it fits into this wrapper." Picking up one of the square pieces of rice paper, he nimbly shaped the piece of dough he'd pinched off to fit into it, with a small border around. "Right?" he asked Nia.

"Yes, sir, I can sure do that," she said eagerly.

"Good. Now, Mr. Irons, would you kindly shred this cabbage? And chop the onion very fine, please."

"Be glad to," Shiloh replied, picking up the cleaver and enthusiastically severing the cabbage into two precisely equal portions.

"And, Dr. Duvall, would you fill the wrappers? You take some of the meat, you see—oh dear, it is rather chunky, isn't it? Perhaps Mr. Irons might chop it a bit finer . . . and some of the shredded cabbage, and some of the onion, and a pinch of salt and a few—a very few!—bits of garlic sprinkled over it. Then you fold and seal the dumpling by pinching it. Right?"

"But . . . that's rather vague, isn't it?" Cheney asked anxiously. "Perhaps your measurements of the ingredients might be a little more . . . precise?"

Shiloh chuckled, Nia giggled, and Reverend Merced struggled to keep from smiling. Cheney frowned. "What's so amusing, may I ask? I believe it's a reasonable question."

"Of course it is," Reverend Merced agreed, "but unfortunately I don't have an answer, Dr. Duvall. I've always just sort of thrown the stuff in there, as did the Chinese lady who taught me to make *jiaozi*."

"Oh dear," Cheney fretted. "Evidently this takes some sort of innate gift, or special tactile sense, that I'm not certain I possess."

Shiloh, still grinning, commented, "Doc, it's not a major military campaign or a brain surgery. Go on, give it a try. Me and Nia will help you."

"All right," Cheney sighed theatrically. "But, Reverend Merced, I expect you to watch me very closely, and at least show me how to . . . um . . . correctly assemble two or three of these . . . infernally complex contraptions."

Reverend Merced threw back his head and laughed gleefully. "I've never heard dumplings called that, Dr. Duvall. But we'll all help you, I assure you, and we shan't let you fall into terrible error."

Shiloh chopped, Nia kneaded, and Cheney eyed and sniffed all the ingredients suspiciously, while Reverend Merced cleaned his wide, shallow cooking pan. Then he poured about an inch of clear oil in it and held it over the small hot fire with a pair of tongs, maneuvering it so that the oil covered the entire inside of the pan.

"I don't believe I've ever seen such a cooking instrument before," Cheney remarked, then said warningly to Shiloh and Nia, "And I don't think we need to hear any comments about my lack of experience with cooking instruments."

Shiloh and Nia glanced at each other with barely concealed amusement, and Shiloh said mildly, "Well, Doc, all I'll say is that it's kinda unusual to call a pan a 'cooking instrument.' "

"Oh," Cheney said uncertainly.

Reverend Merced explained, "It is unusual, because it's a Chinese . . . er . . . cooking instrument. In northern China they call it a *guo*, and in southern China they call it a *wok*. And truly, I suppose it would not be so wrong to call it a cooking 'instrument,' Dr. Duvall," he said gallantly. "For it's not a utensil, and neither is it just a pot or just a pan. It can be used for frying or for boiling."

"See?" Cheney said pointedly to Nia and Shiloh. Neither of them seemed repentant. Turning back to Reverend Merced she asked, "So were you in northern or southern China, Reverend Merced?"

"In southern China. In 1842, after the Treaty of Nanking opened the ports and allowed foreigners—or 'barbarians,' as they call us—to actually live in China, I moved to a small village just west of Canton, called Lin-chow."

"*They* call *us* barbarians?" Cheney exclaimed.

Reverend Merced smiled. "Yes, they do, and the longer I stayed there, the more I agreed with them. Begging your pardon, Dr. Duvall;

it's just that, in many ways, Western culture is more primitive and savage than that of the Chinese."

Cheney's expression was one of cool disbelief, and she made no comment. Shiloh glanced at her as he skillfully chopped cabbage into uniform thin slivers, then asked politely, "Well, how is that, Reverend Merced? I'd like to understand what you mean."

Sighing, he answered, "It took me years to understand the Chinese, and even now they still mystify me at times. They are an ancient culture, you know. They made gunpowder while our ancestors were still throwing crude spears, and for a thousand years they used it only for fireworks, not weaponry. They made printing presses with movable type four centuries before Gutenberg thought of it. They smile when we think they should cry. Their ideal of true heroism has nothing to do with physical prowess or military might; their ideal man is humble, generous, upright, and honest in all ways. Their lifelong search is for tranquillity and harmony."

"Yeah," Shiloh commented dryly, "that's pretty mystifyin' to me. Not exactly what Westerners long for, is it?"

"Just out of curiosity," Cheney put in acidly, "how do women fit into this tranquil and harmonious society?"

Gravely Reverend Merced studied her, then answered gently, "They are not a tranquil and harmonious society, Dr. Duvall, and they never will be. I was just commenting that these attributes, these qualities, are what they glorify in their arts, in their poetry, in their dreams. But Chinese women have probably the worst lot of any culture in the world—in my opinion, at least. They accept their place with stoic courage, which I think is the secret of the Chinese people's great inner strength."

Still Cheney looked skeptical, but Reverend Merced concentrated on maneuvering his hot pan, while Shiloh diced the onion carefully, at arm's length, so he wouldn't start crying.

The old missionary stared blankly down at his wok, then murmured with a poignant sadness, "When I first went to China, they called me 'Horse That Sweats Blood.' "

"It sounds as if you were a courageous and daring man," Cheney remarked.

"So I thought, and I was proud. I didn't realize until many years later that it was actually an insult." Reverend Merced's mild blue eyes were clouded. " 'So foolish was I, and ignorant: I was as a beast before

Thee.' Only after I had been ministering in China for almost twenty years did they begin to call me 'Always White Bamboo.' "

"And that was a compliment?" Cheney asked, mystified.

"Much more than that. It was a term of deep respect, and through the years came to be a term of endearment for some of them. 'Always white' for mourning, because I lost my wife and mourned her for so long, even longer than the Chinese mourn their dead. And 'bamboo' for a man who has, at long last, grown into a gentleman, who is upright and humble and yet finds a way to stand firm." Reverend Mercer studied Cheney for a long time, watching her struggle for comprehension. "I know it's difficult to understand," he finished quietly. "It is Chinese."

16

Dragons and Pearls

Nia, who had finished kneading the dough and had deftly prepared a pile of the wrappers, asked Reverend Merced if she might make some tea. He smiled and motioned to the kitchen. Feeling more at ease every moment, she rose and busied herself preparing China tea. As Shiloh gleefully chopped, Cheney frowned and measured cubes of pork and vegetables and spices piece by piece, grain by grain.

"That was a compelling story you told to Little Wren the other day, Mr. Irons," Reverend Merced said, his brown cheeks flushed bronze from the heat of the blue flames. "I suspected, since you obviously have a strong connection with this lovely and mysterious Oriental girl, that you might like to know a little more about the Far East."

Thoughtfully Shiloh chopped the cabbage into tiny slivered strips. "Yes, sir, I am curious about the Orient, as I suppose most Westerners are. But there's another reason I wanted to visit with you."

"Yes?"

"Yes, sir. You see, I have two items of . . . well, we suppose of Far Eastern origin," Shiloh said with a touch of unease. It was difficult for him to speak of personal things to anyone, even though Reverend Merced was the type of man who immediately made a guest feel a part of his home and life. "These two items were found with me when—you remember what I told Little Wren? About the Oriental girl who saved my life?"

"Certainly."

"May I tell you the entire story?"

"Of course," Reverend Merced said instantly. "I'm most curious, though naturally I would never press you."

"I'd like to tell you," Shiloh said firmly, "and then I'd like to ask you a favor, sir."

"Mr. Irons, I'll help you in any way I can," Reverend Merced said quietly. "It would be a pleasure."

Dispassionately and succinctly Shiloh told Reverend Merced how Navvy Wingo had found him and the Oriental girl he'd called Pearl, who was already dead. He told him about the wreck of the New Orleans freighter that belonged to Shiloh Ironworks, the *Ahava*, and the clipper ship *Day Dream*, and about finding the home registries of the two ships. He told Reverend Merced about Behring Orphanage, and about the crate from Shiloh Ironworks that had given him his name, and finally he told him about the scarf and the metal fish that were found with him.

"What an exciting story," Reverend Merced declared, vigorously and absently shaking his pan.

"Here is tea," Nia announced, coming out onto the terrace from the kitchen.

"I have one finished!" Cheney announced.

All eyes turned to her. Flushed and triumphant, she proudly held up a single forlorn-looking, mushy, misshapen dumpling.

After a few moments even Cheney was laughing.

★ ★ ★ ★

Everyone was stuffed and the table was cleared. Washing up had begun with many difficulties, as all four of them crowded into the one-person kitchen, with Cheney issuing orders and getting in the way, Shiloh ducking and stooping to keep from bumping his head on the various pots and pans that hung from an overhead rack, Reverend Merced vaguely taking clean dishes first here and then there, forgetting where he usually stored them, and Nia doing the bulk of the work while tactfully trying to shoo the others away. Finally she flatly told them that they were as helpless as little mewling kittens, and Cheney, Shiloh, and Reverend Merced trooped sheepishly back out onto the terrace to have more of the mild herbal China tea.

With a flourish Reverend Merced produced a tin of Ghirardelli's chocolate thins, and the three companionably sipped tea and nibbled at the rich wafers. As they talked, Nia softly sang a hymn in the kitchen, and the serene sound floated through the open door, its accompaniment the feathery whispers of bamboo stirring in a refreshingly damp afternoon wind.

"Now, Mr. Irons, why don't you bring out your treasures?" Reverend Merced asked, his eyes bright. "I'd love to see them."

"Yes, sir, I'd sure like for you to take a look at them." Shiloh retrieved the canvas knapsack he'd set down by the door. Wordlessly he opened it, took out the curious fish, and handed it to Reverend Merced.

With both hands Reverend Merced took the fish, hefted it slightly to judge its weight, turned it upside-down and back again, and then bent down to study it closely. About eight inches long, the fish was fashioned of two pieces of thin metal. Reverend Merced ran his finger down the body of the fish; the scales and fins were etched so finely that they actually felt real, like a bass's prickly skin. He touched the eye, with the epicanthic fold, and smiled slightly. "It's tin," he murmured. "Fine workmanship."

Then he touched the fish's "belly," which was an inset piece of the same metal, mounted on a pin. The circumference was engraved with regular groups of what looked like tally marks. When he touched it, the round piece of metal shivered fragilely. "Hmm," he muttered. "Is this—"

Suddenly he jumped out of his chair, cradling the fish securely in front of him with both hands. He turned to the side. Then with military precision he made a quarter-turn, which put his back to the table.

Shiloh and Cheney stared at him and each other doubtfully.

Finally he made another quarter-turn, which faced him toward the house. He sat down again, smiling broadly. "I've got it, I believe," he said with satisfaction. "Watch."

He set the fish down in the center of the table, and then adjusted it slightly until the simplest group of tally marks—one long vertical line, two short lines, then one long line—was lined up exactly along the fish's eye. As the others watched, he slowly turned the fish a quarter-turn. The movable center lightly floated until another group of tally marks lined up.

"It's a compass," Shiloh said with wonder. "A compass! Of course!"

"Correct," Reverend Merced rumbled. "And a fine one too. A fisherman probably wrought this himself—it's lovingly done, and the fish is decorative, made simply to please the eye. The compass-piece is rubbed over a magnetic lodestone to give it the north-magnetizing properties. This, too, is a time-consuming process, as the piece of tin must be equally magnetized throughout in order for it to be true."

"A compass," Cheney murmured with impatience. "Of course it is. How could we miss it? So these marks are directional markings, yes? They aren't alphabetical characters."

"Exactly," Reverend Merced answered. Stealing a quick glance at Shiloh's absorbed face he went on, "I believe it is Chinese, but in truth this design is typical of almost any Asian culture: Siamese, Javanese, Burmese, Japanese, Korean . . . and also, Mr. Irons, I'm afraid there's nothing here to indicate any family identity."

Shiloh smiled at him. "Oh, I didn't really expect that, Reverend Merced. I'm just so glad to know what the blinkin' thing is! And now that I see—how could I have been so blind? It's so obvious!"

"Ah yes," Merced commented gently. "A common human failing, Mr. Irons. We are all blind sometimes." He caressed the surface of the tin fish for a moment. "It's certainly fine craftsmanship. And—you said this was found with you in 1843? Twenty-four years ago?" He shook his head in wonder. "It's amazing that it's still retained its magnetic charge—and it does appear to still be fairly precise. Simply amazing."

"I suppose, like Navvy Wingo said, this compass, and the Behring sisters, were so I could find my way," Shiloh said quietly.

"I'll bet he knew exactly what this was," Cheney said warmly. "I'll bet he understood as soon as he saw it."

"Yes," Shiloh agreed. "Well . . . here, Reverend Merced. See what you think of this, would you?"

Shiloh took out a long piece of flame-colored satin from the knapsack. It was carefully rolled up; now he unrolled it and laid it horizontally across the table in front of his host. It looked like a long table scarf, about six feet in length and twelve inches wide. The entire expanse was embroidered with satin thread and was a breathtaking work of fine needlework. To Cheney and Shiloh, the design itself was a meaningless jumble; many of the creatures depicted were like none they'd ever seen or imagined; some of the human figures were turned this way, that way, upside-down; dragons, lions, birds, trees, clouds, flames, ships, seas, moons.

"Ah," Reverend Merced breathed with appreciation. "This is exquisite work." He bent closer and fingered the glossy, limber fabric. "You were found wrapped in this? So it was soaked in sea water?"

"Must have been." Shiloh shrugged.

But Cheney said quietly, "Navvy Wingo said it was dry when he found Shiloh and Pearl. She was soaked, her hair had turned to ice, but Shiloh was warm and dry."

"Doc, that part of the story must have been . . . uh . . . you know . . . apocalyptic."

"Apocryphal," Cheney said evenly, "and I don't think so."

"Miraculous," Reverend Merced murmured. "Either way it is miraculous. If it got soaked in brine, it shows absolutely no sign. This is fine delicate fabric, and under normal circumstances immersion in sea water, even for a short period of time, would have ruined it. It's not faded, no water-spots, no brine stains, no unraveling. I'm sorry, Mr. Irons, but it does appear that you are alive today because of God's miraculous intervention." Shiloh said nothing but looked vaguely uncomfortable, so Reverend Merced went on. "This is most definitely Chinese."

"It is?" Shiloh asked with a trace of excitement. "We didn't know. We had no way of knowing."

"Oh yes, definitely," Reverend Merced repeated firmly. "But . . . I suppose it's just a big muddle to you, is it not? I mean, you haven't seen the story unfold, have you?"

Both Cheney and Shiloh looked utterly mystified, and Reverend Merced smiled gently. "Yes, I see. As you said, you had no way of knowing." He rose and began to shift the long scarf around so that it lay vertically on the table. "Come around here."

Cheney and Shiloh hurried to stand on either side of him. He pointed to the top right-hand corner of the scarf. "You see, the Chinese write from top-to-bottom, right-to-left. I believe if we study this tapestry—for that is what it is, one panel of a tapestry—you will see that the figures are in scenes, which are in a coherent pattern. In effect, I believe this tapestry is going to tell us a story."

"Oh my goodness, oh my," Cheney cried. "Shiloh, look, look! It must be Pearl!"

Cheney pointed to the first scene that, once they viewed it vertically instead of horizontally, seemed suddenly to snap together as if made of close pieces of a magnetic jigsaw puzzle. The first scene in the upper right-hand corner of the tapestry piece depicted a figure, clothed in white, surrounded by swirls of color and clouds of flame.

"Yes . . . yes . . . let me see," Reverend Merced muttered, bending close over the tapestry. "If you would just give me a few moments to study this. . . ."

As he bent over the tapestry, Shiloh's and Cheney's eyes met over his rounded shoulders. Cheney's eyes sparkled with frosty green points of light, while Shiloh's calm features were animated, his expression one of barely contained excitement. Cheney thought with a pang that he'd never seemed so vital, so strong, so alive . . . so heartbreakingly attractive.

His eyes grew heated with awareness, as if he knew her thoughts, which he seemed so often to do. Quickly she dropped her gaze and leaned over toward Reverend Merced, who was humming and muttering to himself.

Shiloh and Cheney waited impatiently. Restlessly Shiloh pulled the three chairs close around the end of the table. Reverend Merced absently sat, never taking his eyes off the tapestry, while Cheney sank into the chair with relief. Shiloh remained standing, leaning close over Reverend Merced, propping one hand on the back of the missionary's chair and one hand on the table. Cheney found herself studying Shiloh's rugged, scarred hands with more interest than she felt for the tapestry.

"Yes, I think I've got it now," Reverend Merced suddenly announced. "You see this first scene, with this figure at the center. Even though it's rather a simplistic figure, you can see that it is a woman or girl, and she has black hair and Oriental eyes. This girl—and I'm certain she is the artisan who made this tapestry—was the daughter of a poor fisherman. Her home was probably a crude boat in the South China Sea. She was an only child, and she was illiterate. Then she was orphaned."

"You can tell all that?" Shiloh barely breathed. "How?"

"Well, obviously I think that your compass was her most prized possession, and therefore I imagine it would have been made by her father—a fisherman. Now look at the self-portrait. Do you see how unproportioned the feet are? That's not careless artistry, it's deliberate. Her feet were unbound, and she was ashamed. That's why she's depicted them so large—to her, I'm sure they appeared huge and ugly."

"Unbound feet?" Cheney repeated. "I don't understand."

Reverend Merced turned to her. "In China, all girls of good family have their feet bound, beginning at the age of about five. Her mother and aunts tie the feet, and by increasingly tight bandaging through the years, her heel bone and forefoot are brought closer together. They strive to shape them so that they are no more than three inches long; then they could be called 'Golden Lotuses,' which is most desirable."

Cheney looked appalled. "You are telling me that these women *deliberately* make themselves club-footed?"

"Yes, they do," Reverend Merced answered calmly. "It's not only considered the ideal of feminine beauty. Without 'Golden Lotuses' a girl is unmarriageable. Even the life of a concubine—please pardon me, Dr. Duvall, but in China they are considered honored members of society—is not open to a girl with unbound feet."

"I thought you were a Christian," Cheney rasped. "You sound so . . . calm, so matter-of-fact about it! How could you countenance such a thing?"

A jolt of deep pain marred Shiloh's face at Cheney's harsh words, but she ignored him, gazing accusingly at Reverend Merced. He met her anger with a beatific smile and a kind voice. "Dr. Duvall, I certainly did not intend to offend you, and if I did I most humbly apologize. The topic is, of course, offensive to American ladies, and I—"

"No," Cheney countered. "It's not the topic. I'm not stupid. Of course I know of the existence of prostitutes. It's just that you're so . . . so . . ."

"Calm?" Shiloh suggested with a sharp edge to his voice. "Kind, maybe?"

"It's quite all right, really," Reverend Merced ventured. "Believe me, I understand—all too well—Dr. Duvall's indignation. I, too, was shocked and enraged when I came face-to-face with my first little six-year-old girl, who was already in continuous pain from her feet being so cruelly and constantly bound."

"Oh really?" Cheney said with frosty politeness. "But you do sound inured to it. You even seem to admire it."

"Oh no, never," he said firmly. "Of course I care, very much, just as much as I did then. It's just that my wife, and the Lord, carefully pointed out to me that I wasn't going to do much good if I stayed furiously angry with my brothers and sisters all the time."

"Really," Cheney said coldly, and now Shiloh began to look angry, his eyes slowly narrowing to blue slits.

"Yes, Dr. Duvall," Reverend Merced said respectfully. "It took many years for me to learn such a grievous lesson, and for the Lord to cleanse me from such unprofitable anger. After all, our blessed Lord Jesus must be constantly and continuously appalled by our wickedness, our blindness, our stupidity—but does He stay angry with us all the time? No, of course not. He loves us so much that He gently leads us and teaches us. And I—even though I spent many, many years being chastised for my proud wrath, stubbornly refusing to change—believe that finally I learned to have a measure of patience and some understanding."

"I will never understand such ignorant cruelty," Cheney said stiffly.

"Oh, yeah?" Shiloh finally spoke up, his tone carefully controlled. "Hey, Doc, you wear whalebone corsets? You know, the kind where you tie yourself up so you can have a seventeen-inch waist?"

"What!" Cheney snapped. "How dare you, Shiloh!"

"Yeah, you know," he went on relentlessly. "The kind where it makes you faint? And sometimes even cracks your ribs? How many ladies have you treated with problems like that?"

Cheney sat rigidly in her chair, staring at Shiloh, her face set in hard lines, her eyes flashing dangerously. Shiloh met her gaze stonily, and Reverend Merced looked uncomfortable.

Abruptly Cheney wilted. "Oh, dear, I'm behaving badly, aren't I? How can I possibly apologize to you, Reverend Merced . . . and . . . and you, too, Shiloh for my unforgivable rudeness?"

"Apology accepted," Reverend Merced said briskly. "It's forgotten."

Shiloh watched Cheney, and to her deep dismay, he still looked mutinous. In an instant, however, as she stared at him with misery plain on her face, he deliberately smoothed out his expression and made his tone clear and casual. "Please go on, Reverend."

With a measure of relief Merced continued, "So this girl was from a poor family, one that could not afford the luxury of a child—a worker—with bound feet. She's wearing white, and that's our next clue—white is the mourning color in China. Now look, do you see these two odd figures here?"

Shiloh commented, "They're scary-looking, aren't they? A cloud, like fire, and those faces."

"Yes, I believe these are 'hungry ghosts,' " Reverend Merced told him. "You see, the Chinese worship their ancestors. They offer sacrifices to them, which they believe feed their spirits. If a person is too poor to offer sacrifice, the dead become 'hungry ghosts,' pitiful, frightening, and frightened spirits who wander aimlessly, without hope, without love."

"Sad," Shiloh said quietly. Cheney was conspicuously silent and kept her eyes trained on the tapestry.

"Yes," Reverend Merced agreed. "Anyway, I think that these must be this girl's parents. I think, since there is no indication here of any siblings, that she must have been an only child. This, too, would have been a terrible reproach to her and the parents, not to have a son to continue the line. I think the parents must have died. She was a poor, ugly orphan, and only a girl. So her parents became 'hungry ghosts.' "

He waited, but neither Shiloh nor Cheney made a comment, so he continued, "Now look here. Do you see what the girl is doing?"

"It's . . . the sea, isn't it?" Shiloh speculated. "And that—it's kind of a funny-looking boat, but—"

"Yes, it's a Chinese junk," Reverend Merced replied. "Their sails are shaped differently, and the body of the junk is low and squat, because generally they are used on the wide, slow rivers, or only close in the bays of the seas. So now the girl, alone, is at a port, and she's—"

"That's—she's diving, isn't she?" Shiloh interrupted. "And that's a pearl!" He looked at Reverend Merced, his eyes shining. "She was a pearl diver!"

"Yes, I think you're correct, Mr. Irons," he said, "and that's why I think she must have been in southern China. Most of the pearl diving is done in the South China Sea. Now look very closely at the face of the girl. It's small, but do you see? She has a mouth, and it's turned slightly down. Also, she has depicted her eyebrows in a slant, upturned to the center."

"She was sad," Shiloh murmured.

"Yes. It's interesting. This girl obviously couldn't read or write, though she had absorbed, for instance, that her story should be aligned top-to-bottom, right-to-left, as Chinese characters would be. But here, in this picture, she shows some knowledge of drama, which is a complex and formalized art in China. This expression she's depicted is the one used on the Chinese stage to portray sadness, regret, bitterness. And do you see these figures on the junk? They are simple, yes, obviously intended to portray two men—and they're clothed in white. Now I don't think that she meant to convey that they were in mourning, as she was. I think she was using a stage device."

"The actors dress in white to symbolize what?" Shiloh asked curiously.

"Treachery," he answered.

The three were silent for long moments. Finally Reverend Merced pointed to the next series of pictures. "Now the next scene. Here are two huge people, much bigger than the figures of the girl or the men in the junk. A woman and a man. Whom do you suppose they could be?" he asked, his eyes twinkling.

"They're white people, aren't they?" Shiloh ventured. "A . . . couple? Maybe . . . maybe my parents?"

"I think it's very possible," Reverend Merced answered. "Because of what the tapestry depicts later on."

"But . . . but . . . gracious, just look at these figures," Cheney put in hesitantly. "They look . . . evil. And . . . surrounded by dragons!"

"Yes, to our Occidental eyes, they do appear to be symbols of evil," Reverend Merced said gently. "But you must try, Dr. Duvall, to see this story through a young Chinese girl's eyes. I would imagine, to her"—he looked up at Shiloh appraisingly—"a tall blond man and woman with blue eyes would be somewhat frightening, and so she depicts them with wild, shocking white hair and round outraged eyes. The fact that they are dressed in black doesn't have the same connotation to the Chinese as it does to us. For again, the color black is used in drama to illustrate a bold character, a person of strong beliefs and the inner strength to stand up for them. Such people may be intimidating, but not necessarily wicked. And then there are the dragons."

"Surely you agree that dragons are a symbol of evil," Cheney began, but Shiloh gave her a penetrating glance, and she quieted.

"Again, Dr. Duvall, in western culture, they are," Reverend Merced said.

But Cheney couldn't contain herself. Rudely she burst out, "No, Reverend Merced, in biblical teachings they are."

"Yes, I know, Dr. Duvall," he said patiently, for he could sense the tension growing in Shiloh again. "All I'm attempting to do is interpret these symbols as the artist intended."

"I think Dr. Duvall must be overly tired," Shiloh said coldly. "Perhaps, Cheney, you would like me to get the carriage for you?"

Cheney was stunned by the frigid tone of Shiloh's voice; she couldn't recall his ever speaking to her in such a hateful tone. The thought crossed her mind that perhaps she was the one being hateful—after all, this was an important clue to Shiloh's past that he needed to understand—but impatiently she rejected the guilt this half-realization brought to her. She debated whether to leave, but some part of her couldn't bear the thought. Confusion rose up in her, dark and heavy, and before it could take hold of her mind she firmly shut a mental door, closing it out. For a while, anyway.

"No, I apologize . . . again," she said stiffly. "Please continue, Reverend Merced."

The elderly missionary was watching her gravely, his eyes flickering. As always, however, his voice was patient and kind. "Then, to continue, the dragon, to the Chinese mind, is a symbol of great power. The five-toed dragon, of bright yellow gold, is the emblem of royalty, the mark of the emperor or empress. Traditionally it is a symbol of good fortune, and also of a long and prosperous life. These three-toed, black-and-red dragons this girl has depicted, I think, are to reinforce that the two people are strong and powerful."

"I hope they were my . . . my . . . mother and father," Shiloh said hoarsely.

"I believe they are, Mr. Irons. Look here. You see that the girl again draws herself—only now she's lying down, beneath the couple, and the dragon below them? Now the girl is wearing red, which is a symbol of loyalty. Her eyes are closed, which means she is at rest. Her hands are folded, which means she is at peace. She has come under the protection of the strong and bold man and woman."

"I see," Shiloh said thoughtfully. "Yes, I see. And look . . . in the next series, there are ships—four ships. She's tried to make them look . . . more . . ."

"Seaworthy," Reverend Merced suggested. "They are more streamlined, more elegant than junks, although she has still made the sails look a little awkward. But you see the significance of the human figures here?"

"It's the couple and the girl," Shiloh observed. "But they're riding some kind of bird."

"It's a crane," Reverend Merced told him. "The Chinese revere them. They believe they are captive spirits of beauty, of wealth, of good fortune. I think she was trying to show that the couple sailed in a fine ship, a wondrous ship, that was far better—or above—the fleet."

"A fine clipper?" Shiloh suggested, his eyes warm.

"Perhaps so," Reverend Merced nodded. "Now here is an interesting scene. Look at this symbol."

"I know, I have looked at it a lot," Shiloh said wryly. "It's the only thing on this tapestry that looks something like an alphabetical character."

"Yes, it does, but I don't think it is," Reverend Merced said with a trace of excitement. "I know it's not a Chinese character. Look here—oh, I need something—a pencil—" he muttered vaguely. Suddenly he jumped out of his chair and hurried into the house, talking to himself.

Shiloh studied Cheney impassively, and she could feel a discomforting heat in her cheeks. Moments seemed to drag by, and finally she muttered, "I'm sorry, Shiloh. I don't know what's wrong with me today."

"Well, I do," he muttered darkly.

"Wh-what?" Cheney stammered.

But Reverend Merced reappeared, happily clutching a pitiful stub of a pencil and a forlorn scrap of paper. "Look at this, Dr. Duvall. Perhaps you can help me see if my observation is feasible. Do you see this geometric symbol? Now look." He drew three crosses, the one in the middle large, the two on either side smaller, but with the crossbeams at equal heights. "You see, I don't think she would have realized that the crossbeams would be closer to the top, instead of the middle," he said enthusiastically. "Crucifixions on a cross are Roman inventions, you see, so she would never have conceived of such a thing. Now—" He connected the crossbeams into a straight horizontal line, then drew straight serifs at the end of each line, the three vertical ones and the single horizontal one. "There!" he said with pride. "What do you think?"

"I think," Cheney said slowly, "that your interpretation is absolutely correct. I think it's three crosses. And . . . and . . . this dead dragon underneath . . ." She gave Shiloh a cautiously pleading look, then went on. "Do you suppose that that was the best way she could think of to depict a dead Savior? A dead—emperor, if you will?"

"Yes, yes, I certainly do!" Reverend Merced vigorously declared. "It must be! And look! Then there are three sunrises—the Chinese usually show the rising sun as red—and here is the dragon again! Alive, strong, glowing! Note that it is the imperial yellow—but with seven toes, which would be her way of adding all the majesty and nobility that she could to her vision!"

"She became a Christian," Cheney said softly. "And this was the best way she knew to show it."

"Isn't it wonderful?" Reverend Merced exclaimed.

"More than wonderful," Cheney murmured quietly. "Miraculous."

"Yes, it is. Always, with all of us," Reverend Merced agreed.

Shiloh was studying the series of scenes, his face absorbed, and Reverend Merced quickly said, "Now, this last set of pictures. This, Mr. Irons, is why I'm certain that this tapestry depicts a Chinese girl's life with your parents. First we have another flock of cranes, with the girl and the couple riding the largest. The flock, if you will note, goes in all directions of the compass."

"Yes, north, south, east, west," Shiloh noted, pointing to each lead bird in the groupings. "And this scene is bordered by the same kinds of ships she did up here."

"Yes, so I think that the couple owned more than one ship, but because they always traveled on a special one, a wondrous one, the girl shows them flying on the most revered bird, the crane," Reverend Merced speculated. "And so they traveled, everywhere. Now look at this very last series. These two birds are mandarin ducks. They are, perhaps, the most beloved birds in all of China. They are always used to symbolize true and perfect love. They are always painted in pairs."

"So . . . this . . . these are my parents?" Shiloh wondered.

"I think so. Because look here, at the last finished picture. It's our little maiden, and what is she doing?"

"She's kneeling by some water—" Shiloh began hesitantly.

"Still water, denoted by the gentle widening circles, which means she was at peace," Reverend Merced explained. "And she's feeding a duckling."

"A baby," Cheney breathed. "Shiloh."

"Yes," Reverend Merced said simply. "Shiloh."

The three stared long at the last scene the Chinese girl had so poignantly depicted. Shiloh's face was tender, vulnerable. Though she fought it fiercely, tears burned Cheney's eyes; she turned and surreptitiously brushed all traces of them away, and by a sheer effort of will swallowed the overwhelming sadness and regret she felt for him. When she turned around, her face carefully set in a tranquil pose, he was watching her knowingly. He smiled at her, which threatened to make the tears flow again. But with a superhuman effort Cheney stifled them and managed to give him a tremulous smile in return.

"Well, Mr. Irons, I think that tells us your story," Reverend Merced murmured in a deep voice. "But I am so sorry—I see nothing here, nothing at all, that gives us perhaps the most important clue—a family name."

With an effort Shiloh drew his gaze away from Cheney's strained face and frowned. "I guess that'd be too much to ask. Since she couldn't write, and all. She did a great job of telling the story."

"Yes," Reverend Merced said absently. His brow wrinkled as he grew deep in thought, and Cheney and Shiloh waited in silence. After a few moments he took a deep breath, then said quietly. "There is, perhaps, a clue to *where* your parents lived. But you must understand—I'm not certain of this. It's just a speculation on my part."

"I understand," Shiloh said kindly. "But I'd be glad to hear any ideas you might have, sir."

"Well . . . you see. Up here, as part of the background, when this girl is in China—you see the mountains? This is the typical way Chinese artists depict mountains. Steep and elongated with a narrow base. Many of the mountains, at least in the southern part of China, look exactly like this."

"Not like our mountains," Shiloh observed. "Thinner, taller."

"Exactly," Reverend Merced agreed. "Now look down here. Beginning here—at the scene with the Christian symbols—you see these mountains here? They are wider at the base, with more gentle slopes."

"And they're black," Cheney noted. "Those others—in China—they were gray."

"Yes, they're black . . . but look here, at this final scene, behind the mandarin ducks," Reverend Merced pointed out. "The same mountains, black, wide at the base—"

"With fiery red summits," Shiloh said with an edge to his voice.

"Volcanoes?" Cheney breathed.

"I think so," the missionary replied.

"So . . . volcanoes would most likely be in—" Shiloh began hesitantly, as if he were afraid of voicing it out loud.

"Hawaii," said Reverend Merced.

17

Temperament and Taste

Dr. Cheney Duvall was having a most troublesome night.

For one thing, she had adjusted to night work and day sleep so well that on her nights off it was impossible for her to rest. But the setting of her physiological clock was not the only reason Cheney was lying in bed, eyes squeezed stubbornly shut, bedclothes tangled, nightgown twisted. Without her consent, her mind kept doggedly returning to Shiloh Irons: the expressions on his face, the tension between them that day, things he'd said, the way he'd said them. In spite of her most determined efforts, her thoughts honed in on him, and Cheney seemed helpless to constrain them.

"Ohh!" she groaned in exasperation and bounded out of bed. With roughly impatient movements, she lit a single candle and pulled on a heavy velvet dressing gown and soft velvet slippers. Opening the double doors that led out onto the generous balcony, she hurried outside and stood by the balustrade. Crossing her arms, she frowned at the feeble city lights below. In spite of the warm day and a cleansing wind, a fog had crept in after sundown. It lay heavy on Cheney, like an old, damp, smelly wool cloak. She shivered. "Cold as winter," she murmured darkly.

Returning to her bedroom, she closed the glass balcony doors softly so as not to wake Victoria, whose bedroom was next to hers. Then she left her room to cross the half-lit hallway into the room opposite. The second floor of Steen House consisted of four immense bedrooms with baths *en suite.* Cheney and Victoria had taken the two bedrooms that opened onto the balcony overlooking the gardens. The two front bedrooms had no balconies, but they had the corner turrets. Cheney decided to sit in the north turret for a while and try to analyze the perplexities that plagued her.

As she entered the extra bedroom, she stood still to allow her eyes to adjust to the darkness and half wished that she had chosen this room. Wryly she smiled to herself; Victoria would be appalled. The two back bedrooms were very feminine, while the two front bedrooms were essentially masculine. This one, which was Cheney's favorite, had a one-hundred-year-old Chippendale bed in a Gothic design with massive posts, a flat canopy with damask tapestry bed curtains in mellow faded colors, and a heavy medieval woodcarving topping the canopy. At the foot of the bed was a lion-footed stool upholstered with an eighteenth-century hunting scene in needlepoint. A genteel George II wing chair, covered in muted green velvet, looked welcoming in a corner reading niche. A massive Gothic mahogany linen press dominated one wall.

This bedroom suited Cheney's temperament and taste much better than her ornate—stifling, Cheney judged—Empire bed with blue and gold satin swags, fringes, tassels, and ormolu crown valance. Particularly she disliked the swan chairs modeled after Josephine Bonaparte's for the Tuilleries Palace. She thought them pompous and useless; the golden swans as armrests, which endowed the chairs with some sort of pretensions to mini-thrones, made them virtually uninhabitable for longer than a few minutes.

"You're an ungrateful wretch," Cheney told herself sternly. The furnishings in her bedroom were costly and elegant, and here she was mentally griping as if they were rush mats and three-legged milking stools. In spite of her inward reprimand, she went into the turret and reflected that she liked it, too, as it was not crammed with furnishings and fragile accessories. Cushioned window seats all around were the only seats, except for a businesslike chair that went with an elegantly simple Queen Anne secretary. Cheney curled up defensively in the window seat and stared out. Very little geography was visible, only the viscous fog undulating somberly outside the diamond-shaped leaded panes.

As Cheney was by nature organized and disciplined, she crisply cleared the clutter from her mind and began a rational scrutiny of the causes of her tumult.

"Really, it all began when Shiloh told me that he wouldn't be at the doctors' staff meeting tomorrow," she whispered, staring into a blurry middle distance. "Why did that . . . unsettle me so?"

With typical thoroughness Cheney formulated hypotheses of this quandary and summarily rejected them until she doggedly found the truth.

Am I afraid to face them without him? Do I feel that I'm inadequate by myself—is it only with Shiloh that I feel confident in my abilities and in my determination to gain respect?

She pondered this for a few moments, then muttered, "That's not it . . . not exactly . . ." Cheney still felt fully prepared to meet with Dr. Baird and the other doctors; her observations of the problems with the hospital and staff were valid; her conclusions were clear; her solutions were intelligent and viable. She felt bold and self-confident.

For two years now—ever since I got out of medical school—he's been there; he's been my ally, my confidante, much more than an assistant. He's more like a partner. In medicine, of course. It's simple, actually. We've been a team, and I feel a little—tentative, I suppose—when he's not involved with every facet of my professional life.

And your personal life? the stern judge in Cheney's head demanded.

"Perhaps," she whispered. "But with the Lord's help I don't have to worry about that. . . ."

Cheney had a separate little compartment in her mind and heart where she kept her feelings for Shiloh utterly, ruthlessly partitioned. It wasn't just a repression of hopeless longing; it wasn't a sacrificial martyrdom; nor was it a denial. Cheney freely admitted to herself that she was physically attracted to Shiloh. The longer they were together, the stronger her desires became. Sudden longings for his touch occasionally jolted her. Unnamed yearnings bruised her at odd times. Sometimes a rush of passion, strong and urgent, engulfed her.

But Cheney had a defense, and a place of peace. In this matter the Lord had granted her a wisdom beyond her years, and certainly her experience, that was her stronghold. Shiloh Irons was a desirable man. She was a young, healthy woman. God himself had endowed Adam and Eve with physical desires and passion. It was not a sin unless, of course, one indulged such feelings until they became lust. Peacefully Cheney reflected that she felt no guilt, no condemnation, because of her human and womanly response to Shiloh.

With the same calculation Cheney reviewed her emotions toward Shiloh, and again she came to the solid, comfortable conclusion that there was no problem here. Shiloh was not a Christian; she had no desire to risk her relationship with the Lord by displeasing Him with thoughts of being unequally yoked. She had found that this decision alone shielded her from feelings of hopeless, tragic, helpless love. Her obedience to the Lord's will was her peace, not only of mind, but of her soul and her heart.

With a small sigh she made herself reflect upon Victoria's words yesterday. *He's in love with you, Cheney. Surely you know that.*

But she didn't.

Shiloh, in many ways and at many times, was still a complete enigma to Cheney.

He likes me, he enjoys my company, he's comfortable with me, he respects me. . . . I think he admires some things about me. . . . But sometimes he does show . . . a certain desire, a strong attraction to me. Just as, I'm sure, he sees in me sometimes.

Cheney frowned and struggled to know and understand Shiloh's feelings toward her. But there seemed to be no way to find a definitive answer to the question. All she could do was wonder. *I haven't fallen in love with Shiloh—but only because I choose not to, and by the strength of the Lord Jesus Christ I've kept my heart from harm.*

But what about him?

If he's in love with me, then what keeps him from showing it, from declaring it?

Cheney brooded upon these things for a long time. Outside the mists wandered, sometimes aimlessly, sometimes seeming to aim for the window, then break as ghost-waves on the shore of diamond glass. Desultorily she breathed upon one of the panes, and with her little finger wrote "Shiloh" in the delicate steam. It was silly and fatuous, and she knew it, but she didn't care. The evidence of her foolishness was formed of less than breath and less than air, and would soon disappear altogether.

★ ★ ★ ★

Dr. Ansel Tasker, twenty-two and fresh out of San Francisco's three-year-old Toland Medical College, was a meek and shy young man with curling brown hair already receding away from his wrinkled forehead. He had a small, inquisitive nose and fast, clever hands. Cheney had never worked with him; in fact, she'd only met him twice in passing since she'd come to work at St. Francis. He was seated—huddled, almost—in one of the club chairs in Dr. Baird's office. Dr. Werner sat with a proprietary air to the right of Dr. Baird's desk, while Walker wearily slumped in the straight chair to the left.

When Cheney arrived at 9:58 for the 10:00 A.M. meeting, everyone was already present, so with a calm and unhurried air she settled by herself onto the couch. With deliberate casualness she arranged her skirt, then placed her report and notes—which were in an expensive leather case she'd bought just for the purpose—beside her.

Dr. Baird cleared his throat, a deep growl, and got right to the point, as was his custom. "I called this meeting because last Friday night we had some confusion, and I've received some unclear and unsatisfactory reports about the events. In my view this implies that there are some problems that need to be resolved."

With a jaundiced eye he studied each of the doctors' faces. Dr. Tasker quickly dropped his gaze to study his slender hands, Cheney tilted her chin slightly and met Dr. Baird's gaze head-on, Walker nodded wearily. To Cheney's surprise, Dr. Baird's discerning stare lingered on Dr. Werner's face, and Dr. Werner's angular jaw tightened. "I am the man who's going to solve these problems," Dr. Baird muttered, then leaned back in his chair and crossed his arms.

"Dr. Baird, I have prepared a full report, in writing, of the events of last Friday night, along with my recommendations for some changes in hospital procedures, some additions to the attendants' training, and an evaluation of some of the hospital's unused facilities," Cheney said in a clear and concise voice.

Dr. Baird appraised her with narrow eyes. Dr. Tasker gave her a startled glance, then chewed nervously on his bottom lip. Walker glanced at her quizzically but smiled warmly at her when she met his gaze. Dr. Werner's steel-gray eyebrow shot up as his Arctic blue eyes raked over her with ill-concealed disapproval.

A time of silence weighed on them, and the tension grew heavier with each long second. Finally Dr. Baird said, "I appreciate your conscientious work. I will read your report, and I will take into consideration your recommendations."

"Thank you, sir." Cheney couldn't keep a snide little note of triumph creeping in as she saw Dr. Werner's open disdain at Dr. Baird's speech.

"But," Dr. Baird said heavily, "we're not here to evaluate the staff or the hospital's rules. Today we're here to review you—the doctors. Particularly where it is pertinent to last Friday night."

Dr. Tasker swallowed hard, then ventured, "But I didn't have any patients involved in anything, Dr. Baird."

Impatiently Dr. Baird replied, "Not directly, perhaps, but you had patients in the hospital, Dr. Tasker. Our decisions here will affect them, too, as much as any patient."

Cheney made a quick mental shift during this exchange. She had come prepared to critique the staff, the rules, the unused wings of the hospital—but she also had included in her report a scathing criticism of some of the doctors' written orders, which had put her in so many precarious positions last Friday night. Dr. Tasker's notes were always clear as to the prescriptive: dosage, frequency, possible adverse reactions, and so on, but he never made any evaluation of the patient. Walker's notes were thorough, but so hurriedly written that Cheney and the nurses frequently had trouble deciphering them. And concerning Dr. Werner, Cheney had several comments that she felt needed to be discussed.

While she was busily reorganizing her thoughts, she suddenly noticed that, again, the other doctors were watching her in silence. She cleared her throat, a weak, uncertain sound.

Dr. Baird said gruffly, "Dr. Duvall, I have already interviewed the other doctors and several staff members. Some things came to my attention that need to be discussed, and this is your opportunity to give me your explanation."

At first Cheney was unable to comprehend the implications of what Dr. Baird said. When she finally absorbed it, she was stunned. *This meeting is a critique of—me? It's an investigation of me? Dr. Baird can phrase it however he wants to, but it's still a . . . a . . . hearing! As if I'm guilty of something! I've done nothing—nothing!—except my job as well as I could under such needlessly difficult circumstances!*

Cheney became aware of a heated ache in her back, and an objective voice in her mind dully recited, *You are sitting up much too stiffly erect.* Still she was motionless. She felt anger surge in her chest, hot and stifling, and resentment, deep and powerful, seep into her as if she'd been submerged in a bath of oil. Her cheeks were pale. In her eyes was a hard glitter.

At long last she said in a brittle voice, "I understand, Dr. Baird. I'm fully prepared to explain any, or all, the events that transpired last Friday."

Ignoring her curt tone, he said with gruff calm, "There are three areas that I think all of the doctors need to consider carefully. First, I want to discuss the authority of the physicians at St. Francis de Yerba

Buena, in relation to the nurses and attendants." He studied the four doctors shrewdly and continued. "I want an improvement on how we supervise the staff. I want the physicians to be in complete control of their activities at all times, and I want them closely supervised."

Dr. Baird was watching Cheney, so she shrugged with elaborate carelessness. "Very well."

"Very well," Dr. Werner sarcastically echoed her. "What that means is that medical attendants do not decide upon and order prescriptives. Drunken dressers do not perform surgical procedures. And an apothecary never issues a diagnosis."

Cheney tried to control her ire, but still she sounded strained. "I assume you are referring directly to events that transpired Friday night."

"Yes."

Cheney's jaw clenched so tightly that she might have chipped a tooth, but she answered smartly, "Shiloh Irons merely facilitated orders that he knew I would give as soon as I could attend the patients. Mr. Irons also knew that it would be some time before I could even see these patients, much less diagnose and prescribe treatment. Therefore he assigned Mr. Florey—who was perfectly sober—to stitch Mr. Fain's wound. I believe he did a total of eight stitches, which I would hardly term a 'surgical procedure.' Mr. Indro merely confirmed, with the use of an autolaryngoscope, my own diagnosis. Which, I might point out, was the correct diagnosis. Yours, Dr. Werner, was incorrect."

Dr. Werner's severe features remained impassive, though his eyes narrowed slightly. Before he could respond, Dr. Baird asserted, "I understand that there were extenuating circumstances affecting your decisions, Dr. Duvall. Nevertheless, I must insist that you maintain an absolute control over the attendants." Staring at her, he waited for her response.

"Yes, sir," she said. She realized that she sounded rebellious, but it was the best she could do at the moment.

"No nurses or attendants will order treatments or prescriptives. Mr. Indro, though an expert apothecary, will not be consulted on diagnoses. If it is necessary to discuss a particular case, the attending physician will be called. As for Mr. Florey"—he gave Dr. Werner a hard glance—"I have no problem with his stitching up injuries; he dresses wounds very well, so in cases of necessity, as I believe this was, any attendant who is capable may perform such emergency treatments if they are deemed necessary."

Cheney was beyond repentance, and she gave Dr. Werner a sidelong glance of triumph, but Dr. Baird quickly deflated her. "But only as a *physician* directly orders," he continued sternly. "I'm sure this is clear to everyone now."

"Well, I do have a question," Walker said. "The rule is clear, of course, but the reality is sometimes not as objective. What about verbal orders? Are they valid? What about when a physician directs a certain prescription"—he gave Cheney a warm look—"as Dr. Duvall did in ordering ephedra for Marlett Fair, but is uncertain of the dosage? She had made it clear to Mr. Indro that Mr. Fair would need ephedra if, in fact, he had diphtheria. Then she was called away into a life-and-death emergency. Doesn't this constitute a good reason for taking the initiative, and fulfilling the spirit of the physician's orders, if not the law?"

Cheney gave Walker an intensely grateful look.

Dr. Werner answered evenly, "No. There can never be any nonsense about attendants reading a doctor's mind and then just starting treatment as they *feel* it should be done. Mr. Indro and Mr. Irons never should have given Mr. Fair anything without orders. Clear, concise, written orders."

"In emergency situations such as we—particularly Dr. Duvall—faced the other night, I don't believe that rule is enforceable. In fact, I don't believe it's conscionable. If Dr. Duvall had obeyed this rule, she would have been at the nurses' station for hours writing orders and instructions. Patients would have suffered," Walker mildly persisted.

Werner gave a small exasperated sigh. "It's difficult for me to comprehend your argument, Walker. Either nurses are allowed to decide on a patient's treatment, or they must be required to wait for a doctor's instructions. I understand, and agree, that Mr. Irons' expertise and medical knowledge are exceptional. But can we, here, arbitrarily decide that he may perform a physician's tasks? Why, then, should anyone bother to become a physician? We could stop fighting it and just let the surgeons and dentists and hacks and abortionists hang out a sign when they decide that it is time they start calling themselves physicians."

Walker looked thoughtful and had no answer. Neither did Cheney, but she argued anyway. "Mr. Irons's expertise is exceptional, and I still maintain that the circumstances dictated the correctness of his actions."

"His actions are not in question here, Dr. Duvall. Yours are," Werner shot back.

"Let's move on," Dr. Baird said heavily. "I have decided upon an unambiguous rule that must be followed at St. Francis de Yerba Buena. Attendants and nurses must only provide such treatment as prescribed by a physician. Written orders, initialed properly, by the responsible doctor, whether it is the primary physician or a staff physician. Any questions? No, I thought not. So now I want to discuss a corollary to this situation we've just brought up: the rules and policies of St. Francis. Last Friday night, rules were broken."

"Now what?" Cheney muttered to herself, but the words seemed loud in the tensely quiet room.

Dr. Baird gave her a hard look. "You disobeyed the primary physician's orders for Mrs. Callister, Dr. Duvall. You changed the diagnosis and subsequent treatment for Mr. Marlett Fair, and then performed a surgery upon him—all without even an attempt to consult with his physician. And"—he squinted down at a single sheet of paper squarely in front of him on the desk—"you took a patient out of the general ward and put her in an expensive private room without permission."

"I would have moved Mrs. Irby, too, Father," Walker declared, his eyes darkening to a stormy navy blue. "Now I wish I would have written orders to that effect so Dr. Duvall's judgment wouldn't be in question."

"But you didn't," his father countered, "and it is."

Cheney was dangerously close to losing her temper. If she had been overcome with anger, she would have simply gotten up and swept out of the room. As it was, at Dr. Baird's comment, she abandoned all attempts at reasoning and became reckless. "I gave Mrs. Callister something to eat! Her prescribed diet, I felt, was much too stringent! And if I hadn't diagnosed what was really wrong with Marlett Fair, and performed that emergency surgery, he would have died! And as for Mrs. Irby, I will be happy to personally pay the difference between her general ward rate and the private room rate for that night," she finished defiantly.

"Do you see, J. E.?" Dr. Werner commented coolly. "They always take a narrow, personal view, and then they react emotionally."

"Women, you mean," Cheney retorted angrily.

Werner appraised her in a supremely detached manner. "Yes. Female physicians, particularly."

"Dr. Duvall, please calm down," Dr. Baird said with carefully controlled patience. "I realize this is difficult for you. You have always worked alone, never in conjunction with other physicians. We've all been through this, all of us. Every time there is a problem at the hospital, we must decide how to solve it together."

With the merest hint of a smile, Dr. Werner said blandly, "It's nothing personal. It's a professional necessity. There is no need for hysterics."

Because he was so calm, Cheney abruptly, painfully saw and heard herself through his eyes. She was nowhere near hysteria, but she certainly was . . . tempestuous. With a sharply indrawn breath, she squeezed her eyes shut for a mere second and ordered herself, *Be calm and quiet and cold. Right now. No matter what happens, no matter what is said, be cold. Speak softly and unemotionally. All this criticism—this is the one thing that you can control. You can win on this count.*

With a supreme effort she sat back a tiny bit and positioned her hands gracefully in her lap. Her tone was neutral, though her mouth felt curiously stiff as she spoke the words. "Pardon me, Dr. Baird. Please go on."

"Thank you, Dr. Duvall," he said dryly. "Quite simply, the hospital does not allow the attending physician's orders to be changed. If a material change in a patient's condition—or a discovery of a diagnostic error—requires changes in treatment, the patient's physician should be consulted. Of course, all of these rules are governed by whether the situation is a quick, life-or-death emergency, and then each patient will be treated as necessary to sustain life. I think we all comprehend that."

He waited until all of the doctors nodded, although Cheney could only manage one curt bob of her head.

"And as far as assignment of private rooms go, that is to be decided by the patient's physician, and then he—or she—must get my permission."

"I understand," Cheney responded evenly. "Is there anything else?"

"Yes, Dr. Duvall, there is one more item that I must stress to you," Dr. Baird said in a warning tone. "This hospital is a private hospital, and what that means is that we limit our patients. We cannot afford to take in any patient who walks in the door. Also, a certain standard of medical care is expected by our patients."

A clear warning of what was coming was signaled to Cheney by Dr. Tasker dropping his head and flushing slightly, and by Walker's sudden refusal to meet her eyes. Still she didn't understand what Dr. Baird was saying. "I understand those principles," Cheney said coldly. "But just to assure that I have a complete understanding of what is required, Dr. Baird, perhaps you'd better give me examples."

"Very well." He leaned closer over his desk to direct his intense gaze directly into Cheney's eyes. "We take no Chinese patients, Dr. Duvall. For last Friday night, I would have made an exception, because Mr. Dare Dunning is a personal friend of mine and Walker's. But in the future you must understand and agree to abide by this rule. Also, we do not ordinarily send the ambulances to the Barbary Coast. Again, in this case, I approve of your decision because the patients were medical students, known to us. But unless it is an exceptional circumstance such as that, no St. Francis ambulances go to the Barbary Coast."

"Yes, Dr. Baird," Cheney said, sarcasm heavy in her voice and expression.

"You understand I am not reprimanding you for those two instances," Baird said, scrutinizing her carefully.

"Yes, Dr. Baird."

He grimaced at her tone but went on grimly, "But for this you must be subjected to a formal reprimand, Dr. Duvall: no Negro attendants are on staff here at St. Francis de Yerba Buena. None will be hired. None will be allowed to fill in under any circumstances."

"But, Dr. Baird, my maid Nia—" Cheney began stubbornly.

"I won't contemplate any extenuating circumstances for this, Dr. Duvall. It was inexcusable. Even if you felt you could not call in Dr. Werner, there were two other attendants available, who live only a short distance from the hospital," Dr. Baird said, his eyes harsh. "Again, no Negroes attend the patients in this hospital. As I clearly stated, our patients—the patients that we are all working so hard to serve—expect a certain standard of medical care. Regardless of our personal beliefs or feelings, colored attendants are not acceptable here. Do you understand?"

Cheney's eyes narrowed, and it seemed a long time before she answered. Finally she muttered darkly, "Oh yes, Dr. Baird. I understand perfectly."

★ ★ ★ ★

"That," Cheney pronounced irritably, "was not an enjoyable experience."

Walker gave her his most endearing boyish smile. "Those doctors' meetings never are. We always know someone—or everyone—is going to be raked over burning coals before it's over."

Cheney looked up at him with open disbelief. "Oh, really? I was certain that your father's supposed inclusion of all of the doctors was just to camouflage some pretty harsh judgments of me personally."

"That's just not true, Dr. Duvall," Walker answered mildly. "All of us have been subjected to review meetings. All of us have made mistakes that required evaluations."

"Even Dr. Werner?" Cheney asked darkly.

"Yes."

"Even your father?"

"Oh yes," Walker replied lightly. "When his practice was much more active, he made many mistakes. Dr. Werner was just as strict with him as he was with you."

"I don't believe it," Cheney scoffed. "Dr. Werner dislikes me. Personally. His criticism of me was unfair."

Walker was silent. They had left Dr. Baird's office together, and Walker had quietly asked her if he might speak to her for a few moments. They wandered out into the courtyard and stopped near the great fountain, where they watched the gleeful play of the water and the fat goldfish lazily swimming at their feet.

When Walker spoke, his voice was so low and soft that Cheney almost didn't catch the words. "I'm afraid you are much mistaken, Dr. Duvall. Dr. Werner has no personal vendetta against you. He merely stated his observations and opinions."

"He insulted me," Cheney argued stubbornly.

"How was that?"

"He said I took a narrow, personal view. He said I react emotionally."

"Ah," Walker said gravely. "But you are not taking this personally?"

"No!"

"And certainly you are unemotional about this observation."

"Yes!"

Walker watched her, his eyes dancing merrily, and Cheney regained some insight into her reaction. Still, she had no intention of acknowledging this to Walker—or to herself. Hastily she said, "You look very tired, Walker. I believe this is the first time I've seen you with any signs of fatigue. As your physician, I prescribe a cup of hot, black coffee."

"Sounds good," he sighed. "Last night was difficult. Shall we go to the doctors' hall?"

As usual, the little cottage was dingy-looking with opened bags of coffee, spillings of tea, and half-empty cups. The cook, Mrs. Raymond, cleaned the cottage thoroughly in the mornings, and Li Bai or Li Shen cleaned it at night, but the doctors came and went at such odd times throughout the day and evening that it was generally in disarray. Mrs. Raymond was careful to keep a fresh pot of coffee and hot water available throughout the day and usually left some pastries or fresh fruits in the kitchen. Walker wearily began cleaning up and preparing a tray, but Cheney sternly ordered him to sit down. "I'm the doctor, and this is my prescriptive," she said. "I'll prepare this for you. Then I'll make sure and write it down," she added mockingly.

He gave her a quizzical glance. "You understood the underlying implications of what my father said about written orders, didn't you?"

"Hmm? I suppose not. I was too busy worrying about what was being said outright to think about hidden meanings," Cheney complained.

"Yes, I know," Walker agreed—too readily, Cheney thought—but he went on before she could comment. "He said the rule is that the doctor's orders must be in writing. He didn't say they had to be in the doctor's writing. Do you recall that initialing was mentioned?"

Cheney brought in a tray of two cups of hot coffee and two small peach tarts and set it on the rickety three-legged tea table by the sofa. "Yes, I do recall it now. Do you mean that all of that punishment about Shiloh issuing doctor's orders could have been avoided if I'd just made him write it down, and then initialed it?"

Walker sighed, then picked up the cup of coffee and sipped it slowly, inhaling the richly acrid steam with appreciation. "I'm trying to make you understand, Dr. Duvall, that none of this was intended as a punishment to you or anyone. You see, all of us know that everything must be written down. We try to document it ourselves, but in emergency situations my father turns a blind eye if it's in an attendant's handwriting and properly initialed by a physician."

"I wasn't aware of all that," Cheney complained.

"Well," Walker commented gently, "now you are."

Cheney was mute, and her expression was clouded with the remnants of her anger and resentment. Walker searched her face anxiously, then went on carelessly, "All of us have been corrected from time to time, Dr. Duvall. Sometimes for things we didn't know, sometimes for rules we broke, sometimes for ignorant mistakes. It's just a part of being in a working environment where you have an interdependency with other people."

"Is that so?" Cheney scoffed. "Somehow I find it difficult to believe that Dr. Werner has ever been through a session such as I just endured."

"But he has," Walker persisted. "Not too long ago he was so harsh to Bethena Posey and Sallie Sisk that they both were reduced to tears. We had a meeting just like the one this morning, and my father demanded that we treat the nurses and attendants with courtesy and respect, and if they required strict correction, Mrs. Tilden should be advised to do it—in private. He particularly reprimanded Dr. Werner."

"How did he react?" Cheney asked curiously.

Walker shrugged. "The way he always does. Objectively, dispassionately. He clinically agreed that his actions had been too harsh, and that he had made a second mistake by dressing them down in front of the patients. He sounded just like he was standing outside himself, observing, and agreeing on that person's just reprimand."

"I don't understand it," Cheney grumbled. "I just don't understand people like that."

"No, it doesn't appear that you do," Walker candidly agreed.

Ignoring him, Cheney complained, "And what about all that about Mrs. Callister? All I did was give her a little food and a little more wine than Dr. Werner prescribed! What harm was there in that?"

"None, in itself," Walker said gently. "But you did change Dr. Werner's orders, did you not?"

"That's ridiculous."

"Is it? Suppose I give you another example, Dr. Duvall. You ordered a new, untested treatment for a dangerous illness—gangrene—for Ike Trimble."

"It's working," Cheney interrupted.

"Yes, it is. But we all—especially Dr. Werner—had serious reservations about it," Walker said gravely. "And did you know who was the most stringent about carrying out your precise orders, to the exact letter, Dr. Duvall? Do you know who, when he was on duty, usually performed the irrigation and debridement, instead of allowing the attendants to do it?"

Cheney was quiet for a long time. Staring out the window, she absently pleated her skirt between her fingers. Finally she said in a distant voice, "Dr. Werner?"

"Yes, Dr. Werner," Walker replied. "He is German, and for years he has adhered to the German philosophy of medicine that is very cautious. They observed that many doctors and treatments and prescriptives not only do not work, but many of them are positively harmful, and they evolved an attitude toward medicine that is extremely conservative."

"But sometimes that is harmful too," Cheney argued.

"Perhaps." Walker shrugged. "But who can say which is most harmful? Who can quantify the practice of medicine so that it is an exact science—*this* is correct in all situations, *this* is wrong, *this* will work forty-eight percent of the time—"

"I see," Cheney said quietly. "But I am trained to be a physician, and I cannot contemplate standing by and doing nothing, just . . . just . . . blessing a patient with my attention!"

Walker didn't answer, which in itself was a reply to Cheney's remarks. She knew Dr. Werner didn't simply refuse to treat patients, and no one expected her to behave that way either. But Cheney was angry, and the light in her heart had gone into the murky shadows of resentment and bitterness. After a long uncomfortable silence she muttered, "And I see that this policy of non-treatment extends to certain peoples and races, does it not? At least at St. Francis de Yerba Buena."

Walker studied Cheney's face with compassion and a touch of pity, but she refused to meet his honest eyes. Finally he answered wearily. "Not at all, Dr. Duvall. Refusal to treat the Chinese is simply an extension of the general hospital policy: no one is admitted who is not a patient of one of the physicians here."

"So all of you refuse to treat the Chinese," Cheney snapped.

"No," he replied patiently. "They refuse to come to us. They have very little confidence in Western medicine, you know. Their own medical traditions are . . . oh . . . about a thousand years older than ours."

"Older traditional treatments aren't necessarily the best," Cheney said hotly. "I've heard they actually stick needles in people! And burn them with hot irons!"

"Acupuncture and moxibustion." Walker nodded thoughtfully.

"We find it savage and primitive. But, Dr. Duvall, suppose you try to explain to them about leeches and cupping?"

Cheney was taken aback. "But . . . but we don't do that anymore!"

"Of course you and I don't. But many so-called doctors still do, and you know it. So do the Chinese," Walker said regretfully. "They would be frightened to death to go to a Western doctor. It's not our policy to deliberately exclude them, Dr. Duvall. Ask Reverend Merced if they'll allow us to treat them. Ask him where they insist upon going, even with traumatic injuries. To their own practitioners."

Cheney considered this for a while, then decided on another attack. "That still doesn't explain my reprimand about Nia."

He shot her a glance with the first hint of impatience he'd shown. "That had nothing to do with treatment of a Negro patient, Dr. Duvall. I have, in fact, seen very few Negroes in San Francisco, and I've never had one come to me and request treatment. And besides, don't tell me you didn't comprehend why you were reprimanded. Nia is not, after all, on staff here."

"I don't care," Cheney cried. "Negroes have a right to be here! And so do those poor people down in the Barbary Coast!"

Walker laughed humorlessly. "Yes, they deserve medical treatment. So have you been to the Barbary Coast yet, Dr. Duvall?"

"Yes, I certainly have."

"Then I know you saw at least one person—probably many more than one—who was injured, or passed out," Walker declared. "And did you treat them? Did you stop and ask them if they'd be interested in being your patient?"

Cheney's silence was answer enough.

He went on indignantly, "You haven't seen City and County Hospital emergencies. They take all cases, all people, any ailment, any complaint, any injuries, anytime. It's filthy, it's dangerous, it's like a train wreck and an earthquake and Bedlam, all at once. Particularly on weekends. I should know. I, and Dr. Werner, and Dr. Tasker all volunteer for alternating Friday and Saturday and Sunday nights. Last Friday night, Dr. Werner was at City and County while we were here dealing with our genteel emergencies. Do you know what he was dealing with? A drunk, brought in from the Barbary Coast by some of his buddies—one of whom had shot him in the gut. None of them seemed to know which one it was. They were quite jolly about it, even the man who'd been shot. He still had his gun, and he waved it around and fired it just to show how he was still full of spit and vinegar. He almost shot two of the attendants, and he did shoot out four windows."

"What!" Cheney exclaimed, appalled. "How—aren't there police, or someone, to deal with such things?"

"Of course," Walker told her. "The ratio of policemen to people on the Barbary Coast on weekends is approximately one to one hundred fifty. Two policeman are on duty at the hospital each night. They're still outnumbered."

"Oh," Cheney said in a small voice. "What happened to the man who was shot?"

"Dr. Werner had been operating on him for about an hour when he died," Walker said evenly. "And then his friends threatened to kill Dr. Werner."

"They did?" Cheney gulped.

"Yes, they did," Walker answered quietly. "But he handled them exactly as he handles everything else. He told them that they were so drunk they probably couldn't hit Telegraph Hill with buffalo shot. He said that he'd take offense, however, if one of them did try to shoot him, and he would certainly defend himself. And since he was sober, and also a fairly good shot, he figured he'd probably be able to drop two or three of them before they could get him. He said all this as if he were discussing possible courses of treatment for catarrh," Walker finished with amusement.

"I suppose they changed their mind about trying to kill him," Cheney remarked.

"Yes, they slunk off," Walker said. "And Dr. Werner just went on to the next drunk, the next gunshot wound, the next knifing, the next alcohol poisoning."

They sat in silence for a while, and Cheney sipped her lukewarm coffee listlessly. "I must be going home," she murmured. "I need to rest before tonight."

Walker rose and stretched achingly, then offered Cheney his hand. "May I have the great honor and pleasure of escorting you home, Dr. Duvall?"

Cheney rose and smiled at him for the first time that day. "Dr. Walker Baird, I would enjoy your company, and thank you for your solicitations."

"Of course, m'lady."

Cheney took his arm, then murmured, "And besides, I should like to continue our discussion of Nia and her training."

Walker sighed, then boyishly asked, "But can't we talk about something else besides work today?"

Cheney looked up at him blankly. "But what else is there," she asked, "besides being a doctor?"

"What else, indeed?" he muttered darkly.

"I beg your pardon?"

"I have decided, Dr. Duvall," Walker dramatically announced, "that I am finished with discussing anything or anyone involved with medicine today. From this moment, until I sadly take my leave of you, we shall discuss something else of much greater import."

"And what is that, may I ask?" Cheney countered.

He gave her a sly and warm glance. "Your beauty, Dr. Duvall. I do find that most women are always happy to change the subject of conversation to that topic. And also, I wish to alert you as to how I propose to persuade you to allow me to be your escort at the grand party for the hospital Mrs. de Lancie is sponsoring at Steen House."

Cheney blushed slightly and started to demur, both because she had no wish to talk about her physical appearance, and because she had an uneasy feeling that Dr. Walker Baird was beginning to view their relationship as much more warm and personal than Cheney wished. But as she had done so often all morning long, again she ignored her better judgment. With a wry smile she said, "Very well, sir. You may proceed."

A foolish woman is clamorous…
For she sitteth at the door of her house,
On a seat in the high places of the city,
To call passengers
Who go right on their ways:

Whoso is simple,
Let him turn in hither:
As for him that
Wanteth understanding,
She saith to him,

"Stolen waters are sweet,
And bread eaten in secret is pleasant."

But he knoweth not
That the dead are there;
And that her guests
Are in the depths of hell.

Proverbs 9:13, 14–18

18

Just Plain Miracles

Mrs. Brookshear Irby, after the premature birth of her son and his death twenty-two minutes later, went into an alarming decline. She refused most food and would drink only water and apple juice. Her rich brown hair grew dull, her still-youthful complexion suddenly showed signs of age and wear. Most of the time she stared listlessly out the window of her fine private room. Once, in the middle of the night, Cheney caught her pretending to sleep. But Cheney knew she was awake, for a tiny forlorn sob escaped her. Cheney spoke soothingly to her and gave her a drink of cool water but felt helpless to comfort the woman, who suffered not from physical ills but from grief and guilt. Cheney studied Dr. Werner's notes, but they never gave any hint of his method of dealing with such sickness of soul. Cheney had no solution either.

Surprisingly, Victoria did.

"Why didn't you tell me about Viola Irby?" she demanded one morning when Cheney came in from work. Victoria was having her usual lack of breakfast out on the terrace, and Cheney tiredly threw herself down at the table and asked Mrs. O'Neil for strong tea with lots of honey and cream.

"First of all, I would never betray any patient's confidence, Victoria," Cheney said with an irritability that seemed to plague her often these days. "Secondly, I wasn't aware that you were acquainted with her."

"Only slightly," Victoria replied. "I called upon her when we first arrived, and she received me. It was obvious she was expecting, so I thought it unusual that she wasn't in confinement."

"I expect she dared not refuse a call from a Steen," Cheney commented. "How did you find out about her?"

"I was at the hospital yesterday, going over some plans for the party with Dr. Baird."

"What party?" Cheney wearily asked.

"The party that we're giving for the hospital staff and patrons."

"Oh. Oh yes. That party. Um—what do I need to do?" Cheney half-heartedly volunteered.

Victoria smiled. "Noble of you to ask, but you can drop that long-suffering martyred look. Mrs. O'Neil and I have it under control. I rather like planning parties. It's fun, particularly when one doesn't have to do any of the actual work."

"Poor Mrs. O'Neil," Cheney murmured. She'd forgotten that the housekeeper stood right behind her, at the buffet that Victoria always had set up for breakfast and rarely ate. Mrs. O'Neil's politely disinterested expression didn't change at Cheney's comment.

"Don't worry about her, Cheney, I'm going to have an army of maids and cooks and footmen for the party," Victoria said, making a graceful dismissive gesture with one tiny white hand. "So you don't have to worry about anyone or anything—except what you will wear, and I shall help you with that, of course."

"You mean you'll give me my orders," Cheney teased.

"No, I'll give Nia your orders," Victoria replied briskly. "So you won't have to worry about that, either. Anyway, to get back to Mrs. Irby. I want you to accompany me to the hospital. I want to see her, but I'm really not an intimate enough friend of the family's to just go marching in there uninvited. If, however, I happen to be at the hospital on business, accompanied by my friend, Dr. Cheney Duvall, it would surely be acceptable for me to visit a patient who is a slight acquaintance."

"Well, this is the first time you've needed *me* to be a social excuse for *you*," Cheney said with amusement. "But, Victoria, why all this . . . trouble? Why do you want to make it appear so casual? And why do you want to see Mrs. Irby, anyway?"

Victoria hesitated, then answered softly, "Why, I should think you, of all people, would understand, Cheney. After all, you were my physician when . . . when . . . before I became a Christian, and I . . . I . . ." She swallowed hard and struggled to say the words.

"Oh. Yes, of course, I see," Cheney said matter-of-factly, which helped Victoria to regain her composure. The first time Victoria had come to Cheney, she had thought she was pregnant and had requested an abortion. It turned out that she wasn't pregnant at all; she had ovarian cysts, which necessitated removal of her ovaries. Victoria would never have children now. "So you feel that you'll be able to cheer up Mrs. Irby?" she asked politely.

"I don't know about that," Victoria answered quietly. "But I can certainly sympathize with her, particularly with her guilt. And I know, Cheney dear, that you've been praying for her—I know you always pray for your patients—but I feel that the Lord is directing me to pray *with* her. If she'll allow it, of course."

Cheney suddenly grew very still, and her gaze withdrew sharply inward. Her mind was quiet except for a voice, weak with shame, that repeated, *Pray? Did I pray for Mrs. Irby? For Mr. Fair? Have I been praying for them? For someone? Anyone?*

Stubbornly Cheney put the uncomfortable thoughts away, telling herself that she was a Christian, and of course she prayed . . . sometimes. "You know, you've reminded me of something, Victoria," she said crisply. "After two years, I just found out that Shiloh is almost incapable of assisting at childbirths. Isn't that odd?"

Victoria looked at her curiously, and after a moment replied, "No, not really. Not if you consider Shiloh's point of view."

Cheney shrugged. "He's a dedicated and capable medical attendant. I think it's very strange that he can't abide childbirth—he's certainly seen much, much worse."

"But don't you see?" Victoria asked gently. "It's not the physical part of it that bothers him. It's the mental and emotional strain."

"What do you mean?" Cheney asked with a hint of impatience.

"I think he's probably afraid," Victoria replied quietly, "not of childbirth, but of the deaths of the mothers . . . leaving an orphan."

Cheney stared at her in disbelief. "Shiloh's stronger than that. He's not—he doesn't—he isn't subject to that kind of vulnerability."

Victoria said intently, "Cheney, he's a man. Just like all the rest of us, he has fears and insecurities and frailties and weaknesses."

Cheney shrugged dismissively and said no more.

They went to the hospital that afternoon, and Victoria was pleased that Mrs. Irby allowed her to pray with her, though she was unresponsive. Victoria persisted, however, and called upon her every day until her discharge the next week and often after she returned home. Mrs. Irby had not yet regained her strength and was still struggling to come to terms with the death of her son and her own guilt. But eventually she—with the help of Victoria's nonjudgmental compassion—came to understand that she still needed healing. Mrs. Irby had been a Christian for many years, but Victoria helped her to understand that the Lord was not only the Savior of her soul, He was also a Savior of mind and heart.

Meanwhile, Victoria's comment about praying for her patients kept coming back to Cheney in an oddly roundabout and tentative way. When Mrs. Callister was discharged with her healthy eight-pound son, Cheney said a dutiful thank-you to God. When Mr. Dibley struggled with his serious pneumonia, Cheney asked the Lord, rather formally and stiffly, for healing for the kind, gentle man. But by the time Mr. Dibley recovered and was released a week later, Cheney forgot to say thank you to the Healer.

Eight-year-old Molly Costanza had only a slight case of pneumonia and was released after a few days. The Fighting Five, as the hospital attendants dubbed them, suffered various fates. To everyone's—particularly Cheney's—amazement, four of the injured boys requested Cheney to be their physician. Guy Fain insisted upon Dr. Werner attending him—he never allowed Cheney to touch him—but his closest friend, Joe Ryman, who was uninjured that night, asked Cheney to be his physician.

Guy Fain was released the next day, as his knife wound was slight and, as Cheney triumphantly observed, Mr. Florey had done excellent stitching. She took the .22 bullet out of Laban Smith's leg, and within two days he was well enough to be released. Wesley Nance and Daniel Van Toll, who had sustained minor injuries, were released the next morning. Hudson Kramer, who was beaten rather badly and had a severe tearing knife wound to his foot, remained in the hospital for ten days and was obliged to use crutches for six weeks. He made an ironic comment to Cheney to the effect that he'd learned one lesson: to stay out of knife fights and stick with guns. Her answer to him was that perhaps he'd better consider just dragging a cannon along when he went on his next junket to the Barbary Coast with the Fighting Five.

Marlett Fair's tracheal tube was removed the following morning, and he slowly recovered from the devastating diphtheria. Dr. Werner attended him very closely and visited him at least once each night of his two-week hospital stay. Cheney didn't see much of Mr. Fair and his mother after the fateful Thirteen Friday, other than perfunctory checks during her night shifts. But both of them thanked her profusely and told her that they knew she'd saved Mr. Fair's life.

The revolutionary treatment Cheney and Shiloh devised for Ike

Trimble's gangrene worked, though it was painstakingly slow. He had to stay in the hospital for over two weeks and suffer painful debridement and excision two or three times a day. After he had been in the hospital for four days, Mrs. Trimble came to Cheney in tears.

"Ike, he's talking about leaving the hospital tomorrow, Dr. Duvall. We . . . we don't have much money put back, you see, and since Ike can't work—"

Cheney frowned. "You mean you can't afford to stay here? It's the money? You're not dissatisfied or upset with Mr. Trimble's treatment, are you?"

"Oh no, ma'am," she exclaimed, her brown eyes widening with distress. "Ike and me think it's just a plain miracle, a miracle of God, Dr. Duvall, that he ain't gonna have to lose his leg. Ike says he thinks I can take care of him, if you'll show me how to . . . to . . . tend to him."

"Nonsense," Cheney scoffed. "This treatment is difficult and complex, and only a skilled medical person should do it, and he requires constant monitoring. Listen to me, Mrs. Trimble. I'll see if we can make some arrangements with the hospital about your bill. If not, I'll discharge Mr. Trimble, but I'll come attend him in your home."

"But . . . but I don't think we can afford that, either, Dr. Duvall," she said. "Mebbe you better just show me what to do."

"Mrs. Trimble, you just work on keeping Mr. Trimble's spirits up, and both of you stop worrying," Cheney said firmly. "I'll make sure that Mr. Trimble gets the care he needs. You trust me, don't you? Then just leave it to me."

When Cheney approached Dr. Baird about making some arrangements for Mr. Trimble's bill, he considered for a long time. Then he said, "I have a proposition for you, Dr. Duvall. This treatment you've invented for gangrene is most interesting, and if it is truly a cure, it should be published. If you will agree to give lectures on Mr. Trimble's treatments, and if he will agree to be a test case for observation and study by the other doctors and medical students from Toland College, I will forego his hospital charges."

"All charges?" Cheney demanded. "Even the cost of the carbolic acid and bandages?"

"You drive a hard bargain, Dr. Duvall," Dr. Baird said with dark amusement. "Yes, I will agree to forego all charges if you will give, say, four lectures on the treatment. That should be enough to get all of our doctors, and any who care to join us from the other hospitals, and all of the medical students. Also, I shall require you to write a thorough report of the treatment and submit it for publication in several medical publications such as *The Lancet* and *The New England Journal of Medicine*."

"Agreed," Cheney declared happily. "You set up the schedule for the lectures, Dr. Baird, at your convenience. I'll be happy to do them at any time. And I've already done an informal paper on the treatment for my own use. I can easily turn it into an article."

"Good, Dr. Duvall," he said encouragingly. "You are, I must say, a clear and concise writer. Your report on—what does everyone call it?—the fateful Thirteen Friday was very well-organized and presented. I didn't agree with all of your arguments, but I am considering some of your suggestions. The report was presented in a most impressive, capable manner."

"Thank you, sir," she said quietly. "In retrospect, I believe I was too harsh in some of my conclusions about the other doctors."

"Yes, you were," he said gruffly. "Those are the parts I disagreed with. I know you won't listen to me, Dr. Duvall, because you're a doctor and you're young. But I'm going to tell you anyway. I've learned one thing about people, especially doctors—even you. There's good in them, and there's bad in them. You have to figure out how to see and utilize the good"—he gave Cheney an understated half-grin beneath his ferocious mustache—"and punish them severely for the bad."

This made Cheney think hard—not about herself, as she should have done—but about Dr. Carl Werner.

★ ★ ★ ★

In the weeks that followed, Cheney slowly found herself being drawn into the life of the hospital in ways that she hadn't foreseen or planned. She was amazed at the turnout for her lectures on Ike Trimble's treatment, and though many of the medical students were still rude, most of the other doctors treated her with cautious respect. Even Dr. Werner attended one of her lectures, and she was so distracted by his presence that she could barely make herself coherent at first. But she saw him taking notes and managed to complete the lecture capably. He said nothing to her afterward, but she heard him in the hallway that encircled the amphitheater, discussing the treatment with another doctor.

"I know she's a woman," he said coldly, "but the treatment works.

At least it did for the test patient. And she was realistic about the limitations. She stresses that the time required for the treatment may not be feasible in certain cases, for example, where the necrotic material is too close to the torso, so the option of amputation is only available for less than twenty-four hours."

"I know," the short, grumpy-looking Dr. Haley replied, "but she's a *female physician*, Werner! How can you trust in anything she cooks up in her little kitchen?"

"Because it worked, Haley," Dr. Werner snapped in a tone that implied the man's name might as well have been "Idiot." Then he turned to walk away, and Cheney quickly scampered out of sight, her cheeks flaming. But she was secretly gratified.

Walker Baird began to spend time with Cheney. Admittedly, it was almost always on hospital business. First, Dr. Werner did one of his semiannual dissections, and Walker insisted Cheney attend with him. Carl Werner, for all the shortcomings in his bedside manner, was perhaps the foremost anatomist in the West—possibly in America. The dissection was attended by hundreds of people. Cheney was amazed to see Bethena Posey and Ionia Tilden there, along with several other women she didn't know.

"He allows nurses—women—at his dissections?" Cheney whispered to Walker as they managed to find enough room for the both of them to sit together in the stuffed amphitheater.

"He encourages it," Walker replied. "He believes that the entire secret of practicing good medicine is understanding the human body and how it works—or doesn't work. This dissection will take about six hours. That's because he doesn't just concentrate on one specific part of the body, or one system, or the symptoms of one illness. He will dissect the entire body and—you won't believe it—but he can name each part of each system."

Cheney's face registered her astonishment.

"That's right," Walker continued. "Respiratory, muscular, reproductive, urinary, the nervous system, circulatory, digestive. He also spends about an hour just on the skin. And for the skeletal system he'll actually dissect half of the body and name each bone."

"How wonderful!" Cheney exclaimed. "I've never had an opportunity to attend such an extensive dissection! It's exciting, isn't it!"

He watched her with amusement. "You certainly are unusual, Dr. Cheney Duvall."

"Hmm? But it is exciting, Walker! Dissections are usually so specific, with such narrowly defined applications."

Walker gave up on trying to communicate to her how odd it was for a well-bred, genteel lady to find dissections an entertaining pastime. "Yes, well, that's why all of the medical students are required to attend," Walker replied. "And that's why so many of the doctors try to attend at least one of Dr. Werner's dissections. I try to attend them both. Just to keep sharp, you know."

This began a discussion of the difficulties in keeping up with all of the latest discoveries in pharmacopoeia, and in new instruments, such as the autolaryngoscope. Walker and Cheney began having twice-weekly sessions with Mr. Indro, who was an obliging and thorough teacher. This, in turn, led Walker to start drifting in when Cheney was giving Nia her "classes." For two hours each weekday, Cheney was teaching Nia the rudiments of medicine. Soon Walker was a faithful member of the "class," although he and Cheney were soon taking turns being the teacher. While Cheney was very good at diagnosis and prescriptives, Walker was better at explaining anatomy and the nature and results of illnesses and injury.

Nia was an attentive and dedicated student, but because of her complete lack of training in any field remotely connected with the discipline of medicine, her education progressed very slowly. Cheney chafed at the fact that Nia would have no opportunities for hands-on application of the knowledge she was slowly absorbing. But aside from seesawing back and forth between irritation and anger, Cheney could think of no way to remedy the situation. Walker flatly told her that Nia would never be able to get a position with a hospital, or in any doctor's private practice.

"I suppose she could open an office herself for her own people," he said thoughtfully. "But I should think that she'd have the same trouble you have. Maybe even worse."

Immediately Cheney was defensive. "What do you mean by that, Walker? I'm a perfectly capable and conscientious doctor! Just because I can't name skeletons in my sleep, and I can't seem to understand the difference between a pituitary gland and a pineal gland doesn't make me any less of a competent doctor than you . . . you . . . men!"

To Cheney's puzzlement, Walker didn't seem to be upset by this tirade. On the contrary, he seemed to be amused. In fact, he appeared to be so amused that he was having difficulty speaking without laughing. Finally he managed to say with a semblance of gravity, "But, Dr. Duvall, I wasn't saying that Nia won't be a good doctor, as are you. I was just trying to say that . . . humph . . ." He almost laughed, but by a terrific effort managed to choke it down. "I was just saying that she might, perhaps, face the same assumptions about being a female doctor that you do. You know, the . . . um . . . humph . . . much mistaken idea that you're emotional? Defensive?"

"Ridiculous," Cheney muttered. "I am no such thing, and neither is Nia."

"No, no, of course not," Walker hastily agreed.

Cheney suspiciously searched his face, which was positively radiating laughter, and finally a slight glint of amusement flashed in her eyes. Blandly she added, "And it does so infuriate me whenever someone accuses me of being emotional. But at least," she sighed theatrically, "after a good cry, I can usually get over it."

Walker finally released his boyish laughter, and Cheney smiled with him. Still chuckling, he said warmly, "Dr. Duvall, you are a jewel. A radiant, precious jewel."

She said, "Thank you, Shiloh."

He started, but Cheney didn't notice. And Walker Baird never corrected her.

★ ★ ★ ★

Regardless of his apparently light reception of the news that Cheney had seen a clipper called *Locke's Day Dream*, Shiloh had in fact felt a surge of hope and excitement at the news. The next morning he hurried down to the Embarcadero to talk to the harbormaster.

To no avail.

Courteously a clerk in the harbormaster's office told him that all rented wharves and docking records were recorded under ownership names. Any ships in the San Francisco Bay registered with the harbormaster were therefore recorded by the name of the company or individual owning the craft, not the name of the ship.

The pang of disappointment and the discouragement he felt surprised Shiloh. *Maybe this whole thing's just a delusion. Maybe the* Day Dream *was never here, has nothing to do with San Francisco. Maybe Pearl was never here, maybe she was never in Hawaii. . . .*

Maybe I ought to forget the whole thing.

Brooding, Shiloh considered this bleak option. Finally common sense took over. He could no more stop speculating about and trying to work out the mystery of his past than he could stop being Shiloh Irons.

Oh, that's a real good analogy, he reflected ruefully. *Considering I'm not really Shiloh Irons. . . .*

But then again, I guess that's exactly who I am—all of who I am.

Being a man with a strong will and a good measure of self-discipline, Shiloh dismissed his philosophical wanderings and reviewed the problems and solutions he could deal with in the present. *If I can get another class of four and add a session, I could save all of that money and have enough for passage to Hawaii by the first of the year, maybe . . .*

Eight men were now enrolled in pugilistic training sessions with Shiloh "Iron Man" Irons, and three more men were clamoring to join. Shiloh's training and sparring sessions were divided up into two groups of four men each. He trained them in the afternoons, alternating groups, six days a week. He decided that he would try to enroll another student so he would have another group of four, and then add a morning session every other day. This would be an exhausting schedule—impossible for a man without Shiloh's natural strength and stamina.

Walker Baird waited for him to come to work one night and cornered Shiloh in his office to ask him about the wisdom of adding another class.

"Simple," he told Walker. "I need the money. They're paying me seven cents per man per session. Right now that's a little over thirteen dollars a month. If I add another session, it'll put it up to sixteen dollars a month. Nice bit of change."

"Yes, but, Shiloh, I don't think anyone can work every night and all day too for very long," Walker worriedly replied.

Shiloh shrugged carelessly. "I can do it. I'm going to do it."

Walker was thoughtful for a long while. "Are you sure you wouldn't like for me to arrange for a fight for you? It wouldn't take much promotion, because you are a well-known pugilist. We could raise a handsome purse—probably a couple of thousand dollars, at least."

"Nah. My fighting days are over. The doc doesn't like it."

Walker gave him a sharp look, and Shiloh quickly added, "She's my doctor. She was when I was fighting too."

Slowly Walker asked, "So as your physician, she advised you to stop fighting? For medical reasons?"

"Uh . . . not exactly." Shiloh shifted restlessly in his desk chair. "She just thinks it's stupid."

"Ah," Walker gravely remarked.

"She thinks fighters are low-class thugs," Shiloh continued carelessly.

"Most genteel ladies do," Walker said carefully. "But I'll say one thing about Dr. Duvall. She's what I call 'class-unconscious.'" He watched Shiloh carefully to try to gauge his reaction.

Though his light blue eyes flickered with interest, his tone and demeanor were casual. "Whaddya mean?"

"I mean that Dr. Duvall is not what the Bible calls a 'respecter of persons,'" Walker explained. "She's one of those rare people who seem to be able to form her opinion of a person without regard to their race or social status or wealth."

"True," Shiloh agreed. "Her father is much like that, you know. He's a fine man. Honorable and just. Takes people for who they are. Treats everyone with the same kind of easy respect."

Walker grinned slyly. "Well, I would say that Dr. Duvall treats everyone the same . . . only I'm not certain I'd term it 'easy respect.'"

Shiloh returned Walker's infectious smile with a lazy one of his own. "You're right about that, Walker. I'd say the doc's not a respecter of persons, 'cause she treats everyone with the same sauce."

"You've told her that, have you?"

"Not hardly," Shiloh grunted. "And don't tell her I said it, either."

Walker's smile faded, and he asked with intense casualness, "You two have worked closely together for a long time, haven't you?"

Shiloh suddenly looked wary. "Yeah. Little over two years now."

"And . . . uh . . . you don't have any kind of . . . understanding?" Walker asked uncomfortably. His naive brown eyes wandered about the room.

"No, we don't understand each other at all," Shiloh joked with determined lightness. "Why? You interested in the doc?"

Walker grimaced slightly and gave Shiloh a quick glance. But Shiloh seemed merely to be mildly interested. "She's really . . . special," Walker finally said a little hoarsely. "She's smart, she striking, she's captivating, she's amusing."

"Yep," Shiloh agreed congenially. But his eyes were darkened to a stormy blue, and the V-scar under his left eye seemed suddenly very pronounced.

Walker searched his face, and Shiloh met his gaze directly. In desperation Walker said, "Look here, Shiloh. I have a lot of respect for you, and I think you're a good sort. I wouldn't want to offend you or barge in where I'm not wanted."

Shiloh abruptly sat back in his chair and jerked his head around to stare out the window. He said nothing for what seemed a very long time. Walker was beginning to think that Shiloh wasn't going to reply when he finally muttered, "Walker, it's just not my call to make. I don't have any claim on Dr. Duvall. Couldn't even if I wanted to."

Walker cleared his throat and asked with difficulty, "Are you so sure of that?"

Shiloh shrugged, a curiously violent, jerking gesture. "Yeah," he rasped. "I'm a penniless orphan with no prospects. She's from a fine family—did you know that her great-uncle is a vicomte? Yeah. On her mother's side. And the doc's rich. She's not as crazy rich as Mrs. de Lancie, but she's got money."

Now Walker Baird was in a quandary. He liked Shiloh Irons and thought him an honorable man. He also was getting very fond of Cheney Duvall and knew that he was close to falling in love with her.

So should I tell Shiloh that's all nonsense? That Cheney doesn't care about any of that, that she isn't at all that kind of person? That it wouldn't make any difference to her one way or the other if she loved a man? Should I tell Shiloh all this . . . which would be like . . . encouraging my competition?

But immediately the absurdity of this train of thought struck Walker. Cheney Duvall was not a woman to be won. She certainly wasn't the type to swoon into a man's arms just because he managed to fight off the competition. In fact, she might just take a swing at the man who hit her with the good news that he'd "won" her because he was the biggest Neanderthal. The vision struck Walker as funny and he chuckled. Shiloh gave him a hard look, and Walker quickly sobered. "Sorry," he said. "I was wool-gathering. Short attention span, you know. I've got to be going."

Shiloh said, "See you in the morning, Walker. Don't worry about the boxing classes. I can handle it. I won't let my work here at the hospital suffer."

"I know that," Walker said uncomfortably, shifting from one foot to the other in the doorway. "Uh . . . Shiloh. I think you've gotten kind of wrong-headed. About Dr. Duvall. People like her don't worry about lineage or how deep your pockets are."

Shiloh made a quick cutting gesture. "I know her better than you do, Baird. I know her better than anyone."

"Probably true," Walker persisted, though he was hesitant to intrude upon Shiloh's private thoughts any longer. "But in that case, you of all people should know better. Later, then." He disappeared.

Shiloh returned his enigmatic gaze to the barren view outside.

19

Traps and Trappings

Mrs. Victoria Elizabeth Steen de Lancie
requests the pleasure of your company
at an Evening Party
on Thursday, July twenty-seventh
at half-past seven o'clock.
Dancing. Steen House, Russian Hill

" . . . And then Mrs. O'Neil devised a plan to have two seatings for dinner, which I thought was a stroke of genius," Victoria prattled on. "So I sent out two invitations, one for seven-thirty and one for nine-thirty, and seated those people who wouldn't object to dining with Chinamen at the early dinner. Of course, no one is likely to fuss now, not after all of the nattering that's gone on. But some guests, such as that awful Mrs. Rand and her daughter Calliope—isn't that the most absurd name for a girl?—it was intended to evoke the Greek muse of heroic poetry, I believe, but really, who can possibly keep from thinking of sawdust and elephants? They really are the most obnoxious social climbers, and they could treat Li Bai and Li Shen abominably. In the most genteel tradition, of course.

"Anyway, Cheney, you are to preside over the first seating, if you don't mind, and Walker volunteered to act as host at head of the table. I really wanted to take the first seating, with most of the staff, because I think that will be much more fun, but I'm afraid I'll be obliged to dine with the stuffy old patrons, as I'm supposed to be representing my father, and Dr. Baird has agreed to host. So you will wear your lavender. I've ordered lavender sweet peas and stephanotis and lilies of the valley for your hair, and I insist you wear those pearls I bought from Gump's—"

"Stop," Cheney finally said desperately. She had been dressing for work, but Victoria had come sailing majestically into her bedroom, talking like the sirocco, and Cheney had been lost since way back when Victoria had uttered the phrase "dining with Chinamen."

"I beg your pardon?" Victoria said icily.

Smiling, Cheney amended it to, "Stop—please. Victoria, you have been speaking gibberish ever since you came into the room."

"I never speak gibberish," Victoria sniffed. "You just hear it."

"You get so excited about parties and balls and things, don't you?" Cheney said affectionately. "Very well. You've excused me from all duties in preparation, so I shall do whatever you wish at the party. But are you saying that you've invited Li Bai and Li Shen to dinner?"

"Of course," Victoria piously replied. "The party is in honor of St. Francis and in celebration of some generous donations by the patrons, and is for the doctors and all of the staff and their families."

"How in the world did you pull off this hat trick?" Cheney asked, her eyes glinting. "Are you telling me that the board of directors and their families are actually going to have dinner with . . . with . . . Li Bai and Li Shen? And Hubert and Sallie Sisk? Oh, how delicious!"

"Delicious," Nia echoed darkly from the floor. She was down on her knees, brushing the hem of Cheney's navy blue skirt.

"Actually, I can hardly take credit for the society harridans' response," Victoria said with evident enjoyment. "When the invitations were sent out two weeks ago, there were many malicious whispers and dark mutterings about a gathering of such low persons. But then Dr. Baird came up with the inspiring idea of printing a card in all of the newspapers, announcing the party and presenting it as an exclusive and grand charitable function.

"Soon after that," she went on with a preening cat's smile, "fashionable ladies started hinting for invitations when I attended the theater or opera. I heard that Mrs. Rand's invitation occupies a casual but permanent place on the vestibule table by the calling card salver. I started receiving some rather frantic morning callers. Dr. Baird started getting visits from persons who were suddenly interested in patronage of St. Francis de Yerba Buena. Walker and Shiloh have been prodded for invitations at the Olympic Club by some henpecked husbands, I believe."

"Isn't it funny!" Cheney exclaimed, giggling. "It's one thing to consider yourself above socializing with certain people, but it's quite another to be excluded from socializing with them! Particularly by a Steen!"

"I suppose so," Victoria said in a bored tone. "But still, I wasn't sly enough to think of presenting it in such a way. Dr. Baird is a cunning diplomat, you know."

"You'd never pull it off in New York," Cheney remarked.

"No, I'd be cut off for years. Maybe forever," Victoria breezily agreed. "But this is San Francisco. Here they're still making up the rules, and I decided I should make up one of my own."

Cheney was searching about the room with a distracted air. "Nia, these are my black shoes. Don't I have some navy blue ones?"

"Yes, ma'am, but I can't find them anywhere," Nia answered. "Where do you s'pose you left them?"

"That's absurd, Nia. I don't go places and leave my shoes," Cheney scoffed.

"But you do, Cheney. You left them on the terrace last Monday. I instructed Zhou-Zhou to collect them and clean them, so they might possibly be in my dressing room, Nia," Victoria replied.

"I left my shoes?" Cheney murmured distractedly. "I came through the house and upstairs barefooted?"

Victoria and Nia exchanged worried glances as Nia glided silently out of Cheney's bedroom to go in search of Cheney's shoes—again. Cheney, in the last couple of months, had left gloves, reticules, parasols, shoes, cloaks, hats, and hat pins littered around downstairs in the mornings. It was unlike her; normally she was meticulous and organized. She had been so distracted and absentminded that Victoria was genuinely concerned.

"Never mind, Cheney, you're always so exhausted in the mornings," Victoria said lightly. "Are you feeling quite well these days?"

"Of course," Cheney declared with a tinge of irritation. "Now, what was it again—oh yes. You say you want me to wear the lavender? Surely, Victoria, you can't be imposing upon those poor people to have full evening dress?"

"Of course not. In fact, some of them will be coming directly from the hospital—I've arranged to send the landau to pick them up—and some of them will be leaving the party to go back to work. So through Dr. Baird I've made certain everyone understands that it's to be dinner dress. But they will expect you and me in fine evening dress, Cheney. You understand. And besides, I should think you'd be glad to wear something pretty for a change. You always look so dreary and forbidding."

"I do?" Cheney asked uncertainly, staring down at her plain navy skirt and unadorned white blouse. "Yes, I do. All right, the lavender. So . . . did you say Walker will be acting as host at dinner? And Shiloh?" she asked very casually. "Is he at first seating or second?"

"Second seating," Victoria replied apologetically. "It was the only way to work it out with lady-gentleman seating, and he's one of the few on the staff that wouldn't be cut by the Rands and the Cumberleys and the Youngers."

"Oh," Cheney said a little forlornly.

"At least he's coming," Victoria said softly.

"Yes," Cheney sighed. "At least."

★ ★ ★ ★

"Ooh!" Angelina Cassavettes practically swooned into Shiloh's arms, waving her cheap paper fan vigorously. "Ooh, Mr. Irons! You are such a energetical dancer! I have quite lost my air! I fear that I am suddeniciously vaporizing!"

Admirably hiding his amusement, he bowed solicitously over her plump, hot hand, managing to take a long backward step as he posed. "Allow me to seat you, Miss Cassavettes, and fetch you a fruit ice."

"That would be delicious of you, Mr. Irons," she said plaintively, taking his arm in a grip that would have done one of his pugilistic students proud. "I should find a raspberry ice ever so delicious!"

"Then a raspberry ice it is," he said gravely, handing her into one of the fine Louis XV chairs from the City of Paris that lined the wall in the great hall. With great relief he hurried into the dining room where a buffet was set up and gave his order to one of the blank-faced footmen who had been retained for the party. With less eagerness he returned to Miss Cassavettes. She made him uneasy. He'd had a bad—a very bad—experience with a foolish young girl in his visit to New Orleans the previous winter. The sultry cook's helper at the hospital reminded Shiloh somewhat of Chloe, which made him very glad to have his obligatory dance with Angelina over and done, and in an indecent hurry to get away from her.

"Please, Miss Cassavettes, you must take this slowly and stay seated for a while," he advised her. "You look a little overexerted."

"But golly's goat, I am so exerted!" she clamored. Then, recalling her grandest society manners and mannerisms, she lowered her voice, flapped her fan, and flitted her lashes up at Shiloh. "It is so an excitable night, don't you find it? And don't Mrs. de Lancie and Dr. Duvall look so grand, like dutchies?"

"Er—is that 'duchesses'?" Shiloh murmured half to himself.

"Yes, duchesses," Miss Cassavettes chattered. "Such smashing gowns! The awfullest fine house! The elegantest persons!"

"Yes, so they all are," Shiloh gravely agreed. "There, I think Hack Venable's coming this way. He expressed to me his great desire to dance with you, Miss Cassavettes. Perhaps I should—"

As it turned out, Shiloh need not have worried that Miss Cassavettes' smoldering dark eyes were dwelling too hotly upon him alone. Before he could finish making his polite excuse, Miss Cassavettes appeared to find her air and stop her vaporizing, for she jumped up out of her chair to run to the swarthy medical attendant before he could reach Miss Bethena Posey, whom he seemed to be aiming for. Shiloh, with an inordinate measure of relief, made his escape back toward the buffet.

He paused in the doorway leading into the dining room to watch the dancers idly for a few moments. The gathering of people in the great hall was odd, indeed, and gave the candlelit room, with the haunting music of a Strauss waltz, a surreal cast. Women in gray and black skirts and plain white blouses danced with men dressed in everything from copper-riveted denim Levi's pants to old shiny black wool suits. Ionia Tilden, wooden-faced, glided by, dancing with Mr. Tilden, who appeared to be much older than his wife and was dressed in an interesting brown-and-yellow checkered suit with a red satin waistcoat. Bethena Posey looked like a wraith, her pale, thin face floating in the ghostly light a full six inches above Jesty Tukes' unruly brown bob. Even as he glanced at the couple, Miss Posey stumbled over Jesty's feet, and a terrible disaster nearly occurred. She blushed furiously and gave a hunted-small-animal glance around the room. Shiloh determined to dance with her again. Though he didn't dwell much upon it, he knew that it would give Bethena Posey a certain status, for he was a much-sought-after partner. Shiloh Irons was a kind man and was careful to pay attention to people he could help.

He lingered, watching the dancers circle the floor in a stately waltz. A finely dressed, imperious-looking man glided by holding his elegant wife, whose haughty features were fixed in a stiff smile, at an uncomfortable arm's length. In a dark corner, where they had stood motionless all night, were Li Bai and Li Shen. Their crescent-hooded eyes were black and inscrutable, their hands always hidden in the sleeves of their identical blue tunics. Dr. Carl Werner, resplendent in a black dinner suit with a royal blue waistcoat, danced by. He was actually smiling down at his wife, who, surprisingly, was sweet-faced and delicate-looking.

Shiloh's eyes were drawn to Victoria de Lancie, glowing in a white dress with scarlet feather trim and gold spangles. In her alabaster blond hair was an arrangement of white and gold feathers. She was at her most charming, the height of translucent loveliness, and she was unreachable and untouchable. Shiloh found it fascinating that Victoria could appear so enticing, yet remain so inaccessible.

Cheney, in contrast, looked vivacious and exciting in a dress of a frosty lilac color, long silvery-lilac gloves, and white and lavender flowers in her hair. A magnificent set of pale pearls set off her dramatic coloring. She was the lady that men wanted to walk up to and talk to and listen to and try to make smile. She looked interesting, she looked interested, she looked amused, she looked amusing. As she was dramatically swept around the room by Walker Baird, she looked up at him and laughed. Shiloh felt an unwelcome jolt of jealousy.

Quickly he turned on his heel and stalked into the dining room, where he grabbed and emptied a full glass of mineral water. Then he asked for a tangy lemon ice, which was refreshing when sipped in very small doses. The sharp flavor stung his mouth and nose, and he determinedly put the vision of Cheney and Walker Baird dancing out of his mind.

He returned to the great hall, ostentatiously sipping his fruit ice, hoping that none of the ladies would slip up to him and oblige him to ask them to dance. He felt slightly guilty, for he did somehow feel that he should try to make the staff of St. Francis feel comfortable in this glittering night that was so alien to their lives. *Mine too*, he reflected ruefully. *Why should I feel like some kind of baby-sitter? Why should I feel like some foreign diplomat or something?*

He could answer his own question, and he did. *Because I just do, and because I can. I'm kinda like the governess—between-stairs. Dunno how I ended up like this. . . . I sure don't fit into this world any more than Angelina Cassavettes does, with what she thinks is fashionable conversation, or poor Ionia Tilden, with all her stilted expressions of exaggerated gentility and her embarrassment over her husband. They haven't figured out yet that these people, like Mrs. de Lancie and Cheney and even her parents, have this sort of unspoken code, this ease, this sure knowledge that they belong . . . can't learn it, I don't think. Either it's inside you or not. . . .*

For some reason he remembered when he'd been introduced to Mrs. Andrew Fain, who was the wife of the man who had sold him Balaam, and the mother of Guy Fain, the obnoxious and spoiled medical student and the rudest of the infamous Fighting Five. He had been introduced to Mrs. Fain when he had bought Balaam, and had suspected her to be one of those ladies who were scratching and clawing to get out of the middle-class echelon into the upper class. Normally they were the worst snobs of all. Still he treated her with the same unaffected gallantry with which he treated everyone. As he was examining Balaam with Guy Fain, he had heard Mrs. Fain talking to her husband. She had a piercing, intrusive voice, and Shiloh couldn't help but catch, "He's Shiloh Irons, that vulgar fighting person? Impossible! He must be someone else!"

With a dry smile Shiloh thought that she was right.

Though he didn't pursue the idea, Shiloh was aware deep down that somehow he presented the same air of careless gentility that was so characteristic of the upper classes. It was a sort of self-possession, and still yet an unprepossession. He had it, unbidden, unconscious, and unforced.

Finding himself standing still, watching Cheney again, Shiloh turned with irritation and made his way along the back wall of the huge room, nodding and smiling and saying an occasional quick word to someone. He went into the music room, which had been converted to a game room for the party. About twenty people were there, mostly the older people, playing at the small gaming tables Victoria had brought in. Pretty Miss Calliope Rand was playing the piano, with two hopeful suitors loitering about, but she looked up and smiled invitingly at Shiloh. He lifted his crystal goblet in a slight salute, smiled, and hurried along. Sallie Sisk and her silent husband, Hubert, whom she called "my Hubie," were engaged in a rather loud and energetic game of dominoes with Miss Rees, who looked almost happy, and Baltimore Florey, who looked a little drunk and very happy.

"Mr. Irons! Care to play?" Sallie called, positively beaming with excitement. "Me and my Hubie's beatin' the stuffin' outta Miss Rees and Mr. Florey!"

With a sly grin Shiloh said, "Then I better not. Mr. Florey beats me every time, so if you're beating him, I'm a sure loser. How are you tonight, Mr. Florey?"

"Fine, fine, Mr. Irons," he replied too heartily, dropping his eyes.

"You're not on tonight, are you?" Shiloh asked in an offhand manner.

"No, sir," Mr. Florey said in a barely audible voice.

Shiloh clapped his hand on his shoulder and said kindly, "Then have fun, and you better shape up and beat Mrs. Sisk, or she'll never let you live it down."

Mr. Florey sat up a little straighter and smiled weakly. Shiloh moved along.

Again he smiled dutifully at people and stopped to speak to Mr. Indro and his wife, who was as bright-eyed and lively as her husband. They were playing a quiet game of cribbage with Mr. and Mrs. Younger, who were patrons of St. Francis de Yerba Buena.

He wandered into the drawing room with some relief. Victoria had left its somber furnishings, and for the party she had courteously set it aside as a sort of men's hideout. A snooty butler met any wandering lady at the door and with exquisite politeness asked if he might assist her. A errant escort, a mislaid glove, some water, some fresh air on the terrace? The butler fixed everything, while never allowing a lady to enter the semidarkened room, which was filled with lazy blue cigar smoke and the aroma of after-dinner brandy. Shiloh slowly made his way through the groups of men toward the butler, who was standing unobtrusively behind a white-draped table where tall crystal decanters and businesslike squatty glasses twinkled in the candlelight. The men were standing or sitting in comfortable groups of three or four and talking in low tones, mostly about silver and gold and all the traps and trappings of them.

". . . had a woman wiretapping, intercepting the confidentials from the mine superintendents at the Comstock! Woman was a coding expert, too, and could decipher the information. . . ."

". . . first bonanza, then borrasca, then nothing but steam and hot water! He's still plump, though, got his wife's money to run through. . . ."

". . . everyone knows—now—that Steen was smarter than most everyone. Didn't have any gold claims, you know. Made it selling the supplies and hardware to the miners, so he ended up with a pile he never had to dig for. . . ."

Then Shiloh heard something that jarred him to an abrupt stop, his face drained of all color.

". . . wanted me to bet *Locke's Day Dream*! Man's got sand, doesn't he? He's tried to buy her at least half a dozen times and finally thought he might sucker me into betting her."

"So you didn't bet the ship?"

Shiloh barely heard the second man's voice, filtered and faint in the rumbling din of the room.

A derisive laugh. "Of course not! I told him I'd bet one of my Sandwich Islands"—rumbling laughter all around—"which I told him was as good a bet as his chits. Which were collectible in—shall we say—chits?" Raucous laughter drowned out the rest of his words.

Sandwich Islands—Hawaii?

Shiloh's sharp eyes searched the crowded room. Finally he singled out the man who was telling the story. He was standing by the door leading into the vestibule, still saying something about "chits." Shiloh was too distracted to comprehend exactly what he was saying, as he was fiercely concentrating on memorizing the man.

He didn't stand out in the room, for he was not noticeably tall or handsome or commanding. He was of average height, with dark brown carefully styled hair and long sideburns, with a full and smooth complexion. Perhaps twenty-six or twenty-seven, Shiloh calculated, a little surprised, for from the man's tone of bored sophistication he had expected him to be older. Now he saw the man check his pocketwatch, and Shiloh noted that he was in full evening dress—a tailed coat, white waistcoat, white tie, white gloves.

He must be waiting for his hat and cloak, Shiloh thought with alarm. *They're all dressed in evening clothes . . . natty young bucks, aren't they? Must be going to the opera.*

With quick decision he turned and went back to the great hall. Stopping immediately inside the room, he stood up straight and scanned the whirling couples' heads. Hurrying onto the crowded dance floor, he went straight to Victoria de Lancie, who was dancing with elderly, doddering Mr. Cumberley. "Pardon me, sir, but may I take the liberty of cutting in?" he asked.

Seventy-two-year-old Mr. Cumberley wheezed, "With my blessings, and my thanks, Mr. Irons. Your pardon, madam. I'm not as spry as I once was." With undisguised relief he toddled toward the nearest chair.

Shiloh caught Victoria up in his arms, gave her a businesslike whirl, and said, "Would you please come with me right now, Mrs. de Lancie?"

Victoria, who was busily deciding on a suitable censure for Shiloh's rudeness, stared up at him indignantly. "I beg your pardon?"

"Please," he said gravely. "It's important."

"Yes, of course," she said instantly, her face clearing.

He took her arm and hustled her toward the door. All along their path, faces turned in their direction as if they were blown that way by a strong wind. Watching Victoria and Shiloh with greedy curiosity, one couple barged into another and all four of them almost piled up, but somehow they managed to right themselves.

Victoria nodded and smiled with queenly elegance as Shiloh practically dragged her through the music room and straight into the drawing room. Men punched each other and made awkward little chin-jutting gestures and furtive pointings toward her, and they all sheepishly hid their cigars behind their backs and set their brandies down somewhere, anywhere. It was ludicrous, really—after all, Victoria had paid for the brandy and cigars and had supplied the comfortable room and the silently efficient butler. Certainly she would have a vague suspicion that men might be in here smoking and drinking. But it was customary for gentlemen to pretend women didn't know these things, and it was customary for women to pretend they didn't know these things, so with sly delight in her blue eyes and an angelic expression Victoria nodded and smiled and greeted everyone.

"Can you hurry up and think of a way to introduce me to that man?" Shiloh whispered furiously. "That one—the one who's just put on his top hat, and—there he goes, out into the vestibule—"

"Come along. Hurry," Victoria hissed.

"Gentlemen," she said in a low, pleasing tone as they neared the group of four men who were carelessly making their way, adjusting satin-lined opera cloaks and sorting canes, still laughing and talking, out into the vestibule. As they all turned, Shiloh now saw with a start that one of the group was Dare Dunning.

"How very rude of you to take your leave without bidding me farewell!" Victoria teased, majestically keeping her satin-gloved hand lightly positioned on Shiloh's arm as she moved toward them so he was obliged to walk her along.

Hurriedly and guiltily they all tore off their hats and made low bows. "Mrs. de Lancie, please accept my most anguished apologies."

The young man with whom Shiloh very much wanted to speak stepped forward. "We are committed to Westin's box at the opera, and we couldn't contemplate depriving your partner of his dance with you. That might be cause for a duel, and I shouldn't blame any fellow for taking grave offense if your attention was distracted from him!" He made a mocking bow in Shiloh's general direction.

"You are too kind, and entirely too charming," Victoria protested prettily. "Perhaps if introductions are made, no duels will be necessary, hmm? May I present to you a friend of mine, and Dr. Duvall's, the Supervising Attendant at St. Francis—Mr. Shiloh Irons. Mr. Irons, may I present to you a longtime friend of Dr. Baird's, and a generous patron of the hospital. This is Mr. Winslow. Mr. Bain Winslow."

20

Inquiries, Investigations, Information

"He just listened."

Victoria and Cheney stared at Shiloh, Victoria with polite curiosity and Cheney with impatience. Unconcernedly Shiloh took a bite of fish, chewed ruminatively, and pronounced, "This fish is deliciously vaporizing."

Victoria giggled, but Cheney continued to stare at Shiloh, her sea-green eyes darkening to a smoky jade. "Do you mean to tell me that that's all you're going to say? That he *listened*?"

"Whaddaya wanna know?" he drawled.

Clearly and slowly Cheney answered, "Generally, in order to repeat a conversation, one must first tell what one party said, and then how the other party responded. Then one usually relates what the first party said, and how, in turn, the other party—"

"Okay, I got it," Shiloh interrupted. "The party of the first part—which is I—said, to quote David Copperfield, 'I was born.' Then the party of the first part—I—continued . . ." Cheney was staring at him with such keen irritability that he sighed and began again somewhat repentantly. "Okay, Doc. It's just that there wasn't much to it. Really. I just told him that I was an orphan and I was trying to find out something about my parents. I told him I thought they might have owned a clipper called the *Day Dream.* I told him that they might have had an Oriental girl as a servant, and that they might have lived in Hawaii."

"So what did he say?" Cheney demanded.

Shiloh shrugged. "Not much. He asked why I was telling him all this, so I told him that I knew he owned a ship called *Locke's Day Dream*, and I thought that was an unusual coincidence. And I told him I'd overheard him say something about Hawaii." With deliberation Shiloh put down his fork, took a long drink of iced cherry water, and touched his mouth with his blue silk napkin. "He told me that, yes, the name of his family's clipper was *Locke's Day Dream*, and, yes, they live in Hawaii."

He fell silent, and Cheney insisted, "So? Is that all?"

Shiloh dropped his eyes to stare blankly at his half-eaten fish and buttery new asparagus shoots. "I just came out and asked him if his family had any connection with the *Day Dream*, the clipper that wrecked in South Carolina in 1843, or if they knew anything about it. He got kinda mad then."

"Mad!" Cheney snapped. "How dare he! When you are just making some inquiries to try to find out about your own family?"

Victoria asked softly, "I suppose after that he wouldn't tell you much of anything, Shiloh?"

"Well," he said dryly, "he did tell me the name of his solicitor. Said from now on I'd better not show my ugly mug in Winslow Brothers' office. That if I had the guts I'd best try my flimflammery on the solicitor."

Cheney was outraged. "Perhaps I should go talk to this fine gentleman and teach him some manners! No, on second thought, Victoria, you must go speak to him!"

Shiloh raised his eyebrows and said mockingly, "Gee, thanks, Doc, but I think I can handle this by myself."

"Obviously you can't," Cheney replied hotly. "Obviously you didn't."

Victoria and Shiloh now stared at her, and she met their gazes defiantly. Shiloh asked evenly, "What is wrong with you, Doc?"

"I'm sure I don't know what you mean."

Shiloh shook his head. "It's like talking to someone else. It's not like talking to Cheney Duvall at all these days."

"I just think that this Mr. Winslow is acting like a cad," Cheney blustered. "And I think that you're intimidated or afraid or something."

"I'm neither," Shiloh replied sharply. "I'm reasonable. Which some people at this table aren't."

"Victoria, tell him," Cheney insisted.

Regarding Cheney coolly, Victoria responded, "No, Cheney, I have no intention of telling Shiloh what to do or how to do it. Perhaps you should rethink your position? This is not really our affair, except that Shiloh, as our friend, wants to confide in us. Which, I must say, you are making very difficult for him to do."

"Well, please pardon me," Cheney said stiffly. "I was merely expressing my opinion of what should be done."

"Doc, you've been doing an awful lot of that lately," Shiloh said, though now his voice was gently teasing. "But sometimes people just have to figure things out for themselves. You can't know it all and fix it all for everybody and everything."

"At least I try," Cheney muttered ungraciously. "At least I care."

An uncomfortable silence fell on the three diners, and they all awkwardly resumed eating. Mrs. O'Neil, as usual, stood silent and unnoticed at the end of the dining room by the kitchen door.

Victoria had invited Shiloh to dinner after he had told her he'd arranged to meet with Bain Winslow. As Winslow and his companions had been leaving the party the previous evening, Shiloh had no opportunity to speak to him then, but Winslow had agreed to receive him that afternoon.

"What is this fish, anyway?" Shiloh asked politely. "It's really good. Different."

"Yes, it's a delicacy particular to San Francisco, I believe," Victoria remarked. "It's called sand dab. It is tender and flavorful."

"I like fish," Shiloh announced thoughtfully, "that's not too fishy. This, I would say, is not too fishy."

"All right, all right, I'm sorry," Cheney said with agitation. "Please forgive my . . . suddenicious vaporizing." She gave Shiloh a weak smile.

He returned it, warmly. "Forget it, Doc."

"I really would like to know, Shiloh, if you have any plans to contact Mr. Winslow again, or . . . or . . . how the meeting was concluded," Cheney said tentatively.

After only a brief hesitation Shiloh said, "Well, after Winslow finished about the solicitor, I told him that I wouldn't be calling on any solicitors, because I wasn't interested in anybody's money. I said that all I cared about, and all I would ever care about, is finding out about my parents. He kinda calmed down then, but he was still pretty wary." Shiloh made a careless gesture, and his expression was placid, but his eyes were veiled.

Cheney, with a shock, realized that for all Shiloh's apparent offhand manner, he was upset—even grieved. She felt helpless and hurt for him, and then felt anger rising in her again. Swallowing hard, she fought it down. It was difficult for her to understand why her pique, which she regarded merely as empathy for him, offended him. But it did, so she determined to keep her composure. "And so you left it at that?"

"Yeah, pretty much. I just said I'd give him a couple of days to try to think if he could possibly help me," Shiloh said in a low tone. "I told him I'd call on him again on Sunday."

"I just don't understand it," Cheney said, careful to keep her voice even.

Shiloh looked at her quizzically. "Think about it, Doc. You would have acted exactly the same way."

"No, I wouldn't have," Cheney replied. "Either I would have said, 'Of course, you're So-and-So, I know all about it,' or I would have said, 'I can't help you.' Wouldn't you, Victoria?"

Victoria delicately shook her head. "I don't think so, Cheney. Your problem is that you're only looking at it from Shiloh's point of view. Try to see from Bain Winslow's point of view."

"I'm not acquainted with him, so I can't possibly know how he thinks," Cheney argued.

"Then figure what he thinks, Doc," Shiloh said impatiently. "Suppose some guy that you'd never heard of, that you knew nothing about, showed up at Duvall Court to see your father. Suppose he said he was Devlin Buchanan's long-lost brother, and he was looking for his family. What would be your reaction?"

Cheney's face blanched, and she started to retort, then closed her mouth tightly.

Victoria said quietly, "Something very similar to that happened to my family. I had an uncle who died when I was very young. He'd never been married, and he died when he was not yet thirty. Mother told me that a young man showed up twenty years later, saying that Uncle Bret had married his mother just before he died. He claimed to be his son."

"Bet I know exactly what your father did," Shiloh said sturdily. "Had him thoroughly investigated."

"Yes, naturally, he was obligated to do so," Victoria replied, though she spoke more to Cheney than to Shiloh. "The marriage license was a forgery, and my father could never find any evidence whatsoever that my uncle and this man's mother had a . . . liaison," Victoria finished delicately. "She was his nurse for the last two years of his life. He died at a sanitorium in Switzerland, of consumption. Evidently when this woman found out she was with child, she decided to arrange everything so that Uncle Bret would appear to be the father."

"But he wasn't?" Cheney asked in a low tone.

"No, probably not, though, of course, there is no way to prove such things," Victoria replied. "But the sad thing is that the young man did appear to believe it. Evidently his mother had told him, as truth, that she had been married to Bret Steen, who had died. The young man lived with his mother until she, too, died of consumption, then came to America to find us. But my father—" Victoria made a dismissive gesture. "There wasn't much he could do. Even though this young man believed what his mother had told him, he seemed to be a lot more concerned with his rightful share of the estate than he was with finding family. He was not at all like Shiloh." She smiled warmly at him.

Gratefully he said, "Thanks, Mrs. de Lancie. At least you know I'm not trying to scamp anyone."

Cheney sighed. "Fascinating story, Victoria, but I still can't see why Mr. Winslow didn't just tell Shiloh if he knows something about his family. Or else just come out and say that Shiloh was wasting his time. Instead he told Shiloh nothing at all."

"But he did," Victoria said quietly. "Don't you see? If he really didn't know anything at all about Shiloh's story, he would have said so. He would have had no reason not to. But what he did do is very significant. By his actions we can gather that there's a very good possibility that he does know something, but he's merely being cautious."

The three sat quietly for a while, everyone's face a study in deep thought. Cheney murmured, "Yes . . . yes . . . you're exactly right, Victoria. It might be . . . it just might be, Shiloh, that you are a Winslow."

He shrugged carelessly. "Can't prove anything. Never will be able to. But I kinda hoped I wouldn't have to."

Cheney searched his face, and her throat burned with sorrow and compassion for him. *He thought . . . he really hoped . . . that it would be someone who'd smile, or cry, and say, "Oh, how wonderful! It's you, you've come back to us!" But I suppose that's not to be. . . . How sad for him! How hard it must be!* As she watched Shiloh toying with his crystal goblet, she desperately tried to think of something comforting to say. But her mind was filled only with tender, disjointed thoughts and wishes.

Shiloh murmured, his voice so low they could hardly hear it, "It's funny . . . nothing's really changed . . . but I feel like I've lost something. It's not true, of course. I'm no worse off than I was before."

Now Cheney was not at all concerned with trying to find something to say; she was totally absorbed in trying to keep from crying. She stole a pleading glance at Victoria, who remained composed, though her fine, delicate features were filled with pity.

When Victoria saw Cheney's distress, her eyes widened slightly, and she said in a matter-of-fact tone, "Well, Shiloh, I know that you would never think of asking anyone any questions about the Winslows. But would you be interested in what I know about them? It's very little, I'm afraid, but it's entirely possible that you have a certain vested interest."

"Hmm?" Shiloh roused himself from his melancholy reverie. "Oh, yeah. Funny, I didn't even think about that. You know him, of course."

"No, not really," Victoria responded. "I've met him several times since we arrived at the theater and operas and parties. My father, I believe, is acquainted with Bain Winslow's father but not Bain. Dr. Baird told me that they have a fleet of four or five freighters in their shipping business. They started out by bringing sugar from Hawaii to the forty-niners. Dr. Baird wasn't sure if they simply are the shippers or if they raise the sugar too. Anyway, now they import sugar, sandalwood, fruits, and also Oriental goods. He said the Winslows have brought in several thousand of the Chinese for Charles Crocker to work on the railroad."

Cheney began to look stormy, but Shiloh gave her a stern warning glance, and she said nothing. He remarked, "So they are a prominent family. Or at least they have a well-established business. By the way, Mrs. de Lancie, do you happen to know who the brothers are in 'Winslow Brothers'?"

"No, and neither did Dr. Baird. He said he met Bain's father many years ago, but he thought Bain might be an only child. At any rate, you're right, Shiloh. They are fairly well-respected businessmen," Victoria said cautiously. "They are philanthropists, in a modest way. Bain Winslow has made some donations to the hospital, and Dr. Baird said he believes they also support the City College and the Mercantile Library Association."

"Sounds fairly presentable," Shiloh said. "Now, let's just hope that what he hears about me won't be . . . the truth!" he finished wryly.

"Nonsense," Cheney declared humorlessly. "You're a perfectly respectable citizen and a gentleman."

"Doc, I'm a penniless orphan, a Confederate traitor, a brawler, and a wanderer," Shiloh said, suddenly quiet and grave. "But that's all right.

Mr. Bain Winslow will either give me a chance or he won't. And that, more than anything, will tell me what kind of man he is."

★ ★ ★ ★

Shiloh and Cheney went on to the hospital, and Shiloh said nothing more about Bain Winslow. On Saturday night Cheney tried time and again, as tactfully as she knew how, to get Shiloh to talk to her about the situation and how he felt. But he kept his normal cheerful, careless demeanor. He ignored her vague hints and skillfully parried her more direct comments.

By Sunday night Cheney was thoroughly agitated and determined that even if she had to mercilessly nag Shiloh, she'd get him to tell her what had happened when he met with Bain Winslow that afternoon.

It wasn't necessary. She was ready, with Eugènie saddled and fidgeting restlessly, when he arrived at Steen House. As soon as they were riding away he said, "He was calm and pretty accommodating, Doc."

With an audible sigh of relief she said, "Please, please tell me."

"Nuthin' much to—"

"Don't even say it, Shiloh!" she asserted with heavy humor, but Shiloh didn't seem amused.

He finally answered, "He asked to see the tapestry and the compass. He said he saw nothing that would directly indicate anything about the Winslows. I agreed. That made him think for a long time, and he kinda just watched me. I kinda just watched him. Then he said, 'Mr. Irons, I have, of course, made inquiries about you. Information about you is scarce.' So I said just ask me anything, and I'll tell you."

Shiloh stopped, and Cheney waited as long as she could, then prompted him. "And? Did he ask?"

"Yeah. So I told him my whole life's story. Took all of two or three minutes," he said ironically. "He just sat and listened. When I finished he thought for a long time, just watching me again. He's a really . . . cautious man. He doesn't give much away. Hard to read." Restlessly Shiloh patted Balaam's neck, and frowned, turning his face up to the dreary gray night sky. "Then he asked me, 'So do you think you are a Winslow, Mr. Irons?' "

Again Shiloh fell silent, but Cheney managed, with a great effort, to be quiet. He finally finished in a dull voice, "I answered him, 'I can't make that claim, Mr. Winslow, because I don't know enough about your family to say such a thing. I don't want to prove that I'm a Winslow. All I want is to find out who my parents were. And I'd like to find out about the girl who died saving my life. That's all.' "

He sighed deeply, his shoulders hunched with weariness. "He got up and paced around the room and then told me that his mother and father had two children—he has a younger sister. His mother's parents are alive. They live in England. But his father's parents died long before Bain was born."

"So . . . so . . ." Cheney swallowed hard, then began again, "So what he's saying is that there's no possible family connection?"

"No . . ." Shiloh murmured and chose his words carefully. "He didn't say that. What he did say was that *Locke's Day Dream* was his father's ship. It seems that it was commissioned a long time ago, when Bain was a child. Something . . . about it . . . caused a rift between his parents . . . he said they're 'estranged.' He finally told me that 'Winslow Brothers' was formed by his father and his father's older brother. But the older brother is dead. Bain said he didn't know much about his uncle. His parents—especially his mother—pretty much refuse to speak about him."

Cheney caught her breath. "Did he—does he—know how his uncle died?"

"Yes." Shiloh sighed and again searched the weak stars. "At sea."

21

At Some Time, Love

The next week—the first week of August—brought a vestige of summer with a brighter lemon-yellow sun and warm sleepy nights. Cheney was off Saturday and Sunday and wearily planned upon resting the entire two days. But after sleeping all day Saturday, eating a light early supper, and retiring again to sleep through the night, she had recuperated enough to attend church Sunday morning and accompany Victoria to the grand opening of the Argonaut Theater on Sunday night.

A company from Philadelphia performed Goethe's *Faust.* Cheney appreciated the dramatic, tragic story of the magician and astrologer Johann Faust who sold his soul to the devil in exchange for power and worldly experience. The rather difficult Teutonic drama was admirably performed. The theater, an old three-story Gold Rush bank that had gone bust, was charming, built entirely out of precious California redwood. Victoria, of course, had a private box, and to Cheney's relief they weren't imposed upon by noisy visitors except during intermission. Walker Baird dropped in, and Cheney and Victoria urged him to stay in their box for the second act. Afterward, they went to a ball at the Cumberleys' and stayed very late. Cheney danced with Walker Baird four times, which was scandalous, though it never occurred to her. She danced with other men, too, and laughed and generally had a much better time than she thought she would.

By the time Shiloh came to escort Cheney to work again on Monday night she felt refreshed and renewed. "I'm glad to be going back to work," she idly commented to Shiloh as they rode along, "which rather surprises me."

"It does?" he asked. "I thought you liked working at St. Francis."

"It's been difficult," she admitted. "Only for the last few weeks have I felt that it's been sort of a . . . rhythm of life. Before, it was a bewildering circle of hazy, exhausting nights, and days that slipped away unnoticed while I slept. Now I'm beginning to feel like a real person, with a job and a life again. Although I must admit it still feels odd at times to be living that life primarily at night."

"Creatures of the black and dark night," Shiloh intoned in a spooky voice. "We crawl, we creep, we cower from the searing sun—"

"Where in the world did you read that?" Cheney laughed.

"Dunno," Shiloh said airily. "I think I made it up. But it fits, huh?"

"Yes, sometimes in the mornings I do still crawl up the stairs," Cheney sighed. "Do you?"

"Nah. I swim. You oughta try it sometime. Cold swim first thing in the morning! Bracing! Refreshing! Good for you!"

"I'm in complete agreement with Dr. Baird," Cheney grumbled. "I don't understand all you men throwing things and punching one another and jumping in icy water first thing in the morning. I believe there's something seriously wrong with the lot of you."

This light banter continued until they reached the hospital and settled into their routine. First Cheney checked to see who was on duty: tonight it was Mrs. Sisk and Bethena Posey, and the male attendants were Jesty Tukes and Baltimore Florey. Li Shen, the younger Chinese brother, was also working, tending the horses and stables and gardens. Mr. Indro had also assigned him to clean and straighten the apothecary's store from top to bottom.

"This is my favorite crew," Cheney told Shiloh as they met in his office to assess the night's work. Methodically she arranged the doctors' orders for the patients on the women's ward. "Mrs. Sisk works harder than anyone I've ever seen. And though poor little Bethena Posey is so clumsy, she is intelligent and has good instincts."

Shiloh nodded agreement, handing her the sheaf of doctors' orders he had collected from the men's ward. "Yeah, I recommended a raise for both of them. A pretty good one for Mrs. Sisk 'cause she's been here since the hospital opened, she's always worked nights, and she's only missed work a couple of times. She's still working for the same wage she started out with—three dollars a night."

"What!" Cheney exclaimed. "She hasn't gotten a raise in three years?"

"No. Guess it's 'cause she can't read. I recommended—"

"Oh! How . . . irritating!" Cheney blustered. "Sometimes I could just shake people! Couldn't you?" Shiloh started to reply, but Cheney ranted on, "Well, I am certainly glad that my contract is up next month. I'm going back to New York to start up a hospital of my own! I've already spoken to Victoria about it, and she will support it, and of course I know Dev will. And I think what you should do, Shiloh, is come back with me. I considered seeing if you would be interested in going to Toland Medical College, but they only offer one- or two-year programs, and I think you would get better training either in New York or Pennsylvania."

He stared at her in disbelief. "You've decided all this, have you, Doc?"

"Well, of course I was going to ask you."

"Ask me what?" he asked evenly. "Or maybe I should say, ask me what . . . first?"

"What do you mean?" Cheney asked, genuinely puzzled.

Shiloh replied, his eyes glinting frosty blue points, "For instance, ask me if I even want to go to medical school? Then maybe ask me if I have the money—and if I did, would I want to go to medical school with it? And then maybe just for curiosity ask if I want to go on trailing around after you all my life like I'm some kind of stray dog you've taken pity on?"

Cheney's eyes grew round, first with distress and then with vexation. "That's all nonsense, Shiloh—especially about the stray dog. I'm not even going to acknowledge that with a response. So why wouldn't you want to become a doctor? You practically are right now anyway, and—"

"Bain Winslow left yesterday," Shiloh abruptly interrupted. "He went back to Hawaii. You look surprised. I guess you just didn't think to ask me about little details like that—my entire past, my life, what I might consider is important."

"But . . . I . . . I thought that you wanted to be with—" Cheney was confused and almost blurted out something she would have regretted very much. Desperately she managed to stop herself in time, and was so flustered she didn't see the flame of hope, and something else, fire Shiloh's eyes. But his expression immediately settled into neutral lines when she exclaimed, "Bain Winslow left? Without so much as a by-your-leave?"

"That's not the point, Doc," he said quietly. "The point is that you'd kind of forgotten about him, hadn't you? Making all your plans, settling on everyone's future, deciding everyone's wants, discarding their hopes and wishes if they don't suit you."

Cheney looked up, startled, and Shiloh met her gaze with shadowed eyes, his mouth grim and hard. "I'm going to renew my contract next month, if Dr. Baird will have me. I'm doing some extra work, saving my money. By the first of the year I figure I'll have enough to take a short leave of absence to go to Hawaii."

A harsh indrawn breath was the only motion Cheney made. Still she and Shiloh stared at each other, the aura of their contact changing from moment to moment; now it was with animosity . . . now with hurt . . . then fear . . .

At some time, love.

Shiloh leaned over the desk, an urgency in his movements. "Cheney . . . Cheney, listen . . ." he said hoarsely.

"N-no," she whispered, then roused herself with a jerk, dropped her eyes, shuffled papers busily, and chattered, "No, no, Shiloh, I'm not stupid, of course I understand why you want to go to Hawaii. But I think it's a waste of your time and money. If Bain Winslow refuses to have any more contact with you, why should you go chasing after him like . . . like . . . some stray dog? You said it, not I."

Shiloh immediately and completely withdrew into himself. His eyes became a blank blue, his face was free from any expression, his posture deliberately careless. He even smiled, though it was far from his usual easy, genuine grin. "I guess you don't need to worry your pretty little head about it, Doc. I also said I'm just a brawler and a gypsy. When I get ready I'm going to go to Hawaii—and from there, who knows? Who cares?"

"I do," Cheney whispered, her eyes still averted.

"Yeah, thanks, Doc. Big of you. Now, how about the patients? You wanna be their doctor tonight or not? Okay, we only got nineteen men on the ward tonight, with two new admissions. . . ."

★ ★ ★ ★

Cheney knew it happened at 11:38 exactly, because she was staring at her watch, taking a pulse. First came the flash of light, a disturbing caldron orange that shot through the squares of the opened windows and leered between the slats of the shutters. In less than a second a subterranean thrum thudded into their ears.

Cheney ran outside. Shiloh was already there.

Directly to the east was a sky-coal, red in its heart, fading to a dull terra-cotta around the edges.

"Fire," Shiloh said.

"I wonder what exploded?" Cheney murmured.

"I don't know. That's right downtown."

They watched in silence for a few moments. Smaller explosions sounded occasionally, some deep and humming, some like quick crackles. "Sounds almost like a battle," Shiloh said in a peculiar faraway voice. "Artillery . . . small arms . . ."

"I think we'd better send the ambulances," Cheney said.

"Yeah." He turned and hurried back into the hospital.

Cheney followed him, though he went on down the hallway toward the back exits, and Cheney went to the men's ward. Jesty Tukes and Baltimore Florey were both standing at a window, their faces outlined with flame-lit dread.

"Mr. Tukes!" Cheney said sharply. All of the patients were awake, with several of them standing at the east windows. "You're going to need to drive an ambulance. Go now and help Mr. Irons and Li Shen get them supplied. Take anything Mr. Irons tells you, and do everything he tells you. I'll make certain that everything is properly documented later."

"Yes, s-sir," he stammered as he skittered toward the back door.

Cheney didn't notice his gaffe, as she was already issuing more orders. "Mr. Florey, go into the amphitheater, light all the lamps, and turn them up full. Then set up twenty—no, make that thirty beds. Put them at one end of the floor. At the other end move in two operating tables. I'll send Mrs. Sisk to help you. When Li Shen comes in, put him to work making up beds and bringing extra towels, basins, and all the jugs of water he can carry."

Mr. Florey looked a little distressed, but he gamely asked, "Will that be all, Dr. Duvall?"

She gave him a small spare smile. "That will be enough to begin with, Mr. Florey. But I think we've a long night of hard work ahead of us."

"Yes, Dr. Duvall." He still didn't move as he fidgeted with a button on his white coat, staring down at the floor.

"What is it, Mr. Florey?" she asked impatiently as she turned to leave.

"Um . . . er . . . about the ward, ma'am. There's two patients that need medication—"

"Miss Posey will be taking both wards," Cheney said. "Hurry up, Mr. Florey. I don't think we have too much time."

Cheney went to the women's ward to give Sallie Sisk and Bethena Posey their instructions. She had finished and was going to the operating theater when she heard the clatter of the ambulances leaving the hospital. *Shiloh's so quick. . . .*

On impulse she went instead back out to the front steps and watched the two lumbering wagons traveling at a dangerously fast clip in an arrow-straight line to the east. She stood on the steps for a few moments, gathering her thoughts and making her plans, when she saw a glimmer in the darkness straight ahead. Straining, she finally saw that a rider was thundering toward the hospital, a man on a gray horse. He was bent almost double over the saddle, and his head was bare. When he drew near Cheney saw that he was dressed in solid black, with a billowing gray opera cape. The horse pulled up to a dancing stop at the foot of the steps. One corner of Cheney's mind observed that he seemed too young to be so somber.

"Did you come from there?" Cheney asked, pointing.

He didn't look back. "It's the Argonaut Theater. It caught on fire and caused a panic. There's a sea wind . . . it blew cinders across a narrow alley. A three-story house. On the top floor fireworks were stored. Chinese fireworks."

"The explosion?"

He watched her gravely. "It is a house of prostitution. In the basement were men and women, smoking opium. The top floor exploded and then fell in."

Grimly Cheney asked, "Do you know how many injured?"

"Many," he answered sadly.

Cheney suddenly thought he was much older than she judged at first.

"Don't be afraid, Dr. Duvall," he told her. "You'll have help."

"What?" she asked, bewildered.

But the man turned his horse and was preparing to ride away. Cheney called out, "Wait! Please, wait a moment, sir!"

He turned back around, and his face was anguished. "People are burning."

Cheney was struck dumb, and he rode away.

★ ★ ★ ★

The amphitheater was hot. Although it was past midnight, it was the first night of August, and two dozen gas lamps glared harshly, each a small oven. But Cheney knew they'd need the light. Assessment of serious injuries was mostly visual.

Cheney, Mr. Florey, Mrs. Sisk, and Li Shen were still frantically making preparations when they heard the rumbling of wagons and stamping horses just outside. Hurrying to the door by the side of the seats that led out into the main courtyard, Cheney was surprised to see Dr. Werner come striding in first, his face grim and dirty, his evening clothes filthy.

He stopped at the basin of carbolic acid Cheney had set up at the doorway and scrubbed his hands viciously. The acrid odor of singed wool drifted around him. "Can someone get me a coverall?" he barked. "Here's the first lot, Dr. Duvall. There are going to be about thirty in all, I think. Maybe more."

"Are you hurt, Dr. Werner?" Cheney asked.

"Of course not," he said brusquely. "I was at that accursed theater. *Faust.* Didn't know we were going to experience firsthand the fire and brimstone." His hawk-gray eyes searched around the operating theater, observing the basins of carbolic acid waiting by the two operating tables. "You've got a good start setting up here, I see."

"Yes, because of the messenger—oh, you must have sent him," Cheney said with a little confusion. "He said I'd have help."

"Not me," he answered shortly. "But I was praying that somehow word would get to you that there'd be serious casualties, and a lot of them. Burns require fast work and special treatments."

"You didn't send him?" Cheney said dumbly. "Then who—" Dr. Werner was watching her with barely concealed impatience, so she quickly said, "I'll get Mrs. Sisk to get your coverall."

She went to instruct the nurse, then hurried to the casualties. One man, dressed in evening clothes, walked in by himself; he had a rough, bloody bandage around his head, and he was holding his left arm in a sheltered, defensive position with his right hand. Cheney directed him to a bed in the farthest corner. Two more men, both with visible bruises and one with a singed face and hands, brought in a makeshift stretcher that was merely a board with a horse blanket thrown over it. A woman groaned and shifted restlessly on it. Behind them came two more men supporting a staggering, obviously blinded man between them. Anxiously Cheney looked outside; these people were arriving in private carriages. More people formed a rough line to come into the hospital, some walking, some helping others. Two men, she saw, were lying on the ground, waiting for a stretcher.

She went back to Dr. Werner. "Did you see the ambulances? I sent them."

"Yes, they're coming. Mr. Irons was just about finished loading them when I left. And there'll probably be more coming in private carriages," he answered, pulling on the coverall that Mrs. Sisk had brought him. "I tried to direct only the least injured to City and County, because it's going to take them a long time to get there. About a hundred or so carriages ended up crashed and piled up and burning, blocking two of the north streets, and the fire wagons blocked another north-western. Straight east was the fastest way."

He subjected her to a flinty appraisal. "Dr. Baird and Walker will come soon, I'm sure, and so will Dr. Tasker, but he lives just south of Clay and he'll have trouble getting through. So until then it's just you and me, Dr. Duvall. You're going to have to be very careful in your initial assessments."

"I understand that, Dr. Werner," she said rather stiffly. "I have some experience with trauma cases."

"I'm aware of that, but do you have experience with burns? Third-degree burns?" he demanded.

Cheney wavered and opened her mouth, but she could not make herself admit to this arrogant man that she had no hands-on experience with severe burn cases. She knew what the textbooks said, and she had prepared the supplies and medicines accordingly. She felt that he was trying to maneuver her into a position to admit her ignorance. While she was still dithering, he said flatly, "All right. Just remember that most severe burn cases won't make it through the night. Do you understand what that means?"

"Yes," she said, although she didn't. Before the night was over she would understand all too well.

But at this moment she was still blithe and blind, and she said to Dr. Werner, "Perhaps, sir, you might see about getting everyone safely inside? I saw two men lying on the ground out there—"

Without a word he whirled on his heel and called out, "Li Shen! Mr. Florey! Get a stretcher and check outside!" Then he hurried toward the operating tables, calling instructions to a skittering Sallie Sisk.

With a callous shrug Cheney started assessment of the patients. She directed the ones who could walk to get into the beds at the back and the far end of the theater. The ones on stretchers she stopped to hurriedly check their breathing, then directed the bearers where to put them.

Eleven people had arrived in three carriages. Cheney was still busy with them when the ambulances arrived. Shiloh had taken as many people as he possibly could. Each ambulance held four stretcher cases, four injured sitting on the floor in the wagon, and two on the seat with Shiloh and Jesty. Through the door Cheney heard Shiloh's harsh order, "You people who can walk make way! We need to take the stretchers in first!"

He and Jesty came in with the first stretcher. Cheney hurried to them and saw that they carried a Chinese woman. Her eyes were closed, and her hands were folded peacefully on her abdomen. Cheney looked up at Shiloh questioningly.

"Legs burned. One's broken," he muttered harshly. "I hope she's unconscious."

"Put her up there," Cheney directed. "Put all of the burn cases up there on the right. Put the emergency surgery cases over here close to the tables."

"Right," he said. He and Jesty went to the beds Cheney had indicated and gently laid the girl down, stretcher and all, on the bed. Cheney watched closely—if the girl's legs were painfully burned, how would they lift her? But Shiloh already had that problem solved; he had put a sheet underneath the burn patients, so that he and Jesty just took the corners of the sheet and lifted it. Neatly Cheney slid the stretcher out from under. Without speaking Shiloh and Jesty hurried back outside.

Cheney bent over the woman and saw that she was still breathing. She was so pale, and so still, Cheney thought she might have died, but she was passed out, probably from pain. Cheney left her, for she had to finish getting the supplies and medications she'd need arranged on the table that had been set up in the area she'd designated for burn patients. Then she went to do a quick check of the people who'd been less seriously injured to make certain that none of them were in immediate danger. Cheney knew that many times a person can be gravely injured, but in shock will walk, talk, appear to be fairly coherent—then suddenly will collapse and die from internal hemorrhage or a heart attack or a traumatic stroke.

She catalogued broken bones, mild burns, abrasions, two head traumas, and four ladies with injuries that were painful, but not life-threatening, but who were going into shock. She gave Mrs. Sisk crisp instructions on whom to deal with first and what to do. By this time Shiloh and Jesty had brought in four more burn cases. Cheney searched the room and saw Dr. Werner beginning surgery on a man, and she saw with relief that Walker was assisting him. Dr. Baird was setting up the other operating table.

She decided to go check on the burn cases and hurried over to them. Shiloh stopped her at the bed of a man who was screaming hysterically. Cheney saw his flailing, burnt hand clawing at empty air. "I'll try to give him something for the pain, Doc," Shiloh said. "You can't examine him while he's like this. Check on the others, okay?"

"Those three pitchers on the table are water with morphine sulphate dissolved in it, Shiloh," she told him hurriedly. "Try that instead of laudanum."

The Chinese woman was still unconscious. The second patient was a man whose right arm and chest were burned. He was conscious, but evidently he had been given a good amount of morphine, or else he had smoked a great quantity of opium, because he appeared dreamy and unconcerned.

Cheney stopped in her tracks at the third bed.

The form in it was small, so small, and too still. "Oh no, not a child!" she moaned to herself. Finally she made herself walk to the side of the bed. It was a child, a girl, maybe fourteen years old. Her eyes were open but lifeless. Her lovely sheen of black hair was burned to stinking cinders on one side. A sheet covered her all the way to the chin. Cheney swallowed hard and walked to the girl's bedside. The lovely uptilted eyes followed her, focusing on her face as if she were a vision of a savior.

"Hello, I'm Dr. Cheney Duvall," she said softly. "Do you speak English?"

No response.

"What is your name?" Cheney tried again.

The girl merely looked at her. Mutely pleading.

Cheney lifted the sheet.

When she saw the extent of the little girl's injuries, Cheney felt a sickening numbness, then she felt as if she'd been turned to cold stone. She couldn't think. She couldn't move. She couldn't talk.

Her eyes dull, shocked, moved slowly up to the girl's face. The girl still watched her, now with almost lifeless eyes, except for a tear at the corner. Cheney watched with horror, with fascination, with dread, as the single jeweled drop trickled slowly down the girl's perfect white face. It was the only movement in the pathetic scene.

Cheney didn't know how long she stood, her mind a blank stupid white nothing, her stomach heaving, her eyes burning. She didn't think she could blink. The girl never looked away from her.

Cheney felt a hand, heavy and comforting, on her shoulder. "Dr. Duvall," a voice said evenly, "why don't you let me help you?" Two hands appeared in her tunnel vision and were laid gently on top of her two lumps of fists that held up the sheet. With insistent pressure the hands—the live, warm hands—loosened her whitened stiff fingers. "Here . . . let me . . . let's just lay this back down. That's good. Good evening, my dear. I am Dr. Werner. Here, I want you to drink this."

Cheney stood dumbly, numbly, and as if she were insidiously drunk, she laboriously made herself look away from the girl's face. Dr. Werner bent over the bed, holding a cup to the girl's lips. On the other side of the bed stood Reverend Justice Merced. He spoke quietly in Chinese and took the cup out of Dr. Werner's hand. "I can do this, Doctor," he said softly. "There will be others who need you more."

Dr. Werner firmly took Cheney's arm and led her to the door. "Dr. Duvall, I want you to go outside and get some air. You look faint. You won't do anyone any good if you get ill."

Cheney stood stupidly at the door, staring uncomprehendingly at him. He turned and started to walk away, then turned back to her. "That was bad, Dr. Duvall. She was bad. The worst I've ever seen. I don't find it at all surprising that you had a reaction to it. Now just go outside until you can collect yourself. That's all we can do when this happens."

Cheney ran, blindly, because her eyes were suddenly flooded with stinging salty tears.

The scene outside the east door was still a tumult of ambulances, carriages, and people. Cheney ran across the courtyard, past the night-dead fountain, in between the pharmacy and the kitchen, which were both garishly lit. In the back of the apothecary were the gardens, and they were dark. Cheney went to the far end, to a small stand of pines that half hid the stables behind. Throwing herself down to the ground beneath one of the trees, she sobbed helplessly. Her nostrils were filled with the dusty smell of old earth, her eyes were filled with salt, and her heart was overrun with bitter grief and shame.

This dreariness went on for a long time, but in people with sound hearts and minds there is always an end to the tears and hysteria, if not to the sorrow. Wearily Cheney sat up against one of the trees, pulled her knees up, and hugged her legs as if she were a frightened child. Which, in a manner of speaking, she was.

"Dr. Duvall, may I sit down here with you?" a grave, kind voice asked out of the darkness.

Cheney was too dulled to even start. "I suppose so, Reverend Merced."

He sat down by her, a thin gray ghost in the darkness. But she could feel his warmth and sense his compassion. He said nothing.

After a long time she said, "I don't think you can help me."

Incongruously he chuckled. "Oh, there's no doubt in my mind about that, Dr. Duvall. Of course I can't help you. But I know Someone who can. And so do you."

Again there was a long silence, which Cheney finally broke. "I don't know what to say."

"You don't have to say anything to me. I'll just sit here with you, if I may, and I'll pray for you."

Cheney started crying again, only this time it was with quiet sadness. "I have been so stupid. I have been so arrogant. I thought I . . . knew everything, could do everything, could . . . control everyone. Now I find I can't even control myself!"

Reverend Justice Merced was very matter-of-fact. "When God gives people very demanding ministries, they often fall into that trap. You have a special gift from God, Dr. Duvall—the power of healing. As it is with those talents that are most demanding and require the utmost dedication, they also have a tendency to give the person a false sense of power. You can't do it alone, Dr. Duvall. You never could. Perhaps you had forgotten this for a while. But now you're remembering."

"But I've been so . . . stupid! So . . . beastly!" Cheney miserably searched the darkness for a comforting glimpse of his kind face. "What . . . what was that scripture you quoted the first time I came to your house? Something about being . . . a beast?"

"Ah, that's my own personal reminder of when I had to go through something similar to this. It's a psalm of Asaph. 'So foolish was I, and ignorant: I was as a beast before thee.' "

Cheney sighed fitfully.

Reverend Merced went on, "But the second part of the passage is the answer to us foolish ones, Dr. Duvall. 'Nevertheless I am continually with thee: thou hast holden me by my right hand.' "

Awkwardly, Cheney scrubbed away the tears from her face and rubbed her eyes with the palms of her hands. "He holds my right hand," she murmured, then held her hands up close to her eyes so she could see them. They looked white, ghostly, frail in the darkness. "Still, I . . . failed. I've failed, Reverend Merced. When I saw that poor child, she was so horribly . . . so terribly burned! And I . . . just froze! I felt ill! I'm supposed to be a *doctor*!"

"You are a doctor, and an excellent one, I understand," he answered. "So you felt horror and revulsion, and you were unable to get control of it for a time. Humans falter. Humans fail. Humans are weak. Even doctors. Even . . . you."

Cheney slumped and dropped her head. The old missionary had to strain to hear her voice. "Yes. Yes. This was . . . a lesson . . . I simply had to learn. I wanted so badly to be strong, but instead I became—headstrong, instead of . . . heart-strong. I understand, Lord. Please forgive me, Father, for my terrible pride, arrogance, my foolishness. Please help me, always, to remember that only You are the Healer, that only You are my strength, that only You are my knowledge and wisdom and understanding."

Cheney and Reverend Justice Merced prayed together for only a short time. Then they rose and started back to the hospital. "I . . . don't know if I can . . . face . . . it," she said, her voice still tense and strained. "I'm afraid, Reverend Merced."

"Yes, it's terribly frightening," he agreed quietly. "But, Dr. Duvall, may I make a small suggestion?"

"Yes, of course."

"If you could just say a very short prayer, just—take hold of God's hand a little tighter before you go to each patient."

"Yes, of course," Cheney muttered. "I stopped doing that. I forgot about it. Of course! I'll start again, right now!"

"Then you'll be fine, I know, for God has given you a marvelous gift, Dr. Duvall. And all of His gifts are without repentance. He will never take it away from you."

Before they reached the hospital, Cheney stopped and turned to face Reverend Merced. "The girl . . . the little Chinese girl . . ."

"She died," he said sadly.

"Did you get to speak to her about the Lord?" Cheney asked. The tears almost flowed again, because she thought, *If I hadn't been standing there, wasting her last few minutes, like some sort of accursed idiot . . .*

"Yes, I did, which I'm sure is why the Lord let her live as long as she did," Reverend Merced answered, his voice lighter. "It's so difficult with the Chinese. So many of them have never heard of Jehovah, Our Father, or His Son Jesus."

"Then . . . then how do you tell them? What do you say?" Cheney wondered. "Especially when you know you may only have minutes . . . seconds . . ."

He smiled beatifically. "The simple truth, Dr. Duvall. I tell them that there is only one God, great and mighty, the beginning and the end. I tell them that He sent His only Son, His one precious Son, to die for us, for we are all sinners from the moment of our birth. I tell them that even at the moment of our death, Jesus can still cleanse them and save them and take them to heaven to be with Him and His Father. Then I tell them that all they must do is know this and ask Him to save them and to come into their hearts."

"And that little girl?" Cheney asked sadly. "Do you think, Reverend Merced, that she turned to Him before she died?"

"She said His name. As it was her only and last word," he replied calmly, "I think it must have been the most important thing in the world to her then. I think she is in His arms right now."

"Pray for me," Cheney pleaded, clutching his arm tightly with both hands.

He smiled and patted her long-fingered, capable, healing hands. "Oh, I will, Dr. Duvall. As you do your job, so I will do mine. And our blessed Lord Jesus Christ will give us strength and rest and peace."

22

BECKONING SIRENS

"I had thought you would be returning to New York with me," Victoria sighed. "You, too, Shiloh."

"I had thought I would too. I thought I would be returning in triumph, the great physician, ready to do the world a favor and open the perfect hospital," Cheney said wryly. "I also had Shiloh's future in New York all planned."

He nodded. "Yeah, but I just couldn't go along with it. I mean, she wanted me to go to medical school! Me—Dr. Shiloh Irons!"

"Doctor?" Victoria echoed.

Cheney's brow furrowed, and she said in her best lecturing voice, "Now, Shiloh, you know perfectly well that I can't certify you as a doctor, even though you have been my assistant for over two years. This apprenticeship tradition must stop." She saw the amusement on Shiloh's and Victoria's faces and finished blandly, "So now you can be my secretary, Shiloh."

"Or your bootblacker," he suggested.

"Bodyguard?" Victoria offered slyly.

"How 'bout if I get this acupuncture thing down, and we could open a parlor?" Shiloh went on. "You could be the doctor, and I could be the acupuncturist."

Cheney's eyes sparkled. "No, how about if we make Nia the physician, I'll be the animals' and servants' surgeon, and you be the acupuncture and moxibustion specialist?"

Shiloh settled back in the landau's sumptuous velvet seat and put his arm carelessly around Cheney's shoulders. He told Victoria solemnly, "We're going to be rich. Maybe as rich as you, Mrs. de Lancie."

Victoria smiled but said sadly, "I'd rather you were coming back to New York with me."

Cheney grew somber. "I know, Victoria, I shall miss you very much.

But you know that I really believe the Lord would have me stay at St. Francis for a while. If He can get me to keep my mouth shut and my ears open, maybe I can learn some things."

"That would be a miracle, all right," Shiloh teased.

"Wouldn't it," Cheney agreed complacently.

Victoria studied her. "You've changed. I've seen you, talked to you, and watched you growing and learning so much. Ever since the fire."

"Yes," Cheney said quietly. "That night I had a life-changing experience with the Lord. I know people sometimes don't believe in that, but I can testify that it's true. Oh, I know I still make mistakes, I still lose my temper, I still don't have a lot of wisdom. But I have changed. I will learn."

Shiloh listened to her intently. "St. Francis really has been good for you, hasn't it, Doc?"

"Yes, it has. I'm proud to be a part of it. I'm proud of the opportunity to work with such eminent physicians, and I'm so blessed to be able to learn this way about private hospitals. Because one day I will come back to New York, and if it is the Lord's will, I'll open a hospital like St. Francis."

"I'm going to hold you to that, Cheney," Victoria said seriously. "Look, there she is. The *Maiden of Zanzibar*." They all looked out the carriage windows at the clipper ship floating restlessly in the bay.

"She's a beauty," Shiloh said appreciatively. "All clippers are."

Victoria busily began gathering her reticule and parasol, straightening her gloves, adjusting her hat. "Would you like me to buy her for you, Shiloh?" she asked innocently.

Shiloh's bright blue eyes widened with shock, but he recovered nicely. "Aw, shucks, my birthday's already over. Maybe for . . . um . . . All Hallow's Eve? Michaelmas? Hanukkah? Chinese New Year?"

Giggling, Cheney told him, "You really mustn't make such jokes with her, Shiloh. You might find that blooming ship with a big red bow on it, floating in the pool at the Olympic Club on All Hallow's Eve."

Victoria made a tiny almost-yawn, then patted her lips delicately. "Impossible. I dislike red bows."

The carriage came to a stop, and Shiloh, Cheney, and Victoria got out on the pier close by the ramp leading up to the *Maid of Zanzibar*'s main deck. The captain, clothed in blinding white, fidgeted impatiently at the foot of the ramp, watching the carriage. There were no other passengers on the wharf, only a few seamen hurrying here and there.

Cheney asked hesitantly, "Victoria—is this—you don't own this ship, do you? Not really?"

"Why, no, Cheney. Why do you ask?"

"Well, I don't see any more passengers."

"Oh no, there aren't any," she said airily, "except for Zhou-Zhou, of course, and she boarded early this morning and brought all my luggage. Actually, the *Maid of Zanzibar* makes regular runs from my father's holdings in South Africa to San Francisco, and her sister ship, the *Maid of the Caribbean*, runs from South Africa to New York. Technically they're not passenger ships. But my father arranged for the *Maid of Zanzibar* to take me to Panama, and for the *Maid of the Caribbean* to take me to New York, so that I might get back home in a month, rather than two months on a steamer."

"So you mean your father sent these ships to pick you up? To . . . to . . . give you a ride?" Shiloh asked in amazement.

"Well . . . yes," Victoria replied with puzzlement.

"But . . . but . . ." Shiloh stuttered, staring up at the elegant—and obviously expensive—clipper with amazement.

"Give it up, Shiloh, dear. She lives in a different world, you know." Cheney patted his arm comfortingly. "It's a good thing Victoria likes sea travel, or I'm sure Mr. Steen would have finished the transcontinental railroad in order to bring her home."

"That's absurd. I hate trains," Victoria scoffed, her eyes gleaming. "Anyway, I simply must get home before Dev does. I . . . I'm quite anxious to see him."

Cheney glanced at her, then threaded her friend's arm through her own. "You must miss him terribly, Victoria. And I know he can't wait to be reunited with you."

Victoria smiled beatifically, and Cheney thought that her face glowed. Her creamy complexion seemed translucent, her lips warmer, her eyes like jewels, when she spoke of Devlin Buchanan. "Cheney, I don't want to sound like a foolish schoolgirl, but it has seemed forever since I've seen him, and it seems forever until we'll be married." She gave Cheney a stern look. "You promised—"

"I know, I know." Cheney laughed. "I promised, Victoria, that I would come help you with the wedding. And I will. Of course, I must see what arrangements I can make with Dr. Baird for such an extended leave of absence."

"I've already made those arrangements," Victoria said haughtily.

"You didn't think I'd leave something that important up to you, did you?"

"Of course not," Cheney said dryly. "Poor Dr. Baird."

Grandly ignoring her, Victoria looked up at Shiloh and said softly, "Dev and I both would be honored if you would come to our wedding, Shiloh. We've spoken of it, and although I will, of course, send you an invitation, I would like for you to consent now to attend."

"I consent, Mrs. de Lancie," he said quietly. "It will be my great pleasure."

"Good." Slyly Victoria looked at him beneath her delicate lashes. "If there are any more like you at home, Shiloh, bring them too."

"Victoria!" Cheney scolded. "You are an engaged woman!"

Victoria indignantly replied, "I didn't mean that, Cheney. I meant—"

"I know," Shiloh interrupted, grinning. "Matching footmen."

★ ★ ★ ★

On September 15, 1867, Cheney Duvall, M.D. made formal application to Dr. J. E. Baird to renew her contract with St. Francis de Yerba Buena Hospital for one year. Dr. Baird accepted Dr. Duvall's application with great pleasure, gave her a raise, and offered to change her hours so that she would only have rotating night shifts one week a month. This Dr. Duvall respectfully declined and requested to continue working nights. Her request was granted, with gratitude and an immense sigh of relief from Dr. Baird.

That night Cheney was off. She put on a lovely, comfortable "at-home" dress, a satin skirt with a matching satin sacque in a rich burgundy that was, indeed, the color of old, fine wine. In spite of the fact that she missed Victoria, who had returned to New York at the end of August, she was enjoying this evening alone. Mrs. O'Neil had built her a fire and made her some hot cocoa, and the homey crackle of slow-burning oak and the rich milky smell were poignant reminders of her home and her parents. She wrote a letter to them, then one to Victoria, and then one to Dev. Then she began reading—again—Charlotte Brontë's *Jane Eyre.* It had been one of her favorite books since she was a child, but it had been years since she had read it.

Before she had finished the first chapter, however, she had put it down and was staring at the fire, thinking. *This book . . . it's really about Jane Eyre's search for a home. It's so strange that I feel so at home here—*

Steen House is not my home, not really, I don't care how long I stay here or how much Victoria presses me to regard it as my own. How is it that I feel that I belong here? How is it that this does, finally, feel like a home?

The answer, of course, came to her so quickly and so clearly that she smiled. " 'My flesh and my heart faileth,' " she quoted softly, " 'but God is the strength of my heart and my portion forever.' You are my home, Lord."

She resumed her reading.

At almost eleven o'clock Cheney heard boots on the veranda and a soft knock on the front door. She knew it was Shiloh, and without waiting for Mrs. O'Neil, she jumped up and ran to answer it.

"Hello, I just knew it was you," she said lightly. "Come in! I have a fire and hot cocoa I'll share. If you're nice to me, I might share my book too."

He smiled, but it was forced, and Cheney was unsettled for a moment. But she went on, "Here, let me help you with that—goodness, these canvas coats are heavy! And cold! Is it raining?"

"No, but it's awfully foggy and mushy," he answered in a distracted manner. "D'you suppose Mrs. O'Neil could do me some hot coffee? I am kinda chilled."

From behind them, Mrs. O'Neil's somber lilt sounded, "Yes, sir, t'would be a pleasure, Mr. Irons." Her skirt whispered softly as she floated back through the darkened dining room toward the kitchen.

"I don't think there truly is a Mrs. O'Neil," Shiloh intoned as they went back into the drawing room and he took his pose in front of the fire. "I think she's the ghost of Steen House. You never see her coming. Her footsteps make no sound. Her voice is like a soft whisper on the air."

"Trust Victoria to have a ghost who is an excellent servant," Cheney laughed. "But no, Mrs. O'Neil is quite real. And very nice, besides being a wonderful housekeeper. I'm so glad she stayed with me."

He gave her an odd look. "She told you, didn't she?"

"About her husband? Having the distinction of being the first man hanged by the Vigilance Committee back in 1851? Of course, she told Victoria and me just before she left. Finally," Cheney scoffed. "I can't imagine why she didn't just come out and tell us in the beginning, instead of stewing and worrying about it until she was almost a nervous wreck."

"Yeah, it is hard to figure," Shiloh angelically agreed.

"Oh! You—you know I've changed! You know I'm trying!" Cheney scolded.

He grinned, genuinely this time. "I know, I know, Doc. You've just been so good lately, I don't hardly have anything to tease you about."

"Have I been? Really?"

"Yeah, really." A single tiny clink behind Cheney made her jump. By the time she turned around, Mrs. O'Neil was already coming around the sofa with a steaming cup of coffee in one of the fine Sèvres cups. "Thanks, Mrs. O'Neil," Shiloh said politely. "I appreciate your trouble."

"Not at all, sir." She bobbed, a sort of cross between a nod and curtsy, and left the room.

"I think you're right," Cheney said, staring at the open doorway through which the housekeeper had soundlessly disappeared. "Do you think she just dissolves into a mist when she's not in the room with us? Or . . . I've never touched her, you know. Do you think my hand would just go right through her? Is she a wraith?"

"Don't be afraid, Doc. I'm a big strong man, I'll protect you from Mrs. O'Neil."

Cheney smiled at the vision of Shiloh valiantly shielding her from the somber, dignified Mrs. O'Neil. Shiloh took a sip of his coffee, then put his cup down and came to sit down on the sofa, close by Cheney. Automatically she moved over to make room, but he reached out and caught her hand, and she stayed still, watching him.

He searched her face, slowly and deliberately. He looked at her hair, her eyes, her mouth, and he smiled a little. With one finger he reached up and traced her cheekbone and lightly touched her lips. "Bain Winslow came back yesterday," he said quietly. "He's asked me to go back to Hawaii with him."

Cheney's mind began whirling, but uppermost was a single loud insistent word: No!

She stared at him, her face stricken, and when he saw it he grimaced. Turning away, he picked up his coffee cup again but only stared straight ahead. "He didn't say much, didn't give me much. Said maybe I should come try to talk to his mother."

Cheney swallowed hard and took a deep breath, but her voice was still weak and quavery. "He . . . didn't . . . say anything about you? About your . . . family?"

"No."

Cheney hesitated, then laid her hand on his arm. He jerked a bit, as though it stung him, but then he put his cup down again and turned to her. "I know you're not going to like this. You've never seemed to want to give him a chance."

"Shiloh, I just don't trust him," Cheney said, but it sounded more like a plea than an argument.

"I know," he bit off. "But I have to."

"No, no, you don't," she said, openly beseeching now. "Shiloh, you . . . you're a wonderful man, a strong man, so strong that you can do anything you want! You're intelligent, you work hard, you have determination and courage! You can make a good future for yourself!"

His face turned bitter. "Cheney, you do not understand what I want, and you do not understand what I need."

"Then just tell me!" Cheney cried.

He jumped up and stalked to the fire. Turning his back on her, he laid his hands on the mantel and leaned heavily over to stare into the greedy, hissing flames. "I can't explain it," he said darkly.

She was silent, stricken.

After long moments he turned, and his face was wistful. "I want to know my name. I want to have a past. Who . . . what . . . am I? What kind of man just appears on the earth with no beginnings? I've never had a direction, because I never had a starting point. Mrs. O'Neil is not the ghost here. I am."

"That's not true, Shiloh," Cheney said quietly. She looked up at him, and her eyes shimmered, tears dancing in them with the flickering light. "You've been real, so real, so solid, a rock. For me you've been a fortress, strong and invincible, since the first day I met you."

He almost smiled. "It was at night. You were the most beautiful creature I ever saw. You were horribly frightened, and you ran, so fast and so lightly, and your hair fell all about your shoulders down to your waist. I thought that you were a ghost, a lovely ghost who ran away and I'd never see the like again on this earth. . . ."

The tears fell, hot and heavy, now. "Maybe sometimes we all are ghosts. Something has to happen to make us be real again. For me it is, and has always been, the Lord. He's the one who touches me, and makes me know that I'm flesh and blood and strength and weakness and sorrow and joy and laughter—"

"And love," Shiloh said. "I know."

"You always know," Cheney said, smiling through her tears.

"Will you walk me outside?" he pleaded. "I'd like for you to say good-bye to me there. I don't want to walk away and leave you sitting here alone."

"Of course." Cheney unashamedly brushed her tears away, and they walked to the door in silence. She held out his heavy canvas coat, savoring the rough feel of the canvas and the leathery outdoor smell. They went outside into the damp and misty night. She walked down the steps and rubbed Balaam's neck affectionately. "Leave him at the club, please. I'll send for him and take care of him while you're gone."

"Thank you." He moved close to her and turned her so that she faced him. "I'll be back, you know. As soon as I can."

"Will you?" she whispered.

"Yes. I promise." He stared into her eyes as if he were searching for something and said in a deep voice, "It's because of you that I have to go, Cheney. And it'll be because of you that I'll come back."

He kissed her, softly and sweetly. Cheney closed her eyes and slid her hands gently beneath his coat to rest them over his heart. She felt its strong, sure beat. Their lips were moistened by Cheney's fresh tears.

Quickly he pulled away and mounted. He looked down at her, his face shadowed by his wide-brimmed hat and the night. "Good-bye, Cheney. Don't forget me."

"I won't," she said. "Ever."

He rode away, and Cheney turned and stumbled into the house, blinded by her tears. She ran up the stairs and into the empty bedroom. Almost feeling her way, sobbing, she went into the turret and pressed against the delicate diamond-shaped window panes. She watched him ride down Russian Hill and disappear into the beckoning siren of the mists.

EPILOGUE

For the ways of man
Are before the eyes of the Lord,
And He pondereth all his goings.

"Reverend Merced, just look at this letter!" Cheney burst into the chapel and burst out talking at the same time. The reverend was kneeling at the altar in prayer, but Cheney steamed right on. "I just received this letter from Shiloh, and I think it's disturbing, don't you?"

With a rueful smile Reverend Merced got to his feet. "Well, Dr. Duvall, I shall likely find it disturbing if you say so. But probably not until you tell me what it says."

"Here! Read it!" Cheney thrust the letter toward him as accusingly as if it were a wanted poster with his picture on it.

Obediently he took it, fumbled in a pocket for his spectacles, fumbled in another pocket for his spectacles, and finally sighed, "I apologize, Dr. Duvall, but I don't know where I've put my spectacles again. And I'm not too certain I could read this in here anyway. The lighting is so—" He made a helpless, all-encompassing gesture.

Cheney looked around vaguely, as if she were surprised to find herself in the hospital chapel. "Oh, dear, no, I'm the one who must apologize, Reverend Merced. After we finally persuade you to be the hospital chaplain . . . I come charging in here like a madwoman, stopping your prayers and ordering this and that!"

"Yes, well, you always will have a . . . er . . . forceful . . . er . . . personality, Dr. Duvall," he said diplomatically.

"Hmm. What a delicate way of putting it," she murmured, then smiled at him. "Could we please go into the office for a few moments? Then I'd like to return here with you, if you'll pray with me before I start work."

"Of course, Doctor, that's my job."

They went into Shiloh's office. As he had asked Dr. Baird if he might take an indefinite leave of absence, it had remained "Shiloh's office." But Cheney used it at night, as much as she had when Shiloh had been here. For the last two weeks it had seemed that here in his office, she'd missed him more keenly than anytime or anywhere. They settled in, Reverend Merced's eyeglasses were located in a maliciously hidden pocket, and he read the letter. After he finished, he took off his glasses and polished them meticulously with a handkerchief. It was a bright red handkerchief with a loud blue paisley design on it, which made Cheney smile.

"So . . . his tapestry and his compass were stolen, hmm? How very odd." With deliberation he polished and polished and then looked up at her, his blue eyes coldly shrewd, an expression Cheney hadn't seen on Justice Merced's face before. "Do you believe it was just aimlessly pillaging thieves at Honolulu?"

"No, sir," she replied spiritedly. "I think it's too much of a coincidence. First Bain Winslow makes Shiloh little more than an unpaid sailor on that ship. Then Winslow obligates Shiloh to fight in a pugilistic match, making Shiloh think he must do so to pay for his passage to Hawaii! And now? Now the only tangible evidence that Shiloh had, the only possible link to his family, has mysteriously been stolen?" Her voice rose in anger, and for once she didn't berate herself.

Neither did Reverend Merced. He frowned, deep in thought, and then said slowly, "I think I must tell you something. It is a bad thing, a terrible thing, and I had convinced myself that it would do no one any good to repeat it. But now, perhaps, we should consider everything we know and pray, for it might be that the Lord would have us do something to help Shiloh."

Cheney waited, her curiosity almost unbearable at his cryptic words. But Reverend Justice Merced was a careful and cautious man, and he never repeated tales about people, even true ones, without good reason and without choosing his words carefully. "You remember Zhu Xinlan?"

"Of course," Cheney said softly, sadly. "I'll never forget that poor child." Zhu Xinlan was the fourteen-year-old Chinese girl who had burned to death in the August 7 fire.

"I went to the Chinese Six, and I made them tell me who her parents were," Reverend Merced said with sudden harshness. "They live in a little village outside of Shanghai. She was writing to them, sending them every penny she made."

"I . . . don't understand," Cheney said.

"She was in Lillian Fontaine's brothel that night, Dr. Duvall. Her parents had sold her to an American for his brothel."

"S-sold her? But . . . she was just a child! She was just a little girl!"

"They have four other little girls," he went on relentlessly. "She was just another mouth to feed. They sold her when she was twelve."

"But . . . do you mean . . . they knew she was going to be a prostitute?" Cheney's mind reeled. She could hardly form the words, and they left a horrible taste in her mouth.

He shrugged. "Maybe, maybe not. They knew she was sending them more money than the coolies make in the mines."

Finally Cheney said, "All this is . . . just . . . horrendous, Reverend Merced, but I'm afraid I don't quite understand—"

"The American who bought Zhu Xinlan," he said in a throaty rasp, "was Bain Winslow."

Cheney sat in stunned silence for a long time, and then slowly a cold, shriveled knot of fear and dread chilled her heart. "Oh, Reverend Merced . . . this is bad, this is very bad . . . I'm . . . frightened for Shiloh. . . ."

"Let's go pray, Dr. Duvall," he said. "We must first seek God, and know that He will tell us what we must do."

The next morning Cheney waited for Dr. Baird to arrive at the hospital.

She wondered how she would explain to him that she needed a leave of absence. It was imperative that she go immediately to Hawaii.

Notes to Our Readers

First, thank you for being our readers! We appreciate your loyalty and hope that you'll join us next year as Cheney travels to Hawaii to be reunited with Shiloh.

★ ★ ★ ★

Gump's is still one of San Francisco's most elegant department stores. It is particularly famous for its oriental antiquities, especially jade and pearls. In 1948 its interior design department, the Design Studio, became famous under the auspices of Eleanor Forbes and the McGuires, who designed innovative furniture of rattan and wood. Gump's has recently relocated to Post Street.

★ ★ ★ ★

The *City of Paris* was a victim of the great San Francisco fire of 1906. It sustained massive damage; only its steel framework remained intact. Blackwell and Broun were commissioned to rebuild it. They used the strong framework and added a rotunda and an elegant amber-colored skylight above it. This skylight bears the arms of the city of Paris, a ship with a Latin motto, *fluctuat nec mergitur:* "It is tossed by the waves but does not sink."

But the *City of Paris* is gone. Demolished in 1982, it had still been the city's most elegant and renowned store at the beginning of the century, and vigorous protests from the citizenry forced the builders to preserve the rotunda and skylight. Though it is now Nieman Marcus, it bears the arms of the city of Paris, which indeed has been tossed by the waves but never lost.

★ ★ ★ ★

Watch for the sequel to
IN THE TWILIGHT, IN THE EVENING
in the Fall of 1998!